Also by Jill Marie Landis

HEAT WAVE
SUMMER MOON
MAGNOLIA CREEK
LOVER'S LANE

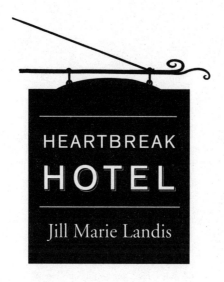

HEARTBREAK
HOTEL

Jill Marie Landis

A Novel

Ballantine Books New York

Copyright © 2005 by Jill Marie Landis

Published in the United States by Ballantine Books, an imprint of The Random House Publishing Group, a division of Random House, Inc., New York.

Ballantine and colophon are registered trademarks of Random House, Inc.

ISBN 0-345-45330-1

Printed in the United States of America

Text design by Laurie Jewell

Maggi Davis a.k.a. Mom.

B., K., and T.
Here's to hot Anini nights.

The Tiki Goddesses of O'Kauai
You all know who you are.

Lis and Bran
Beth and Sean
Robin
Jeffrey
Ellen Marie
Abby
Jack
"It's never too early to start
sucking up to Auntie."

HEARTBREAK
HOTEL

CHAPTER ONE

Wade MacAllister had spent most of his life wishing he had more of everything—more luck, more talent, more money.

He had money now. More money than he'd ever imagined. If he'd been blessed with real talent, maybe his luck wouldn't have run out.

Steering his Harley into a scenic turnout with a view of the Pacific, he killed the engine and set the kickstand. The heavy black and chrome bike listed to one side, poised above the pavement, heat radiating off of the pipes. Though silent now, the growl of the engine still hummed in his ears.

Beyond the lookout, the ocean rose and fell, its rough surface surging in every direction, pulled by the tide, the wind, and the swells. Gathering twilight made it harder to see. Wind gusts off the water matched the rhythm of the waves. The chill in the air cut through his leather jacket, reminding him that he could still feel. That he was still alive.

The night was moonless and melancholy. Restless like him.

"Make up your goddamned mind." The mumbled words were quickly swept away, carried off on the wind, drowned by the roar of the waves. "If you're going to do it, get it over with."

He glanced up and down the highway. There were no cars in sight. He was ever conscious of the gun in his saddlebag, a classic Colt .45, Gold Cup Trophy model he had picked up from a dealer in Phoenix. He'd practiced at a firing range to make sure he knew how to use it, though for his purposes, a good aim wasn't important.

Tonight, like every other night, his fertile mind conjured up memories of things best forgotten. He tried, God knew he'd tried, but there was no way he could ever forget the twelve women murdered in unspeakable ways. Lovely young women who had died violent, heinous deaths. Acts spawned by a sick and twisted mind.

His sick and twisted mind.

Do it right now. Right here. Get it over with.

But there was more than a whisper of daylight left. His mind spun out the what-ifs. What if an unsuspecting driver pulled over? What if a car full of people drove by, saw his body lying there? What if there were kids in the car? What then?

He needed to go somewhere off the beaten track, somewhere lonely and solitary. A secluded place more in keeping with the way he'd always lived his life.

He'd know it when he saw it and when he did, maybe then he'd find the courage to put an end to everything.

The twelve women.

The constant moving. The disguises.

He'd find the right place and then maybe he'd find the courage to bring the story of his life to a close.

CHAPTER TWO

After dark, the lobby of the Heartbreak Hotel seemed to expand, like the walls of a carnival fun house. At night, the persistent pounding of the waves against the shoreline filled the rooms like the amplified beat of a solitary heart. Except for an occasional passing car, there was no competition for the echo of the waves.

Loneliness filled the rooms in the evenings, too. Tracy Potter didn't notice it as much during the day when she was running in all directions. But at night, after the workmen left, the sun had set, and her nine-year-old son, Matthew, was tucked in bed, she would struggle with an ache so deep, so raw, that it took everything she had to convince herself that circumstances change—that life was bound to take a turn for the better.

She still found it hard to believe that in a couple more weeks, her husband, Glenn, would have been gone six months.

Gone.

The word made it sound as if he had just stepped out to meet a client and would be back any minute.

Her footsteps echoed against the scuffed hardwood floors of the wide-open lobby, falling silent whenever she paused to pick up a sticky wad of used masking tape or carefully sidestep a pile of drop cloths the workmen had left on the floor.

Six months ago, if anyone would have told her that she'd be a widow at thirty-three, or that she'd be renovating the Heartbreak Hotel, let alone living in it, she would have laughed and called them crazy.

A few days after Glenn's death, when his accountant, David Sylvester, informed her that Glenn had been deep in debt, she thought he'd been joking. But David had been dead serious and the joke was on her.

It was a morning she'd never forget, sitting there in David's office, listening as the accountant outlined the bleak details.

"There's no easy way to put it, Tracy. You're broke. As far as I can tell, there's enough left in your joint checking account to pay expenses for the next six months, if you're careful and if you're lucky."

She knew things had been tough. She'd confronted Glenn about the mounting bills. She'd wanted to go back to work, gladly offering to renew her real estate license. She would have done anything to help keep them from going under, but he'd been adamant. He wanted Matt to have a full-time mom. There were listings about to close. Things were just tight right now. Things were going to change soon.

Still she'd worried, and with good reason. What the accountant told her after Glenn's death made that quite clear.

"Glenn refinanced the Canyon Club house to the limit," David explained. "There's no equity left. Your credit cards are maxed out, too. In fact, he made your last two house payments with his American Express Card. And unfortunately, he was underinsured. You'll be able to cover the funeral expenses and, if there's anything left, I'd advise you to pay off your car, and Chelsea's."

Luckily, hers was free and clear.

Chelsea's wasn't. Chelsea was Glenn's daughter by his first marriage. Nineteen now. A freshman at the University of Southern California. Tracy had sat in stunned silence, thinking of Chelsea, of the hefty tuition Glenn had been paying. *What now?*

"Sell the house," David had advised. "Get the bank off your back before they foreclose."

The luxurious house had been Glenn's dream, part of an upscale development he'd spearheaded. Cabrillo Canyon Club was a gated community of sixty high-end homes scattered around a golf course designed by Rex Burrell, one of the West's premier course designers. They were well built but overpriced, even in a good market. The homes all sold eventually, but not overnight.

"There is one bit of good news, I guess," David had quickly added, as if aware that she was quickly slipping into a self-induced coma. Anything to escape.

"And *that* would be?"

"That the IRS and the banks can't touch your inheritance from your grandparents. It's not much, but it'll help. And there's that old hotel on the coast road. Glenn put the title in Matt's name, with you as trustee."

"Matt? When? Why?" Matt was only nine. What had Glenn been thinking?

At first she couldn't even remember the place, and then it came to her. The Heartbreak Hotel. Perched on the coast off the old Route 1. Glenn had purchased the derelict, nineteenth-century hotel a handful of years ago, planning to tear it down and replace it with elegant condos. The project had quickly bogged down in California Coastal Commission hearings.

After the Twilight Cove Historical Society and the Central Coast Preservation League entered into the fray, he had tabled the project altogether, too busy to spend time and money fighting them all.

She had left David's office that morning determined to sell the white elephant. But prospective buyers couldn't walk away fast enough once they learned that the hotel was to be registered as a historic landmark—thanks to the Twilight Cove Historical Preservation Society—and that the Coastal Commission had deemed the prime oceanfront land beneath it off limits to any new development.

She'd looked into renewing her real estate license, then realized that it might be months before her first escrow closed, if and when she got a quick listing and actually sold something.

Forced to do the only thing she could under the circumstances, she'd taken a leap of faith, relied on her ability to see things the way they could be, not the way they were, and had used her inheritance from Grandma and Grandpa Melton to clean up the Heartbreak.

Now darkness was quickly gathering as she walked over to a bank of wall switches behind the desk, flipped on the lights, and surveyed the progress. Though the place would never be a five-star hotel, it was finally coming along.

Six guest rooms were already completely finished. There were three left to paint and furnish. The painting was nearly finished in the lobby. The adjacent sitting room was no longer as dingy and derelict as it had been the day she took her first hard look around.

Even she, a consummate optimist, had been hard-pressed to envision possibilities for the place. If Matt hadn't been with her the first time she walked through, she'd have been tempted to break down and bawl her eyes out.

Old wallpaper had to be stripped. Thankfully, the hardwood floors were still solid, but needed refinishing. An army of termites had taken up residence in the walls. She'd handled the damage with spot repair and fumigation. Basic cosmetic renovations and a race to open for the coming tourist season would never have been her first choice, but she'd seen no quicker way out of her financial crisis.

Walking away from their home at Cabrillo Canyon Club, selling off almost everything, including the designer furnishings hand-chosen for the house, hadn't hurt anything but her pride. But then, she'd never really felt as attached to the Canyon Club house as Glenn. It had been his dream to live in an impressive showplace—one that left no doubt as to his success.

It wasn't like her to look back, so, counting on the future to bring change, she glanced out the wide bay window that curved around the entire front wall. It was gloomy out tonight. Not a single star brightened a heavy sky.

She was headed for the sunroom and small kitchen area off the lobby when she heard the deep-throated rumble of a motorcycle on the coast road. When the sound abruptly stopped, she froze.

Alone in the empty room, she was suddenly all too aware of how vulnerable she and Matt were, living out on this deserted stretch of road. It was one thing to have considered running the Heartbreak all by herself, but the cold, stark reality of it chilled her blood. She held her breath, hoping to hear the motorcycle start up again.

CHAPTER THREE

He couldn't have conjured up a better place to stop.

Poised in isolation on a remote stretch of road bypassed by the main highway, the huge two-story wooden hulk had been visible from a quarter mile away. Reminding him of the Bates Motel in *Psycho,* it rose stark and ominous against the night sky. The place beckoned him, compelled him to slow down as he neared.

Complete with a widow's walk, the old hotel clung to the bluff above the Pacific. It might have been abandoned, except for the neon sign out front that blazed EAR EAK HOT L in hot pink. Below that, in aqua letters, glowed the word VACANCY.

Once he saw the place at close range, there was no way he could ride on. No way he could leave.

Perfect.

He rolled the bike beneath the eave of the building where it would be out of a slow drizzle that was making a halfhearted attempt to turn itself into rain. Quickly he unsnapped the saddlebag, pulled off his helmet, clamped it beneath his arm, and ran splayed fingers through his short hair, forcing it to spike up in front. Taking a deep breath, he headed around the corner of the building along a path nearly covered by weeds.

Hoping like hell that whoever was manning the front desk wouldn't recognize him, Wade cleared the worn treads on the front steps and stared at the oval, etched glass window in the front door. He gave in to an overpowering need to step inside.

CHAPTER FOUR

She knew all along that she would be obliged to greet late arrivals and that she'd be vulnerable every time she opened the door to a stranger. Thankfully, she'd always been a firm believer in the innate goodness of people and had been all her life, but the minute she heard footsteps thudding on the porch outside and then an insistent knocking, Tracy found herself slipping her cell phone out of her pocket. Clutching it in her hand, she crossed the lobby. Through the window set in the front door, she saw the silhouette of a man.

He stood beneath the golden glow of the porch light—tall, not thin, not heavy. Solid, with wide shoulders beneath a black leather jacket that glistened with moisture. His deep-set dark eyes stared back.

While he waited for her to open the door, he wiped his face with the back of his hand and she realized it must be raining. She stepped closer to the window in the door and noted the shiny black helmet beneath his arm and motorcycle saddlebag dangling from his left hand.

"We're not open for business." She raised her voice so that he could hear her through the oval pane.

He leaned closer. He was smooth-shaven and his clothes appeared to be clean.

"Your sign says vacancy." His voice was low, but she easily heard him through the window and suddenly realized that she must have accidently hit the switch for the neon sign when she turned the lights on.

"We're not open yet," she told him again, damning the sign. Fixing the thing hadn't made it to the top of her to-do list yet, nor did she have the money. So many letters were burned out that the first time Matt saw it lit up, he asked who would want to stay at a place called Ear Ache Hot-L and she'd collapsed into gales of laughter.

"Come on, lady. Give a guy a break. It's raining." He shifted his weight and the helmet before he reached into his pocket.

Before she could react, he moved the helmet and pulled out a wad of bills and flapped them back and forth, then pressed them against the window.

"I've got cash. I just need one room for one night."

Tracy sucked on her upper lip and frowned.

He was a good head and shoulders taller than her. Stronger, obviously. Wet. Possibly tired.

He had the money, he needed a room, and she had an abundance of those—not to mention a bank account in need of an injection.

"It's one twenty-five a night." She quoted what she thought was an outrageous fee for a room in a place still being renovated.

He leaned closer to the oval pane. "I'll take it."

She'd always thought you could tell a lot about a person by their eyes. Though this man's appeared to be open and honest, there was something else in them she recognized. Something she'd seen looking back at her from the mirror lately—a deep, abiding sadness that no amount of positive pep talks could erase.

That underlying sadness moved her more than the fact that there were day laborers to pay tomorrow, additional paint yet to buy, not to mention extra bedding and linens on order. At the rate she was going, she'd have very little money left to fall back on if the Heartbreak didn't immediately take off.

She wasn't exactly desperate. Not yet anyway. Besides, desperate wasn't a word she ever used. It conjured up hopelessness and despair. She certainly wasn't hopeless or desperate. She was still determined to start over, to make something of the Heartbreak.

And she could certainly use the extra cash.

Besides, she was going to have to act like an innkeeper sooner or later. Why not start tonight?

She pasted on a big smile, opened the door, and indicated the torn-up lobby with a flourish and a little too much exuberance.

"Welcome to the Heartbreak Hotel. You're our first official guest."

She found herself wishing he would at least smile back.

CHAPTER FIVE

He noticed a smudge on her nose and a streak of white paint in her blond hair. The minute he stepped into the lobby, her megawatt smile dimmed slightly, as if she'd suddenly thought better of letting him in.

He shot a glance around, noted the paint cans and battered aluminum ladder, the recognizable shapes of two sofas smothered by huge drop cloths near a river rock fireplace that nearly covered the entire wall of an open sitting room across the lobby.

His gaze drifted back to her face with its finely drawn features, her aquamarine eyes, her plump lower lip. She was wearing a pastel silk blouse and fitted khaki pants that showed off a trim figure softly rounded in all the right places. Her white Keds were still clean. Even with the paint smudge on her cheek, she looked as out of place here as a pile of French fries on a diet plate.

"Right this way." As she headed for the reception desk, he followed, watching her cross the room. Her blond ponytail bounced against her shoulders and, oddly enough, his pulse seemed to beat in time with her step. His stomach knotted.

How long has it been? Incredibly, he couldn't remember the last time he'd slept with a woman. So long he couldn't remember.

She pulled a huge, worn, leather-bound register out from under the counter, swiped the dust off it with her palm.

"This is the original hotel register. I—" She stopped abruptly, then started over. "*We . . . we'll* be getting online for credit cards, naturally, but since I . . . *we're* planning on making this a traditional sort of inn, I thought it would be nice for guests to sign in."

He made no effort to respond. He didn't want to know her. He didn't *need* to know her. It was the place itself that had drawn him here, this timeworn monstrosity of a hotel wearing a new coat of paint.

At a tall oak desk, the woman watched him count out the cash. He pushed the bills toward her.

"That's one twenty-five." He noticed how rough and unused his voice sounded.

"Thank you. Now, if you'll just sign in here, Mister . . . ?" Suddenly efficient, she spun the huge register 180 degrees and offered him a pen.

He hesitated, then gave her an alias for his last name. "Johnson. Wade Johnson."

"I'm Tracy Potter." As she handed him the pen, he couldn't help but notice her wedding ring. The diamond almost blinded him, even in the dim light. It was impressive enough to warrant a second glance.

So where in the hell was her husband? Her *rich* husband?

What kind of guy would let her open the door to a stranger? Some idiot upstairs watching reality TV?

Quickly, he took the pen and signed the name Wade Johnson. Instead of handing it back, he carefully placed it in the spine of the register.

"Would you please add your license plate number, too? You rode in on a motorcycle, right?"

"Yeah." He must have looked curious about how she knew.

"I recognized the sound. We had a neighbor who had one," she offered.

"I parked close to the building, out of the rain. Is that all right?"

"Of course."

He closed his eyes, pictured the license plate, scribbled the number behind his name. When he looked up again, he caught her eyeing him carefully, and for a second he was afraid she might have recognized him. But aside from her direct gaze, she didn't let on that she had a clue who he was.

He couldn't tell her age. There was barely a line on her face, though she looked a little tired.

As an awkward silence lengthened, her smile wavered uncertainly.

"Unless I miss my guess, this is the part where you give me a key and show me to my room." The old Wade would have smiled at his attempt at humor. The new one didn't remember how.

She blinked, a mere flick of long gold lashes, almost as if she were awakening from a trance, and her smile turned shaky as she reached into the open drawer and took out a room key, an old brass original. The key ring sported a plastic dolphin with the words Twilight Cove printed on its blue gray sides—a trinket from one of the many tourist stops in the nearby hamlet he'd blown through on the Harley.

"Right this way," she offered, stepping out from behind the desk.

He followed her through the lobby and down a narrow hallway lit by a series of dim lights, their flame-shaped bulbs a reflection of the past. They passed a series of tall doors fitted with old-fashioned glass transoms above them. A chilly breeze fluttered the sheer curtain over a long narrow window at the far end of the hall. The place had an empty, eerie feel to it, yet he felt oddly comforted, as if the building itself were drawing him deeper inside. As if he were being seduced by the Heartbreak.

"I'm sorry about the paint smell," she apologized, breaking the spell, reminding him that he wasn't alone. "Fortunately, it's not as strong back here as it is in the lobby."

When he didn't immediately respond, she glanced back over her shoulder expectantly.

He mumbled, "No problem."

"Great." She slipped the key into the lock and opened the door.

Wade walked in, tossed his saddlebag and helmet on an upholstered chair just inside the door. He expected her to leave, but she hovered, uncertain, while he gave the room a cursory glance.

Stark white walls adorned with splashes of color from framed crate labels depicted scenes and the names of various fruit orchards of old California. The atmosphere was warm and inviting without being gaudy, fussily old-fashioned, or overblown with floral prints.

"This is fine. Thanks." He held out his hand and she finally dropped the key into his palm before flashing him another awkward smile and hurrying out.

She closed the door softly behind her.

CHAPTER SIX

Outside the room, Tracy collapsed against the wall beside the door and pressed her palm over her racing heart. The damn thing was thumping along worse than a flat tire on a rutted road.

Doubt and fear had almost turned her into a complete, bumbling idiot the minute Wade Johnson had walked through the front door, but she had to give herself credit. She didn't think she'd done all that badly, seeing as how this was the first time she'd welcomed a complete stranger.

At night, no less.

How on earth am I going to do this over and over again?

Damn you, Glenn.

She reminded herself that she wasn't a quitter. She was a woman with goals and objectives. She always had been and she didn't intend to change just because her luck had soured. She'd moved to California straight out of college and had landed her first job selling real estate on her first interview. She'd made a success of it, too, right up until two years ago when Glenn finally convinced her to stay home and take care of Matt.

She wasn't in the habit of failing. Making a go of the Heartbreak was not only a matter of survival, but a way to gather the pieces of her own life back together.

When she heard Wade Johnson moving around inside his room, she tried to conquer her nerves. Stepping away from the wall, she walked to the end of the hall and closed an open window before she headed back to the lobby. The old floorboards creaked and complained beneath her as she passed the door to his room. She hurried by, hoping he didn't think she was hanging around in the hall for some reason. Hoping he didn't step outside to ask why.

Upstairs in their second-floor apartment, she found Matt sound asleep, stretched out on the couch with the television on. She sat down beside him, brushed his shining rust-colored hair back off his smooth forehead. How often had they laughed about Matt being Glenn's clone with his sandy hair and freckles, his blue eyes?

Whenever she looked at her son now, she saw Glenn again—his smile, the way he walked, the way he shrugged. She heard Glenn's voice in Matt's laughter. It wasn't until she slipped her arms beneath him, picked him up to carry him to his room, that she realized not only how heavy he'd grown, but how infrequently Matt laughed these days.

He was nine, after all. Certainly not her baby anymore. She thought of the not-too-distant future when he'd be too heavy for her to carry. No matter what Glenn had been into, no matter how he'd wound up disappointing her, it still broke her heart knowing that Matt wouldn't have his dad around to watch him grow into a teen, to tease him about his first date, his first kiss, or to teach him to drive.

She walked down the short hallway that led to one of the apartment's three bedrooms. She'd given Matt the brightest corner room, decorated it with his favorite posters, model boats, his nautical navy-and-white-striped spread.

She'd tried to make the move a smooth transition for him and, though the Heartbreak was home to them now, it still didn't quite feel like one. She tucked Matt in, brushed her fingertips over the sheet after she drew it up around his shoulders. A falling mist teased the canvas curtains over his window. Once more, she shut out the night breeze. Before she closed the curtains, she glanced out at the moonless night. Low-lying clouds hung heavy over the water.

She went into her own room and turned down the bed, used to climbing into the vast emptiness alone. Long before Glenn died, she'd grown used to going to bed alone. He'd tried to convince her that his expanding developments like the La Hacienda project in Santa Barbara's redevelopment area forced him to stay overnight in the area. Once she'd spent the night with him in the studio he kept there, intending to make it a romantic getaway.

Equipped with a utilitarian leather sofa bed, a desk, his computer, and piles of paperwork, the crowded space had been nothing more than an office with a bed in it. Glenn had been preoccupied that weekend and spent most of the time fielding phone calls. She'd never made the trip again.

After that, she'd tried to make up for his time away by making his nights at home special, but more often than not he was exhausted and running on empty. Seeing how hard he was working, she hated doubting him, but resentment and worry slowly set in.

She had never asked for the Canyon Club house. She didn't see why he had to have a new Mercedes every year or why he was so driven. She would have given it all up, gone back to working alongside him just to have him home more.

Finally, pushed to the limit, she'd confronted him shortly before he died, asking him point-blank if he were having an affair. He'd been so angry, so hurt and insulted, that she'd ended up apologizing. Over and over he had always insisted, *"I love you, Tracy. I'll always love you. You're my rock. My oasis."*

With a sigh, she walked into her private bathroom, a quarter of the size of their walk-in dressing room at the Canyon Club house, and leaned against the sink. For a moment or two she stared down at the drain. When she finally raised her eyes and looked in the mirror, she hardly recognized the woman looking back.

She'd always looked younger than her years, but she thought she'd definitely aged over the past months. There was no denying it. Shadows were lodged beneath her eyes. There were a few new lines here and there that definitely hadn't been evident before she'd lost eight pounds.

She knew that Glenn had been having money problems. He was always talking about deals about to close, for lenders to come through for clients. He had contractors to pay. He made excuses for why he wasn't paying off the credit card bills. She had offered to do all the bookkeeping and help shoulder the load. He told her he was happy with David Sylvester and bought her a diamond tennis bracelet. Two months ago, she'd turned it over to an upscale consignment shop.

They used to share everything, but slowly he became more and more distant. So distant that just before he died, they were constantly arguing.

For Matt's sake, they'd settled into an unspoken agreement to live under an illusion of normalcy.

Once Santa Barbara is behind us, things will get back to normal.

That was his mantra. But coinciding with the La Hacienda project was the new tract of upscale homes inland from Avilla Beach. Later there came another golf club homes development plan.

She understood his need to succeed. He'd told her stories of a childhood lived in poverty, of his vow never to be hungry or poor again. He didn't want his children to want for anything.

He gladly paid Chelsea's tuition and all of her college expenses. He was making payments on her car. The girl had been so distraught at Glenn's funeral that Tracy had decided to wait until after finals to tell her that unless they could find a scholarship, there would be no tuition for the University of Southern California next year. In what little spare time she had, Tracy had already started researching possible scholarship opportunities.

She whispered to the woman in the mirror, "What in the hell really happened? What were you into, Glenn?"

She had almost convinced herself that he was doing drugs. Afraid that he was too proud, or too deep into them to ask for help, she'd surfed the Internet, looking up everything she could find on drug addiction. Determined to confront him, she never had the chance. The autopsy proved that he'd died of an aneurysm. It also clearly stated that there were no drugs in his system.

Whatever happened, for whatever reason, it all happened. Glenn was gone and she was starting over.

How many people even get another chance?

She was lucky, she reminded herself. She still had her life to live and a boy to raise. For what it was worth, she had the Heartbreak and enough money to dress it up and make it livable.

She opened the medicine cabinet, picked up a jar of facial cleanser, began to smear cream on her face. She removed her mascara, her lipstick, what little foundation she wore. Then she scrubbed her face with soap and water, patted it dry with a towel.

Bone tired, she brushed her teeth and turned off the light. Bathed in darkness, she walked down the hall to a small, dark stairwell that led to both the attic and the widow's walk. She loved to go outside at night, inescapably drawn by the sound of the sea.

The light rain had stopped, so she stepped onto the narrow walk that spanned the house. In the daytime it afforded a panoramic view of the ocean and the coast in both directions.

Why wasn't it called a wife's walk? she wondered. *Why was it just for widows?*

She couldn't resist escaping up here once or twice a day. Tonight, buffeted by the chilly wind, she drew her robe close and wondered if there had ever actually been another widow living here, one who used this walk to escape and think about her life. Perhaps another woman facing a new start, a woman who took time to stare out to sea and dream of better days to come.

She felt strangely comforted high above the rolling surf, beneath the wide-open sky. Alone on the widow's walk, she'd even managed to find moments of profound peace.

But not tonight. Tonight her thoughts drifted to the man downstairs.

Who is he? she wondered. *What is he? Where is he going? Why stop here when there are plenty of other places, less expensive, far better places to stay up and down the coast?*

She couldn't help but remember the haunted loneliness in his eyes, as if he carried the weight of the world on his shoulders. That look made her feel as if they were somehow connected on a level neither of them could escape.

Had he felt it, too?

She decided it was a fanciful thought conjured by an overworked mind. She let the night wind carry it away.

When a shiver passed through her, chilling her, she wrapped her arms around herself. It didn't matter who or what he was, or where he was headed.

He was only passing through.

CHAPTER SEVEN

D ownstairs, Wade pulled a new bottle of tequila out of his saddlebag, filled one of the glasses he'd found on a white Lucite tray on the dresser, and downed half the drink.

Refilling it to the top, he carried it and the bottle over to the nightstand and sat down on the edge of the bed. Reaching for the gun, he laid it across his lap and knocked back another shot of tequila.

He snapped off the light and let his eyes adjust to the dark and the weight of the gun on his lap. Instead of focusing on whether or not to use it, he found his thoughts straying to the woman.

The twenty questions game was ingrained in him now, as much a part of him as breathing. It was an occupational hazard—playing twenty questions.

Who is she? What drives her? What does she want?

What's she most afraid of? How did she get here?

She was definitely uncomfortable with him. He'd seen it in her eyes, heard it as her words rushed out the nearer they got to the room. There was a considerable amount of cash in his pocket and he'd bet all of it that there was no one but her on the premises.

No husband waiting for her upstairs. No one to protect her.

If she were *his* wife, he'd never let her open the door to a stranger.

She would make a perfect victim. A lovely woman all alone in this cavernous, run-down shell echoing with bone-chilling emptiness. It was the perfect night for a murder, too. Moonless and misty.

He stroked the barrel of the gun lightly, the way a man might run his fingers along a lover's spine. Though bottomless self-loathing coursed through him, he knew that he'd never have the courage to use it. Not ever.

He didn't deserve to take the easy way out. Not when fitting justice would be to live out the rest of his life facing his demons.

He poured himself more tequila—liquid courage that numbed the senses but unfortunately not the mind. His thoughts strayed to the woman again.

What was her name? Suzie? Patti? Mitzi?

Definitely something preppie. Something that ended with an *i* she had probably dotted with a big fat heart in high school.

She looked like the type who actually meant it when she told people to "Have a nice day."

He shifted, leaned against the white lacquered headboard, closed his eyes, and tried to imagine shooting himself. What a joke. He was afraid to get a flu shot. Besides, it would be a damn shame to mess up these freshly painted walls.

He pictured Mitzi? Patsi? Trixi's? face when she chased the sound of a single gunshot and found him lying here with his brains spattered all over her white walls and pristine new bedspread.

Why kid yourself?

He couldn't do that to her or anyone else any more than he could do it to himself. He set the gun on the nightstand, listened to the sound of the ocean filling the room. His mind refused to turn itself off. There was really no rest for the weary—or the guilty.

Resigned, he sighed heavily, turned off the light, and sat there staring into the darkness.

A terrible ache, a tearing, ripping asunder. His heart feels as if it is about to explode with the pain. Unlike anything he's ever experienced before. Deeper than physical hurt, the longing tears into him, pulsing, matching the pull of the tide, the sound of the sea that surrounds him.

Dream or reality? He has no idea, and yet he sees her clear as day, standing on the bluff. A raven-haired woman in yellow silk. The gown is old-fashioned. Long. It presses against the length of her legs, caressing the juncture of her thighs, outlines her high, full breasts. The sea breeze teases wayward strands of her hair, tangles it gently in her lashes. She brushes it back, draws a wisp of it across her lips with hands that he longs to feel caressing him.

He can taste her lips—and yet he hungers for her like a starving man. Suddenly his world turns upside down. She's no longer there. Blackness engulfs him. He is blinded by the sun's rays blazing down through fathoms of water. He stares at the refracted sphere and shafts of light shimmering all around him. His lungs are bursting. He knows better than to gasp for air until he's fought his way to the surface.

When he does, he is surrounded by emerald water capped with frothing white. He bobs on the crest of a swell, his life reduced to nothing more than the pieces of wreckage floating all around him.

I'll survive.

The promise is for her, not to soothe himself.

I'll live to touch you again. To taste you.

Nothing can keep me from you.

Not even death.

Wade awoke with a start, fighting for breath. He swallowed air in huge gulps, wrapped his hands around his throat as if he were choking. Disoriented, he glanced around the dark room, struggling to remember where he was. Words came to him in a bright neon memory.

EAR   EAK. *Heartbreak. The Heartbreak Hotel.*

He ran his shaking hand through his hair and over his eyes. His pounding heart outraced the rhythm of the waves that filled the room. The smell of paint lingered, not heavy enough to make him nauseous, but perhaps enough to account for the nightmare. Or was it a dream that had seemed all too real?

Shit. Even with all that had gone down in the last couple of years, he'd never suffered a full-blown panic attack, but he had a hunch that's what was happening. Doubting his ability to stand, he sat and listened to the thunder of his heart ringing in his ears.

He closed his eyes and immediately had the sensation that he was being rocked by ocean swells—not the greatest feeling in the world for a guy prone to seasickness. Over the beat of his heart, he thought he heard a woman crying.

He strained, listening closely, and decided that somewhere nearby, a woman was definitely sobbing. The sound was deep and intense, dredged up from the depths of her soul. It drew him off the bed. He tested his legs, found standing far easier than he expected.

He rubbed the tightness in the back of his neck as he walked over to a narrow French door set with a series of rectangular windowpanes. It opened onto a wide porch overlooking the Pacific.

He opened the door and the chilly night air hit him like a slap. The first thing he noticed was that the rain had stopped.

And so, evidently, had the sobbing.

Had the mournful sound been a remnant of the nightmare? A figment of his overly fertile imagination? The voices of the Even Dozen tended to haunt him, too. Voices he'd only heard in his own mind.

He drank in gulps of night air. Filled his lungs with it. As his heartbeat slowly settled into a normal rhythm, he closed the door, pulled the drapes. Wandering back to the bed, he felt surprisingly calm despite what had just happened. More so than in a long, long while.

It wasn't until he turned on the light and found himself digging through the drawer in the nightstand for a pad of paper and pen that he realized he had an overwhelming urge to write again—and that scared the hell out of him, more than the dream. More than the panic attack or whatever the hell had just happened.

He slammed the drawer shut. Then he reached for the clock on the bedside table. Two hours had passed since he first checked in.

He pulled off his boots, turned off the light, and stretched out on top of the comforter. Stacking his hands behind his head, he lay in the dark staring at the ceiling. He needed more than tequila.

He needed a damn laptop.

But he had vowed that when, and if, he ever had the urge to write again, he would fight it.

Easier said than done.

He closed his eyes, let the sound of the ocean fill his head. Forced himself to inhale and exhale keeping time with the waves, counting each breath.

The next thing he knew, someone was knocking on the door.

Knocking incessantly.

His head was pounding. The knocking didn't help. Neither did the harsh sunlight invading the room through the cracks between the white curtain panels. Wade rubbed his eyes, glanced at his watch.

Eight-thirty already? The damn thing must be fast. There's no way I slept through the night.

But the clock on the bedside table concurred. He got up and headed for the door, if for no other reason than to put an end to the infernal sound of bare knuckles rapping against hardwood. He was halfway across the room when he remembered the gun.

He hurried back to the bed, slipped the Colt into the drawer between copies of Gideon's and *The Wisdom of Buddha.* When he caught sight of the notepad beside the phone and recognized the tight scrawl filling the top sheet, he picked it up.

Every single sheet of paper in the four-by-five notepad was filled with his handwriting. Notes that made little sense now. Notes he didn't recall writing.

Confused, appalled, he tossed the pad inside and closed the drawer.

Shit. The knocking started up again.

Before he got to the door, his instep came down hard on the heel of the boot lying beside the bed. He cursed and hopped the rest of the way, then flung the door open.

There she was, cheerfulness personified, her blond hair pulled back into a perky ponytail that bounced as she jumped back. Her eyes were far bluer than he remembered. Her plush lips formed a silent "O." High color bloomed on her cheeks, but she didn't turn tail and run. She didn't even budge. But her smile quickly bloomed the same.

"I'm sorry, Mr. Johnson . . ." She glanced down at his stockinged feet, then slowly raised her eyes to meet his again. She didn't try to speak until she'd run her tongue across her lips, a quick, unconscious move that made his gut tighten.

"Last night . . . I forgot to tell you that I'd be serving you coffee and pastries in the sunroom. They're complimentary. It's still a bit of a mess, but the back porch is really nice and it has a view, too. Or if you'd like, you can bring your breakfast back here."

She glanced at her watch, a slim, gold Rolex. "It's getting late and I'm expecting the workmen to arrive by nine . . ."

"Coffee?" Now that he thought about it, hot coffee sounded pretty damn tempting. Almost as tempting as she looked. He got a whiff of a tantalizing aroma wafting down the hall. Maybe a good cup of coffee would clear the cobwebs. Give him the courage to open the damn nightstand drawer again and read what was on the notepad.

"Fresh ground," she informed him.

"Plain or flavored?"

"Oh. Just plain. I'm sorry, I—"

"I hate flavored coffee."

Her megawatt smile quickly rebounded. "Me, too. But I'm planning to offer choices, though, when I'm *officially* open."

"Choices are good."

This morning she had said I, not *we*. He glanced at her ring finger again, at the boulder sparkling on it. At the moment she was twisting the ring round and round.

He *was* hungry.

"Give me a minute, okay?" He shoved his fingers through his hair again, figured he had camel breath, took a step back.

Her gaze flicked past him to the bed. "Did you sleep well?"

"Yeah. Fine." Slowly he ran his gaze over her, studied her eyes. There was a sadness that belied the heroic effort she was making. Had she been the one he'd heard crying in the night? Had that been real or inspired by a dream?

For fear of being recognized, he'd made a habit of spending no more than a couple of nights in any one place. He usually paid cash and left well before dawn, before anyone else was stirring. But here, not only had he overslept, but for some damn reason he found himself in no hurry this time.

Hell, he even found himself considering her feelings. She was new at this, that much was obvious. Maybe that explained why he didn't want to disappoint her.

"Look," he said, hoping he wasn't going to regret it, "give me a minute, okay? I'll be right there."

She looked so pleased he almost didn't regret accepting the invitation.

"I'll see you in the sunroom," she said softly. "It's down the hall, just beyond the lobby."

CHAPTER EIGHT

Matt Potter watched his mom fuss with the pot of coffee, the basket of muffins, even the fancy white napkins she used to use at the Canyon Club house on the golf course.

He sat on the tall swivel stool beside the high registration desk and twisted the stool back and forth. It squeaked something terrible. If his dad were here, he'd say, "That thing needs some WD-40. Wanna help me fix it, Matt?"

Thinking about his dad made him sad, so Matt stopped moving the stool and rested his cheek on his arm as he spied on Mom.

She'd been acting really weird all morning. The banana-nut muffins had been cooling on the kitchen counter before he was even out of bed. That's how he knew something was up. Then Mom told him that their first guest had checked in last night.

He'd followed her into her room, watched her put on mascara and lipstick and comb her hair. She always fixed herself up right before his dad came home, too, even though she never got very messed up. She always wanted to look good for Dad.

But this morning she'd done the exact same thing for the first time in a long time, and he couldn't figure out why she cared so much about some guy they didn't even know. The idea made him feel creepy way down deep in the bottom of his stomach.

He looked around the lobby, at the dark wood walls and scratched floor, and for a couple of minutes was content to watch dust motes sift and shimmer like flecks of gold in streaks of sunlight by the windows.

He hated the Ear Ache Hotel even more than he had the Canyon Club house. He wanted to move back to Twilight, where they used to live. What he *really* wanted was a house by his best friend's, Christopher Montgomery's, up on Lover's Lane. He begged Mom all the time, but she just said they had to live here for a while longer—at least until she got the hotel running and maybe they'd have some luck finding somebody to buy it.

Maybe *then* they could move to another house, a real house, close to his blood brother, Chris.

He checked the watch Dad had given him for his birthday last year. It was a way cool G-Shock, the kind all the surfers wore. Since it was waterproof, he never took it off, not even when he took a bath.

It was almost nine. Almost time for Chris and his mom, Carly, to pick him up. She was going into San Luis Obispo to do some shopping and had invited him to go along to see the new Disney movie. He'd wanted to go until Mom told him about the guest. Now he didn't know what to do.

Just then, the guy walked in. Matt slipped off the stool and slithered along the tall registration desk like one of the Spy Kids. He looked at his watch again. 9:03. It was important to check the time when you were spying on someone.

At least that's what Chris had told him. Chris's dad, Jake, was a private investigator who used to spy on people from inside his car and other cool stuff like that, but now he mostly wrote books on how to be a detective so that he could stay home with Chris and Carly.

He eyeballed the guest, who was pretty tall. Taller than Mom anyway. He had on old black cowboy boots with pointy toes and heels. They weren't shiny and they looked pretty worn out. He was wearing Levi's and a black T-shirt tucked into his pants, but no belt. And he had muscles.

Dad never had muscles. He always talked about wanting to lift weights at the spa at the country club, but he was always working and never had time.

Maybe if he'd have worked out he'd have been healthier and he wouldn't have died. Maybe.

Afraid he might start crying, he concentrated on the guest instead.

The guy wasn't carrying a suitcase or anything as he walked over to where Mom was still messing with the coffee cups and napkins and re-arranging the muffins on a pink glass plate with a paper doily on it.

How many muffins did she think the guy was going to eat, anyway?

Matt watched the man stare at Mom until she finally looked up and noticed him. She smiled up at the guy in a way that she never smiled any-more. It was a kind of nervous, grown-up smile of some kind.

Something about the way she was fussing and talking and smiling and pumping coffee for the guy made Matt's stomach hurt even worse, so he pushed off the side of the registration desk and walked over to Mom, then he leaned up close to her side, trying to make himself look taller. He stared at the guy without smiling, hoping the man would take the hint and go away.

CHAPTER NINE

Matt, this is Mr. Johnson." Tracy automatically finger-combed Matt's hair. When he didn't respond immediately, she gently nudged him with her hip. "Honey—"

"Hi," he mumbled. "Nice to meet'cha."

She didn't press for more. He'd had so many adjustments to make that now wasn't the time to ride him about his manners.

With her hand on Matt's shoulder, she concentrated on Wade Johnson. His dark hair was still damp from the shower and if he'd tried to comb it, it didn't show. It was obviously died rock star black and just long enough for the front to spike up in an artfully mussed, retro style. His jeans were faded, worn thin over knees and thighs. From the looks of it, his cowboy boots were the real deal. The leather was cracked and aged. They certainly didn't look like he wore them only to cowboy bars.

There was a swagger in his slow easy stride, and she embarrassed herself by staring at the way the jeans perfectly fit his butt when he turned around to choose a muffin.

"Mom?"

Startled, she looked down into eyes exactly like Glenn's.

"What, hon?"

"It's almost time for Carly and Chris to pick me up."

"I know. You can wait outside, if you want, but stay on the porch."

"I'll wait right *here*." He was staring at Wade Johnson.

"How old are you, Matt?"

The man's casual interest surprised her. Up to now he'd been silent but observing, giving little indication that he cared about conversing with either of them. She waited for Matt to respond, pleased when he spoke up this time.

"Nine."

"You recommend these muffins?"

Matt shrugged. "They're okay."

"They're banana," Tracy added. "My grandmother's recipe."

"Sounds good." He put two on one of her dainty flowered dessert plates that was dwarfed in his hand, picked up a china coffee cup, and headed out to the porch. The fragile cup and plate looked ridiculous in his hands, and she made a note to bring down some of her white ceramic mugs, too.

She watched him carry his coffee and muffin outside. In the light of day, he didn't seem the least bit intimidating.

This morning his reticence seemed far less sinister, as if he were deliberately quiet. Maybe even a bit shy. His face was rugged—certainly not pretty-boy handsome—but good-looking all the same. She was about to follow him out onto the porch to make sure he was comfortable when the front door opened and Christopher Montgomery came bounding in.

Matt stepped closer and whispered, "Maybe I should stay home, Mom."

She smoothed her palm over his cheek and wanted to cry for all the joy that had gone out of his life when Glenn died. "I thought you wanted to see the movie."

"I do, but—" he glanced toward the French doors that Wade Johnson had just passed through.

"No buts. I've got a lot to do today and, besides, Diego and the workers will be along in a few minutes."

"You *sure* you'll be okay?"

She gave him a quick kiss and laughed when he quickly scrubbed it off.

Chris came bounding across the lobby. Carly waved as she came through the door and followed Chris in. Tracy reminded Matt to run upstairs and get his sweatshirt, and the boys hurried off together.

California casual in jeans and a sleeveless shell, Carly brushed back her long blond hair, her smile infectious, her friendship never in doubt. She'd shown up the morning of Tracy's moving sale with a thermos of coffee, price stickers, and marking pens, and stayed all day fending off rude shoppers, keeping an eye on the boys, and helping raise Tracy's spirits. That night she'd even insisted that Tracy and Matt join the Montgomerys for pizza.

They'd shared the holidays, too. Their friendship was the only thing that had kept that first Christmas without Glenn from being a complete nightmare.

"How's it going?" Carly asked, looking around the lobby. "It looks a heck of a lot better in here every day."

"The painters are almost done and, as of yesterday, I've got six rooms finished." Before she could go on, Carly reached into the leather backpack over her shoulder and pulled out a stack of envelopes tied with a piece of polka-dot grosgrain ribbon.

"I was afraid I'd forget these."

Tracy recognized the invitations to the open house celebration she had planned for mid-June. Carly had volunteered to hand-print the addresses in precise, graceful calligraphy. They were perfectly lettered works of art. She gave her friend a quick hug.

"Thanks, Carly. You'll be back before the party, won't you?"

"You sure you'll be done in time?" She glanced around, frowning.

"I have no choice. I'll make sure the lobby is finished. I've only got this tourist season to make it. Failure isn't an option. Please tell me you'll be back in time."

"We wouldn't miss it. Besides, Chris really wants to be home for the last day of school. I feel bad enough that he's missing the last few weeks, but he's finished all his important tests and his teacher is sending along some assignments."

The Montgomerys were heading for an art showing in Taos, where Carly was almost as well known for her distinctive painting style as she was here along the coast.

Tracy watched proudly as Carly scanned the lobby, noticed the muffins and coffeepot laid out with linen napkins, jam, a crystal honeypot, and little silver spoons on a pretty white tray.

"Help yourself," she offered.

"What's up? All this isn't just for me."

Tracy glanced toward the wide French doors opening onto the veranda and pulled Carly aside.

"Our first guest checked in last night. He's outside having breakfast . . ."

Carly glanced over her shoulder. "Is that *his* Harley parked outside?"

"Yes."

"Did he check in alone?" Concern crinkled her brow as she added, "You aren't even open yet."

With a sigh, Tracy tried to pretend she hadn't had plenty of her own misgivings last night.

"Look, it was late when he got here. It was raining. Besides, he seemed perfectly harmless." She knew *that* was stretching the truth, but so far her intuition had proved right. Wade Johnson might not be very congenial, but he seemed perfectly normal.

"But, you had no idea whether or not it was safe to let him in."

"How am I ever going to know who's okay and who isn't?" She sighed and absently twisted her wedding band. "God knows, I needed the extra cash."

She looked around the half-finished lobby, visualizing it the way it would be when everything was finished.

Unconvinced, Carly shook her head. "I wish you'd have called us. Jake might have been able to check him out."

"I have to stand on my own two feet, you know? I can't depend on you and Jake, or anyone else. I'm going to have to go with my gut, and last night it told me this guy was to escape."

"Are you suddenly psychic?"

"Okay, I'll admit that at first I was nervous, but it turned out all right. I can't have Jake running ID checks on every guest, can I?" She didn't want Carly to think she wasn't grateful for her friendship—even her over-protectiveness. "I appreciate how much you care, both you and Jake. I don't know how I'd have made it through these past few months without you."

"Enough of that. You'd have done the same for me."

"I know, but—" At a loss for words, Tracy fell silent.

As Carly picked up a muffin, Tracy wondered if she really would have been there for Carly had their situations been reversed. Their lives had changed with lightning speed once Glenn had become involved in the Canyon Club and other projects, but Carly had always made it a point to keep in touch, to see that the boys saw each other as much as possible over the summer.

"By the way," Carly sniffed the muffin before she broke off a morsel. "Jake said he'd have time to go over Glenn's accounts while we're in Taos, if you'd still like him to."

Months ago she had voiced her concerns to Jake, wondering how Glenn had managed to lose everything so relatively quickly. Jake said that he'd be happy to help and offered to go through the books, but there had been so many other pressing details that she hadn't thought about taking him up on it.

"I hate to have him working while he's away," Tracy admitted.

"Hey, he'll have little else to do but keep Chris amused while I'm getting the gallery show pieces together. Besides, he loves following money trails. It was one of his investigative specialties, you know. It'll keep him from getting rusty."

When Carly headed for the porch, Tracy dogged her heels. "Where are you going?"

"I want to get a look at your guest."

Just then, Wade Johnson appeared in the open doorway with his empty coffee cup in hand. When he noticed Carly, he gave her a nod, a quick once-over, and headed straight for the coffeepot.

Undeterred, Carly followed him, offered her hand, and introduced herself.

He shrugged, shifted his coffee cup, and shook Carly's hand and said, "Wade Johnson."

"Are you from around here, Mr. Johnson?"

Tracy's face caught fire as Carly got right to the point.

"Just passing through."

"Why don't we wait for the boys outside?" Tracy suggested, afraid Carly would give him the third degree, but her friend didn't budge.

Wade helped himself to more coffee and Tracy was relieved when, as if on cue, the boys ran back in, all arms, legs, and impatience bundled into two very hyper packages.

"Let's go, Mom!" Chris was halfway to the door with Matt trailing slowly behind. "We gotta have lunch before the movie."

Carly turned to Tracy and sighed. "He just had breakfast."

"I know what you mean. Bottomless pits."

Tracy walked Carly out to the front porch. The midmorning sky was so bright with sunshine that it was almost impossible to believe that it had been gloomy the night before.

"I can see why you let Mr. Johnson in," Carly said as she dug the car keys out of the pocket of her jeans. Out at the curb, the boys were already climbing into her Volvo wagon.

"What do you mean?"

"He's hot. Even has a bad boy look about him. But not real bad, though. Strong, silent type, maybe? But what's with the hair?"

"Have you watched MTV lately? Dyed hair is in. The more obvious, the better." Tracy laughed, unwilling to admit that on Wade Johnson, it looked better than interesting.

"He's not exactly a kid."

"I kind of like it."

"How much?" Carly cocked an eyebrow.

Tracy immediately blushed and stared down at her hand where the diamond on her ring finger glimmered back.

"Oh, damn. I'm sorry, Tracy."

"Hey, that's okay." Tracy shrugged. "I noticed his looks, is all."

"You'd have to be blind not to—look, Tracy, there's no need to feel guilty. Glenn's gone. You've got the rest of your life to live." Carly took her hands, forced her to look up.

"It's too soon."

"Hel-lo, it's *me* you're talking to. Carly. You've admitted things weren't that great between you and Glenn the last couple of years. Your marriage wasn't any bed of roses."

Her hope of a fantasy fairy tale marriage had been just that—a fantasy built on deception, overextended credit, and, if not outright lies, then evasion. A world of glamour without substance. Near the end, her marriage had been as bankrupt as their money market accounts.

"I get nervous when I think about . . . dating anyone."

"Who's talking about *dating*?" Carly laughed and hugged her close. "Hey, do what you feel like doing, Tracy. You'll know when you're ready."

"Maybe I should stop wearing my wedding ring." She stared down at the diamond that she was wearing not out of loyalty, but habit. It reminded her of their wedding day, when their vows were fresh and new and real. When life seemed filled with endless possibilities.

"Wear it as long as you need to," Carly advised. "Besides, if you're going to continue to check in late-night guests alone, you might as well let them think there's a *Mr.* Potter waiting for you upstairs."

Tracy glanced out at the car. The boys were already buckled into the backseat, heads together.

"You'd better go. No doubt they're plotting something." Tracy waved back when she saw Matt waving to her. At least he was smiling now, which made her feel better about insisting that he go along.

"I'll have my cell on. If you need anything from town, call me and I'll pick it up," Carly offered. "And plan on coming over for dinner tonight. You can bring the account books."

"I will. Be careful." The panic that set in whenever she was about to be separated from Matt these days came swift and sure, surprising her as it always did. Just as he was reluctant to leave her, she had to fight her own reservations about letting him out of her sight.

Life seemed so very fragile now. Still, she refused to let unfounded fear smother Matt.

Just as Carly was backing out of the driveway, Diego Rios pulled in with a minivan full of day workers from nearby San Luis Obispo. When six men piled out of the car instead of the four she'd agreed to pay, Tracy sighed and hurried down the steps to head them off before they all went inside.

CHAPTER TEN

Alone inside, Wade wandered across the lobby to the front window. He found the view down the coast road spectacular, but just as compelling were the snatches of conversation between the women that he'd heard drifting through the open door.

His hostess was alone —except for the boy. Alone and living unprotected. Ms. Potter's friend had questioned her about letting him in last night, having more sense, it seemed, than Tracy Potter.

Tracy sounded matter-of-fact rather than desperate when she claimed that she had to have the hotel up and running because she had to make a success of it this season. The fact that she was strapped for money surprised him, especially with that ring on her finger. It was worth plenty, and proof that women could be far more sentimental than practical.

What had happened to the husband? he wondered. *Separated? Divorced? Widowed?*

He couldn't help but think of his mother, of the way she'd always scrimped and saved to make it on his dad's military benefits. It had been just the two of them for as long as he could remember, just he and his mom living in a crowded one-bedroom walk-up above a Korean-owned minimarket and deli in New York.

The Heartbreak was a far cry from the dingy place he remembered growing up in. Tracy Potter's circumstances were obviously quite different; still, it was just her and the boy. At least right now that was the case.

His attention was drawn to the small parking area off to one side of a rose garden gone wild. Hands on hips, her ponytail swayed back and forth like a pendulum as she spoke to what appeared to be the foreman of the crew loitering nearby.

The silver-haired Hispanic man kept gesturing toward the side of the building where six men in faded jeans, T-shirts, and baseball caps were slouching in silence. Their postures pretended disinterest but their eyes spoke volumes. They needed work and desperately needed the discussion to go their way.

Wade stepped out onto the porch, leaned back against the wall, and listened to the exchange.

"You see, Missus, you like to be finished on time, you need them all."

"I *know* I need them. That's not the issue. I can't *afford* all of them. Four." She held up four fingers. "I can pay four today. I told you that yesterday."

"Okay. Okay. Maybe you pay five, okay?"

"Four, Diego. *Quatro.*"

Wade pictured his mother bartering with the grocer downstairs, something he hadn't thought of in years. There was nothing she hadn't done to keep food on the table. She took in ironing and mending to supplement her military dependents' allotment, cleaned and ran errands for the elderly man who lived across the hall. The one job she loved most was writing confessions. She had a file folder full of clippings, stories she'd sold to *True Confessions.* Stories of love, lust, and betrayal. All fiction. She never dated. Never had affairs. She worked hard, wrote for fun.

Over in the parking area, Tracy still hadn't backed down. The foreman had walked over to where the men waited and after a spate of Spanish he came back to talk to her again.

"Okay. You pay six—"

Wade gave her credit for her tenacity. He almost went to her rescue, but she held her ground and smiled, though she emphatically shook her head no.

"I can pay *four.*"

Diego nodded vigorously. "*Si!* But you *get* six. You pay for four."

She shook her head. "That's not fair, Diego. I can't ask two of them to work for nothing."

"Ah, but you don't ask. I ask. They say okay." He shrugged, "That way, everyone makes some money today. Okay, Missus? A little is better than nothing."

Wade watched Tracy stare over the hopeful workers who were more than ready to put in a full day's work and settle for whatever cash they could make.

"I'll give them all lunch," she offered.

Diego's smile quickly reappeared.

"Lunche," he called out to the men in Spanglish, a combination of Spanish and English spoken all over California. Satisfied, the men headed inside, obviously already familiar with the place as they made their way up the front steps.

Each nodded politely to Wade as they went inside. He had no desire to follow them. Instead, he waited for Tracy. When she finished talking to Diego, she finally noticed him in the doorway.

"Nice going," he complimented as she came up the steps. He meant it, too.

She seemed as surprised by his sudden willingness to talk as he was. It was the first time in a long while that he'd dared to exchange more than a few obligatory words with anyone, but watching Tracy Potter's little drama unfold had reminded him of a life he hadn't lived since childhood, and made them seem connected somehow.

"I feel guilty." Her gaze flicked to the sunroom where the men were already setting up for the day. A team of two carried paint rollers and pans down the hall where the guest rooms were located. "I wish I could pay them what they deserve."

"A little is better than nothing," he quoted.

"Still . . ."

"Their foreman knew exactly what he was doing when he brought too many men."

Finally, she turned her gaze on him. It was liquid blue. Her stunning eyes were wide and full of such promise that for a moment he almost missed the shadow of sadness he'd seen there last night. Looking deeply, he saw it hadn't entirely left her.

He was mesmerized and at the same time bereft, knowing that, unlike Mrs. Potter, he no longer had a dream to fight for. He no longer possessed a single drop of hope for a better day.

Time stopped as he stared down into her eyes and momentarily, he lost himself. Her nearness warmed him, awakening something inside him that he'd thought long dead, something he'd convinced himself he didn't deserve to feel anymore.

Mentally he shook himself and finally looked away. He held up his empty cup.

"The coffee was great," he said.

"Would you like some more?"

"I've had plenty, thanks."

"How about another muffin?"

"They were great, too, but no thanks."

When she dropped her gaze, when her eyes left his, he felt the kind of chill that comes whenever a cloud passes in front of the sun. Amazed, he was a little resentful to think that she'd awakened such feelings in him at all.

He didn't deserve to feel anything anymore. Certainly not anything this good.

"Checkout isn't until noon." Though she said it casually enough, she was studying him intently, assuming he had somewhere to go, some destination in mind.

He had nowhere to go. No one was waiting for him.

Because of this place, maybe because of her, he was still alive.

He thought of the notepad in the nightstand, square slips of paper covered with cramped scratches, the start of something. Notes? Sentences? He didn't even know what he'd written yet. Words inspired by dreams. Probably middle-of-the-night nonsensical rambling.

"I'd better see if the men need anything." Tracy shoved her hands in the back pockets of her jeans.

The move was totally innocent on her part, but it emphasized her breasts. She was too preoccupied with the workers, with her need to get the hotel ready for her grand opening, to be trying to seduce him. She had no idea the effect she was having on him, which made her even more enticing. He stared at her flawless profile, her trim waist and hips outlined in casual jeans, her spanking white canvas shoes.

He'd be a fool to think about the luxury of hanging around, crazy to risk being recognized, no matter how greatly he was tempted.

"Thanks for opening up for me last night. I appreciate it."

The fingers of her right hand twisted the wedding ring on her left in an absentminded gesture. "Are you on your way home?"

Home? He didn't have one anymore. "No, just traveling the coast."

"What do you do?" Though she had plenty to do, she didn't appear to be in a hurry to leave.

His mind quickly touched on possible answers the way a steel ball clangs around in a pinball machine. It finally landed.

"I'm in advertising." He had no idea where that came from, but he went with it.

"Where?"

"In L.A." *General enough.*

"Do you come up with jingles? Like Barry Manilow?"

"Not really."

"Do you write commercials?"

He shook his head, tried to think of a way to smoothly segue out of the conversation. "Just copywriting. That's all. Pretty tame stuff."

"Well, good luck then. If I don't see you before you go, just leave the key in the room."

"I will."

"Be safe."

He pictured himself going back to his room, showering, changing into a clean shirt, wrapping the Colt in his dirty one, and shoving it into the bottom of the saddlebag. Last night he'd put to rest the notion of suicide. He was too big a coward to take the coward's way out. He thought of the string of months he'd spent aimlessly wandering the countryside on the Harley. Of all the sleepless nights and restless days he'd spent roaming around alone.

He thought of the way she'd taken a chance last night, opening the door to him, trusting that he was one of the good guys when she had no reason to. He thought of the Even Dozen murdered women and the guilt that never left him.

Most of all, he thought of how fate had led him to the Heartbreak Hotel last night, and now he was in no hurry to leave. Not yet, anyway.

She was concentrating on one of the painters who was carefully masking off the molding around the floor.

"Tracy?"

"Yes?" She turned, hesitated.

"I'd like to stay a few more days."

She brushed aside a wisp of hair that had slipped artfully over her left eye. "You're staying?"

He nodded. "If it's no problem." He started toward her, digging in his pocket for cash. He counted out nine hundreds—enough for a week's lodging.

"Of course not." Her gaze flicked down to his hand.

He rolled up the bills. Their eyes met as he handed them over.

"You plan to stay a whole week?"

He said the first thing that came to his mind, probably the closest thing to the truth that he'd told her since he'd arrived.

"I really have no idea."

CHAPTER ELEVEN

He's staying.

She didn't know why she felt so relieved. Perhaps just knowing he was downstairs last night had taken the edge off her loneliness.

"I'll be in to make up the room in a few minutes," she promised.

"No hurry. I'm going out for some supplies."

"There's a grocery store near the Plaza in Twilight Cove. Take the coast road a couple of miles south to where it hits the main highway. That'll take you right through the center of town."

"Thanks." He gave her a fleeting smile.

The "William Tell Overture" pealed out of her pocket as her cell phone went off. Wade nodded good-bye and headed for the door. She flipped the phone on and watched him walk away.

"Hello?"

"Tracy? It's me. Chelsea."

Hearing the tone of anguish in Glenn's daughter's voice, she jogged up the stairs to the apartment. She walked into the kitchen, heard the Harley start. Beyond the front window, Wade pulled out of the drive, headed toward Twilight. "How did finals go?"

"I think I did all right." Chelsea was less than enthusiastic.

"You sound down today."

Chelsea sighed heavily. "I really miss Dad."

"I know. It's tough."

Tracy had no idea whether or not Chelsea had been aware of the strain between them before Glenn died. If she had, the girl had never let on. Though she and Chelsea had never shared the close relationship Tracy once hoped for, her heart naturally went out to her. She had never expected to take Glenn's ex, Monica's, place in Chelsea's life, but before she married Glenn, she had hoped that she and the girl would at least become friends.

It took a few years before Chelsea accepted the fact that her father was never going back to Monica. If there were times when Chelsea acted self-centered and spoiled, it was because Glenn and Monica had continually competed for her loyalty.

"Mom married the dweeb and went to Austria for the summer." Chelsea laughed, but the sound didn't cover her bitterness or her heartache.

Tracy wasn't surprised. Five years ago, Monica had moved in with a stockbroker ten years her senior. The only thing that had kept Monica from marrying him sooner were Glenn's hefty alimony payments. Tracy propped her elbow on the desk and rubbed her temple.

"When did they get married?"

"Over the weekend. They went to Vegas. Mom didn't even call and tell me until today. She knows I can't stand Chuckie."

Tracy had never met Charles Strauss, until Glenn's funeral where Monica paraded him around like a trophy, introducing him to all of Glenn's old friends.

"I know you don't much care for him, but he's married to your mom now."

"He's too stupid to see that she married him only because Dad's gone and so is the alimony."

This wasn't the time to tell Chelsea that she'd been looking for a way to help pay her tuition next year. Before Tracy could say anything, Chelsea asked, "Can I come and stay with you and Mattie this summer?"

The request caught her off guard. Chelsea had never asked to stay past her three weeks' visitation every summer. Now that she was eighteen and Glenn was gone, Tracy hadn't held much hope of Chelsea spending much time with her and Matt, but she'd prepared an extra bedroom for her anyway.

"Of *course* you can stay with us. We'd love it. But what about your mom? What will she say?"

"As if she'd care. They'll be gone all summer, and I feel weird staying at Chuck's alone."

"As long as you're not doing this to upset your mom, Chelsea, you know you're always welcome here. Matt will be thrilled."

"Mom hinted that I should live in the sorority house this summer, but everyone's gone until fall and I didn't want to ask you for extra money."

Truth couldn't wait any longer. There was no extra money on this end.

"Listen, there's something I need to talk to you about." Tracy knew there was no easy way to say it, so she jumped right in. "After your dad died, I found out that almost all of our money was gone."

"What do you mean *gone*?"

"That's exactly what I asked the accountant. The house was mortgaged to the hilt, the credit cards were maxed out. Your dad owed money on all his projects."

"But you guys had that big house. And Dad's new Mercedes . . ."

"All I have left is this place, and a little money that my grandparents left me. When the hotel is up and running, I'm going to list it for sale and try to get back into real estate. For now, it's providing us a place to live, and hopefully some income." The view outside the window drew her gaze again. She'd always wanted to live on the water, but never imagined this.

"I thought you were just resurrecting that dump because you missed Dad so much you needed a project. I thought you moved out of Canyon Club and sold everything because it reminded you of him. I can't believe this has happened to you."

"It happened to you, too, honey . . ."

"But Dad left me a trust fund."

"He did, but it doesn't allow for any withdrawals of funds until you're twenty-five, not even for tuition. I guess he figured there would always be plenty of other money. I've talked to a trust attorney about it and we're trying to get things worked out, but it'll take time . . ."

"How much time?"

"She said it could be months. In the meantime, there isn't any money for your tuition next year."

"But . . . I have to come back to SC in the fall!"

"Let's not panic yet. We've got the whole summer to figure something out. I've been looking up scholarships on the Net, but I don't have a whole lot of extra time yet. I figured you could help once finals were over. Maybe your mom and Charles will help."

"Oh, *sure*. Mom didn't want me to go off to school in the first place."

"We'll find a scholarship."

After a brief silence she added, "I don't have a clue how I did on my finals. I probably screwed up big time. It's so hard to concentrate right now."

"I know." Tracy took a deep breath and leaned against the kitchen counter. "Listen, pack up and come up here, okay? Things will work out. You'll see." *Somehow. Some way.*

Another sigh, and then Chelsea said, "Okay, I'll see you in a few days, if you're sure it's okay."

"Of course, it's okay. This is your home, too."

She wasn't absolutely sure about anything else anymore, but welcoming her stepdaughter with open arms was what she'd always done. Chelsea was Matt's half sister. She would never turn her away.

As Tracy negotiated the coast road on the way home from the Montgomerys later that evening, she looked forward to seeing Wade Johnson again with mixed emotions. During dinner, Jake Montgomery had successfully raised enough questions to instill doubt about the wisdom of having let Wade Johnson stay at the hotel as her only guest.

She pulled her black BMW into the dilapidated garage, once a carriage house beside the hotel, and nudged Matt awake. As the two of them walked up the path to the side door, she noticed the Harley parked beneath the porch overhang. So did Matt.

"Hey, way cool! Where did this come from, Mom?"

"It belongs to our guest, Mr. Johnson."

Matt stepped away from the bike. "The guy with the cowboy boots?"

"Yep."

He admired the bike with his hands on his hips, strutting around it just the way Glenn would have. Tracy pulled out her cell phone and hit the automatic dial. When Jake answered, she lowered her voice.

"Jake? It's Tracy. Here's the license number you wanted."

The ex-P.I. wouldn't take no for an answer earlier. He'd insisted she let him run a check on Wade's plate, just to be safe. She read him the number while Matt circled the bike, engrossed in the chrome and the flame design on the gas tank.

"Thanks," Jake said before he added, "I didn't want to head to New Mexico and leave you there alone without checking this guy out. I'll call back as soon as I follow this up."

She thanked him and said good night.

Matt was right beside her. "Can I sit on the Harley?"

"Of course not. Come on, honey. It's late." She put her hand on his shoulder as they continued along the path to the side porch. The garden on either side of the brick walkway was overgrown with ancient rose-bushes, misshapen and wiry, pushing up through a tangle of weeds. She forced herself to ignore them every time she walked by. There was just too much to do inside to worry about the outside yet.

"Do you like him?" Matt asked as they stepped inside the entry. The solid door closed behind them with a resolute click. Since Wade was obviously in, Tracy turned the lock.

"Who?"

"Mr. Cowboy Boots. Do you like him?"

She'd left the lights on in the lobby. They were old fixtures, like the ones in the hall. At some point they'd been converted from gas lamps and, because of the small size of the bulbs, they gave off little more than weak, muted light.

Looking down into Matt's eyes, she realized what he was really asking and quickly knelt down on one knee and framed his face between her hands.

"Oh, honey. I don't even know him. He's just a guest. That's all. We're going to have lots and lots of guests checking in this summer."

"You were being real nice to him this morning."

"I plan on being nice to all the guests. They'll be paying to stay with us, and that's where we're going to get money for all the things we need from now on. I need you to help me welcome them to the Heartbreak, too. This is our home now, and I want them to feel as if they've come to visit. I want them to feel at home, have a wonderful time here, and tell their friends about this place."

He was quiet for a minute, digesting what she'd said.

"Just because I'm nice to Mr. Johnson, that doesn't mean we'll ever forget about your daddy. You know that, don't you?"

He mumbled something she couldn't hear.

"What, honey?"

He looked up, his eyes bright with tears that sparkled even in the dim light. "Yeah."

She took his hand as they walked through the open lobby. He may have grown, but his hand was still small in hers. Small, warm, and very, very trusting.

"You can really help me, you know," she said. "When it gets crowded, it's going to be hard for me to make everyone feel at home, so I'd really appreciate it if you'd be friendly to the guests, too."

"Be nice to *strangers?*"

The question gave her pause. "Once they've checked in, technically they won't be *strangers,* but you are *never* to go into a guest's room, okay?"

He nodded. "What should I do?"

"Be polite. Talk to them. Answer questions about Twilight Cove and tell them about all the things there are to see and do around here. You know about the beaches and the trails and the shops, just as much as a tour guide would know."

"If Chris is around, can he help, too?"

"As long as you are both polite and don't get silly."

Tracy slipped her apartment door key out of her pocket.

"I've got a surprise for you." The minute she said it, Matt stopped walking.

"What?" He turned and stretched his arms wide as if he could block her path.

"Chelsea is coming to live with us this summer."

"She comes to stay with us every summer. That's no big deal."

"Yes, but she usually stays for only three weeks. This time she's moving in for the whole summer."

"Into the empty bedroom?"

Tracy nodded. "And guess what? I'm going to let you help me vacuum and dust and get it ready for her."

"Big wow, Mom."

"Big wow that she's coming?"

"No. Big wow that I get to clean."

He focused on something over her shoulder.

"Mom?" His voice was low and troubled.

"What?"

"It's that guy," he whispered.

CHAPTER TWELVE

Tracy turned and found herself staring into Wade's unreadable dark brown eyes. He'd walked in again without making a sound and, seeing him there, filling up the entrance to the hallway, everything Jake had cautioned her about earlier came back to haunt her.

"I didn't mean to startle you," Wade said softly. "I heard you come in."

"Mom?" Matt stepped close to her elbow, hovered there. She gently laid her hand on his shoulder before she handed him her keys.

"Why don't you go on upstairs and get ready for bed?"

"But, Mom . . ."

"Go on, hon."

He looked as if he wanted to argue, then glanced over at Wade before finally heading for the stairs. Her cheeks caught fire, even before she turned around and caught Wade staring at the neckline of her blouse. Her hand strayed to her throat. It had been forever since a man had looked at her with desire.

Perhaps the look should have frightened her, but when she realized that it was having the opposite effect on her, she was doubly shocked.

"Is everything all right?" she asked.

He paused, then slowly nodded.

"I was just wondering if you have any paper I can use. I'll replace it tomorrow."

"I have some copy paper right here in a drawer somewhere." She walked over to the registration desk, opened one of the lower drawers, and pulled out a stack of paper. "Is that enough?"

"Plenty, thanks." He curved it into a crescent in his hand. "Like I said, I'll replace it tomorrow."

"Don't worry about it." She assumed he would walk away and found herself wishing that he wouldn't. Not yet.

Carly and Jake had done a successful job of planting doubt about him, and yet she still found herself attracted to this man, even though the safest thing, the right thing to do would be to quickly tell Wade good night, retreat to her own quarters, and lock herself in with Matt.

Until now, she always did the right thing. That had been her way since childhood. She grew up trying hard to please her grandparents. After both her parents were killed in a pileup on an icy interstate, she'd made a bargain with God. In exchange for her being good enough, and smart enough, she asked Him not to take her grandparents the way he'd taken her mom and dad. She'd kept her end of the bargain, and her grandparents had lived long and happy lives.

Doing the right thing had always been easy—until tonight.

Tonight she was tempted by something else altogether, even though she had no idea if Wade Johnson was who or what he said he was, but he'd given her no reason to doubt him.

His rugged features were softened by the gilding of lamplight. He was a good-looking man, she noticed, younger than she first thought, though the shadows of lingering sadness in his eyes made him seem older. She wondered: *What was behind the melancholy that never left him? Where was he headed? Was he married? Where was he from?* All of the unanswered questions were as intriguing as he was.

"Are you planning to burn the midnight oil working?" she asked.

"Sort of."

She found herself smiling. "Sort of? How do you 'sort of' write?"

The corner of his mouth lifted with an almost smile. "That's the easy part. Actually *working* on something is another story altogether."

Alone with him in the semidarkness, caressed by the deep, warm sound of his voice, she realized how much she had missed sharing intimacy with a man—and here was this attractive, intriguing man who left her mind filled with more questions than answers.

She brushed her hair back over her shoulder. "How long have you been a writer?"

"A long time." An answer that revealed nothing, really.

"How long have you owned this place?"

"My husband bought it a few years ago. He . . . died quite suddenly, and I didn't have any recourse but to move in and fix it up."

His eyes latched on to hers, held her gaze. "You're a widow."

"Six months now," she repeated.

"I could tell you were new at this."

"I'm sure I'll get better at it. I've never run a hotel before."

"I meant that you're new at being alone with a man."

Now her cheeks were frying. She dropped her gaze to her hands, saw that she was nervously twisting her wedding ring and stopped. When she looked up again, she noticed that he had taken a step closer. His penetrating, deep brown eyes never wavered. He was so close she noticed he wore contacts.

"Do you know anything about the history of the Heartbreak?" He leaned against the registration desk, his stance casual, his stare intent. "Like when the place was built, or who owned it?"

Was he just making small talk? Trying, like her, to keep the conversation going?

She shook her head. "I haven't had time to do much of anything but get moved in and start the renovations. The local historical preservation society has made it their cause to put the place on the National Historic Register. When that happens, it won't look very promising to potential buyers unless I can make a success of the place exactly the way it is." Her forehead creased into a slight frown. "I think Glenn mentioned that the hotel was built around 1900."

"Glenn?"

"My husband."

"How long were you married?" He shifted, settled in.

"Ten years." A decade. Long enough to know someone intimately, to have a son with him. A decade, and yet near the end she had begun to realize that she no longer knew Glenn at all.

"Were you happy?" He didn't seem in the least embarrassed by the personal nature of his questions.

The fact that she barely knew him and that he would be walking out of her life at the end of the week made it easy to be honest.

"The last couple of years were rocky. If it hadn't been for Matt, I'd have probably filed for divorce."

He made no comment. She read no judgment in his eyes.

"How about you? Were you ever married?" She thought about it and then quickly added, "Are you married now?"

He laughed, as if the notion were somehow ridiculous. "No. I'm not married. Never have been."

Her gaze touched his dark hair. It looked as if he'd been raking his hands through it.

"Why not?"

"I was married to my work."

"But now you're taking time off."

He nodded. "That's right."

"So what's the paper for?"

She watched him shrug. Again, half a smile, no more. "I'm just dabbling."

"What is it you're 'sort of' writing?"

"I'm not sure yet."

Just then the stairs creaked behind her. Wade's gaze flicked over her shoulder.

"Mom?" Matt sounded more uncertain than impatient.

She turned, saw him standing on the stairs in his pajamas, waiting.

"Are you coming to tuck me in?"

When she turned to Wade again, she noticed that he'd put space between them.

"Thanks for the paper."

"No problem."

Neither of them moved.

"Mom?"

"I'm coming," she promised. Then to Wade she added, "Coffee will be ready at 7:30. Since it's Sunday, the workmen won't be around, so it'll be a lot quieter."

"Why don't you sleep in?" he suggested. "There's no hurry."

His simple act of thoughtfulness moved her. "How about 8:30 then?"

"That would be fine."

"Great. Good night, Wade." She found herself completely at ease, even smiling for no good reason at all.

"Yeah. You, too."

It was the first time he'd heard her say his name aloud, and he was shocked at how such a short, simple word coming from her lips could send such a wave of desire through him. Headed down the hall alone, he warned himself to not go there.

Don't even think about it.

But it was already too late. Ms. Potter had taken up residence in his mind.

He hadn't wanted to admit that he was worried about her and the boy earlier. When he hadn't seen them around the hotel that evening, he found himself wondering where they were, what they were doing out so late.

She had left the front door unlocked and the lobby lights on for him, but there was something desperately lonely about the place with her and the boy gone. Every creak and groan of the old wood walls and floors seemed amplified. The surf was loud as a freight train when it crashed against the jagged rocks below the bluff.

He'd been to town that afternoon, bought packaged fast food, a styrofoam cooler stocked with sodas, and a new bottle of tequila. He'd purchased the only notebook left at the small Twilight Cove market—an old black-and-white composition notebook complete with faded blue lines and a few years of dust on the cover.

He'd filled it in no time at all, jotting down sensory impressions about the hotel. The sounds, the tang of salt air, the slight taint of mildew that the night's dampness inspired. The cries of the gulls in flight. The hurried *whoosh* of passing cars on the road. The stillness, the aching loneliness that seemed to permeate the very walls.

When he had heard Tracy come in, he'd left his room with the excuse that he needed more paper, but who was he kidding? His urge to see her again was so undeniably strong that it shocked him. Almost as much as the fact that her hesitance to walk away earlier seemed to be driven by something other than a mere need to be polite.

He walked into his room, deposited the copy paper on the desk littered with notepad scraps, the composition notebook, plastic wrapping from a deli sandwich, and an open pack of ballpoint pens. Staring at the cluttered desktop, he thought about his compulsion to stand in the lobby and stare at Tracy. *What would she do if she knew who I really am?*

It wasn't as if he were desperate for a woman. There had been plenty of them in his life. None that he'd ever fallen for, though. None that inspired loyalty or commitment. They'd been flirtatious attractions that had led to physical encounters, short-term relationships that never lasted more than a few days, a month now and again.

After the murders, the string of lawsuits, the trials and publicity, women had still been attracted to him, but they'd been drawn by his notoriety, seduced by his wealth. He never knew if a woman really cared or if she was simply twisted enough to be dazzled by the three-ring circus his life had become overnight.

Eight months earlier he'd changed his looks and walked out on his old life. Since then he'd had one or two infrequent encounters while on the road. Safe-sex one-night stands that hadn't given him pause. He'd never looked back, never thought about the women again.

He'd found it easier to drop off the radar, to avoid contact with anyone rather than live his old life, and by some miracle he'd managed to keep his identity secret.

Just because he was attracted to Tracy Potter, that didn't mean he could get cocky and press his luck. If he were smart, he'd pack up and leave tonight.

Was he willing to take a chance, to risk exposure, to risk it all—just to get to know Tracy Potter a little better? To be near her awhile longer? Was it worth it?

Something told him that it was.

The same something that had brought him to her door.

Upstairs, Tracy made sure that Matt brushed his teeth, and then she tucked him in before she closed his door, took her cell phone into the kitchen, and hit redial. Jake answered immediately.

"The Harley plates are registered to a literary agent in Los Angeles," he said without preamble.

"That was fast."

"It helps to know people in the right places."

"He *said* he was a writer."

"Not an agent."

"Maybe he borrowed the bike." Relief sluiced through her as she leaned against the kitchen counter. She shook her hair out, rubbed her temple. It had been a long day and a very productive one. She should be dead tired, but her exchange with Wade had rejuvenated her as much as knowing that he was indeed connected to the writing world.

Jake hadn't said anything else, but she could almost hear him thinking.

"He's a writer on hiatus," she nudged.

"Right."

"So will you stop worrying now?"

"I'll call the agency in the morning and find out if they represent Wade Johnson." Jake sounded determined to go ahead.

"Please don't, Jake."

There was a moment's hesitation on the other end of the line before he said, "Look, Tracy—"

"The man deserves his privacy. Hopefully he'll recommend the hotel to friends when he goes back to L.A. This is the perfect spot for a writers' retreat, don't you think?"

"You're sure you don't want me to make a few calls?"

"I'm sure. I promise, I'll call you if I change my mind. Okay?"

"Did Carly give you our number in Taos?"

"I've got it. Will you call when you finish going over the books?"

"Of course."

"Thanks again, Jake."

"See you soon."

She hung up, feeling better for asking Jake not to delve into Wade's background.

She very much *wanted* Wade Johnson to be exactly who and what he said he was.

CHAPTER THIRTEEN

The room was dark as pitch, yet Wade had the distinct feeling that someone was there. Someone was watching him. Someone silent, and still.

He lay in the middle of the bed, trying to decide whether he was awake or asleep. He remembered spending a couple of hours making notes. Feeling brain-dead, he'd finally turned off the light.

Now, groggy, he pushed himself up to a sitting position, disentangled himself from the spread. As usual, he'd fallen asleep fully dressed, but his feet were bare.

Drinking in air, he snapped on the light. He was alone. The door was still locked. The French doors to the porch were closed.

There was no intruder. He had no idea what time it was, except that it was still night, still dark out. The clock on the bedside table read 1:45.

He got up and went into the bathroom, turned on the light. It blinded him. He blinked, ran water in the sink, and splashed it over his face by the handfuls, soaking the front of his black T-shirt down to his navel.

"You look like shit." He shook his head at the man in the mirror. After all these months, he was still unaccustomed to the harsh black tint on his hair, the ragged "in" style he had fashioned himself with gel, his smooth, beardless face.

At eighteen he'd grown a beard and worn one ever since, right up until the day he dropped out of sight.

There were few if any photos of him without one. He'd purposely kept the beard all through the trials, for he'd begun to plan his rebirth as Wade MacAllister again. For the first time in his life, he'd been thankful that he and his mom had moved around so much. He'd missed more picture days at various elementary schools than he'd actually made, and by the time he was a sophomore in high school he dropped out, studied at home, and passed the GED at sixteen. His mother was gone now. There would be no unearthing of old yearbook photos, no classmates, friends, or relations cashing in on his nightmare.

He left the light on, stumbled back into the room. The intense chill had left the air. Light from the open bathroom door spilled out across the bed, accented the amber liquid in the tequila bottle on the bedside table.

He walked over and picked it up, screwed off the cap, lifted the bottle to his lips.

"Jose Cuervo, you are a friend of mine . . ."

The tune filtered through his mind, collided with volumes of minutiae trapped there.

The walls of the room were closing in on him and, suddenly claustrophobic, he stepped out onto the porch, closing the French doors behind him without making a sound.

His bare feet hit the wooden floorboards of the wide covered porch that was cool and slick with moisture. The paint was peeling, the surface rough and uneven.

Yet another task for the lovely Mrs. Potter's work crew.

The sound of the waves beckoned him. The sharp sting of the salt-laden breeze cleared his head. He was drawn through the garden filled with overgrown hydrangeas and marguerites—or maybe they were daisies. He never could tell the difference.

He stubbed his toe on an uneven brick, mumbled a curse under his breath, walked on until he was standing high on the edge of the sandstone bluff above the water. A fine sheen of mist shone on the surface of the dark rocks below, glistening like a woman's tears.

It was a long, long way down to the rocks. He rubbed his hand over his eyes and took a quick step back away from the edge.

Breathing deeply, he closed his eyes and let the sharp, cold mist off the water, the even tempo of the waves, soothe him. A vision filled his head, one of tall-masted ships and billowing sails, of rolling hills of green and gold and yellow, and under it all the sound and scent of the sea.

When he opened his eyes and turned around, a flash of white up near the roof of the hotel caught his eye. Hurrying toward the ramshackle garage off to the side of the yard, he slipped into the shadows where he could see but wasn't likely to be seen.

Staring at the roofline, he thought for a moment that he was hallucinating, that he was seeing the woman in his dreams, the raven-haired beauty whose loss he felt as deeply as if her life had been his own.

But the woman walking along the widow's walk in the long, flowing nightgown was Tracy Potter. With her blond hair shimmering around her shoulders, she walked to the railing, clasped her hands around it to brace herself, and leaned into the night, facing out to sea. Perhaps trying, like him, to clear her mind, hoping the elements would succeed where she could not.

She was no more than a silhouette against the night sky, a vision out of one of the gothic novels that had been his mother's favorite genre. The wide, ruffled hem of Tracy's gauzy gown billowed in the wind, outlining her trim figure, the curves of her thighs, the tilt of her breasts.

He stared, mesmerized, unable to tear his gaze away, remembered the sound of her voice, the herbal scent of her shampoo. He hadn't missed the reassuring way she'd gently touched her son's shoulder.

She was a widow, prowling the widow's walk in the dead of night.

"The last couple of years were rocky."

It had been impossible to miss the regret in her voice. Was she mourning the man who'd made those last two years hard for her?

His father had been lost to the Vietnam War. Though never outwardly, his mother mourned him for the rest of her life and had never remarried. Working to make ends meet, constantly having to move when the rent was overdue, his mother had never had a chance to date, to meet anyone and find love again.

But Tracy's world was different. Men would be checking in and out of her life as easily as they checked in and out of the Heartbreak. She was lovely. Educated. She could, no doubt, have just about any man she wanted.

The reality of her situation irritated him. It didn't sit well with him.

His feet were cold, his damp shirtfront stuck to his skin. Almost as if she suddenly felt the same chill, he saw Tracy rub her arms. She had to be just as cold, and he was relieved when, a few seconds later, she crossed the widow's walk and disappeared inside.

He counted to ten before he stepped out of the shadows and walked down the path through the untamed garden and back into his room.

CHAPTER FOURTEEN

There was something weird about Mr. Cowboy Boots. Matt was sure of it. Even though Mom said the guy hadn't checked out, they never saw him except for when he had his coffee and when he came in carrying bags of junk food—cool stuff like chips and Snickers bars and Twinkies. Stuff Mom never let *him* have.

She acted like she wasn't worried about the guy never coming out of his room, but Matt could tell she was just faking it.

Before Mom took him to school on Monday, Mr. Johnson hadn't even showed up for coffee. Every time Mom walked past his door, she would slow down and look at it funny, like she wanted to knock or something, but she didn't.

For a while she seemed like she was waiting around for the guy to show until it got late and they had to go. He tried to fake being sick so he could stay home. After all, Christopher was skipping almost three weeks of school—but she didn't go for it.

He hoped that when he got home, the Harley would be gone and so would Mr. Johnson. But it was still parked close to the building, under the overhang.

This morning there was still no sign of their guest even though there were some huge cinnamon buns waiting for him in the sunroom. If Mom wasn't going to do anything, then it was up to him to find out why Mr. Johnson wasn't coming out.

Maybe the guy had slipped in the shower and hit his head. Maybe he had the flu and was dead in there and nobody knew it.

Maybe his brain had exploded like Dad's.

Mom hadn't ever told him what really happened to his dad. She just said that something in Dad's brain had leaked and that's why he died, but Chris told him that it was way worse than that. He said it was just like Dad had a balloon full of blood in his head and it blew up.

Maybe Mr. Johnson had a blowout, too.

Somebody had to find out, and he was the man of the house now. It was up to him. But he had to act fast, before he left for school.

Right now, Mom was busy talking to a man and a woman who had checked in last night, so he told her that he forgot his spelling and had to go get it. She was pouring coffee when he ran out of the sunroom and slipped down the hall toward Mr. Johnson's room.

Outside the room he looked at his watch, then over each shoulder before he pressed his ear to the door. He *thought* he heard something inside, but he wasn't sure.

He snuck outside and took the side steps down to the yard, then crept along under the porch railing until he came to Mr. Johnson's room. The curtains were drawn, but there was a crack between them, so without making a sound, he brought his eyeball close to the window.

The lamp was on inside the room. From what little he could see, the place was a mess. Trash covered the floor, empty potato chip bags, plastic sandwich holders, and Twinkies wrappers. And Coke cans. Lots of them. He saw a couple of empty glass bottles, too.

Finally he spotted Mr. Johnson sitting on the floor, leaning against the side of the bed. He was hunched over a notebook on his lap, writing as fast as Matt had ever seen anyone write before.

Then, almost as if he knew he was being watched, Mr. Johnson's hand suddenly stopped moving. The pen dropped onto the notebook and the man stared *right at the window.*

Matt's heart slammed against his chest. He couldn't tell if Mr. Johnson could see him or not. The crack between the curtains wasn't *that* big, still, he backed away quickly, without making a sound. He almost rolled backward down the steps.

He jumped off the porch and ran back around the way he'd come, climbed through the window, and raced back down the hall, through the lobby, and into the sunroom yelling, "Hey, Mom! It's late! You better get me to school."

By ten, Wade needed coffee in the worst way.

He'd left the room earlier, looking forward to a good jolt of caffeine. He almost walked into the sunroom, but then he heard voices—male *and* female—and immediately turned and walked back to his room.

So much for the cinnamon buns he'd smelled all the way down the hall. As hungry as he was, he was sure he could wipe out half a dozen of them.

He'd run out of supplies late yesterday afternoon, so technically, he'd had nothing substantial for dinner. Not even he could call chips, nuts, and Cheetos, a meal.

As soon as he was back in his room, he pulled up the blanket and bedspread. Then he grabbed the white plastic wastebasket in the bathroom and carried it around with him, hastily picking up trash.

Two empty tequila bottles were sticking out of the top, but the floor looked a little better by the time he was finished.

He set the can down and looked around to make certain the place was presentable enough. Then he opened the curtains and stared out across the garden, out toward the horizon.

There were no passing ships. Even so, he had no problem imagining what one might have looked like a hundred years ago with its sails billowing in the wind, cutting through the foaming green water. His eyes stung. The taste of salt water filled his mouth. Rubbing his temples, he turned away from the view and walked over to the bed where his papers and the composition notebook lay.

The notebook's pages were swollen with ink and sweat. He'd accidently spilled Coke and tequila on some of them. There were telephone notepapers and paper napkins covered with writing stuffed inside the notebooks, too. Some pages had been ripped out entirely, balled up, rescued, hand pressed, and shoved back into place.

Never one to waste words or paragraphs that could be recycled, he always saved every draft.

It wasn't that every line was that terrific—or that precious.

What's more, he hadn't even reread what he'd written yet. Not one word. It was bad enough that he was even writing again, let alone revising. With any luck, he'd toss the damn pages over the cliff, move out, and be done with this.

Two years ago he swore to himself that he would never, ever write again. He couldn't, even when he tried.

And he'd kept that promise to himself until the night he walked into this place and woke up and started scribbling on the phone notepad, completely unaware of what he was doing.

He'd hoped that he could have stopped this idiocy by now. He had no idea if what he'd written even had any merit. The urge to write had come to him so powerfully, poured out so insistently—and yet he had barely any recollection of what he had written.

Not that it mattered. Nothing would ever come of the work he'd done here. He'd make certain of it.

When he heard a quick knock at the door, he was thankful that he'd taken time to clean up the floor. He opened the door and saw Tracy nearly hidden behind a stack of fresh white towels so high that she had to peer around it to see him.

"Is this a good time? May I come in?"

"Of course." He stepped aside to let her pass and instead of closing the door, left it open while she was alone with him. He realized with blinding clarity that *she* wasn't the one that he didn't trust.

Her movements were swift and efficient as she gathered up the dirty towels and hung fresh ones. It made him uncomfortable, sharing such a small, intimate space with her. His thoughts would have probably sent her running from the room.

She had on fitted black capri pants and a sleeveless black top. The outfit wasn't meant to be provocative, but her shapely figure brought them to life, filled them with gentle curves that tempted and fired his imagination.

He still had no idea how old she was. Thirty-two at the most, he guessed. He really didn't care as he watched her move across the room, attending to the little details of life.

His gaze was drawn to the wisps of blond hair that had escaped her ponytail and trailed across the pale, delicate skin at the nape of her neck. Lost in her, he forgot about the damn notebooks until she picked them up so that she could make the bed.

He held out his hand.

"I'm sorry."

"Don't be." He smiled, trying to put her at ease.

"That's nice." Her tone was light, her eyes shining.

"What?"

"Your smile. You don't smile enough, you know."

"I know." Shy as a kid, he'd never exactly become the life of the party. Over the last couple of years there had been little to smile about.

"Looks like you're still 'sort of' writing." She nodded toward the notebooks on the nightstand.

He laughed. "Sort of."

The hell of it was that he *was* writing again. The weird part was that he had no idea why or how. He felt like a dog having lied to her about being in advertising.

Then again, he hadn't *exactly* lied to her.

He *was* a writer.

He was a novelist. Or at least he *had* been, until twelve innocent women were murdered.

"It takes me an hour to write a thank-you note. I worry over every word, but Matt's a good writer." Tracy gathered up the bedsheets and blanket, completely unaware that she was giving him an outstanding view of her trim behind.

She had the figure of a much younger woman. He'd bet a hundred bucks that she was as firm and supple under her clothes as she looked inside them.

He walked across the room, ashamed of himself for taking advantage of the view when she had no idea that's what he was doing, and all the while she was innocently talking about her kid.

"Of course, all moms think their children have talent."

His mom certainly had, too. She'd believed in him and in what she called his instinctive talent for writing. So much so that she'd encouraged him to submit a piece when he was only twelve. By the time he was sixteen he not only had a file folder of rejections, but another of check stubs, none of which amounted to much, but enough so that he tasted the hope of actually becoming a working writer able to support himself one day.

Hopefully, all mothers believed in their children.

"What's Matt written?"

"Oh, lots of poems and stories. Mind you, the spelling is a bit creative—he's still sounding out a lot of words—but he's got a great imagination. He used to write a lot before . . ." she stumbled on the words and fell silent.

He turned around, noticed her hands had paused in the act of smoothing the sheet. Their eyes met.

". . . before Glenn died," she finally finished.

"How'd it happen? If you don't mind my asking."

"Aneurysm. It was very sudden. He collapsed and was gone without regaining consciousness."

It sounded like a good way to go to him. He could think of worse. Much, *much* worse.

Outside, the morning sky was still overcast. On the far horizon, it was hard to tell where the gray sky ended and the ocean began. His stomach rumbled, reminding him that he hadn't eaten a thing since a dried-out Twinkie last night.

"I thought I heard someone talking in the sunroom earlier. Did someone else check in?" He tried to sound casual, as if it didn't matter. Until now he had felt at ease, almost complacent here. That wasn't a good sign.

When he turned around, she was tucking in folded corners of the sheet, making perfect angles of it.

"Just for one night. I hope they didn't disturb you."

"Not at all. More people will be finding the place soon." He was thinking aloud more than making a comment, but she nodded in agreement.

"I hope so. I just barely made the deadline for advertising in the Chamber of Commerce lodging listing."

"Do you have a Web site?" he asked.

When she laughed, he couldn't help but smile, too.

"Are you kidding? The business cards were just printed."

The bed was finished. She straightened, still smiling.

"Anyone ever mention anything . . . odd . . . about the place?" he asked before he could change his mind. Asked on the off chance that she would say yes and then he'd know he wasn't losing it.

She shook the pillow out of the case and then lined it up to shake it down into a new one.

"Odd? Termite infestation in some walls and not others. Then there's the fact that no one painted any of the rooms for about thirty years. That kind of odd?"

"Not really." He shrugged. "Sometimes old places like this have some folklore attached."

She finished bagging the second pillow, laid it in place against the headboard, stood back, and straightened it again. "Like what kind of folklore?"

"Like ghost stories."

"Are you looking for a ghost story?"

"Not really."

At least he hadn't been, not until he couldn't explain what was happening to him.

But then again, he had been paid for making things up for most of his adult life. His imagination was trained to work overtime.

She was watching him closely. "You don't believe in that sort of thing, do you?"

"What sort of thing?"

"Ghosts."

"Not really." At least, he never had before.

"Good." She glanced around the room, assessing, and must have decided it passed muster. "Well, I'm all finished."

She crossed the room, pausing just inside the door.

"Are you ready for that coffee now?"

Was she inviting him to extend their conversation or merely being polite? He found himself weighing the consequences of getting any further involved.

She was a widow of only six months.

He was a shadow, hiding behind a disguise, hiding from the world at large.

But he was a shadow who wanted to be with her more than he needed that cup of coffee or one of her damn cinnamon buns.

"Sure, I'll have some coffee, if it's not too late."

"Of course not. I made a fresh pot a few minutes ago."

He volunteered to carry out the dirty sheets and towels for her.

She waited for him in the hall.

He decided maybe she was as hungry for his company as he was for hers.

CHAPTER FIFTEEN

The anticipation Tracy felt whenever she thought about seeing Wade again was ridiculous. At least that's what she tried to convince herself of, but it didn't help calm the spike in her heart rate or cool the flush on her cheeks when he opened the door and ushered her into his room a few minutes ago.

When he looked directly into her eyes, she'd almost forgotten what she was doing there.

Until she'd come in to straighten up his room, she hadn't really spoken to him except in passing since Saturday night. By sequestering himself behind a Do Not Disturb sign, he'd managed to fuel her fantasies. Even though she hadn't seen much of him, it was oddly comforting just knowing he was downstairs when she turned off the lights at night. Both comforting and arousing.

This morning he looked worn out—surprising for a man who ostensibly hadn't done anything but laze around his hotel room. There were violet shadows beneath his eyes and a droop to his shoulders, though it made her blush when she couldn't help but notice what fine, solid, well-defined shoulders they were.

"Something smells great." Wade walked behind her, as closely as the narrow hall would permit.

She glanced back over her shoulder and wondered if she was imagining the intensity in his stare or not. Unable to look away, she almost tripped over her own feet as the two of them entered the lobby.

Workmen were everywhere; on ladders, kneeling on drop cloths, touching up yards of white wooden molding, scraping paint speckles off windowpanes, buffing the floor where the painting was finished.

She was proud of the sitting room, nearly finished except for a few decorator touches. Overstuffed sofas with white slipcovers and bright red and blue throw pillows faced each other, inviting guests to sit and chat. The fireplace mantel held two tall blue-and-white vases that flanked a huge mirror with a rustic crackled frame.

Soft oldies music drifted on the air as did the heady scent of the cinnamon buns she'd made at dawn. All in all, the hotel was beginning to look just the way she'd imagined it.

"Where should I put these?" he asked, slightly lifting the sheets and towels.

"The laundry is just off the sunroom, to the right. I'll get you some coffee."

"That's okay." He paused just outside the door to the sunroom. "I can get my own. I'm sure you've got plenty to do."

Nothing that couldn't wait until she made certain he had what he needed.

She was headed for the sideboard when she heard the familiar sound of her stepdaughter's voice calling from the lobby.

"Tracy?"

"You're here!" She left the sunroom and hurried to greet the striking redhead toting a heavy duffel bag through the lobby. The minute Chelsea saw her, she dropped the bag and it hit the floor with a heavy thud.

Tracy closed the distance between them and wrapped her arms around Chelsea, holding her tight.

"I'm so glad you're going to be staying," she said softly.

Chelsea drew back, obviously embarrassed by the show of emotion. "Thanks, Tracy. I really appreciate this."

"Don't even mention it. As I said before, this is your home, too."

Chelsea looked around slowly. "Wow. It's bigger than I thought."

Tracy laughed. "The more we paint, the bigger it seems to get. At first I didn't think it would ever get finished."

"Is it?" Chelsea looked around skeptically.

"Almost."

Chelsea dropped her voice to a husky whisper. "Who's that?"

Tracy saw Wade framed in the wide sitting room doorway holding a mug of coffee. She drew Chelsea across the room and introduced them and added, "Wade is our first official guest."

Wade and Chelsea exchanged pleased-to-meet-yous before he quickly excused himself and went back to the buffet for cinnamon rolls.

"Let's get your bag and I'll show you to your room upstairs." Tracy started for the duffel but Chelsea beat her to it.

They had reached the top of the landing when Chelsea glanced down the stairwell and asked, "So, what's a guy like that doing in a place like this?"

"Is it that bad?" Tracy's heart sank.

"I meant, how did he even find the place? He looks more like a rocker than someone who'd stay in a trendy new inn."

"Trendy new inn? Really?"

"Okay, so that's a stretch. But it looks a lot different than when I saw it over President's weekend. It's just not the kind of place I pictured a guy like that staying in."

"He showed up at the door a few nights ago needing a room and, to be honest, I couldn't turn down the money. Thanks to him, the rates are up."

"Is that it?"

Tracy paused, frowning. "What do you mean, is that it?"

"I don't know. You kinda lit up when you introduced us."

"Lit up?" She couldn't control her blush.

Chelsea eyed her suspiciously. "Yes. Like right now. You're blushing."

"He's just a guest."

"So you say."

Tracy couldn't decide whether Chelsea was merely teasing or actually uncomfortable with the idea as she showed her to the room she and Matt had prepared. Fresh flowers filled a vase on the student desk in the corner, and a new brocade comforter covered the bed.

Chelsea tossed her duffel on the end of the bed and, noting the size of it, Tracy hoped that everything inside would fit in the chest of drawers and small closet. Chelsea didn't seem a bit concerned as she brushed her long auburn hair over her shoulder. Strikingly beautiful, she was a quintessential redhead with deep-rust-colored hair and ivory skin dusted with freckles.

"It's weird to be here without Dad." The girl's voice sounded thick with tears, but her eyes were dry.

Tracy crossed the room and tried to hug her, but Chelsea stiffened and shrugged her off. "Don't, Tracy. Don't make me cry."

Chelsea sat down heavily on the edge of the bed, her hands clutching the bedspread. She stared up hopefully. "Have you had any luck researching scholarships?"

Tracy shook her head and answered honestly. "I haven't had time."

"I went to the counseling office and asked. The deadline to apply is passed."

Hopeless, the girl looked around the room, and Tracy suddenly saw it through her eyes. The four walls were covered in 1940s chintz paper that was faded except where pictures had once hung.

The carpet, matted and flat, had a footpath worn through it. It had been cleaned and vacuumed, and she had fresh curtains at the windows. Still, the room was a far cry from what Chelsea was used to at Monica's. She'd had her own room at the Canyon Club house, too. One that Glenn had decorated for a princess.

Looking around, Tracy refused to let Chelsea give up hope. Nor could she afford to get depressed herself. Not now.

"We'll find a way to manage."

"SC is one of the most expensive schools in California." Chelsea dropped her gaze to the floor and scrubbed the toe of her sandal against the carpet. Once pink, it had faded to a sickly color.

Tracy crossed the room and sat down beside her. Chelsea wiped a tear from beneath her eye.

"You can get a summer job while you're in Twilight. There have to be some scholarships that are still open—"

"It's too *late*," Chelsea moaned.

"It *can't* be. There are always funds available. You just have to know where to look. And I'm not counting out your mom. Have you talked to her?"

"You don't really know Monica, Tracy."

She knew enough about Monica to know that Glenn's ex was resourceful when it came to looking out for herself, but whenever Chelsea needed anything, Glenn had supplied it.

"I called her in Austria." Chelsea's voice faltered. She fell silent, swallowed, fighting tears.

"It's okay, honey."

"She said she can't do anything about my tuition and she won't ask Charles for the money. She said she just married him and that she doesn't want to screw up this marriage." Chelsea swallowed again. "She didn't even talk to me for more than eight minutes. The last thing she said was 'Work it out.' "

"You might have to go to junior college for a semester or two . . ."

Chelsea jumped up and started pacing the room.

"That's easy for you to say, Tracy. Your whole life isn't over. You've got this place. And Mattie. First I lose Daddy and now, school. And two weeks ago, I met a great guy from Orange County!" She took a deep breath and looked panicked. "Where am I going to get spending money?"

Whenever Chelsea cried, her complexion turned a bright, mottled pink. She sat slumped on the bed, knees together, fingers clenched tight.

"I can give you a little money," Tracy offered, calculating in her head. "And you can find a summer job. As soon as guests start checking in, I'll need help with the rooms. I'd planned to hire a part-time maid and was thinking maybe you could—"

"A *maid*?" The word came out as a high, strained squeak.

"I'd never ask you to do anything I'm not willing to do myself," Tracy said softly. She'd worked at the Dairy Queen all through high school and managed to not only make straight A's but made the cheer squad and the swim team. Chelsea was every bit as capable. But was it asking too much too soon to have her take on so much after losing her father?

"Daddy would never, *ever* make me clean up after strangers in a dump like this! I . . . I just can't believe this is happening!" She grabbed her purse, slung the long leather strap over her shoulder, and walked out.

"Chelsea, wait." Tracy followed her out of the room. "Please don't drive while you're this upset."

Chelsea repeatedly wiped her hands over her cheeks, mopping her tears. Finally she stopped in the lobby and turned to Tracy, somewhat collected.

"I'll be okay. I promise. I just need to get out of here for a while. I don't want Mattie to see me like this."

"Where are you going?"

Chelsea shrugged. "Twilight, I guess."

"When will you be back?"

Another tear slipped down the girl's cheek. The feeble smile she gave Tracy nearly broke her heart.

"I don't know," she whispered. "But I won't be late."

"Be careful, okay?"

Chelsea managed to nod before she walked out.

CHAPTER SIXTEEN

A gull swept up the bluff, dropped the clam it was holding in its beak, and attempted to break it open until another bird—noisier, stronger—swooped down and stole it. Their cries sounded almost human. The screeches intensified until the smaller of the two gulls gave up and flew off.

Wade watched from the footpath behind the hotel as the remaining gray gull rode the air currents. It twirled above the rocks below the bluff. He wanted to get far enough away from the building so that he could use his cell phone without being seen or heard.

The wind off the water was picking up as he sat down on a boulder that gave him a great view of the coast. A gray cloud bank gathered on the horizon. He pulled his phone out of his jacket pocket and autodialed the number for the only person in the world he trusted—his literary agent, Bob Schack.

Bob had taken him on ten years ago when no one else in the publishing world would give his work a second glance. They'd both been young and hungry then, both lacking in experience.

Schack, balding at twenty-seven, had been personable, honest, and willing to treat each client as if he or she was the only one he represented.

That in itself was a major juggling act, but somehow he'd not only managed to build a stable of working writers, but had gathered other agents together as well. Ten years later, Bob Schack had offices on both coasts and represented some of the top writers in the country.

When Bob's secretary answered, Wade gave the name Horatio Alger. He was put straight through.

"Where are you?" Schack always asked. Wade never told him.

He found himself smiling, the familiarity comforting after weeks of anonymity. Bob was probably the only soul left on the planet who truly gave a damn about him.

"I'm looking at the ocean as we speak."

"Atlantic or Pacific?"

"That I'll keep to myself."

"Doing all right?"

"Great. I'm going to need a draw though."

He'd given Bob power of attorney over his considerable estate and depended on him to wire him cash whenever, wherever he needed it. Considering all the money he'd made for the Schack Agency in the past three years, Bob would have probably been willing to deliver anything Wade asked for, in person.

"How much?"

Wade named a figure he thought should last awhile, enough to cover him for a couple of months at least.

"Wire it to Western Union in San Luis Obispo."

"Is that where you are?"

"No. Not at the moment. I'm not even close."

"How are you doing?" There was genuine concern in Bob's voice.

"Actually, I hate to go so far as to say I'm doing better, but I'm doing okay, actually."

"No one's recognized you?"

"Nope."

"Celebrity only lasts as long as a shooting star in this country, buddy, you know that. Maybe it's time you turned back into Edward Cain before it's too late to cash in on it."

"Edward is history."

"Oprah's people are still calling."

"I can hear you salivating over the phone. Eight months later and they still want to interview me. Edward Cain is never going to rear his ugly head again."

"Speaking of ugly heads, are you still using that black dye?"

"Afraid so. I've added some gel. You should see me."

"Spare me. That stuff kills brain cells."

"I wish." If he knew for certain that hair dye killed off memory, he'd start using it twice a day instead of every couple of weeks.

"Sally's been calling, too."

"Please. No." Sally Reinhart, known by both authors and associates as Psycho Sally, was undisputedly one of the biggest predators in the publishing pool. She sniffed out moneymaking projects the way a shark smells blood in the water.

"She wanted to know if you were working on anything yet."

"What part of I'm-not-ever-writing-again doesn't she understand?" *What part don't I understand?*

"She said she could sell a week-old salmon inside a puke green cover if it had Edward Cain's name on it."

"Just goes to show you where people's tastes are."

His own ass was going numb from sitting on the rock. He tried shifting, gave up. After a glance back at the hotel, he got up and walked along the deserted path again.

At nineteen, after having sold magazine articles and short stories for years, and having grown up on the streets of New York, where the publishing heart of the USA beat the loudest, he became determined to complete a novel and break into the business.

He grew a beard to make himself look older. His mom agreed it gave him literary aplomb. He took to wearing dark turtlenecks, cable-knit sweaters, and tweed jackets like the best-selling male novelists wore in their publicity photos.

Then he landed a day job in the mailroom at Ballard, a small-press publishing house, moved out of his mother's apartment, and rented a room in a run-down building in Brooklyn. He started submitting his work to both agents and publishers at the same time.

After a stack of rejections from both, he sent his proposal to one of the newest agents in the business, hoping the guy was as anxious to discover raw new talent as he was to gain representation.

That's how he and Bob had hooked up. The first thing Schack told him was that he did have some talent, but no voice. He'd penned two westerns that Bob likened to lackluster imitations of Larry McMurtry.

"Romance and mysteries are hot right now," Bob advised. "Put together a proposal and I'll shop it around."

Refusing to even think about writing a romance, he went to a used-book store and walked out with a bag of paperback mysteries, read enough of them to get the idea, and came up with his own series of connected books.

Determined to do something offbeat that hadn't been done, he eschewed the usual run-of-the-mill hard-boiled male detectives as well as the smart-mouthed new breed of sarcastic female P.I.s and decided on a lecherous dwarf detective with a lesbian partner.

Together, the unlikely pair—after the obligatory 250 pages—eventually solved crime after crime.

Wade was determined to become the biggest name in mysteries to hit the stores in a decade.

True to his word, Bob shopped the proposal around and, finally, a publisher bit. With the contract pending, Wade did something he'd been waiting all of his life to do: He legally changed his name, choosing the pseudonym Edward Cain.

He even planned what he'd wear when Oprah called.

He did make a name for himself, not a household name by any means, but his publisher continued to offer him three- and four-book contracts. He slowly accumulated some money and a bit of celebrity, but he was certainly not notorious.

Finally, six years and twelve books later, Bob thought the midget mysteries had run their course and encouraged Wade to write a breakout novel.

"Thrillers are really outperforming everything else. Suspense is the ticket, Wade." Bob was the only one who ever called him by his real name. The only one who even knew it. To the world at large, he was Edward Cain.

Because Bob had been right before, and because he certainly wanted to "break out" of the mystery genre, he went back to the lucky used-book store, bought a bag of thrillers, and inhaled them.

His writing credentials gave him entrée to police squad rooms and ride-alongs with cops that exposed him to such grisly scenes that he couldn't sleep for weeks.

He interviewed prison inmates to get accurate glimpses into the workings of a criminal mind, took extension courses in forensic science. Then he sat down and pounded out the most violent, most suspenseful, the goriest serial-murder thriller he could conjure.

With only 250 completed pages, Bob was able to generate an auction. Three publishers bit on the proposal for *An Even Dozen,* and Edward Cain was offered just under six figures—a fortune as far as he was concerned.

Bob had been disappointed in the money, but assured Wade that the publisher would make up for the lack of advance with promotion.

Psycho Sally had won the auction, but held firm. Any special promotion for *An Even Dozen* was out of the question. Bob threatened to buy back the book and walk. When Sally told him fine, pay her back and they'd be square, Wade stepped in and told Bob to back off. He'd already spent part of the advance as a down payment on an apartment in a better area.

Unfortunately, after a long struggle with lupus, his mother passed away before the book hit the stores.

An Even Dozen was published with a minimum push. Initial sales were flat, but Bob was certain that if Wade started a second book, and stuck it out, an audience would find him.

Eventually, most of the *country* found him—but not until a serial murderer began to copycat—in gruesome detail—the twelve murders Wade had described in his novel.

In the novel, the murders had taken place in Wisconsin, each act completely different from the one before. Someone had copied ten of the murders, in the same state. Readers in the Minneapolis area recognized that the murders reported in the news mirrored those in the novel.

Edward Cain's Web site and the local police agency were alerted, and the authorities realized they had a copycat on their hands.

The FBI showed up to interview Wade, who could prove without a doubt that he hadn't even left the state of New York in the last month and a half.

Then two more women died, bringing the number to twelve.

He moved through life in a fog. The initial print run disappeared off the shelves within days of the first news reports. With every edition of the nightly news, with every episode of *America's Most Wanted, An Even Dozen* went into another printing.

Wade moved into a hotel under his former name and refused to come out. He couldn't eat or sleep. The minute he closed his eyes, he saw those twelve innocent women, all murdered in unspeakable ways that had come from the depths of his imagination.

Things got worse when he began to receive death threats, not only from the serial murderer himself, but from an unstable member of one of the victims' families.

There were low points when Wade just wished someone really would kill him and get it over with.

The Wisconsin police eventually tracked down the killer, a male librarian who had a history of mental illness, but only after the man was stupid enough to check in to a strip motel under the name Edward Cain. He pled guilty to avoid the death penalty and was incarcerated for life without possibility of parole.

Life was bad enough, but then Sally called demanding an Edward Cain sequel, a companion book, maybe even a trilogy. Why didn't he follow *An Even Dozen* with a similar title? Something like *Dead Baker's Dozen*? *Anything,* as long as the word *Dozen* was in the title.

Wade hung up on her. Victims' families sued him for damages. The murderer's brother sued him for preying on an unstable mind. The crowning blow came when one of the inmates on death row accused him of stealing his life story.

One day, while sitting in court, he came up with the idea to dye his hair, go back to using the name he'd been given when he was born— Wade MacAllister—and disappear as soon as the string of lawsuits ended. Thankfully, he was vindicated every time, but the trials were emotional and draining. Over and over he was forced to relive the murders, face the families of the victims, the press, the notoriety, and his own guilt. By the time it was all done, there was nothing left of his soul.

Even though every single jury had found in his favor, he still felt responsible for the deaths of the twelve women.

After the trials, he put his escape plan into action and, with Bob's help, "Edward" dropped off the face of the planet. He legally changed his name back to Wade MacAllister.

It was on the driver's license in his pocket. But when Tracy hadn't asked to see some identification, he'd told her he was Wade Johnson, not MacAllister. He wished now he hadn't lied to her, but that night he hadn't intended to stay. The night he'd checked in he thought that, one way or another, he'd be gone by morning.

"Wade?" Bob's voice was insistent.

"Yeah. I'm here."

Still alive. Still on the planet. Hell, Oprah still wants me.

He had more money than God, but he felt filthy spending it. He'd given much of it away anonymously, had set up scholarships in the name of each of the victims at their former high schools. Royalities and foreign rights kept rolling in.

"I'm worried about you, Wade. This has gone on too long. You ought to see a shrink. Maybe if you started writing again . . ."

"Listen, thanks for wiring the money. I gotta go."

"Wade, wait!"

"Bye, Bob."

Thanks to ID blocking, no one had the number to the cell. Not even Bob. They worked on an I'll-call-you, you-can't-call-me basis.

"Maybe if you started writing again . . ."

He'd come to the end of the path. There was nothing but the bluff and ocean on his left, rolling hills covered in tall waving green grass, blooming yellow mustard, and wildflowers on his right.

The breeze stroked the tips of the summer grass, bowing them before it moved on. Gulls still cackled behind him as if they knew a secret they weren't willing to share.

Shoving his hands in his pockets, he turned around and took in a view so stunning that it almost hurt to see it. An expanse of dark green waters lay under the blue sky above, and there, standing full of silent secrets on the bluff, was the Heartbreak Hotel. For a minute he saw it as it was in the beginning, when it was fresh and new. He saw a woman standing on the widow's walk, young and trim, her long dark hair blowing in the breeze as she stared out to sea.

From the minute he had laid eyes on the place, it had intrigued him, drawn him in.

I should have left after that first night.

But he was worn out, sick of running from the past, from himself. He'd walked in here thinking about ending it all, and now the place was bringing him back to life. Forcing him to write again.

And then there was Tracy.

He admired her courage and her determination, her innate trust. The way she interacted with her son. It was Tracy more than anything, more than the dreams, more than the mysterious night-writing, who was holding him here.

She could certainly use his rent money—not to mention a helping hand. He wasn't fool enough to try and convince himself that helping her out was his reason for staying. He could write her a check to cover her expenses for the next year and hire a big enough crew to have this place finished in a few days.

He wasn't staying just to help out. The dreamer in him wanted to touch her, to taste her lips, feel his skin against hers. She wasn't the type who'd want a one-night stand. She was the kind of woman a man courts slowly, the kind of woman a man marries—and yet she was strong enough to make it on her own. A woman who faced the challenges life threw at her head-on. A woman devoted to her son.

He studied the hotel from a distance. After taking a long, deep breath, he started walking back along the path.

Like twin sirens, the old hotel, and the woman, had seduced him into staying.

CHAPTER SEVENTEEN

Preoccupied, Tracy was downstairs straightening up the buffet when Wade walked in.

She nearly collided with him as he walked in through the French doors. The serving tray listed in her hands. Somehow he managed to catch her and the tray both. His hands were so strong and gentle that she didn't mind that he held her a moment longer than he should have.

She pretended not to notice, but her body responded to his nearness, the warmth of the sun on his clothes and his skin, the masculine scent of his soap mingled with the tang of salt off the sea. His eyes were the color of hot fudge, and right now those eyes were focused on hers.

The spell wasn't broken until the tray in her hands started to droop and teacups slid toward the edge. She flushed and stepped quickly away, but felt him following close behind her as she moved across the room.

He leaned against the low sideboard she'd inherited with the place while she tried to focus on what she was doing. If she didn't concentrate, she risked chipping one of her precious china cups, a gift from her grandmother. She loved the way they looked like a mixed bouquet spread out on her white linen cloths and crocheted doilies.

"Trouble in River City?" So close now, his voice was deep and husky. The sound oozed over her like warm honey.

"Why do you ask?"

"You looked preoccupied when I came in. Anything I can do?"

"I'm afraid not." It was hard to think of anything but his nearness.

"Try me." His gaze roamed her face, connected with her eyes. His intensity moved her to open up.

"I'm worried about Chelsea's tuition for next fall. Her trust is tied up and it may not be available in time. I haven't had a lot of time to track down a scholarship, and most of the applications had to be in weeks ago."

Her gaze drifted to the sunshine pouring through the windows lining the porch. Birds were singing in the orange tree off to the left of the porch and, as always, there was the heartbeat of the ocean.

She sighed. "I'm not giving up, though."

"No. I didn't think you would."

"I try to look on the bright side. Take action. What about you?"

"It's not that easy."

She shrugged. "I've always tried to visualize things the way I want them to be. And I hate giving up," she admitted.

"How do you see this place?"

"All spruced up, full of people enjoying themselves."

"Do you see the best in people, too?"

As she looked deep into his eyes, it was her heart that stumbled this time, not her feet.

"Always," she said softly, sensing that somehow, her answer was important to him.

"I have a proposition to make," he said softly.

"A proposition?" She was almost afraid to hear it.

"I'd like to stay on until you open."

"Why?" she whispered.

His gaze touched on her lips. "The view is great."

"Don't you have to get back to L.A.?"

He looked puzzled for a minute. "I'm on extended leave."

"Oh."

"Yeah. Burnout. I asked for a few months off. So, any objections to me staying?"

"Objections?"

"Do you want me around?"

Are you kidding?

She couldn't believe it. The place still smelled of paint. The crew was milling around the lobby as a cheap radio blared mariachi music. *Peaceful?* No, but the sitting area in the lobby *was* inviting. The sunroom, with its gathering of small tables and brightly covered chairs, was both pretty and functional. There were no curtains at the bank of windows yet, and some of the woodwork was still in need of a touch-up.

"Of course you can stay, but I insist on giving you a break on the rate, seeing as how I'm not officially, *officially* open yet, and things are still a bit torn up."

"That's no way to run a business."

"Maybe not, but I'd sleep better," she said softly.

When his lips lifted and smiled, she fumbled a teacup covered in purple violas.

"I'd like to pitch in. Don't try to tell me you don't need an extra hand. That way, *I'd* sleep better."

She fiddled with the cup handle, thought about what it would be like to have him stay on.

"You really want to help out?"

"Yes. I do," he assured her.

She tried to come to grips with the idea that he'd be here a month more. Having coffee in the sunroom. Walking the bluff. She'd be running into him in the hall, in the lobby, not to mention working with him. She could just hear Jake and Carly now—but they weren't around to talk sense into her.

The teacup was dangling precariously from her hand. Wade reached for it and his fingers brushed hers, sending shock waves up her arm. Her skin tingled beneath his touch. He took the cup, carefully set it on the buffet.

"So is it a deal?" His face was very close to hers, his dark eyes questioning, ever intent.

The sound of his voice ended the debate raging in her mind. She found her own voice at last.

"How can I refuse?"

CHAPTER EIGHTEEN

The next morning, Tracy negotiated the crowded galley kitchen in the apartment, humming the Elvis oldie "Heartbreak Hotel."

With Chelsea and Matt engaged in some good-natured teasing in the breakfast nook, Tracy decided life was settling into a routine and that she had much to be grateful for. She actually enjoyed getting up early, whipping up fresh baked goods, brewing coffee. Only Wade and Diego's crew were enjoying them right now, but eventually the place would be full of appreciative guests.

"You'd better take off," she warned the kids, "or Matt's going to be late."

"I'll get my backpack!" He was used to careening around the spacious Canyon Club house, where huge rooms and luxurious yards separated them from their nearest neighbors.

"Keep your voice down, honey." The reminder was automatic now. As Chelsea walked up to the kitchen sink with their breakfast dishes, Tracy poured hot coffee into an air pot and couldn't help but admire her stepdaughter. Chelsea had grown from a gangly, gap-toothed eight-year-old into a stunning young woman. Her long auburn hair was alive with natural curl and vibrant red highlights, her bright blue eyes outlined with lush, red-gold lashes.

She found herself wishing she could wave a magic wand and make life as easy for Chelsea as Glenn always had.

At least Chelsea had returned from Twilight yesterday with her spirit renewed after running into a friend from Canyon Club. Eric Nichols had told her about an internship opening available at a firm in nearby San Luis Obispo.

"Thanks for dropping Matt off at school."

"No problem. I wanted to get into town early to pick up that application."

Her determination to be chosen for the summer position reminded Tracy of Glenn's dogged persistence. Once he latched on to an idea or came up with a plan, there was no distracting him.

"What's the name of the firm?" Tracy leaned over the end of the counter where she kept scratch paper and an assortment of pens.

Chelsea dug a paper napkin out of her pocket. "Sylvester, Lease, and Lynch."

Tracy put the pen back down. "You're kidding. That's your dad's tax attorney's firm. He hired David Sylvester two years ago."

Chelsea stared down at the neat block print on the limp paper napkin and then looked up again. "Really? Great!"

"I'll give David a call and let him know you're applying for the internship."

"Would you?"

"Of course. Would you mind doing me a favor?"

"No. What is it?"

Tracy pulled the stack of invitations off the countertop and handed them over. "These need to go out today to local travel agents and other people in the tourist industry. I'm holding an open house in three weeks to show the place off."

"No problem." Chelsea shoved them into her bag.

Just then Matt reappeared, dashed through the living room, and called out, "Beat'cha to the car!"

Chelsea rolled her eyes at Tracy.

"Drive carefully, okay?" Tracy cautioned automatically.

Matt was already out the door when Chelsea grabbed her keys off the table. Before she walked out, Chelsea paused and looked back. "Don't worry, Tracy. We'll be okay. Like you always say, 'Everything will be all right.' "

Read it, damn it. I dare you.

Wade awoke at 3:40 from another dream in which he'd been drowning. Unable to go back to sleep, he started wandering around the room. Later, he found himself hunched over the desk at 7:00 A.M. and staggered back to bed.

Now, drained, exhausted, and dry-eyed, he was up again, staring at the composition notebook. He ran his forefinger down the black binding along the spine. If he were smart, if he were true to the promise he'd made himself to never publish again, he'd toss the damned thing out.

The craft had always been in his blood. He'd written ever since he could hold a pencil. Nurtured by his mother, it had eventually taken over his life, and back then he wouldn't have had it any other way. Once he'd sold his first, full-length mystery, his life had revolved around deadlines, proposals, daily page counts, and conferences.

Although he wouldn't have wanted to do anything else, writing had never come easy. *An Even Dozen* had involved months of ongoing research, interviews, and an in-depth study into the minds of psychopathic killers. He'd loved every minute, his energy fed by the quest for information as much as by the actual act of developing the characters and the plot. He never went into writing blind, always following a well-thought-out synopsis.

Now this odd free fall into automatic writing and the fact that he had only a vague memory of what he'd written afterward left him completely unsettled.

Feeling like a schoolboy, he shifted on the uncomfortable straight-back chair, half afraid of what he was about to discover. With his elbow planted on the desk, he rested his forehead on his open palm, took a deep breath, and opened the notebook.

The handwriting inside was definitely his, the letters tight and even, perfectly spaced, clearly executed in his familiar loopy backhand. His mother had always insisted on good penmanship. His fine handwriting was a product of her determination and hours of practice at their Formica-topped kitchen table.

Now, after leafing through the notebook, wondering how he'd somehow filled page after page with barely any recollection, he made himself focus on the first line.

California 1901

As we stand high above the sea on the widow's walk, Violette begs me not to leave her. She places her warm, gentle hands on both sides of my face, forces me to look into her deep brown eyes, and in a voice that nearly breaks my heart, she whispers, "Ezra, please. Don't go."

"It's the last time, darlin'. I promise. The very last and then you can turn me into a damned innkeeper."

"But, Ezra . . ."

I take her hands in mine, hold them, rub my thumb back and forth over her soft skin. My hands, like my face and arms, are weathered and brown, stained from years at the helm, stained by the sun and the wind. They are hard and calloused. But her skin is soft and pale as cream, smooth as the finest silk ever imported.

I don't know how to live life on land. I've been captain of my own ship for near as long as she's been alive and yet, for her, I'll willingly give it all up.

I'll be what she wants me to be.

I love her that much.

"I'm afraid, Ezra," she whispers. Her eyes search my face. Again she reaches up, strokes my bearded cheeks, makes me feel young though I'm already forty-five. Too old to have hoped to have her fall in love with me and yet, she has.

"You've nothing to fear," I assure her. "You're new to being a captain's wife is all." I turn her toward the Pacific. The air is heavy with spray carried on the wind. I can taste the tang of salt on my tongue.

The water is deep blue today, reflecting the sky. The swells roll, driven by the motion of a storm brewing far away. One that will reach our shores in a day or more.

"Look there." I point to a spot on the horizon, one directly across from where we stand on the widow's walk atop the hotel. The place was her father's dream—his folly. It's too far from Twilight Cove. Too far from where they've cut the new road.

She's as stubborn as her father was, though, rest his soul, bound and

determined to run the hotel herself if she has to. To make the place a
success after all.

More the fool, I've agreed to help her, but then I suppose she knows I'd
hang the moon for her if she were to ask it of me. I'd do anything—except
I cannot refuse this one last voyage down the coast and back.

As I point out to sea, I say, "In two weeks' time, stand on the widow's
walk and train your lovely eyes on that very spot on the horizon and I'll
be there. You'll see the Lantana *heaving to under full sail, flying home.*
Have Emilio hitch up the buggy and drive you down to Gull Harbor to
meet me. Wear the yellow dress that turns your eyes as bronze as rich,
thick honey."

I lean down and kiss her cheek. Her skin is warm where the sun
touches it, damp from the mist. Her long, dark hair ripples, alive with
curl. I pull her up against me, press her back against my chest. We are
fully clothed and yet I can feel her round, soft buttocks against my groin
and I want to take her there, out in the open, beneath the sky, beside the
pounding sea.

Resting my cheek upon her hair, I close my eyes. I hear her sigh as she
stares across the bluff, toward the horizon. I know not what she's thinking.
I feel her disappointment, her fear.

I reach around her, rest my splayed fingers against the swell of her
stomach. She lays her open palm atop the back of my hand. We feel my
son move inside her. Deep in my heart I know that the babe is, indeed, a
boy. My pride and excitement know no bounds.

I pull her close and whisper against her lips, "I want our son to play
innkeeper so that I can laze my days away in your arms."

"By the time he's grown and running the hotel, we'll be old," she
whispers.

I realize she is thinking that by the time our son is grown, I'll be the
old one.

"Darlin'," I say, turning her round in my arms until she's facing me,
until I feel her leaning pliantly against my chest, "I'll never be too old for
this."

Wade read on, immersed in the passages that followed. Descriptions of
the California coast at the turn of the century. Each and every detail had
a ring of accuracy to it. Not only that, but—there was much about sail-

ing, cargoes, shipping lanes, and navigation all of which he knew virtually nothing about.

He felt the intense pain of Ezra's leave-taking, the man's resolve, the woman's heartbreak. Unable to bear a last good-bye, Violette refused to accompany Ezra to Gull Harbor where the ship was moored, preferring to watch the *Lantana* sail past the bluff, past the Heartbreak Hotel.

Lost in the story, hunched over the notebook, he suddenly felt a light touch upon his shoulder. He jerked upright and slammed the cover shut.

As if coming back from somewhere beyond these four walls, the hotel room slipped into focus as he settled back into the present, fully expecting to see Tracy standing behind him with a stack of fresh, white towels in her arms.

But there was no one else in the room.

The hair on the back of his neck stood up. A cold chill ran down his spine. He jumped to his feet so fast that the chair toppled to the carpet. He walked into the bathroom, pulled back the shower curtain. There was no one hiding there.

He knew Tracy would never walk in on him—let alone sneak up and touch him.

He glanced into the mirror over the pedestal sink. No matter how many times he'd looked at his face, he still had to remind himself that he was wearing tinted contacts. It was always a bit of a shock when brown eyes, not blue, stared back at him.

"You're really losing it, buddy," he mumbled.

He ran a hand over a day's growth of stubble, reached into the tub, and turned on the shower, hoping that shampoo and lots of hot water would clear his head.

Still a bit groggy, Wade stepped out of the shower and toweled himself dry before he shucked on his Levi's. Buttoning his fly, he crossed over to the window and opened the curtains.

Automatically his gaze drifted to the horizon and he could see a clipper ship under full sail, white canvas billowing against a clear blue sky, the bow cutting through the waves as it headed for Gull Harbor a few miles up the coast.

He was New York City born and bred. He'd lived in his own ego-driven little world for most of his life, intent upon his career, on honing his craft. What he knew about sailing ships at the turn of the century wouldn't fill a thimble, and yet what he'd just read had such a ring of truth to it that he was anxious to research the subject and see if he were actually accurate. For the first time in years he found himself wishing he had his laptop with him.

He gathered up his writing materials and tossed them inside the desk drawer and then shook his head and released an exasperated sigh.

He wasn't ready to accept the fact that he might be losing his mind. Not yet anyway. There had to be some logical explanation for what was happening to him.

Maybe not logical, he amended, but some explanation anyway.

Trying to shake off the lingering melancholy that Ezra's story had instilled, he pulled a clean black T-shirt out of the dresser drawer and imagined Bob Schack laughing.

The bottom line was that, like it or not, he was writing again.

And, like it or not, he was writing a fucking romance novel.

CHAPTER NINETEEN

At ten that morning, Tracy found the coffee and date bread slices she'd set out downstairs still untouched. Apparently Wade wasn't up yet, or if he was, he was still in his room.

Thinking of the films she'd seen where stereotypical lonely young widows and divorcées constantly hounded available men with baked cakes and casseroles, she nearly groaned aloud, but there was no denying that she'd been tempted to hang around in the lobby, hoping to see him again.

When the bell above the front door rang, she buried her disappointment and put a smile on her face. It became genuine the minute she recognized Willa Connell.

"Willa! I'm so glad to see you!" She threw her arms around Willa and hugged her fiercely.

Willa felt as fragile as tissue paper. As breakable as spun glass. The designer had always been as fashionably thin as a runway model, but now, as she hugged Tracy back, she felt like skin and bones.

Willa pulled away first, but gave Tracy's hand a squeeze. They'd become friends at thirteen when Willa moved to Marshall. They'd gone to Indiana State and relocated in California together after graduation. But while Tracy married and had Matt, Willa had stayed single, focusing on her interior design career. They'd gradually drifted apart, their contact reduced to exchanging birthday and Christmas greetings and an occasional lunch together every year or so.

Tracy looked Willa over from head to toe, admiring her trendy haircut. It suited the texture of Willa's sleek, jet black hair.

Somehow, and certainly without trying, Willa always managed to make her feel frumpy. This morning Willa looked chic, totally put together in a slim black sheath, low-heeled sandals, and a black sweater casually thrown over her shoulders. A one-of-a-kind beaded necklace of amber and crystal was both casual and elegant and completed the look.

"I've missed you," Tracy told her.

Willa gently tucked her smooth dark hair behind her right ear. "I think of you *so* often. I had an appointment up the coast today, so I decided to drop by. I hope that's all right. Are you busy?"

"Never too busy for you. Let's go upstairs," Tracy suggested, leading Willa up to the apartment.

When Willa complimented her on what she'd accomplished downstairs, Tracy felt a bit embarrassed because she hadn't once called Willa to ask for decorating advice. She not only hadn't wanted to take advantage of their friendship—but their tastes were entirely different.

Glenn had gently let Tracy know early on that he wanted their Canyon Club house to reflect his success and not so subtly hinted that slipcovers and flea market finds were all well and good for young marrieds in starter homes, but they'd moved beyond that.

He wanted a showplace decorated with the finest furnishings and fabrics available. Tracy knew that Willa instinctively knew how to put that kind of a home together, so she'd suggested that Willa's firm decorate not only their home, but all of the Canyon Club models, and Glenn readily agreed. After the project was completed, he'd used the Santa Barbara–based firm where Willa was a principal partner on subsequent projects.

As they stepped into the apartment, Tracy shut the door and Willa paused to take it all in.

"Oh, Tracy. This is so homey."

"Thanks, but even homey is too polite. It needs new paint and carpeting, I know, but I've had to concentrate on the public spaces and the guest rooms. I'll eventually get to this, unless I'm able to sell the place first."

Over the past few months, Tracy had discovered that it was always like this when she saw anyone who'd known both her and Glenn. Now there were awkward, stagnant silences, gaping voids in conversations whenever friends tried to find the right words to express their sympathy. Usually they wound up saying nothing at all.

She never imagined it happening between her and Willa, though.

"Would you like a Coke, or some iced tea? Have you had breakfast?" she asked.

Willa waved a hand, brushing aside the thought. She looked as if eating were the last thing on her mind.

"Water would be great. No ice."

Willa had always had a quiet reserve about her, one that Tracy knew hid a deep shyness. Though it was hard for Willa to open up, she had always been a good listener.

Though Willa had dated and eventually lived with a stockbroker, after the breakup, she confided to Tracy that, because her father had deserted her family when she was only three, she'd grown up with a strong desire never to be dependent upon a man for anything.

When Tracy walked back into the living room carrying a glass of water and a diet lemonade, she found Willa tucked into the corner of the over-stuffed sofa, her long bare legs crossed at the ankles, her soft leather tote collapsed on the floor at her feet.

Tracy set the water down on an end table where Willa could reach it easily and then settled into an armchair nearby. It was her favorite place to sit and read during what few and fleeting minutes of quiet stillness she managed to steal for herself anymore. From here she had a clear view of the ocean. Glancing outside, she was surprised to see Wade standing on the edge of the bluff, apparently lost in the view of the expansive Pacific.

"Are you *really* doing all right, Tracy?"

Drawn back to the moment, she shrugged. There was no use keeping up pretenses with Willa.

"I'm taking one day at a time and focusing on my endless to-do list." Her gaze drifted to the window again. Wade was sitting on a wide, flat rock, watching the swells roll in. She found herself wondering how he would react if she were to walk outside and sit down beside him.

"You know me, Willa. Always the cockeyed optimist. I know I can make a success of this."

"You've always been the confident one." Willa sounded almost wistful.

"I was raised to believe in myself. I believed in Glenn, too."

Willa took a sip of water, stared down into the glass. Her fingers were long and delicate. The blue of her veins was stark against her pale skin. They'd spoken a couple of times by phone after Glenn died. Willa had called to say how sorry she was that an emergency had come up with her partner and she couldn't make the funeral. Tracy had called Willa to tell her that she was moving into the Heartbreak and to pass along her new phone number. Of course, the reason why and the subject of her finances had come up, but Tracy had explained it all only briefly then.

"He let himself become consumed by the business. He drove himself, spent more and more time away from us. I have to admit, I was worried. Who wouldn't be? I questioned him. I doubted his fidelity. I doubted myself for doubting him. We argued, naturally, but he was so convincing, so sure that things were turning around. I knew things were bad, but not how very deeply we were in debt."

"You still miss him." It was a quiet, sure statement, not a question.

Tracy nodded. "In a sense, I was already missing him before he died." She cupped her hand around the bottom of the glass. Condensation collected in her palm.

It almost felt like old times, having Willa there, listening intently, concerned, and yet now there was a distinct difference. Marriage and widowhood were steps that Willa had never taken. There was no way she could really understand how betrayed Tracy felt, no matter how hard she tried.

"What about you?" Tracy asked. "Did your firm suffer any setbacks because of Glenn's death?" Suddenly embarrassed, Tracy concentrated on what was left of the pink lemonade and bits of ice floating in her glass. "His debts were so monumental. I hope your firm wasn't jeopardized."

She looked up, met Willa's eyes, needing to know the truth, though there was nothing she could do to help.

Willa shook her head. "There were a couple of outstanding bills for orders, but I was able to use the materials on other projects." Her huge, soulful eyes never left Tracy's. "Things worked out."

Relief coursed through Tracy as she sank back into the soft armchair.

"How about Matt? How's he doing?" Willa asked. "They were so close."

"As well as can be expected." Tracy thought of the empty journal in Matt's room. She'd given it to him at the counselor's suggestion, told him it was a place to write down his thoughts and feelings. She'd seen it that morning when she straightened Matt's room. It was still on his desk where it had been for weeks and, she suspected, still ignored.

"He's coping. He has some separation anxiety when it comes to going off to school, but this morning he was actually anxious to go. I think having Chelsea here helps. Even though he had other faults, Glenn was a good father." There was no denying that Matt was the apple of his eye.

"Where is Chelsea?"

"In San Luis Obispo applying for a summer job." Tracy reminded herself to call David Sylvester as soon as Willa left.

Suddenly glancing at her watch, Willa reached for her bag. "I'm so sorry, but I've really got to get going. My appointment is in San Luis Obispo."

They both stood at once. At the door, Tracy rested her hand on Willa's shoulder, shocked at the feel of skin stretched over bone. "Are you sure you're all right? You've lost so much weight."

"I'm fine, really." Willa tossed her head and smiled. "I came to see how *you* were doing, not to worry you."

"I've got so much to do I don't have much time to think about anything else. In fact, I'm holding an open house in June. Why don't you come up for it? You're welcome to stay over so you won't have to drive back to Santa Barbara afterward. It would be so wonderful to have you here and visit the way we used to."

"I'm so sorry. I've been planning to take a little time off in June. Maybe go away for a couple of weeks, but I'll let you know if it does work out."

Willa told her about the client she was going to meet as they left the apartment. In the lobby, where one of Diego's men was wheeling in a floor polisher, Willa waited until the man walked by before she turned to Tracy.

"This place is going to be a great success, Tracy. You'll see. You'll be fine."

"You think so?"

"Of course. You'll make it happen, the way you always do."

"Thanks, Willa."

Willa's gaze shifted to a point over Tracy's shoulder. Her friend's voice lowered. "Looks like someone's waiting for you," Willa said softly.

Tracy made a half turn and her heart collided with her good sense when she saw Wade standing a few feet away with a cup of coffee in his hand. She waved him over and he joined them, though when Tracy introduced Willa, he nodded but didn't smile. There was an undeniable reticence about him as he studied Willa.

"Willa, this is Wade Johnson. He's our first guest." Tracy had to fight to peel her gaze away from Wade as she added, "I guess you could say he's the Heartbreak Hotel's writer in residence."

Willa told Wade it was nice to meet him and then turned to Tracy. "Walk me out?"

"Sure." Tracy expected Wade to excuse himself and return to his room. When he didn't, she said, "I'll be right back."

Again, he merely nodded. "No hurry. I'll wait."

Willa didn't say anything until they reached her car. Tracy noticed it was a new Volvo.

"What's up with this? You said you'd always be the princess of Porsches."

"I guess I wanted a little more metal around me, and this way I can carry interior samples and smaller pieces of furniture."

Willa's gaze touched upon the garden gone wild, then swept up the front of the hotel, over the dormer windows, the Queen Anne features integrated with the California Western exterior, the widow's walk.

Then she said, "He's handsome. He looks familiar somehow. Was he a friend of Glenn's?"

"He's from L.A. He works for an ad agency."

Willa paused before she asked, "Is he living here?"

"He's on R and R. Getting back his muse or something."

"You're attracted to him." It was a statement uttered with calm certainty.

"That's impossible. I hardly know him."

"Physical attraction is a powerful thing. Maybe you should get to know him."

If I'm that transparent, can Wade see it for himself?

Willa pulled her car keys out of her purse and hit the alarm button, unlocking the black Volvo. Her expression suddenly grew pensive before she said, "I know Glenn would want you to be happy."

"You think so? If he had wanted me to be happy, he would have told me the truth from the beginning. He would have let me help him straighten things out."

Willa's gaze drifted to the hotel, traveled up to the top of the building, then out to sea. When she finally looked at Tracy again, she reached for her hands and gave them a tight squeeze.

"Be happy, Tracy. If a fling with your resident writer is what it takes, go for it."

CHAPTER TWENTY

Tracy stepped over the long extension cord connected to the floor buffer in the lobby and was pleasantly surprised when she discovered Wade waiting for her near the registration desk. It was momentarily silent inside, Diego and his crew having taken a break after helping themselves to styrofoam cups of coffee, fresh date bread, and yesterday's pumpkin muffins. She found herself jittery as a teenager and resisted an urge to reach up to see if her hair was in place.

"More coffee?" She glanced at the buffet after Wade shook his head. "Do you need anything else?"

"I'm fine, thanks. I was just thinking about heading into town. Do you need anything from Twilight Cove?"

She shook her head. "Nothing I can think of."

When he didn't move, she took a deep breath. Then she flattened the palm of her hand against her midriff and expected to feel the movement of a hundred butterflies flitting around her insides. She remembered how peaceful he'd looked sitting out on the bluff, staring out to sea.

"I saw you outside enjoying the view."

He studied her for a moment before he said, "It's spectacular."

"You should see it from the widow's walk."

Closing the distance between them, he was close enough to touch. "Is that an invitation?"

"I guess it is. When would you like to see it?"

"How about right now?"

What are you doing? What are you thinking? The butterflies were getting frantic. She glanced around the empty lobby. Showing him the walk meant that she would be taking him through the apartment. Letting him see a more intimate, personal side of her life. Opening up to him.

She couldn't seem to stop herself.

"Why not? Everyone else is on a break."

The intimacy forced by the trip up the narrow stairwell wasn't lost on her as they went up to the apartment. She was aware of his every step as he walked close behind her through the rooms and down the hall to the door at the end. More stairs after that, steeper, just a bit wider than his shoulders. Time and use had worn depressions in the center of each step.

Curious, she found him just one step below her. Their faces were level. His deep brown-eyed gaze locked with hers. Her hand tightened around the handrail. She was able to break the spell, to continue climbing, aware of the sound of the slide of his jeans as he moved. Their footsteps kept time with each other until they reached the top. She opened the door to the rooftop and stepped outside.

She walked to the railing, grabbed it with both hands, and gazed out at the view. The ocean was fairly calm. Swell lines moved toward shore, forming waves in the cove. A slight onshore breeze was blowing.

He followed, stood beside her, his shoulder touching hers. She felt him take a deep breath, hold it, then let it go.

"You were right. This is something."

"I love it up here, above everything. I feel as if I'm floating on the breeze, like a gull." She raised her face to the heat of the sun, closed her eyes. Beside her, he shifted but remained silent. The sound of the workers' voices carried up from the garden below, lyrical Spanish phrases, an occasional laugh that drifted above the sound of the waves.

She let the seconds lengthen into a stolen moment that she savored as the warmth of both the sun and the man beside her slowly replaced the chill that had settled around her heart.

When she grudgingly opened her eyes again, she found that Wade had turned to face her. He was staring at her lips. Her heart stopped jogging and kicked into a full sprint.

"I should probably get back." She realized she hadn't meant to whisper, but she had, almost as if this interlude were somehow sacred. Perhaps it was—in that she would remember it for a long time to come.

"Lead the way." He stepped away from the rail, and as she passed by, she felt his hand riding at the small of her waist. The touch was so light, so fleeting, that she wasn't sure he had actually touched her at all.

"What's that second door to?" He paused at the top of the stairwell after they stepped inside.

"The attic."

She tried the old brass knob but, when it didn't budge, he reached around her to help and his forearm brushed against the side of her breast. Searing, white-hot heat shot through her, radiated down her spine, quickly arousing her, melting her.

She tried to dismiss it. Told herself it was a perfectly natural reaction to his maleness, to the shock of physical contact with the opposite sex.

But she doubted she'd have felt the same way if she had accidently brushed up against the UPS man.

Once they were inside the stuffy little room under the eaves, Wade looked around at the boxes and crates piled on the floor.

"Most of these are full of things I didn't have room for in the apartment. The rest are old boxes that were left here. I don't want to have them hauled away until I've had time to look through them myself." Then she added, "Just on the off chance that one of them might be filled with gold bullion or old bonds worth millions now."

"You've had your hands full." He looked as if he were debating something and then asked, "Would you like me to go through these for you?"

"I couldn't ask you to do that."

"You're not asking. I'm volunteering. You said you'd think of something for me to do in exchange for lowering my room rate. How about if I go through these boxes, sort them all out, and have you look them over? Then I'll haul away what you don't want. If there's anything of interest, I'll set it aside."

"Like a chest filled with Spanish doubloons?"

When he laughed, his whole face lit up. It was such a transformation that she couldn't do anything but stare.

"Be happy, Tracy. If a fling with this guy is what it takes, go for it."

She couldn't help but think that this wasn't only about what she wanted. She was a mom.

What about Matt? And Chelsea?

Would they see her interest in him as a betrayal of their father? Neither of them was completely aware, as far as she knew, of the problems she and Glenn were having. If she were to start dating after only six months . . .

"Who's talking about dating?" Carly had asked.

"What are you thinking about?" He walked away from the window.

You. My kids.

"Nothing," she lied, and then turned the tables. "What are *you* thinking about? Besides this mess?"

"I've been wondering who might have lived here, thinking that a man would be crazy to ever leave, if the place were his." He looked away, as if he'd said too much.

Her gaze lifted to the cobwebs hanging from the rafters. Dust and must were trapped in the air. She was pretty sure that if she held her breath she would be able to hear the termites crunching away inside the walls.

She thought of all she'd accomplished downstairs, of all there was left to do. The Heartbreak Hotel project had started as a means to an end for her. Sure, she'd had enough vision to see it restored, inch by inch, but she hadn't really chosen to live here and probably never would have in a million years. Then she pictured the sunroom the way it looked now, how lovely it looked with the sun streaming through the windows. There was no view comparable to those she had from almost every single window.

And the moments of contemplation and peace she'd found on the rooftop walk were priceless.

"I have to admit," she said grudgingly, "the Heartbreak is starting to grow on me."

He moved closer. "Do you get an odd feeling here? Something that you don't feel anywhere else?"

Slowly she shook her head to deny it. What she was experiencing right now had absolutely nothing to do with the hotel and everything to do with him. The color of his eyes reminded her of chocolate fudge—and there was nothing she liked better than chocolate.

As she studied his face, she made the fatal error of looking at his lips.

His voice was so low she barely heard him when he asked, "What are you thinking about?"

"Chocolate." She felt his hand on her arm. Felt the warmth of his palm as he ran his hand down her arm to her hand.

"Hungry?" His tone caressed.

Her mouth went dry. She licked her lips.

"Starving."

There was a tug on her hand and then she was in his arms, locked in a crushing embrace. His mouth covered hers, his lips relentless, his hands strong and sure as he pressed her hard against him.

A shock to her senses, his touch was rough and at the same time gentle, communicating not only heat, not only desire, but a sense that she had nothing to fear. He would stop if she said the word, she knew it. Instead, she closed her eyes, savored his taste as she frantically kissed him back.

So long.

She hadn't been touched like this for so long. His hands, his lips, his whole body communicated the depths of his desire. His need was evident from the moment their bodies collided. He slipped his knee between her legs. She pressed against him, felt herself growing moist.

His mouth opened, his tongue moved slowly over the seam of her lips until she was compelled to open up to him to kiss him back, to let go and lose herself in him. She moaned when his tongue slid between her lips.

Soaring on sensation, she caught hold of the front of his shirt and hung on as his lips claimed her kiss. Aware of the erratic beat of her heart, of their ragged breathing, she lost track of time and place. She let go of all conscious thought, drowned in sensation—his hard masculinity, the scent of soap on his skin, the musty air around them.

For the first time in what seemed like forever, she felt alive, vital. Young again. Her pulse beat hot and wild in her ears. Her body, inspired by the rush of dampness between her thighs and a tingling pulsation, yearned for more. She ached for him to touch her intimately.

She moaned against his lips, unspoken, unformed words. If she could speak, she would surely beg for fulfillment.

This is insane. This is dangerous.

This is what I want. What I need . . .

Without warning, the floor suddenly creaked behind them. Tracy heard a gasp before Chelsea's voice rang out, "Tracy? Ohmygod!"

She pulled away so quickly that she nearly brought them both down onto the boxes at their feet. If he hadn't held on to her, her knees would have given way and she'd have ended up in a heap.

With her own heart sinking, Tracy watched all the color drain from Chelsea's face as she stood there framed in the doorway, staring at them. Her freckles stood out in bright relief against her pale face.

"Chelsea—" Tracy knew there was nothing she could say, no lame excuse she could make for what had just happened. Chelsea was old enough to see through a lie—though Tracy would never consider lying to her.

Before she could offer an apology, Chelsea turned and ran back down the stairs.

It wasn't until Tracy raised her hands to her lips that she realized her fingers were shaking badly. And that Wade was still holding her.

"Please," she whispered. "Let me go."

"Are you all right?"

She wasn't, but she nodded anyway. "I'm okay, but obviously, Chelsea's not."

He opened his arms slowly, as if afraid she might fall. She clasped her hands together and stared at the empty doorway.

"What in the world am I going to say to her?" She was thinking aloud, not really expecting an answer.

"Tell her that you're sorry she was upset."

"But—"

"There's no need to apologize for what we did, Tracy. It was a perfectly innocent kiss."

She turned to him in shocked amazement. They'd had their hands all over each other. He was fondling her breast. She'd been straddling his leg. A few more seconds and she might have climaxed.

Perfectly innocent kiss?

Innocent? She didn't know whether to be ashamed or disappointed. What she'd experienced had felt far from innocent; it had been an earth-shattering encounter, but she wasn't about to admit that to him now.

"I need to go talk to her." She would rather jump off the bluff at this point, but Chelsea meant too much to her to leave her downstairs alone in an emotional upheaval.

Wade reached for her hand, effectively stopping her in her tracks.

"I'm sorry she walked in on us like that," he admitted, "but I'm not sorry I kissed you. What about you?" His deep brown eyes bored into hers and, in their depths, she saw all the confusion she was feeling. "Are you sorry I kissed you?"

"I'm not sorry, but . . ." She had no idea what she was feeling. Embarrassment, certainly. *Shame?* No.

"Will you be all right?" He reached for her hand. "Do you want me to go talk to her with you?"

"No!" She took a breath. Calmed down. "No. I'll be fine."

She almost laughed. *Fine? Fine?*

"I hate for you to go like this."

"Wade . . ."

"I'm heading to Twilight, but I'll be back." He shoved his hands in his back pockets, meeting her eyes. "I'll leave the next move up to you."

After Wade left the attic, Tracy took a minute to pull herself together. She took a deep breath, pressed her fingertips to her lips. Every nerve in her body was pulsing. She'd never been hysterical before, but right now she felt on the verge of both laughing and crying. Elated, buoyant, she was at the same time heartbroken for inadvertently upsetting Chelsea.

She'd seen the hurt in the girl's eyes and knew without a doubt that Chelsea saw the kiss as an ultimate betrayal of Glenn's memory.

CHAPTER TWENTY-ONE

Tracy found Chelsea in her room and ignored the girl's sullen request for her to go away. She walked in and halted a few feet from the bed.

"Chelsea, I'm so sorry."

"Hey, you don't have to apologize to me," she shrugged. "It's still a free country. Kiss whoever you want." She sat up and slipped off her black sandals. Her toenails were coated with glossy, summer pink toenail polish. "You were so busy with your boy toy you forgot to call David Sylvester," she added.

Tracy felt like a deer caught in the headlights, but she sat down on the foot of the bed anyway. Chelsea scooted away.

"Oh, honey, I apologize again." Her words drifted into silence. "Things got a bit hectic around here. Willa stopped by and then, well, it . . . slipped my mind. Did you talk to David?"

Chelsea nodded. "He gave me an application and said there shouldn't be any problem."

"I'll give him a call the minute we've settled this. I promise."

Chelsea sat up. "There's nothing to settle."

"I'm sorry this happened, honey."

"Sorry you let him kiss you? Or sorry I walked in?" She crossed her arms, stared over at Tracy with more confusion than anger in her eyes. "I'd have expected this out of my mom, but not you. You always tried so hard to be the perfect wife, the perfect soccer mom. I thought you loved Daddy."

"Chelsea . . ."

"You don't even know this guy. He's just using you. How old is he, anyway?"

Tracy shook her head. "I have no idea."

"He's younger than you are."

"A couple of years, maybe."

"So. Don't you get it?"

Tracy stared at her, considering. "Get what?"

"That he's probably just out for sex. You're just lonely without Dad."

"Not enough to make a fool of myself. I wanted to kiss Wade, Chelsea."

She could tell she'd embarrassed Chelsea with her honesty. The girl got up, grabbed her purse off the chair, and dug around inside for the folded intern application.

"I really ought to get this filled out."

Tracy refused to leave with Chelsea this upset. She walked over to the girl and laid her hand on Chelsea's shoulder.

"Look at me," she said softly.

Slowly, Chelsea turned.

She wanted to reassure her that yes, she'd loved Glenn, and she wanted to sound sincere. All the doubt and anger that she'd lived with the last few years of her marriage were not Chelsea's burden. She didn't want to tarnish the girl's memory, so she tried to remember what she and Glenn once had. How much they'd loved each other once.

"I loved your dad. You know that, but now he's gone."

"Have you been sleeping with that guy?"

Tracy shook her head. "No. I haven't."

"Are you going to?"

"I don't know what's happening here. I don't know what I'm feeling for, or about, Wade Johnson. You have to understand that I'd never do anything to purposely hurt or embarrass you." Then she asked, "Are you going to be all right, honey?"

"Oh, yeah. Sure. My dad died, and my life sucks. I'll be fine."

"I can't bring your dad back . . ."

"I know that. I'm sorry, Tracy. I've just been kinda bummed lately."

"Do you need any help with that application?"

Chelsea shook her head. "I don't think so. I looked it over earlier. It's pretty standard stuff. They'll send for transcripts, check my grades and references."

"Then if you're all right, I'll go call David and then fix us some lunch."

Eating was the last thing she wanted to do right now, but it would be a way to get Chelsea out of her room to keep communications open. She left the room praying that she hadn't done irreparable damage to what had sometimes been a tenuous relationship. Unfortunately, there was no easy way out of this. Chelsea had seen what she'd seen. There was no going back.

CHAPTER TWENTY-TWO

School wasn't any fun with Christopher in Taos. Matt wished he could skip school, too. At least Carly had promised that Chris would be back for the class party on the last day.

It wasn't much fun hanging around the Ear Ache either, not with Mom running from room to room making sure everything was perfect for the open house. Today when she picked him up after school, she bought him an ice cream cone like always, but she was in such a hurry to get back that she made him eat it on the way home instead of at a table outside of Sweeties.

He turned off the portable television in his room and headed downstairs. The lobby was deserted, so he wandered down the hall past the guest rooms.

Looking around, he pressed his ear to the door of Wade Johnson's room, but he didn't hear anything. His mom was in another room down the hall pounding a picture hanger into the wall above a dresser. She didn't see him in the doorway, so he walked back to the lobby and out the front door.

The sun had been shining earlier, but now it was overcast, so gray and gloomy that he thought it might start raining. Noticing a ladybug on a bush near the porch, he walked over to see if he could get her to walk up his finger.

The ladybug flew off and Matt sighed, hoping he wouldn't have bad luck for seven years.

Scuffing his Skechers, he trudged along the stone path until he reached the end of the garden. When he turned the corner, he saw Wade's Harley parked beside the building.

Even without the sunshine, the chrome on the motorcycle gleamed like the brightest silver. After glancing around first to make sure no one was watching, he walked up closer to check it out.

He ran his hand over the wide leather seat and touched the glass covers on the gauges. The motorcycle had a kickstand just like his bike, only much thicker. He wondered how hard it would be to kick up the stand.

Reaching out, he gave the bike a little nudge but it didn't even budge, so he pressed a little harder, first with one hand, and then both. Nothing happened.

He glanced up and down the road as far as he could see. There wasn't a soul in sight, so he took a deep breath and climbed up on the Harley, straddling the wide seat. He grabbed the handlebars and wished he could get somebody to take a picture of him.

Leaning forward, gripping the handlebars, he began to mutter low and deep in his throat, trying to imitate the Harley engine's purr.

"Potatopotatopotatopotato." With his eyes closed and the breeze off the ocean stirring his hair, it was easy to imagine cruising along the coast, leaning around the curve that hugged the bluffs, tearing down the stretch of road that turned onto Cabrillo Avenue. He imagined himself slowing down as he rode into Twilight Cove, and the look of surprise on Selma Gibbs's face when he waved to her and rumbled past the Plaza Diner.

Pretending to shift gears, he was just about to burn rubber in front of Twilight Cove Elementary. And his heart stopped when Wade Johnson said, "Having a good ride, Sport?"

Matt's eyes flew open and he froze right there on the big black leather seat. Wade was standing a few feet away with one hand in his back pocket and a black helmet under one arm.

He wasn't smiling, either.

Matt tried to say something, but nothing happened. Finally, when he was able to talk, he could only squeak "I'm sorry" in a voice that sounded just like Mickey Mouse—which was almost as embarrassing as getting caught.

When he was a little kid—a couple of years ago—he had a habit of throwing up whenever he was upset or scared. Right now he was afraid everything in his stomach was working its way north.

He wanted to jump down and tear off into the hotel, but he was too scared to move.

Wade Johnson shifted his scuffed cowboy boots and watched him for another minute before he said, "That model's called a Fat Boy."

"Oh."

"It weighs about six hundred pounds."

"Wow. I'm sure glad it didn't fall over." Matt envisioned himself flattened like a cartoon character beneath the big chrome bike.

"You couldn't budge it if you tried," Wade told him.

"I know. I already tried."

Wade nodded. "I figured."

"You gonna tell my mom?" Matt's stomach lurched again. He tasted mint chocolate chip ice cream.

"Tell her what?" Wade pretended to not know what he was talking about.

The ice cream in his stomach slowly settled as Matt slid off the Harley. He had to tip his head back to look up at Wade.

"You going someplace?" he asked Wade.

"Thought I'd go into town for dinner. Got any suggestions?"

Matt didn't want to like the guy, mainly because he didn't think Dad would want Wade Johnson hanging around Mom, but today Wade seemed a little friendlier than when he first checked in.

Besides, Mom said that he'd have to do his part to help the guests. He didn't really think anyone would ask a kid something like where to eat, or what to see, but maybe Mom was right.

"If you want a good hamburger and fries or some chicken, you can go to Selma's Plaza Diner. Do you like Mexican food?"

Wade nodded. "Some."

"Then you could go to Enrique's. It's on the road out of the town."

"Thanks." Wade nodded.

Wade looked like he was thinking about something really hard.

"How's it going with you?" he asked.

A rush of something Matt hadn't felt in a long time filled him up inside and suddenly he didn't feel like a kid anymore. He felt the way he did whenever he and his dad went someplace by themselves, or whenever he'd looked up into the bleachers during one of his ball games and spotted his dad sitting there watching the game.

Then he remembered he'd never, ever see Dad again, and the good feeling whooshed out of him as fast as air out of a loose balloon.

He hung his head and stared at his Skechers. "It's going okay."

"Just okay?"

He shrugged. "Yeah."

Wade Johnson didn't leave and Matt thought somebody ought to say something. "Mom said you write stuff."

"I do."

"She wants me to write, too. She thinks I'm good at it."

"She told me."

"She did?" That made him feel better, to know Mom was bragging about him. "She wants me to write about how I *feel* in a dumb journal. For *therapy*."

"Do you think you need to?"

He thought about it for a minute and answered honestly. "I dunno. She wants me to write how I feel about Dad dying."

"How do you feel about that idea?"

He shook his head, thinking of the journal with Spider-Man on the cover. It was full of *thousands* of blank pages. More than he could fill if he wrote for the rest of his whole life.

"I don't like to think about it."

"What if you just wrote letters to him?"

Was this a joke? Didn't the guy know his dad was dead?

"He's never going to read 'em."

"You could pretend. You could tell him about how you and your mom are fixing up this place . . ."

"I *hate* this place."

Wade Johnson glanced out toward the ocean and then looked like he just got a great idea. "Write to him about the Harley."

The more Matt thought about it, the more he wished Dad could see him on the Harley.

"I don't spell very good," he admitted.

"I don't either." Then Wade kinda smiled and it made him look much nicer. "Besides, journals are just for you, not anyone else. The spelling isn't as important as what you write."

"I'll think about it."

Wade put on the helmet before he reached into his front pocket and pulled out a key. Matt stepped away from the Harley and stood back, watching closely as Wade righted the heavy bike and straddled the wide seat. He turned the key and pushed a button and the big engine came to life.

Wade gave him a nod before he turned the bike toward the driveway. Matt felt the rumble of the motor down to his toes and wished like anything that Wade would ask if he wanted a ride, but he knew he'd have to ask his mom and she'd *never* say it was okay. No motorcycles. Not ever. That's what she always said.

Wade saluted him with two fingers and slowly rolled down the driveway. When he got to the end, he revved the engine and took off. Matt ran down the driveway after him. Watching the chrome wheels spin and hearing the roar of the engine made him want to fly.

He stood at the end of the driveway and watched Wade ride away.

Later that night, after his mom tucked him in, he waited a few minutes, turned the light back on, and picked up the journal. It took him a minute to find a pen that felt just right in his hand and then, thinking about Wade and the way he'd seen him sitting on the floor writing, he sat down on the floor, too. He leaned back against the bed and propped the journal on his knees, opened it to the first blank page, and in his most careful printing wrote *Matt Potter's Jornul.*

Then he decorated the page with a few rockets and stars and a full moon, then a crooked crescent moon, and a rainbow arcing over some puffy clouds so it looked like heaven.

On the second page he wrote the date in the top right corner and then he wrote *Dear Dad.*

All of a sudden he couldn't see the page because his eyes were blurry. Then a tear plopped down on a line right in the middle of the page.

Matt closed the journal, tossed it on the floor next to him, hid his face in the crook of his arm, and cried.

CHAPTER TWENTY-THREE

For days Tracy had made it a point to not be alone with Wade for more than a few minutes of necessary conversation. She thought that given time and lack of opportunity, her attraction would fade, but unfortunately, the more she avoided being alone with him, the more she wanted to see him. At night she tossed and turned, wondering if he was thinking about her at all or if he was asleep.

Kissing him had been like having one piece of chocolate and trying to ignore the rest of the box.

Alone in the lobby that morning, she turned off the local radio news and weather report and tried to convince herself that meteorologists didn't know everything. It had been raining for two solid days. Not occasional showers. Not drizzle. There had been forty-eight hours of constant downpour, uncommon for California in any month, let alone June.

"What happened to global warming?" she mumbled as she walked over to straighten an already neat pile of magazines on the low coffee table in front of the fireplace. The sitting room was chilly and damp, which encouraged the slight smell of mildew that tended to linger in old buildings by the sea. If she weren't intending to leave for town in a few minutes, she would have started a fire just to dispel the gloom.

She was about to head upstairs to get Matt and her purse when Wade walked in, wiping his hands on a rag.

"I'm finished." He absently rubbed a spot of paint off his thumb as he crossed the room. "The last room is ready to decorate as soon as it's dry. I can set up the bed frame, if you'd like."

"I don't know what I'd have done without you." Three days ago, when Diego called to tell her that Immigration had picked up all but two of his regular workers and bused them back across the border, she had no option but to take Wade up on his offer to help out. Though Diego promised to be back with a crew as soon as possible, she couldn't wait—not with the open house date looming.

"I don't know how to thank you," she said lamely.

"I can think of a couple of ways."

Tempted to follow his line of teasing, she dropped her gaze to the cold fireplace instead. His nearness had quickly dispelled the chill. She knew that the sooner she got away from temptation, the better.

"I'm going into town for the last few linens and baking supplies," she told him.

"Would you mind picking up a pack of spiral notebooks for me?" When he started to dig in his pocket for some money, she raised her hand in protest.

"The least you can do is let me get them for you," she insisted. She wasn't looking forward to driving in the rain or dashing across the parking lots with her packages, but she'd put off the trip to town as long as she could.

The wind outside was howling. Slanting rain pelted the windows. She walked over to a table lamp and turned it on, chasing the shadows out of the room.

"I'll drive," he volunteered.

"I can drive myself."

"I know you can, but I'd like to go along anyway. I can't get out for lunch on the Harley."

"Matt's going, too," she added. *There. The ground rules are clear.* Nothing would happen, nothing *could* happen with Matt along.

"That's fine." He shoved his free hand into his back pocket. "I don't mind at all."

"In that case, I insist you let me buy you lunch."

One corner of his mouth lifted in a half smile. "Whatever makes you happy."

Whatever makes you happy?

She wished her imagination weren't open to so many options.

"Speaking of happy . . ." she smiled back.

"Yes?"

"I hope you like Happy Meals."

Wade pulled the bill of his cap lower and glanced across the front seat as Tracy directed him into the parking lot of the Super Kmart.

"Last stop, guys," she promised.

"Aw, Mom," Matt grumbled from the backseat, where he was almost buried under a mound of packages already.

"I'll bet you're ready to groan, too." Tracy smiled over at Wade as he waited for a minivan to vacate a parking stall near the entrance.

He'd like to groan all right, but not because they'd made stops all over San Luis Obispo. Being with Tracy made him forget to watch the crowd. Every so often he'd look up and realize he was out in public and panic that someone might recognize him. Then he'd try to tell himself to get over it. It had been months. He was old news.

She glanced down at Matt and then turned to Wade apologetically. "I need to check in at customer service. They called to let me know that curtains I ordered are in. Maybe you two could hang out in the toy section until I'm finished?"

Wade turned to Matt. "How about it?"

The boy thought for a moment and then shrugged. "Okay."

"We'll meet you at the checkout in ten minutes. How's that?" Wade asked.

"Great."

He followed Matt through aisles of housewares, sporting goods, and electronic equipment. They stopped in stationery long enough for him to grab some roller ball pens and a three-pack of notebooks.

"You filled up that journal yet?" Wade eyed some with SpongeBob SquarePants on them.

Matt shook his head. The boy had been silent and withdrawn all day. Wade figured that his having come along didn't sit well with him.

"So," Wade attempted to make conversation as they continued on to the toy section, "have you tried writing any of those letters I suggested?"

"Yeah. I tried."

"Well, that's a start."

"Are you almost ready to leave yet?"

Wade glanced at his watch. They'd left Tracy no more than three seconds ago.

"We've got time to look around."

"I mean are you about ready to leave the *hotel*?"

Nothing like a kid to get right to the point.

"Does my staying bother you?"

It was Matt's turn to look uncomfortable. "Kinda."

Though Wade thought he already knew the answer, he asked anyway. "Why's that?"

"My friend Chris's real dad died and he got a new one."

Suddenly all the ramifications of what he was doing hit Wade square in the gut. Tracy wasn't a single woman. She was a widow with an impressionable young boy. A boy who'd suffered a tragic loss.

"I . . ."

Wade had no idea how to respond. Before he could stumble through one, Matt volunteered, "I don't want a new dad. Ever."

Wade glanced at his watch and wished he could come up with a great one-liner. Something prophetic and sensitive, something a character in a novel might say. A few words or phrases that would put Matt's mind at ease—but just then he was a writer without words.

"What do you say we head back to the checkout and get in line?" It was all he could come up with.

Matt looked up. "Can I have a Combo Blaster?"

Wade stared at the display of plastic space-age military toy hardware in front of them.

"What would your mom say?"

He could tell what Tracy's answer would be by the way Matt stalled. "She probably wouldn't care."

"Probably means I'd better say no."

"If you're not sticking around, what do you care if she gets mad or not?"

"I need a ride back to the hotel, you know."

Matt finally smiled. "She wouldn't leave you here. It's raining outside."

"I don't want to take a chance." Wade scanned the shelves. "How about an Operation game?"

"Dumb. I had one."

"Okay. How about Uno? I like Uno." Wade grabbed a deck of Uno cards off the shelf.

"I don't have anyone to play with. Mom's too busy. Chris isn't home."

"I'll play with you."

The kid's expression communicated a "big wow," but Wade added the card deck to the items in his hands. On the way to the check stand, Matt suddenly stopped in the camera aisle.

"Can I have a disposable camera?"

"You like photography?"

"I wanna take some pictures on the last day of school."

"Sure, why not?" He waited while Matt chose a thirty-six-shot camera and then said, "We'd better go get in line."

Matt nodded and led the way.

Wade realized he'd picked the slowest checker in the place, and as they inched forward he grabbed a *People* magazine and started thumbing through it. He glanced at the Pages section and read a glowing review by a well-established writer, which he responded to with mixed emotions. He liked the guy, an affable but not very talented popular fiction writer. The competitive side of him wished he were still in the game, still giving the guy a run for first place.

He flipped through the rest of the magazine and nearly dropped it along with everything else he was holding. He found himself staring down at his own headshot.

In an article entitled "What Ever Happened To Last Year's Headliners?" by Jeannie McCabe, his photo was prominently featured along with a dozen other faces that figured in the news a year ago.

There was a sidebar next to one of his book jacket headshots. He was wearing his signature black turtleneck and tweed sportcoat, and it was a shock to see himself with light brown hair, a full beard, and blue eyes. He quickly scanned the copy.

Edward Cain, object of a spate of sensational murders inspired by his novel, An Even Dozen, *and succeeding court cases, dropped out of sight almost a year ago. Although his agent had no comment, Cain's former publisher, Sally Reinhart, hints that Cain just might be back soon, and with a vengeance.*

"Wade?"

He found Tracy smiling beside him, her arms full of Martha Stewart curtain packages.

"Hi." He snapped the magazine shut and shoved it back into the rack, earning a glare from the checker when the cover tore with a distinct ripping sound. He wished he had the nerve to grab the entire stack of *Peoples* and toss them across the aisle.

"Anything interesting?"

Before he could divert her attention, she picked up the magazine and stared at Prince William on the cover. The handsome young man's photo, displaying features so reminiscent of Princess Di, assured top sales.

"Not much, as usual." Wade held his breath as Tracy set the curtain packages on the rubber conveyor belt.

She stared at the cover a few seconds more, and then sighed. "As if I have time to read." She fingered the slight tear on the cover before she put it back in the rack.

Matt wedged his way between them. "Wade bought some Uno cards. He's gonna play with me—since you don't have time anymore. And he got me a disposable camera, too."

"Did you say thank you?"

Matt shrugged. "Thanks, Wade."

"No problem, Sport." He set the notebooks, pens, the cards, and the camera on the belt and reached for some cash. When he looked up, he found Tracy staring up at him with one hand on Matt's shining sandy red hair. She was looking at him as if he'd just bought the kid a new car.

He shrugged. "Hey, it's just Uno and a cheap camera."

As Matt squeezed between his mother and the counter and walked over to stare at the gumball machines, Tracy touched the back of Wade's hand.

"Thank you," she said softly. "He's having a hard time adjusting and I am always so busy . . ." She looked guilty as hell.

"He's used to having your full-time attention. I hear kids are resilient. He'll adjust." Wade glanced around at the check stand lines, suddenly aware of how many people spent their time waiting by thumbing through *People* magazine. He couldn't wait to get out of the store and head back to the isolation of Heartbreak Hotel.

"Are your parents still alive?"

He realized she was talking to him again. "My parents?"

"You know The people responsible for your being born?" She smiled and tossed her hair back.

He'd almost forgotten that he had a past other than that as Edward Cain. He never talked about his life before the murders anymore. Never. Not even to Bob Schack.

"I never knew my dad. He died in Vietnam. My mom passed away about four years ago." He thanked God every day that she had gone before the murders and subsequent lawsuits. She'd died knowing he'd accomplished his goal of becoming not only a working writer, but one who even achieved a fair amount of success, even before *An Even Dozen* was released.

"You grew up without a father." She sounded thoughtful.

"I never knew what it was to have one." How different would his life have been if his father had come home from Vietnam?

"You're doing a great job with Matt." He wanted to reassure her, even though he'd never been around kids much, but the boy seemed to be getting along all right, given the circumstances.

She sighed. "I hope so."

The checker made a slow and thorough comparison of Tracy's identification with the name and address on her check. Wade forced himself to not look around, certain that if he did, someone leafing through *People* might suddenly realize that Edward Cain was standing right there at check stand four.

He tugged on the bill of his ball cap again before he handed the checker his own twenty as she rang up his items. She took her sweet time counting out his change and then made a point of looking him right in the eye when she handed it back.

"Thanks for shopping at Kmart."

"Right."

Tracy was near the exit, where Matt was lobbying for change for the gumball machine. Wade started toward them.

"Hey, Mister!"

Wade froze when the checker called out to him. He had an urge to run, but slowly turned around while a fantasy scenario played out in his mind.

He imagined the clerk asking, "Are you Edward Cain?" Then she grabbed the microphone above the register and announced, "*New York*

Times best-selling novelist Edward Cain on aisle four. *Edward Cain is on aisle four!"* she shouted.

It wouldn't be the first time he'd been a blue light special. Early in his career he'd done plenty of book signings in stores just like this one.

He took a deep breath and reminded himself that his hair was black and his eyes were brown and he was clean-shaven. He prayed that Tracy and Matt would stay out of earshot.

"Yeah?" He kept his voice low, hoping the checker would do the same.

She picked up a plastic bag by the handles and dangled it over the end of the check stand.

"You forgot your stuff."

He grabbed it and mumbled thanks. As his heartbeat settled back to normal, he walked over to Tracy and Matt near the gumball machine and handed Matt all his spare change.

Rain pelted them as they sprinted for the car. He ran as he pushed the basket along, stood on the bottom rack, and coasted on it a few feet. Matt hooted uproariously when Wade dismounted right into a sizable puddle. Tracy ran along beside them with her jacket over her head and hustled Matt into the car. Together, they laughed as they tossed her purchases in the trunk.

Once they were all safe inside, Matt recounted the shock on Wade's face when he stepped into water up to his ankle. The windows steamed up before he could get the defroster going, and they sat cocooned in the car waiting for the steam to clear. Isolated from the world for a moment, it was almost possible to forget that he *wasn't* simply Wade Johnson, a copywriter with no cares or worries. A man whose guilt wasn't communicating itself into achingly real, sometimes terrifying nightmares.

"Now *that* was fun!" Matt shouted from the backseat. "Where are we going next, Mom?"

"Home!" she laughed. "We're all soaked and it's almost five already." Then unexpectedly, she turned to Wade and said, "Would you like to have dinner with us tonight? I think you've earned a home-cooked meal."

It seemed like the most natural thing in the world for him to accept.

CHAPTER TWENTY-FOUR

Uno!"

Tracy laughed as Wade groaned and feigned frustration when Matt finally slammed down his next-to-last card. She was certain that when he volunteered to play, he had no idea that one round could last over thirty minutes.

Matt jumped up shouting, "I won! I won, Mom!"

Watching from the doorway into the small kitchen, Tracy dried her hands on a dish towel. "Congratulations, honey. Tell Wade good night, okay? It's time for bed."

"Aw, Mom, it's only eight thirty."

"It's ten to nine, actually. Get going. By the time you brush your teeth it'll be nine." She waited while Matt made a few more grousing noises but eventually trudged down the hall. After she'd tucked him in, she walked back out to the living room and joined Wade.

"Can I get you anything else?" She glanced back and forth from the sofa to the easy chair across from it.

"Sit here." He indicated the cushion beside him. She hesitated a moment before she finally joined him.

"I won't bite," he assured her.

"Chelsea will be home from work in a little while."

"How is she doing?"

"So far, she likes the job and the fact that she can carpool with her friend, Eric." She tried to sound casual, as if just the simple act of sitting beside him like this didn't make her all jumpy inside, even though he hadn't moved a bit closer.

"She's not still upset with you?"

"I don't think so. She doesn't act like it, anyway." She tried to relax. Found it impossible.

"What's on the to-do list for tomorrow?"

"I plan to finish hanging some pictures and setting out some flower arrangements. If you could hang the curtain rods and put the last bed frame together . . ."

"No problem."

She wondered if he noticed the way she blushed every time she used the word bed around him. Did the image send his thoughts careening down the same road?

She looked down at her hands, twisted the diamond ring. "I can't believe I'm almost finished. All the rooms will be ready for the open house on Saturday."

She sensed a stillness about him when he asked, "Are you expecting a big crowd?"

"About seventy-five, give or take a few. The RSVP is for regrets only and, so far, no one has called in to say they aren't coming. You know you're welcome to join us."

"Thanks. Maybe I will."

As they settled into an awkward silence, she wished he would pull her into his arms and kiss her the way he had the other day. Kiss her so long and so deep that she would forget about everything but him, but he'd made it pretty clear that the next move was up to her and apparently he was sticking to his word.

After a few more silent seconds she said softly, "I'm not getting any better at this."

"At what?"

"Being alone with you."

"You're doing all right." He reached out, gently took a lock of her hair between his thumb and forefinger, and rubbed it, waiting.

She closed her eyes for a second before she opened them and met his again. "I don't know what I'm doing. I mean . . . I keep finding excuses to be with you . . ."

Her admission was flattering, and yet it only added to Wade's guilt.

"I'd never do anything to hurt you, Tracy."

Unable to stop himself, he reached for her again. He meant every word, and yet he knew that she was bound to feel betrayed if she ever found out he'd lied about his last name and his occupation. There was so much he'd left unsaid about himself that the omissions would surely be seen as lies in her eyes.

She was so trusting that it scared the hell out of him. Creeps and perverts were real and they were out there. He'd not only read about them, he'd interviewed them in prison. He'd inspired a murderer himself.

"If I didn't trust you, I'd have never let you in the front door."

"How do you know you can trust me?"

"Let's just say that I can tell by the way a man plays Uno."

He wished he could stop staring at her mouth. "I want to kiss you again. I've been thinking about it for days."

"Me, too. Maybe you shouldn't keep me waiting."

He wrapped his hand in her hair, gently tugged until her head was on his shoulder and her mouth was there, tilted up toward his, lips parted, waiting.

He meant to kiss her tenderly, to make the kiss last forever. He wanted to explore her mouth with his tongue, to slowly savor the taste of her. He wanted to hear her moan against his lips. But the moment their flesh touched, his blood started pulsing hot and heavy and he was blinded by need.

Slipping her arms around his neck, she hung on tight, pulled him closer. They kissed until they were breathless. He cupped her breast, discovered her hard nipple beneath the fabric of her knit top. He squeezed gently, filled his palm. Heard her moan.

He buried his face in her neck, breathed deep, relished the warmth of her skin, the intoxicating scent of her hair. When she traced his ear with the tip of her tongue, shivers ripped down his spine.

He wanted to make love to her, wanted to take his time undressing her, memorizing her body. He imagined pressing her down into the soft cushions of the sofa, covering her. Sliding into her. Hearing her cry his name.

He pulled away, breathing hard, but he kept his arm locked around her, her breast cupped inside his palm.

A torrent of rain pounded against the roof and yet inside, they were safe and warm.

Though it couldn't last, he found himself thankful for having had a glimpse into real life. A joyful life. Despite everything that had happened to her, she had stayed strong.

Loving her children, accepting love, returning it. Those things were as natural as breathing to Tracy Potter. She'd lost her husband, lost most of her resources, but she was battling back fearlessly, forging a new life and haven for herself, her son, and her stepdaughter.

I have absolutely no business ruining her life.

That first night, when he'd lied about his name, he had no idea that things would ever go this far. If there had ever been a time to make things right, it had already come and gone. If he told her the truth now, he risked breaking her trust in him. And he was certain that someone like Tracy would be as shocked and horrified by what he'd written as by the horrors that had occurred because of it.

Reluctantly, he let her go and moved a few inches away.

High color blazed across her cheeks. Her eyes looked twice as blue as usual.

"I should head back down to my room." He tugged on the front of his jeans and scooted to the edge of the sofa.

She fiddled with the hem of her top before she finger-combed her hair. "I have to be up early . . ." Her words drifted into awkward silence. Then they both spoke at once.

"Tracy—"

"Wade—"

Just then the door to the apartment opened and Chelsea breezed in. Wade had the urge to jump to his feet, but decided that would only make him appear guiltier.

"Wow! Is it dumping out there!" Chelsea laughed as she dropped her purse on the arm of a chair near the door. Water dripped from her hair. A wet circle stained the shoulders of her pastel pink sweater.

She gave her long bangs a swipe, shifting them away from her eyes, and slowly took in the two of them sitting there. Her smile slowly wilted. Her mouth tightened.

"I'm soaked," she said, turning away. "I'm going to take a shower and go to bed."

Tracy started toward the kitchen. "I was worried about you. Are you hungry? There's leftover chicken and . . ."

Chelsea slowly turned. Her tone could have set Jell-O.

"No thanks. I already had dinner with Eric." She shot a withering glance in Wade's direction, then bid Tracy good night.

Tracy was staring down the hall after her. Wade crossed the room and reached for her chin, tried to pull her into his arms, but she stiffened.

"Are you all right?"

She slowly relaxed and sighed. "She and Glenn were very close."

"At least her timing wasn't as bad as last time." He was hoping she'd smile, but she didn't. "What time do we start work tomorrow?"

"I don't want to keep you from your writing."

"You're not. Believe me." He thought of the new notebooks he'd bought earlier. Page upon empty page. Would the dreams haunt him tonight? Would he feel compelled to write at all?

"How about I get to those boxes up in the attic after I put the bed together tomorrow?" he offered.

"If you can spare the time."

"I'll make time. Walk me to the door?"

Alone with Wade on the landing outside the apartment, Tracy was thankful for the low light in the hall. He glanced over at the door, which was closed, before he took her in his arms. She was amazed at how easy it was to step into his embrace. How right it felt. She didn't know what to expect and was surprised when he gave her what was almost a chaste kiss this time. He held her gently, took his time. It was slow, soft, and sweet.

When the kiss ended, she felt the warmth of his breath against her ear. "Thanks for dinner," he whispered.

"You're welcome."

He let her go and she resisted the urge to call him back. As she watched him disappear down the stairwell, she pictured him in his room, shrugging out of his shirt and tossing it aside, imagined the flex of his biceps as he unbuttoned his Levi's.

How would his naked skin feel beneath her palms? Had he any scars? Was he as tan all over as his upper arms and face? Or was his skin beneath his clothes pale as alabaster?

She took a deep breath and when she was calm, when she felt more like the old Tracy, Matt's mom, she opened the apartment door and almost tripped over Chelsea. She was sitting back on her knees on the floor, shoving lipsticks, a mirror, pens, Palm Pilot, and her wallet back inside her purse.

"What happened?"

It was a second before Chelsea looked up. "My purse fell off the chair and everything dumped out." She got to her feet, slipped the strap over her shoulder, and quickly started toward her room.

"Are you sure you don't want any leftovers?"

"I'm positive." Chelsea looked away and fiddled with her purse strap. Tracy couldn't tell if she was angry or not, but something was definitely wrong.

"How was work?"

Chelsea shrugged. "Fine. David's actually kinda weird, though."

Tracy remembered how Glenn had defended his accountant when she'd voiced a similar opinion. "How do you mean?"

Chelsea's brow furrowed. "I dunno."

"Does he make you uncomfortable?" She had never really taken to David, either, and couldn't exactly say why.

"Not really."

Tracy found herself wishing she heard less hesitation and more conviction in Chelsea's tone. "If working there bothers you, then you can always get another job."

"He told me the firm partners award a scholarship to one of the interns every year."

"They do? That's great news."

"I told him I was interested, and he said he'd keep that in mind. He wants me to go out to dinner with him and his wife."

"When?"

"Next week."

"Great, as long as it's not Saturday. I was really counting on you being here for the open house."

"Sure. I'll be here." Shifting uncomfortably, Chelsea started biting her thumbnail.

Tracy pictured Chelsea at eight, the year she'd married Glenn. The girl was at that awkward stage, her permanent front teeth had just come in and they looked too big for her mouth. She was stick thin with deep auburn braids and spattered with freckles the same color as her hair. It wasn't until she was eleven that Chelsea was finally convinced that Glenn wasn't going to leave Tracy and go back to living with her and Monica.

The lovely young woman standing before her now was nothing like the sometimes sullen child she'd met so long ago. But just now, that young woman looked like she'd rather be anywhere else.

"I need to go call Eric. I told him I'd let him know that I made it home through the rain and I forgot all about it."

"You sure everything's all right? You're not upset that Wade was here for dinner, are you?"

"No. Not at all." Chelsea shook her head and even smiled. "Really. I'm not. 'Night." With that she turned and headed down the hall.

Tracy knew her well enough to know that Chelsea might not be upset about Wade, but something was definitely up.

CHAPTER TWENTY-FIVE

W ade tossed and turned. Burning up, he kicked off the covers. A few minutes later, shivering, he tugged them back up to his chin. His dreams were intricate and vivid, so real that his body reacted as if he were living each experience.

At one point, after dreaming that he'd been tossed helpless upon a stormy sea, he was so exhausted he had to drag himself to the bathroom for a glass of water.

Gradually he felt better. He rubbed his face, blinked, looked around the bathroom, and wondered if he had been sleepwalking. Wide awake, he went back into the bedroom and turned on the bedside lamp. A few seconds later he was frantically pawing around the desktop for a pen. Finding one, he then grabbed one of the new notebooks and sat on the bed. As soon as he opened the notebook, his hand started moving across the page.

Almost home.

I was almost home when the storm hit, a monster storm that whipped the seas higher than I'd ever seen them. The wind howled like a banshee, tore the sails off the rigging, brought down the mainmast.

The ocean tossed the Lantana *like a matchstick, threw her high and slammed her low, sending the crew sprawling. We fought like Spartans but eventually she splintered into driftwood, casting one and all into the deep.*

For the first time in forever, I prayed that dark night. Prayed as hard and fast as I could to a God I'd never believed in. I begged His forgiveness, all the time wondering why He should save me over the rest of the crew and spare my life.

All I could think of was Violette and my unborn son. I had to live, for them, if for no other reason. She'd lost her parents. She had only me.

Her words came back to me. "You've given your word to me, too, Ezra. Made a vow to love, to honor, and cherish. We're bound by God . . . I'm afraid, Ezra."

The way she clung to me, begged me not to make this cursed voyage—Why didn't I listen? Why didn't I stay in her arms?

I grabbed for a piece of wreckage, held tight, and gave myself over to my fate. I awoke no better than a dead man with my cheek pressed into wet sand, the foaming tide tugging at my boots. I crawled out of the surf line, spit sand from my mouth as I dragged my weary bones to higher ground.

I slept having no idea if it was days or hours before I awoke again. When I did, the sun beat down on me.

It's been many weeks, perhaps months, by my calculations, since the sea spit me out on this godforsaken island. On clear days I can glimpse the mainland. I see the gold, fertile hills of California as plain as I see my ragged fingernails, my sun-ravaged skin.

I fear I'll starve before I get off this barren rock, fear that I'll not live to see my son. My child has been born by now.

I cannot bear to think of my sweet Violette and know how she's surely suffered. By now she knows the ship was lost at sea. Does she believe that I am dead? Can she feel me here, thinking of her, longing for her?

There are no others on this spit of land with me. I've walked the length and breadth of it, this knoll off Anacapa Island. There's no life here, barely a blade of grass. I exist on mussels and crabs no bigger than quarters. For a man my size it's puny fare. My bones poke through my skin. My teeth are loose with scurvy even though I can see the land of plenty, not thirty miles away.

My mind wanders across the channel that separates us. I imagine Violette on the widow's walk, holding my child in her arms, pointing to a spot on the horizon.

Does she whisper to him? "There! Just there is where we'll see your papa's ship when he comes sailing home to us."

Does she cling to hope that one day I'll return, or has she given me up for dead?

I cannot signal passing ships. I have no fire. I have shouted my throat raw, waved my arms until I cannot lift them. No ship passes near enough to see or hear me.

My hope wanes. I know that if I die here, I will take the love I have for Violette with me to the other side.

Hours later, in a daze, Wade closed the notebook, set it aside. He glanced at the clock on the bedside table and figured he could get a couple hours' sleep before Tracy needed him.

Looking out the window into an ash-colored sky the next morning, Tracy tried to not think about what would happen to the tourist trade if the weather got any worse. She rubbed her chilly arms, tempted to take advantage of one of the sofas and magazines in the sitting room, when Wade came walking in. His eyes were red-rimmed, his jaw covered with a night's growth of stubble.

"You look like a man who could use an espresso."

"I feel like a man who could kill for one."

She laughed. He didn't.

"Did you get any sleep?"

"Some. Did you?"

"Some." Preoccupied, he sat down at one of the tables in the sunroom.

"Maybe you should skip the coffee and catch up on your sleep."

"Sleeping is just practicing to die. Actually, I'm looking forward to sorting through those boxes for you."

"Really? Why?"

"Maybe there's a story up there."

She fixed a fresh pot of extra-strong coffee and knew that if she didn't go back upstairs and pay the bills she'd intended to pay this morning, she was leaving herself open to temptation.

"Help yourself to some coffee and come on up. I'll be in the kitchen upstairs paying bills."

She was proud of the way she made an exit, proving to herself that she did have a shred of both decency and discipline left when it came to resisting him. She was barely settled at the small desk tucked into one corner of the kitchen when the phone rang.

"Heartbreak Hotel," she answered automatically.

"Tracy?"

Tracy recognized Carly's voice on the other end of the line and smiled as she tucked the phone between her ear and shoulder and licked the envelope on the phone bill.

"We're home," Carly announced. She sounded excited.

"You had a good showing."

"Fabulous. I'm really picking up a following in Taos. How about you? Are you finished? Have you got a full house?"

"I'm finished for now, but I've got plenty of vacancies. The weather has been the pits around here lately."

"It's bound to get busy as soon as school's out tomorrow."

"Wade is still here."

There was silence on the other end of the line and then a very speculative, "Oh?"

"He's on some kind of sabbatical. Well, actually, he's been helping around here, too."

"No kidding."

"Most of Diego's crew was hauled off by Immigration last week, so Wade stepped in and finished up." Before Carly could say anything, Tracy asked, "Did Jake have time to look over the books? I'd imagine you had him hopping with the show and all."

"He's right here. I'll let you talk to him."

Tracy straightened, ignoring the rest of the bills. Outside, the sun was making a valiant attempt to break through the clouds.

"Hey, Tracy. How's it going?"

"If you can make the sun shine, things will be better," she laughed. "What's up, Jake? Did you find anything?"

She pictured Jake seated at his desk in his home office. The Montgomerys' 1920s Craftsman home was situated high on a hill on an old dirt road aptly named Lover's Lane.

"If it's all right with you, I'd like to do a little follow-up work before we meet."

"Follow-up?"

Tracy knew his fees were way out of her ballpark. He'd insisted she not mention paying him, but now he was obviously putting in extra time. "Jake, I'm not a charity case . . ."

"You know this is something I want to do gratis, Tracy. For you and for Matt. Don't even mention money and insult me."

"You know how much I appreciate this."

"We'll talk in a few days. I may have something concrete for you by then," he promised.

Concrete.

As she hung up, she found herself wondering what he'd discovered.

What did he find? Something that David Sylvester had missed? Or had David kept the truth from her?

CHAPTER TWENTY-SIX

A gentle but steady rain fell as Wade carefully made his way over to the dormer windows in the attic. The frames were warped, swollen by weather and time, and he was forced to pound on the corners with the heel of his hand until he was able to open them enough to let some air inside.

On the left side of the attic he'd stacked the newer boxes that Tracy had neatly labeled *Potter*. The contents were carefully listed on the outside. Those would definitely stay.

In front of her household things and keepsakes, he lined up the old, weathered boxes with labels of products he recognized. Whatever was inside had probably been packed within the last thirty or so years.

On the opposite wall he lined up the boxes and crates that appeared to be the oldest. Not only were most of the old cardboard boxes falling apart, there were wooden crates tacked shut with nails that had rusted long ago.

These were the boxes in which he was most interested, the ones he secretly hoped might hold a key to the history of the Heartbreak.

He sat on the floor beside what appeared to be one of the three oldest boxes. It yielded nothing but odds and ends—a bent silver candelabra so tarnished it was blue-black, the color of a bad bruise, a frosted glass cream and sugar set, and piles of receipts from department and dry goods stores.

He left the candelabra and glass pieces out in case Tracy wanted them, and then scooped up armsful of paper receipts brittle as fallen leaves, stacked them, and carefully put them back in the box.

Next he opened an old crate full of moldy leather boots and shoes, all used, cracked, and weathered, many with the soles separating from the tops. He shoved them back inside and thought that at this rate, he'd be done in no time.

He carefully opened the top of the next box, and when he saw more mildewed leather, he expected another pile of shoes. After pulling back the top all the way, he realized the box was full of ledgers.

Hopeful that they might contain bookkeeping records or guest registrations, he carefully lifted the first volume, cradled it in his lap, and opened the cover.

Ship's Log
The Lantana
January 1889

As Wade's hands gripped the leather-bound volume, his chest tightened around his heart. For a full thirty seconds he could neither move nor breathe.

1889. The Lantana.

He opened the first page, not knowing what to expect.

It was dated January 27, 1889, and listed the ship's cargo and destination as well as a few other navigational notes. Wade turned the page and there, at the bottom of the second page, the name *Ezra Poole, Ship's Captain* had been signed in thick, bold cursive.

Wade stared at the signature, then rubbed his eyes, hoping the letters might suddenly shift and rearrange themselves into some other name. Any other name.

But nothing happened.

Quickly, carefully, he began to turn the pages. The signature at the bottom of every entry was the same.

He tossed the log aside and grabbed another. By the time he'd scanned through five of them, he was more confused and shaken than ever.

He'd never laid eyes on these logs before, never been inside these walls before. Hell, he'd never even been in Twilight Cove or anywhere near the coast of California until a handful of weeks ago.

And yet here he sat holding on to physical proof that there was nothing fictional about the man he had somehow been induced to write about. Capt. Ezra Poole had been a living, breathing human being.

There was no explanation as to how he had tapped into the captain's heart, mind, soul, or whatever it was he had accidentally tapped into. No logical, *believable* explanation anyway.

He slowly looked around the attic, at the dusty floor, the collection of crates and boxes, the mummified moths trapped in what was left of a few tangled spiderwebs, and began to wonder if any of this was real at all.

Maybe I'm already locked up in some loony bin, being spoon-fed medication and chocolate pudding.

Maybe none of this is real.

Maybe I killed myself and this is hell.

"Wade?"

When he heard Tracy's voice echoing up the narrow stairwell, he realized that if she was here, then this couldn't be hell.

He closed the logbook and shouted, "Come on up."

Her soft-soled shoes padded up the stairs. She paused just inside the door. Her smile faded the minute she met his eyes, and she hurried toward him.

"Are you all right?" Automatically she palmed his forehead, the way she might check her son for fever. "You're white as a sheet."

"As a ghost, you mean." He wanted to tell her that he was fairly certain now that ghosts didn't float around as ethereal apparitions. They took up residence in your head.

"What's wrong?"

"Maybe it's just the light."

"And maybe I'm Britney Spears." She glanced down at the dirty floor beside him, then dragged over a box labeled books and sat down. "I think maybe you should go downstairs. If you pass out, I'll never be able to get you out of here and neither will the paramedics."

"If I pass out, lock the door and leave me up here to rot."

Hearing her laughter settled his nerves, at least a bit. If this whole thing were part of some vivid hallucination, then he was damn thankful she was in it.

"What's that?" She pointed at the leather-bound book on his lap.

"A ship's log."

"It looks old."

"It is." What would she say if he came right out and admitted to losing his mind?

When the candelabra caught her eye, she picked it up.

"This is amazing." She turned the heavy piece over and over in her hands before she set it down on the floor. "I'll see if I can bribe Matt into shining it for me. It would be fun to display it in the sitting room." She then picked up the sugar bowl.

"The creamer is cracked," he told her. It seemed like it was years ago, not mere minutes, that he'd unpacked them. When he looked away from the glass pieces, he found her staring at him intently.

"Your color is a little better, but not much." She sounded relieved. He wished he actually felt better. He wished he knew what in the hell was going on.

Their eyes met and held, until Tracy's dropped to the log again. "Interesting reading?"

"It's from 1889."

"You're kidding." She held out her hand and he gave her the log, relieved to be rid of the thing. Tracy opened the cover, slowly, reverently, like someone who treasured old things for what they were. She leafed through a couple of pages, closed it, handed it back.

Wade ran his hand over the nubby front of the ledger, traced with his fingertip the worn gold leaf letters that spelled out *Ship's Log,* and pictured the signature at the bottom of every entry.

Ezra Poole, Ship's Captain.

"Listen, Wade, you don't have to do this now. I really think you should go lie down."

Go back to his room and get caught up in those dreams again? Go back and perhaps start writing things he didn't know one damn thing about? That wasn't an option right now.

First the copycat murders. Then the lawsuits. The death threats.

If he were smart, he'd burn the damn papers and notebooks and leave Capt. Ezra Poole where he ought to be—ashes to ashes, dust to dust.

"Wade?"

"What?" He discovered that she was no longer perched on the box of books, but kneeling beside him in the dust. Suddenly her hand slid warmly over his, her expression a study in concern.

"Something's wrong," she said softly. "What is it? Please tell me."

Slowly he shook his head, never taking his eyes off of hers, clinging to them, hoping she could help save the last vestiges of his sanity.

"When I checked in here, I was . . . at a low point in my life. I didn't ever want to write again."

"Why? What happened?"

"Too much stress." Better that she thought him a stressed-out copywriter—one of those writers who comes up with catchy jingles and phrases to sell people all the crap they thought they needed—it was better than the raw truth.

"The night I checked in, I started having odd dreams. Odd in the sense that they were more real than dreams. I'd wake up compelled to write. I didn't want to, but I couldn't stop myself."

"That's good, isn't it?"

"The words were pouring out of me, but I had no notion of where they were coming from and very little recollection of what I'd written afterward." He couldn't bring himself to look at her, afraid of what her reaction might be. "It took me a few days before I had the courage to read what I'd written."

When he finally looked over at her, he found her leaning toward him, intent, listening. Caring. She nodded, encouraging him to go on.

"It was the story of a sea captain, a man who owned a sailing ship at the turn of the nineteenth century."

She sat back on her heels and smiled. "We hear the ocean day and night. I've seen you out walking the bluff. Surely the atmosphere inspired you."

He shook his head. "There's a lot more to it than that." Used to stroking a beard, he ran a hand over his lower jaw, wondered if he'd ever adjust to being clean-shaven. "I've written pages and pages, in great detail, about things of which I know nothing."

"You're an educated man . . ."

Like everyone else, she assumed he had a degree, but it didn't take a master's degree in English to be a storyteller.

"But I don't know a thing about navigating a clipper ship, or about life in California in the late 1800s."

Her fingers curled around his hand, her eyes were warm and full of concern. He imagined that this was the way she spoke to Matt when he was upset, the way she'd given her husband unflinching support.

"You probably remember more than you realize from grade school.

Matt's class has been studying early California this year, the settlement of the state, the missions, the gold rush. Kids are immersed in this stuff . . ."

"I wasn't raised in California." *And I was in and out of formal schooling.* "Believe me, I've never studied anything like this before."

She searched his face. "I don't understand."

"I don't either." He held the logbook toward her. "Take a look at the bottom of the first entry."

Her slim, tapered hands reverently cradled the large, musty book. She opened it slowly, taking great care with the yellow, brittle pages, and scanned the first entry. She turned the page, came to the bottom, and read aloud, "Ezra Poole, Ship's Captain."

Then she looked up, expectant.

"The story I've been working on is the first person. The character narrating the tale is Captain Ezra Poole."

"Maybe it's just a coincidence," she said softly, though she sounded far from convinced. "Ezra is an old name. It certainly fits a character from the 1800s."

"*Captain Ezra Poole?* I even nailed his last name and the name of the ship."

She flipped back to the first page. When she looked up again, her expression was no longer thoughtful. She frowned, trying to piece the impossible together.

"You've never seen these logs before today, have you? You haven't been up here going through these boxes before today."

"You know I haven't."

Over the past few days when he'd been working for her downstairs and in the evenings, she'd been up in the apartment. She'd have to have seen him come in, or would have heard him walking around up there. Whenever she left to run an errand, she locked the apartment.

She gently laid her hand on his shoulder. "There has to be a logical explanation for this," she said softly, almost as if talking to herself.

"There is. I'm losing my mind."

CHAPTER TWENTY-SEVEN

H*e's either an Oscar-caliber actor who's lying about this whole scenario, or I'm lusting after a borderline nutcase.*

Tracy didn't know whether to laugh or cry as she sat in the middle of the cluttered, dusty attic listening to him trying to explain something that made absolutely no sense. She realized that *if* he was telling the truth, then he was either insane, or he believed in the impossible.

"Okay," she said slowly, trying to come up with a rational explanation. "So, after you checked in, you had strange dreams and felt 'compelled' to write. Consequently, you just *happened* to name your main character after a real ship's captain who lived in the 1800s."

He nodded. "A man who may have lived right here in the Heartbreak Hotel." His gaze shot to the box beside him, one that contained what looked like many more volumes of the *Lantana's* logs.

"And you've written things you say you don't know anything about."

"I *know* I don't know anything about them. At least I never did before." He was still pale, though not as much as when she'd first walked in. Fabricating a story like this was one thing, but actually being able to make himself appear physically ill was another.

"I think we should go through the rest of the logs."

"I don't." He wouldn't give the box even another glance.

"Why not?" *Because they'd prove he's lying?* She didn't need another liar in her life.

"Because I already know what happens to him."

"To your character, you mean."

"*If* my character *is* Ezra Poole. I've written about how the *Lantana* was lost at sea during a storm sometime in 1901." He looked around the attic. "I think he may have lived here. I think that's why these logs were up here in the first place. Maybe that's why I'm here. Ezra needed someone to write his story."

In some secret spot in her heart, she had wanted to believe he had stayed because he was attracted to her on more than a physical level. That he was falling for her, as she suspected that she was falling for him.

Was he trying to now tell her that he was here because some *spirit* wanted him here?

Slowly she got up and brushed off her pants. His eyes never left her.

"I want to read what you've written." It wasn't a request.

"You don't believe me?"

"I believe that *you* believe what you're telling me. I don't believe in ghosts."

"You don't have time to waste. You have other things to worry about right now."

"Like what? Who's going to rent the eight empty rooms I've got downstairs? Or about how long it might rain? Or if the roads are going to wash out like they did a few years ago? Should I sit around and stew about going broke before I can get this place off the ground?" She offered him a hand up. "Come on. It's still drizzling, the perfect kind of day to make a pot of tea and read by the fire. Maybe your story will keep my mind off of my real worries."

He took her hand but got up under his own power. He didn't let go of her fingers while they stood beneath the eaves, staring into each others' eyes.

He pulled her close. She didn't pull away.

She couldn't have walked away from the desperate need and confusion in his sad, dark eyes, not even if she'd wanted to. She went up on tiptoe and brushed her lips against his.

"Thank you," he whispered.

"For what?" She gently stroked his cheek with her fingertips.

"For not running screaming from the room."

She smiled slowly.

"Hey," she said, squeezing his hand, "give me a chance. I still haven't read what's in those notebooks."

When I think I can take no more, when I'm certain I've endured my final day, my final hours on this desolate rock of an island, a pleasure craft sails into the cove and drops anchor.

Two young men, carefree, with too much time and money on their hands—what shock they must feel, watching me use my last burst of strength to scrabble to the top of the highest outcropping of rocks along the shore and wave the ragged scrap of what's left of my white linen shirt in frantic circles above my head.

I shout, but my voice is weak, like that of an ancient man who has outlived everyone he knows and yet refuses to die.

To have rescue so close, to have them sail away without me is unthinkable. I squint against the sunlight reflected in the dappled crescents that bob on the surface of the ocean.

And I am rewarded when they wave back. They sail closer, as close as they dare without risking their craft. Beside myself, I search the shore for just the right piece of driftwood, one small enough so I can still drag it into the water, one large enough that I can cling to it as I try to kick and float out to the sailboat.

Somehow I make it. Shocked exclamations, wide eyes, and warm hands greet me as the two men pull me onto the sailboat, where I lay like a fish out of water, gasping for breath.

"Where? How? Who?"

Their words and questions swirl around me. So foreign are the sounds of other voices by now that I struggle to make sense of what they are asking.

A year and a day. It sounds ridiculous. A year and a day since the Lantana *went down with all hands and a full hold.*

They recognize my name and that of my ship. Made the news we did, all of us lost souls. I learn that a few of the men survived, lived to tell the tale of the storm that came out of nowhere, of the way the ship broke up beneath us and before we had a chance to man one lifeboat, she was gone.

They turn their craft and under full sail we cross the channel. They want to take me directly to Ventura, for immediate medical care.

I will not have it. I turn into the madman I must appear to be, with my tangled beard and gray hair streaming around my shoulders, with my wild eyes.

I want no doctor, no prodding. None of it. I must get home.

"You want to go sailing," I tell them, "then sail. Take me home, take me back to Gull Harbor." From there I will hitch a ride to the inn on the bluff. From there I'll go directly to my love.

They do not argue, but thankfully sail straight away. The sky is blue as a robin's egg. The wind steady. The young men are on the adventure of a lifetime.

They'll tell their children's children of this day when they grow old. They'll tell of the day they plucked Capt. Ezra Poole off the rocks and saved his life.

At Gull Harbor, old friends drop their lines, stop mending nets, run down the dock to greet my two companions who are shouting and waving their straw hats above their heads.

"He's alive. Captain Ezra's alive!"

I am alive. Over and over I am forced to remind myself that God's little joke is over.

Everyone stares. Surely I must look like the walking dead, but then Refugio De La Raza steps up to me, takes my hand, and pumps my arm up and down before he pulls me into a bone-crushing embrace. The others crowd around.

It's a grand excuse to open a pint of whiskey. A grand way to celebrate a living wake for a dead man come to life.

"I'd love to stay, my friends," I fairly shout above their joyous congratulations, "but I've a fair young wife awaiting me and I've tarried long enough."

I expect them to greet the comment with peals of laughter and ribald jokes, but a pall of utter, deafening silence descends over one and all.

"What is it?" I say, my voice made weak again by the looks on their faces, and then by the way they all turn away without meeting my eyes. Terrified, I find the strength to roar, "What is it?"

Refugio takes my arm. I try to shake him off, but he clings like a wounded terrier. "Come with me, Ezra, old friend. Come along now."

I want to refuse, but the crowd has drifted slowly away, one by one, two by two, with heads together.

Numb, quaking, I let him lead me over to a rotting bench that, like me, has been exposed to the elements, the salt air and the sun, the wind and the sea, for far too long.

He gently touches my shoulder and I slowly lower my brittle self to the bench. Ignoring the splinters protruding from the wood, my fingers wrap themselves around the edge, clinging.

Refugio sits beside me and stares out across the docks, past the boats bobbing at anchor.

"Violette is not there, Ezra." He speaks softly, reverently.

"She grew tired of waiting," I say. She was so young. So much younger than I, and so very lovely. The world would be too tempting for a young woman like her. A young woman believing herself a widow.

Refugio shakes his head. "No. She didn't leave you. She never gave up hope. Long after everyone else was convinced that you were gone, your wife, she clung to hope."

"But then—"

"Then it came time for her to birth the child."

"A boy?"

The dark-eyed sailor nods again. "A boy."

"I have a son." I turn and look into his eyes, old eyes sunken in a face dyed by the sun and creased by time. "Where have they gone?"

"She was a good girl. A good woman, the perfect wife. Every day she waited, watched for you. Every night passersby would see her on the widow's walk, watching for your ship. Long after we all knew the Lantana *had been lost, she refused to believe."*

"Where has she gone? Where are they?" I cry.

"Gone to heaven, Ezra. Gone together. The babe was stillborn. Violette died a few hours later. If it's any consolation, she died with your name on her lips."

I make him take me there, to the inn. He has an old buckboard wagon that bumps and tilts as it lumbers over the pocked dirt road that edges the bluffs.

I see the hotel, her father's folly, jutting tall against the sky. A place that demands to be noticed, the only silhouette where nothing else made by man mars the coastline.

The windows are tightly shuttered. I stumble down from Refugio's wagon and wave him on. "Go! Get away! Leave me!"

I've no use for him now. I've no use for the sorrow on his face. His sympathy means nothing to me. I do not yet believe it's all over.

It's not true. None of this is true. It can't be happening.

The door is locked. I reach over my head, feel along the doorjamb, and find the key. I turn the lock and, out of habit, replace the key before I step inside.

Without the sun streaming in the windows, the lobby is dark. The furnishings are gone, the room cavernously empty.

My bare feet slap against the fir floor as I cross the room, calling her name over and over and over.

"Violette! Violette! Violette!"

The emptiness echoes the sound of my own voice until I'm hoarse. I climb the stairs, search our rooms on the second floor. Where once there was so much love, so much laughter and joy, there is only a hollow void.

Someone has taken out all of the things that were left behind. I don't care. The only thing on earth I ever cared about was my beauty, my Violette, and later my unborn child.

And just as Refugio said, I find they are gone.

I stagger down the dark, narrow hallway to the door that hides the stairs. I take them slowly, one at a time, barely able to lift my feet now that everything I once lived for has been taken from me.

At the landing, I choose the attic door. Her things are piled there, boxes of clothing that still hold her scent. I find her yellow dress, press it to my face, inhale.

I drop the silk into an empty cradle that has already gathered dust, and leave the attic.

I open the door to the widow's walk and step outside. The wind has picked up. It howls around the eaves and dormers, daring to caress this place that is filled to the rafters with heartbreak.

With heavy steps I shuffle to the center of the walk and stare out to sea, out to that spot on the horizon where she must have trained her gaze a thousand times or more, standing firm, clutching for hope with both hands when others tried to tell her to let go.

As I stare out at that far distant place where the sea and the sky become one, I am convinced that if there is a God, he is the most cruel of devils.

Why has he spared me, and not them?

Does he truly expect me to live without them?

The waves pound against the rocks below the bluff, singing a sirens' song, they call to me.

Somehow I make it back down the stairs. I find the strength to shuffle outside and head toward the light of the setting sun.

I look like Father Time standing there half naked on the bluff, my long hair turned silver, my beard blowing in the breeze.

I stand there on the precipice of sandstone and listen to the waves as they crash upon the rocks below. I stare directly into the sun as it quickly slips lower, until it has almost reached that place where it will sink beneath the green waters of the Pacific.

I wait, poised on the edge, knowing there is only one way I can be with them, knowing I haven't the courage or the nobility it would take to live out the rest of my life alone.

I take a deep breath, and at that exact moment when the sun touches the water, I lift my arms and shout, "Violette!" and with her name on my lips, I dive headfirst over the bluff.

And I smile. Finally, I smile again as I plummet toward the rocks below.

CHAPTER TWENTY-EIGHT

Tracy pressed her lips together and slowly closed the spiral notebook on her lap. Tears blurred her vision. The flames in the fireplace wavered and smeared as she watched them dance behind the screen.

Her breath hitched on a sigh. She looked over at Wade, who lay sprawled on the second sofa. He had been watching her from the moment she opened the first notebook. Drawn into the story, she'd quickly become immersed, almost forgetting he was there.

Almost—but with him so near, it was impossible to forget about him entirely.

She could tell he was awaiting a comment. She had so much to say, but struggled for the right words. Running her hand over the cover of the final notebook, she realized there was only so much that mere words could convey.

"It's beautiful," she said.

"It's downright weird. That's what it is."

"It's a wonderful story. But do you honestly have any idea whether or not this is true to Ezra Poole's life?"

He sat up, staring at her across the low, wide coffee table covered with magazines and travel guides. "I have no idea. I never even knew he actually existed until I found those logs this morning."

The shuttered emptiness she'd seen in his eyes the night he'd checked in was back. She made an instant decision.

"I'm going to call Carly and have her pick up Matt when she picks up Christopher. Go get your jacket." She stood up, sore from sitting in one position for so long. She glanced at her watch, couldn't believe how long it had been since she'd first sat down.

"Where are we going?"

"To Twilight, to talk to the one person who might know something about Ezra Poole. If we're lucky, we can kill two birds with one stone."

Palmer Biggs was a fixture in downtown Twilight who spent most of his time in front of the post office with his cronies, but he could almost always be found at mealtime in Selma's Diner.

He was also a past president of the Twilight Cove Historical Preservation Society, one of the groups that had blocked Glenn's bid to tear down the Heartbreak, and he was still on the board in an honorary position.

Palmer's lunch was spread out before him, half a tuna sandwich on wheat toast, a bowl of tomato soup, and a cup of coffee. The cellophane wrapper on a pack of saltines crackled as Palmer tore into it, crushed the crackers in his thick-fingered hand, and then sprinkled them on top of his tomato soup.

The minute Tracy and Wade walked in, Palmer recognized her. His smile revealed a set of teeth yellowed with age beneath a thick, white moustache. A San Francisco Giants ball cap covered his bald head.

"I saw Chelsea in here a while back and she told me to stop by the hotel and see what you've been up to."

"I wish you would," Tracy invited. "I'm having an open house Saturday night. Please drop by, and bring some of the society board members if you like."

He nodded. "I'll do that."

"It starts at six-thirty."

Palmer's gaze strayed to Wade and stalled.

"This is Wade Johnson." She introduced them, looking over at Wade. "Would you mind if we join you, Mr. Biggs?"

"Nope. It's still a free country."

They slid into the booth together and sat thigh to thigh.

"Wade's from L.A. He's here doing some historical research," she explained. "I was hoping that if anyone could help him, you could."

"Maybe. Depends on what he's after."

Wade answered for himself. "I've been dabbling with a piece on turn-of-the-century life in the area."

"Writing something, you mean?" Palmer relaxed a bit.

"Yes. Exactly."

Palmer took a big bite out of the sandwich half, swallowed, and then nodded to Tracy. "I was afraid you were going to tell me he had some cockamamie plan for the hotel like your husband's. Thought maybe you would try to enlist my help in getting some changes past the board."

"Not at all."

Selma interrupted long enough to see if they wanted anything. When Wade ordered a hamburger with fries and a milk shake, Tracy thought: *What the heck? Why not challenge her cholesterol count, too?*

Wade slid to the edge of the seat and leaned on the table. "You know anything in particular about the Heartbreak Hotel?"

Palmer swallowed his last spoonful of soup and shoved the bowl aside. After he centered his coffee cup on the saucer, his gaze slowly drifted over to Tracy, then back to Wade.

"Like what?"

"Are there any records left about who might have built it, or the names of any former owners?"

"All the old building records burned in a fire in 1930."

"You know anything about the California sea trade back in the late 1800s?"

"Some. Want to narrow it down a bit?" Palmer wanted to know.

"Did a Captain Ezra Poole ever live around here?"

"Why would you be asking about old Ezra?"

"Did you actually know him?"

"Hell, I'm not that old!" Palmer chuckled and then sobered. "He lived around here, sure. But I suppose you already know that or you wouldn't be asking. What are you up to?"

Tracy felt Wade's hand on her knee. He gave it a gentle squeeze. When she looked over at him, he was still leaning across the table, toward Palmer, his expression intent.

"I was helping Tracy clean out some old boxes in the attic this morning when I came across some ship's logs that had belonged to Ezra Poole."

For the first time since they had sat down, Palmer perked up and looked genuinely interested. "Ship's logs? From 1900?"

Wade nodded. "Some from the late 1800s. There are quite a few."

The conversation lulled when Selma came back with the shakes. Palmer was ignoring his coffee, pinning Tracy. His eyes were thoughtful beneath frosty eyebrows sprouting every which way like overgrown hedges.

"So what do you know about Poole?" Wade wanted to know.

Palmer finished his coffee and signaled Selma for a refill.

"He sailed the coast for thirty years, lived in a small settlement above Gull Harbor. There's nothing over there now but a small boat harbor and a restaurant."

Tracy felt Wade's fingers tighten on her knee. She didn't know whether to reach for his hand beneath the table and hold on tight or to get up and run as far and as fast as she could. None of the pieces fit anymore.

If Wade had researched Ezra Poole before he knocked on the hotel's door that cold and misty night, why not come right out and tell her? What motive would he have for fabricating this whole bizarre scenario? She would have gladly helped him. Not only that, but the trepidation she felt that first night would have been diminished had she known that he was a writer on a research mission.

"Do you know if Ezra was ever lost at sea?" Wade's voice was low and hesitant, almost as if he didn't really want to hear the answer.

"I thought you didn't know anything about him," Palmer said.

Wade shrugged, noncommittal. "I'm not sure how much of what I've learned is true."

"His ship went down, oh, I can't remember the particulars, I think sometime around 1900. Ezra washed up on one of the small islands near Anacapa. Survived like Robinson Caruso for almost a year. When he finally made it home, he learned his wife had died in childbirth." Palmer stopped, taking a dramatic, pregnant pause. He heaved a great sigh and slowly shook his head.

A shiver slipped down Tracy's spine.

Tracy whispered, "Then he killed himself," effectively taking the wind out of Palmer's sails.

The old man's lips tightened. "Nobody knows what happened to him." He looked at them both. "So what did you come to me for, exactly?"

While they were talking, Selma had slipped up to the table with two hamburger combos. It was a rare moment when Selma was rendered speechless.

She set down their lunch order and wanted to know, "Then how *did* the captain kill himself?"

Tracy was afraid she already knew, but she waited for Palmer to verify it. Palmer was eyeing Tracy and Wade curiously. "Like I said. Nobody knows. He disappeared the day he was rescued. The day he found out his wife and child were gone. Never saw hide nor hair of him again."

Selma shook her head. "Haven't you all got anything better to do? It's gloomy enough with this damned weather," she grumbled. She grabbed a coffeepot from the table behind them and filled Palmer's coffee cup before she turned to Wade and Tracy, indicating their plates. "Eat up, kids."

Then she leaned over the table, winked at Wade, and gave him a flirtatious smile. "Handsome devil like you has to keep up his strength."

Doubting if she could taste the burger now that Palmer had confirmed what Wade had already written about Ezra, Tracy forced a smile. "Thanks, Selma. This looks great."

"I've got some really tasty strawberry pie for dessert. You want some, Palmer?"

"You buying?" he asked Tracy.

"I am," Wade said quickly.

Palmer nodded to Selma. "I'll have a piece." The minute she was gone again, he turned to Wade. "There's more to this than what you're both telling me, I can see it on your faces." He glanced around the near-empty restaurant.

"Don't you wonder why no one has ever made a go of the Heartbreak Hotel?" Palmer looked directly at Tracy. "You aren't the first person to try. The last owners were a couple from San Francisco. Came down here in the late sixties, kept the place open for a year and a half before they went belly-up. They locked up and left without looking back. Never able to sell the place even, not until your husband came along and bought it off them for a song."

Her appetite gone, Tracy picked up a fry, barely dipped it into a puddle of ketchup, bit the tip off of it, set it back down.

"Some folks in my father's generation might have been able to recall

some stories about Ezra from when they were kids. I don't know any particulars, just that they used to say there was something strange about the
place."

Selma arrived with Palmer's pie. He waited until she'd walked away.
Tracy realized she'd been holding her breath. She let it go, fought to relax.

"My father always claimed the place was haunted."

Great. Almost flat broke and I own a haunted hotel.

It was easier to believe that Wade had lied about not researching Ezra
Poole long before he checked in. But did that mean that he somehow
knew about the logs and had gotten close to her in order to have access to
the attic? Had he somehow *known* that the *Lantana*'s logs were there?

How?

And if so, why had he looked so genuinely stunned and shaken when
she'd found him sitting there this morning? Why was he so shocked to
find exactly what he'd been looking for?

Palmer milked the moment, taking time to eat the whole piece of
strawberry pie and then wipe his mouth on the paper napkin before he
raised his eyes.

"You really ought to try some of this. It's great," he urged.

Tracy was ready to leap over the table and choke him. Instead, she
clenched her hands together in her lap.

"Why doesn't anyone talk about the hotel being haunted now? I've
lived here almost ten years and I've never heard that before. Why didn't
anyone mention it to me before I moved in? I would have thought that
someone would have said something, or joked about it anyway."

"Anyone who was alive then is either gone, or was too young at the
time to remember much about it now. The hotel has had a run of bad
luck almost since it was built, with no real explanation for it. The place
was empty for over forty years before you moved in."

*Run of bad luck? A hundred years, give or take a few, is more than a run
of bad luck.*

Palmer set down his fork and stared at the pie plate as if contemplating
licking it clean before he looked at Wade again.

"Whatever made you start researching Captain Ezra anyway? The only
piece we have about him is a short clipping from a San Francisco paper.
Tells about his being rescued, and about how he disappeared the same
day. Never was seen or heard of again. That's it."

Tracy couldn't take her eyes off Wade. This was his chance to prove that she hadn't made a fool of herself by trusting him. He leaned back against the booth, stretched his arm around Tracy's shoulders. She could feel him toying with a lock of her hair. His posture appeared casual, as if he were completely relaxed, and yet she could feel tension radiating from him.

"I stumbled across his name one day and thought he might make an interesting subject."

"You still have the article or piece you 'stumbled across?' " Palmer wanted to know.

"Not with me."

Tracy's heart felt as if it were caught in a vise. She was having trouble breathing. It was all she could do to not get up and walk away.

CHAPTER TWENTY-NINE

She's pissed.

Wade saw all the doubt and questions in Tracy's eyes and wished that he could take her hand and pull her out of the diner, take her to some quiet place overlooking the ocean, and set her mind at ease.

But he couldn't exactly reason with her when there was nothing reasonable about any of this.

Ezra Poole, it seemed, had lived and breathed and died—and if what he'd written was true, he'd jumped off the bluff behind the Heartbreak.

And if, *if* any of this was possible—and he still had serious doubts—then why?

Why me? And, more to the point, *how?*

How had he tapped into the story? How had he gotten all of the facts right?

The old man across the table was eyeing him suspiciously now, perhaps taking a clue from Tracy, who'd gone very still. She'd barely touched her burger.

He kept his arm draped around her, tried to reassure her—pretty impossible when he was a ball of confusion himself. Gently squeezing her shoulder, he watched her turn her wide, troubled gaze his way.

"I should be getting back." There was no smile in her eyes now, none of the warmth in her voice he'd grown accustomed to. "Matt gets out early today."

He nodded in understanding. Matt had nothing to do with her need to get home, and they both knew it. No doubt she was making an excuse, needing to put distance between them.

Wade signaled Selma, and she immediately hurried over to the table. After he asked for the check, the three of them sat in uncomfortable silence in the booth.

Palmer folded his hands and rested his forearms on the table. "Maybe old Ezra will make an appearance at that open house shindig you're throwing on Saturday night," Palmer laughed. "That would sure have everybody talking about him again."

Tracy seemed preoccupied, though Wade watched her attempt a smile. "That's all I'd need."

"Could be good for business," Palmer speculated, "having a resident ghost."

"You think so?" Wade asked.

Palmer shrugged. "It takes all kinds."

Before Tracy slid out of the booth, she looked at each of them in turn and then said, "I'd appreciate it if *neither* of you says one word about Ezra Poole to *anyone* on Saturday night."

It was drizzling again by the time they finally left the diner. A gunmetal gray sky draped with low clouds matched Tracy's mood as she drove back to the Heartbreak.

Her mind was racing faster than the engine of the BMW as she replayed their conversation with Palmer over and over, thoroughly convinced that she obviously couldn't tell the truth from a lie.

Glenn had kept the truth from her, and now Wade? She could understand Glenn not wanting to admit his failure. His ego wouldn't let him admit to her that they were ruined. Perhaps he hadn't even been able to admit it to himself.

But why would Wade lie his way into her life?

Was Chelsea right? Was he looking just for sex? She let her gaze slide over to where he sat silent and brooding in the passenger seat. With his looks and intelligence, he could get sex anywhere.

Obviously, he specifically came to locate the *Lantana*'s logbooks.

How much would he have to gain by getting his hands on Ezra Poole's logs, other than to verify his research? Had he been searching for other documents that might have been stored in the attic? If so, what had led him to believe they might be there?

What did he have to gain from writing Ezra's story?

She waited until they were alone inside the empty lobby before she confronted him.

"Did you come here intentionally looking for those logs?" she asked without preamble, unwilling, unable, to suffer any intimacy. Fearing that if she gave him the chance to touch her first, his charm might melt her anger. "Did you come looking for research material on Ezra Poole?"

She was so upset that she was shaking, so she paced over to the fireplace and took her time straightening its screen until she heard him step up close behind her.

"Look at me, Tracy."

Just as she feared, he reached for her, his hands closing around her upper arms, gently but firmly, forcing her to look at him.

"I never heard of Ezra Poole in my life before I walked through the front door."

"You had to have known something about him. There's no way I can believe anything else."

"Believe what you want. There's no way *I* want to believe what happened, either, but I'm telling you the truth." Frustration creased his brow. When he raised his eyes, there was obvious confusion in them. "I have no idea what in the hell is going on."

"Have you actually *seen* anything?"

"If you mean a ghost? No."

She felt trapped between him and the fireplace, but not afraid. She lifted her chin, dared him to try to cajole her into believing him. He pulled her closer, raking her face with his gaze.

"I haven't lied to you about any of this," he said softly.

"You say that as if you have lied about something." She searched his eyes for the truth, prayed she'd be able to recognize it if it was there. Despite her doubts, her anger and distrust, she wanted to kiss him. She wanted him to make this whole thing go away, to make her forget about the logs and the heartbreaking story she'd read in his notebooks. It was impossible to tear her gaze away from his lips.

He lowered his voice to a whisper. She felt his warm hands on her arms, felt the heat of his palms through the sleeves of her jacket. She could almost taste him. "I wish to God I knew what was going on here."

"And I wish I could believe that, but I find it impossible." She lowered her eyes, hoping to break the spell he had on her.

She refused to be taken advantage of. No matter what else she might feel for him, she *had* to be able to trust him. She wasn't so desperate or so lonely that she would allow herself to fall in love with someone who couldn't be completely honest with her. Not again.

He was so close, she inhaled the scent of the wind and the salt and the sea mingled with his soap and shaving cream. She closed her eyes, wishing they could go back to the easy camaraderie they'd shared before he found the logs. She ached to kiss him. Longed for the thrill, the rush she'd felt last night when he'd held her in his arms.

It hurt to realize that she was already addicted to him even though he'd given her no reason to think that anything would come of their time together. She hadn't planned on falling for him, hadn't thought beyond the moment. She couldn't—not while doubting his motives. She couldn't let him sway her with his hands, his lips, no matter how much she wanted him.

Tugging out of his grip, she started to walk away.

He reached for her, catching her by the wrist. "Tracy, listen—"

A gust of damp air hit them as the front door opened and Matt and Christopher came racing in. Wade let her go.

"Mom! I won a Citizen of the Year award at the last-day assembly." Matt ran around the sofa and thrust a construction paper folder at her.

She opened it, saw the certificate with an official-looking gold seal inside. He had, indeed, been chosen as one of Twilight Cove Elementary's Best Citizens of the Year.

"I'm so proud of you! We'll have to get a frame for this right away." She handed it back and went down on one knee to give Matt a hug, closed her eyes, and held on tight. This was truth. This was real. This was her world.

Fortified, she straightened.

He beamed up at her so proudly that she couldn't resist cupping his smooth cheek and smiling down into his eyes before she greeted Christopher, too.

"Wanna see, Wade?" He held the certificate up for inspection.

"That's great, Sport."

As Matt beamed up at Wade, Tracy focused on Christopher.

"Where's your mom?"

"She'll be here in a minute. She's in the car checking her voice mail."

"How was your trip to Taos?" Tracy hoped Wade would leave. She couldn't face him right now. She needed time to think, impossible with him so close by.

Chris shrugged. "It was okay. Mom had to do a lot of art stuff."

"Wanna go upstairs and play Game Boy?" Matt asked Chris.

"Sure."

"There are some cookies in the jar," Tracy offered. "If you pour yourselves some milk, try not to make a mess."

With a rush of backpacks, rain jackets, and heavy athletic shoes, they ran out of the room. The silence the two exuberant boys left in their wake was deafening.

When Wade took a step in Tracy's direction with his hand extended in open invitation, she wanted so badly to take it, to believe him, that she ached all over—but he was asking her to believe the unbelievable.

"Carly's on the way in." She glanced at the front door, willing Carly to appear. She was mentally exhausted. She could ignore his hand but not his eyes, and as much as she'd like to, she was powerless to dismiss him, to walk away.

"I know it's asking a lot for you to believe me," he said softly.

"Can we just drop this for now? *Please?* I have a day and a half before the open house and I don't need this right now." She met his eyes at last. "Any of it."

"You want me to leave?"

"You mean—"

"Check out."

"That's not necessary." Was her heart showing?

I want you to stay. I want you to tell me this was all some kind of a bad joke.

Instead she said, "You're paid up through Monday."

He closed the gap between them again. "If that's the only reason you want me here, forget it, keep the money."

"Wade, please."

"Please what?"

"Give me time to think this through."

Just then Carly walked through the door. The spell was broken.

"I'm going out, but I'll be back," he promised. He nodded to Carly but didn't smile, and walked out without looking back.

Tracy watched Carly follow Wade with her eyes and answered Carly's question before she asked it.

"Wade's still staying here." She tried to hide her confusion, but Carly knew her too well.

"But something's up. Are you all right?"

"I'm fine." Tracy started toward the apartment stairs. "Come on up and tell me all about Taos. Would you like a glass of wine?"

Carly followed her through the lobby. "Since when do you have a glass of wine this early? I'll take a diet soda."

Since I started acting like an idiot over a guy who communicates with a ghost.

"I guess since it's the last day of school and the open house is almost here. And to welcome you home." Her steps faltered when she heard the Harley start up. It was none of her business where Wade was going. None at all.

Once they were upstairs and settled, Carly kept up a steady stream of chatter, filling her in about the art show in Taos.

Finally able to think of something other than Wade, Tracy commented, "Jake said there were a couple things he wanted to look into before he talked to me about the accounts, but he didn't go into detail. Has he said anything to you about what he's looking for?"

"No. He wouldn't ever do that without talking to you first." Carly finished her soda. "Are you sure everything is ready for the open house?" Carly asked.

"Pretty much. I'm going to start working on the appetizers tomorrow, the ones I can do ahead. We're just having finger food, coffee, tea, and wine in the sunroom. I'll have some guest rooms open for viewing."

"Sounds great. I'll come over early to help you set up."

"You don't have to. Chelsea will be here."

"I know I don't *have* to," Carly told her. "I want to."

"Are you sure?"

"Of course." Carly smiled. "I'm looking forward to it. Jake can join me later and bring Chris. I know everything is going to be just perfect. Pretty soon this will be the hottest place on the coast."

The hottest place on the coast.

Tracy couldn't help but wonder what Carly would say if she told her that not only was Palmer Biggs predicting the hotel was doomed to fail, but that the mysterious hunk living downstairs was trying to convince her that he was channeling the resident ghost's life story.

Wade rode slowly down an avenue where jacaranda trees grew so tall and full of lavender blossoms that their branches arched over the street, creating a tree tunnel alive with color. Well-manicured homes lined both sides of the street.

Sparing them quick glances, he wondered what it would have been like to grow up in a town like this, to know the neighbors, to make friends? What would it have been like to attend the same school for years, go to parties, play on a sports team?

Would he have written *An Even Dozen* if he had grown up here instead of in seedy apartments in New York? Would he have been able to plumb that level of darkness in his soul? Probably. He was a writer. Former housewives from the Midwest came up with equally gruesome thrillers.

He pulled over to the curb near a corner and asked directions to the local library. It was situated on a small grassy park, not much more than a triangular wedge of grass with some ficus trees for shade and a couple of benches. The library itself was light and airy inside. Two walls were a combination of bookshelves and floor-to-ceiling glass windows. The one-story layout was nothing like the old brick-and-mortar libraries he'd haunted when he lived in the city. Compared to those, this one was in its infancy. Still, he found the collection of local archives fairly complete.

But just as Palmer had said, there was nothing on Ezra Poole except for a newspaper article that had been photocopied and added to a small pamphlet detailing the beginnings of Twilight Cove and nearby Gull Harbor. The librarian affirmed that Twilight Cove's original building department records had been destroyed when the old wooden city hall structure had burned down in the thirties.

He spent three hours reading through volumes on the history and importance of shipping up and down the California coast, and then went through a stack of picture books that had detailed drawings of clipper ships and steamers. It should have amazed him when the drawings and paintings validated his descriptions. It should have, but it only stirred more questions than answers.

He couldn't shake the vivid images he'd had of Ezra and Violette. Given all that had happened, there was no longer any doubt in his mind that she had existed, but, unlike Ezra, who had made a name for himself only in that he'd survived the shipwreck, she had joined the legion of others who passed through the pages of history without leaving a discernible mark—unless there was some way to find a birth, marriage, or death certificate for her.

On his way out, he stopped at the information desk again to ask the librarian, "Would the birth, death, and marriage records prior to 1930 have been in the old city hall?"

She nodded immediately. "I'm afraid so."

"There wouldn't have been copies filed anywhere else?"

"Not that I know of."

Another dead end. He didn't know whether to feel frustrated or relieved.

"You're paid up through Monday." Tracy's words echoed through his mind.

He picked up some Thai takeout food before heading back to the hotel. With every passing mile he thought about the doubt, the hurt and confusion in Tracy's eyes. How did he expect her to believe him, to trust him, when he didn't believe what was happening himself?

He had never intended to fall in love with her. He didn't think he had it in him to let anyone in anymore. He'd stayed because he wasn't ready to walk away from her. He'd also stayed in order to help her. He'd never meant to hurt her, and yet he had.

What would she do if he told her he was a novelist? And about his pseudonym and why he hadn't been perfectly honest with her from the beginning?

"You're paid up through Monday."

He wanted to stay and yet he wasn't ready to reveal who he was, not even to Tracy. He thought he could trust her to not tell anyone. Surely she wasn't upset enough to expose him and turn his world upside down. But if he stayed, if she *let* him stay and become more a part of her life, he'd have to tell her everything, and he'd be handing her yet another reason to not trust him.

She and her son were putting their lives back together. If his identity were exposed, he'd be risking their privacy. Seeing that *People* magazine yesterday proved that.

She'd be better off without him around.

CHAPTER THIRTY

At 5:30 on Saturday evening, Tracy made certain that her pearl earrings were on tight and gave her retro French twist hairstyle a last glance before she walked out of the bedroom.

"Chelsea? Carly?" she called down the hall. "I'm going on downstairs."

"I'll be right down," Chelsea shouted from behind her closed door.

On a cloud of steam, Carly stuck her head and shoulders out of the bathroom. "You look great, Trace! I'll join you in five minutes. All I have to do is get dressed." She'd been there since two in the afternoon, helping to set up.

Downstairs, votive candles were scattered all over the sitting area and the sunroom. With the low-light sconces on the walls, the romantic lighting hid the imperfections that no amount of paint would cover.

Carly had picked up flowers at the farmer's market and arranged a multitude of small bouquets. They'd set out wineglasses and put chilled bottles of white wine in an old-fashioned aluminum tub of ice on a side table.

The cold buffet was a combination of appetizers Tracy had made herself along with finger sandwiches and tidbits she'd ordered from the local bakery and deli. It was a splurge, but one she'd carefully budgeted for.

Everything in the rooms and public areas looked just the way she wanted it to. In an hour, the sunroom windows would show off the spectacular sunset view, the bluff, and the coastline. A peaceful, relaxed atmosphere pervaded the sitting room. For a heartbeat she wished she could cancel the evening's affair and sink into the overstuffed sofa with a glass of wine and simply relax.

If she could turn back the clock two days, if she and Wade could go back to the way they'd been then, she would like nothing more than sharing the quiet, romantic atmosphere with him in private.

She'd heard him come and go the past couple of days—the sound of the Harley's distinctive engine hard to miss. Last night she'd almost ventured downstairs to knock on his door, but she was afraid that instead of voicing her concerns again, she would end up in his arms. This morning he'd left around ten and was gone most of the day. She'd been out picking up the party trays when he got back.

It was hard to not be moved by the setting she'd created here tonight. The rooms were perfectly romantic, a candlelit glimpse back to the turn of the century. She'd even talked Matt into polishing the candelabra that Wade had found in the attic. Complete with tall ivory tapers, it graced the middle of the coffee table.

She tried to convince herself that it was the candlelight and flowers, not her feelings for Wade, that stirred such longing in her and had her wishing they could be here alone tonight. She'd been planning the open house for so long that the idea of calling it off to be with Wade took her by surprise.

When the front door opened, she stopped musing and headed across the lobby to greet the first arrivals. Not surprising, Palmer Biggs, accompanied by Eloise Simpson and Vivian Ames, members of the historical society board.

Eloise, the senior of the two, took her time studying the lobby and sitting room and then announced, "I haven't been in here since I was a child. It's a shame this place was hardly ever open. It's such a stunning piece of turn-of-the-century architecture."

"The century just rolled around again," Palmer reminded her. Eloise snorted.

At Palmer's insistence, Tracy began to give them a tour until Carly came downstairs and quickly volunteered to take over. After they walked away, the huge empty lobby echoed with silence. Tracy walked over to the registration desk, straightened the huge registration logbook, then wandered over to the front window and arranged the folds of the lace curtains.

No one else appeared until Jake and Chris walked in a few minutes later.

As Chris took off upstairs to find Matt, Jake gave Tracy a hug and his congratulations. "Where's my wife?" He looked around the empty rooms.

"Giving a tour. Let me get you a glass of wine." Tracy led the way into the sunroom with Jake following close on her heels. Though his greeting had been filled with warmth, she'd sensed a hesitation. An uncomfortable silence stretched between them as she poured him a glass of wine and handed it to him with a cocktail napkin.

He seemed hesitant about something. She watched him take a sip of wine and look around before he said, "I was wondering if you'd have time to meet with me about Glenn's books tomorrow."

She knew by his tone that something was wrong, but whatever he had to tell her about Glenn would be better than not knowing what had gone wrong—and from the look on Jake's face, something was definitely wrong.

What if Glenn was into drugs?

What if that was where the money had all gone?

What had he kept from her?

"Certainly. What's a good time for you?" She tried to sound as if she weren't nervous, as if meeting with a P.I. was something she did every day. But this was, after all, Jake, and he was a friend.

"How about two o'clock tomorrow? We usually go out to breakfast on Sunday mornings."

We.

Two years ago, Carly had been a single mother struggling to make ends meet. Who would have thought their roles would have been so completely reversed? Tracy tried not to envy them, Jake and Carly and Chris. They were a family now, with family traditions to uphold.

"Two is great." She wished they could go upstairs right now and that Jake could lay it all out for her. Two o'clock tomorrow was a lifetime away.

"There's my girl." Jake spotted Carly walking into the sunroom with Palmer and the others. "I'll take her some wine and save her from Biggs."

Tracy watched with mixed emotions as Jake walked over to the tub of chilled wine bottles to get his wife a drink.

"You look beautiful tonight."

The sound of Wade's warm voice so close to her ear sent ribbons of chills unfurling along her spine. Resisting the urge to lean back into him, she took a deep breath and slowly turned around. The moment she laid eyes on him, she was stunned by the change.

Instead of his usual black T-shirt and Levi's, he wore a long-sleeved ivory polo shirt and pleated chocolate slacks that matched his eyes. A pair of designer loafers completed his outfit.

The upscale look was so totally incongruous to the way she'd come to think of him that for a moment she was speechless.

"Are you all right?"

She slowly nodded. "Just surprised. You look . . . you look so . . ."

"Good?" He never teased. Somehow it raised the level of intimacy between them another notch. Strangers didn't tease.

Handsome. Delicious. Sane. She couldn't stop staring.

"Different." She realized that he must have been out shopping most of the day. "You look different."

He stepped closer. "I thought I'd better not show up looking like hired help."

He reached over and straightened her collar for her and his hand brushed the back of her neck. Heat spread from the nape of her neck to her hips, knees, and then toes. She reminded herself to breathe.

"Truce for tonight?" he offered.

"Truce," she agreed softly.

He turned and picked up a small plastic box that she hadn't noticed before. A florist's box. A corsage box.

Her heart started slamming against her rib cage. No one had given her a corsage since her high school prom in Marshall.

"For me?"

He shook his head no. "I was going to wear it myself but it doesn't go with my shirt."

She watched him carefully pry open the corner of the box. The plastic lid popped as the top flew up to reveal a perfect gardenia blossom.

She bit her lips and savored one of his rare smiles, surprised at the care he took as he lifted the corsage and held it out to her.

"Can you . . . would you mind?" She adjusted her collar so he could pin the corsage on her shoulder.

He drew the long pearl-headed corsage pin out of the florist's tape around the stem, and hesitated.

"I've never done this before," he confessed.

"Never?"

"No."

They both moved at once. She stepped closer. He leaned over her and they bumped heads.

"Sorry," she apologized.

"No. I'm sorry."

"Don't be," she whispered, half ashamed of all the things she suspected him of, still afraid that he had lied.

But tonight was special. Tonight was the night she'd worked so hard for. He'd helped her get here, too. Worked alongside her most of the week.

Tonight they'd called a truce and she intended to enjoy the fruits of her labor.

She tried to see the corsage on her shoulder. "It's beautiful."

"No, you're beautiful." His low, husky voice sent another shiver down her spine. "And as much as I hate to let you go, you should circulate." He reminded her that they weren't alone, and for that she was thankful. There was no telling what she'd do if they weren't. No telling what she'd be willing to believe tonight.

She looked over at Palmer Biggs, who was working his way through a tray of appetizers as his friends from the society awkwardly stood by.

Aside from Carly, Jake, and the boys, they were still the only arrivals. Chelsea was downstairs now, stationed in the sitting area near the front door.

"What if no one shows up?" With literally no outside invited guests there yet, she couldn't help but worry.

Wade took her hand, held it between his where no one in the room could see that they were touching.

"Then the others would probably leave early. Would that be so bad?" he said softly.

She looked up in surprise, caught him smiling. His dark hair glistened blue black in the candlelight. His eyes were warm, his smile inviting.

He made it oh-so-easy to forget her concerns. Forget what he'd told her about Ezra Poole.

Seeing him now acting perfectly sane, looking like something out of *GQ* magazine with his hand, solid and warm, around hers, she realized that it wouldn't take much to convince her that maybe *she* was the crazy one for doubting him.

As much as he hoped for her sake that everyone she had invited did show tonight, Wade had been relieved when he walked in and found the room nearly empty.

Though he risked being recognized tonight, the look on Tracy's face when she saw him made taking the chance worthwhile. She'd been shocked by his appearance—which wasn't surprising given that he'd been wearing the same Levi's for two weeks. What astonished him was the depth of his relief when he realized that her anger and doubt had diminished.

He found himself wishing that he could lead her down the hall to his room and make love to her.

Damn the party. Damn Ezra Poole.

Damn his own past.

Since the first time he kissed her he'd fantasized about losing himself in her, slipping the pins from her upswept hair, letting it fall loose and free around her shoulders. Pleasuring her. For the first time in forever, he truly wanted to get to know a woman deeply, not just sleep with her.

He wanted to memorize her skin, savor the touch of her hands. He wanted to hold her close, fall asleep with her pressed against him, their naked bodies aligned from head to toe.

"That would be awful," she said forlornly.

"What?" Shaken out of his fantasy, he looked into her worried eyes and remembered that he'd asked her if it would be so bad if no one showed up.

"It would be just terrible if no one came."

Her disappointment and anxiety were clear as she gave his hand a quick squeeze, let go, and looked around the nearly empty public rooms.

"Why wouldn't they come? Free food and wine, a chance to see a great new hotel right on the water?" As much as he wanted her all to himself, as much as he wanted to hide, he still wouldn't wish this night to be a disaster. She'd worked too hard, planned too long.

"At least it's not raining." He hoped to put her mind at ease, but she wasn't smiling.

"There's always so much going on around here. People are so busy—"

"Give it a while. It's early yet."

She glanced over at the trays of appetizers. "I ordered too much food."

"Palmer looks like he's doing his share to remedy that."

Mentioning Biggs brought back the scene in town, but Tracy's thoughts were obviously elsewhere. He followed her gaze and noticed a well-dressed couple walking through the front door.

"That's Natalie Barnes, president of the Twilight Cove Chamber of Commerce, and her husband," she said in a hush.

When she started to walk away, then suddenly stopped and looked back apologetically, he encouraged her. "Go. I'll help myself to some wine."

"Thank you for the corsage." She reached up, tenderly fingering the blossom.

He didn't move until he'd watched her walk across the lobby. When he turned around, Palmer Biggs and two companions near Palmer's age were bearing down on him.

"Johnson," Palmer nodded, staring up at Wade from beneath his bushy brows.

"Mr. Biggs." Wade introduced himself to the women.

"You able to find out anything more about Ezra?" Palmer wanted to know.

The taller of the two women was beaming at him. "I'm so glad that someone your age has taken up an interest in one of the area's most colorful and least-known personalities, Mr. Johnson."

"Thanks, but call me Wade." He tried to keep his mind on the conversation, but his gaze kept drifting over to Tracy, who was still with the chamber president. They were moving closer, headed for the sunroom. The last thing he wanted was for her to overhear him discussing Ezra again. Not tonight.

He casually glanced at his watch and then tried to appear as disappointed as possible.

"I'm really sorry, but I need to check on something for Tracy. Will you excuse me?"

The ladies looked disappointed, but Palmer was already gazing over at the buffet again.

Wade made a quick exit out the side door.

CHAPTER THIRTY-ONE

Natalie Barnes complimented Tracy on all the progress she'd made and asked important questions about her plans for the Heartbreak. All the while, Tracy was completely aware of Wade as she watched him smoothly escape Palmer, Eloise, and Vivian.

"I'm glad that you've listed the hotel with the chamber secretary. Tourists are always stopping in the visitor center looking for last-minute accommodations. You're sure to pick up some bookings through us. I can't imagine you'll have many vacancies, though." Natalie paused to look around. "This is beautiful. Isn't it, Patrick?"

Patrick Barnes looked more interested in the view outside the sunroom windows. The setting sun performed on cue, staining the sky with red, orange, and peach hues just above the horizon line. The ocean surface was glassy this evening with gently undulating swells rolling toward the bluff.

Natalie took the glass of wine that Tracy offered. "I've never been in here before, then again, neither has anyone else. As far back as I can recall, this place has been boarded up. You're certainly lucky it wasn't a complete teardown."

Lucky? As Tracy looked around, she realized she was lucky. Much more than she thought the first time she set eyes on the interior of the Heartbreak.

Natalie shook her head. "I hope you get a good crowd tonight. We almost didn't make it on such short notice."

Tracy didn't think three weeks was short notice.

Natalie smoothly grabbed a cocktail napkin and an appetizer. "I'm so glad Chelsea called Wednesday to give us a heads-up about the invitation being on the way."

"Did you say Chelsea called?" Tracy thought she had surely misunderstood.

"Yes. Wednesday. To give us a heads-up about the invitation. That was good thinking."

"I'll have to thank her." Tracy glanced around and saw Chelsea beside Carly near the French doors that led out to the porch. They appeared to be in an intense discussion.

Carly looked as serene as always. Though casually dressed in a sleeveless pastel knit top and a long black skirt, her natural beauty and inner glow made her the kind of person that everyone felt comfortable with, old, young, or in between.

Twenty minutes later, Tracy had made all the excuses she could make to the Barneses without embarrassing herself and them. Time and again, Natalie reiterated that earlier invitations would have *certainly* helped fill the room. Tracy walked them to the door and bid them good night.

No one had to tell her that her open house was a complete disaster. The sunroom was dismally empty except for herself and the Barneses and Palmer, and his friends who had taken up squatters' rights at one of the sunroom tables, loaded plates with appetizers, and helped themselves to more wine. The senior contingent was settled for the night.

Jake, Christopher, and Matthew had all disappeared. Wade, too. Even Chelsea and Carly were no longer inside.

She couldn't blame them all for hiding out. If she didn't have to be there, she'd be looking for the exit, too. Tracy lingered on the front porch after the Barneses drove away. She had even lined the steps and railing with cheerfully glowing votive lights here, too. The Heartbreak was all dressed up for a party that wasn't happening.

She refused to give in to despondency as twilight gathered. She thought about Palmer inside stuffing himself on her appetizers and wondered if he would blame this disaster on the ghost of Ezra Poole.

Maybe so, but not her. *She* was going to have a little talk with Chelsea.

"Isn't it the coolest thing you ever saw?" Matt couldn't help but feel proud of the big Harley parked beside the hotel, even if it did belong to Wade, who was only a guest.

He could tell that Christopher wanted to touch it, and if Wade and Jake hadn't both been standing there, he'd have let Chris sit on the bike, as long as he was careful. Heck, they could both fit on the big seat and there would still be room for one more.

"It's waaaay cool," Chris admitted. "Can we get one, Dad?"

Matt was always surprised when Chris called Jake "dad." He did it all the time now. Back when Jake first married Carly, Chris still called him Jake, but things had changed pretty quick.

Chris had always wanted a dad more than anything. Now Matt knew why. He missed his own dad so much that sometimes it was hard not to start bawling like a baby. After a couple of tries, he was finally able to write some letters in the journal, like Wade suggested. Now, sometimes, he found himself looking forward to sneaking into his room to write another one.

Writing to his dad wasn't the same as having him around, but it wasn't as bad as not being able to talk to him at all.

He listened as Jake asked Wade all kinds of questions about the Harley—like how's the mileage and how long has he had it. He was asking so many questions that Matt started to worry that maybe Jake would actually buy one. Then Chris would be able to ride on it anytime—but after Wade left, then he wouldn't even have a Harley to look at, or sit on and pretend.

Just when he was feeling really sad, he felt a hand on his shoulder. He looked up to find Wade standing right there beside him, like they were friends. Like Wade knew how he was feeling.

He hadn't really liked Wade Johnson at first, but the guy turned out to be pretty nice after all.

Besides, his mom smiled a lot more since Wade was around, and if Mom was happy, then the whole place didn't seem so empty anymore.

In fact, when his mom was happy, the whole world seemed a lot brighter.

CHAPTER THIRTY-TWO

When she couldn't find Chelsea or Carly downstairs, Tracy paused long enough to reset the CD player, and instantly Elvis Presley's smooth, mellow love songs filled a silence broken only by Eloise's constant chatter. It wasn't like Chelsea to be vindictive, no matter how upset the girl might be about Wade, but Tracy could think of no other reason for her to sabotage the party.

She forced a smile, waved to Palmer and his friends, and headed for the apartment stairs, but before she could start up, a car horn blared out front. Not just any car horn, either, but one that played the first stanzas of "La Cucaracha."

There was only one person in Twilight with that kind of horn—Joe Caron, the cook at Selma's Diner. Car doors immediately started slamming, followed by the sound of excited chatter. Abandoning her plan to find Chelsea, she hurried across the lobby.

Selma Gibbs came breezing in on Joe Caron's arm. As soon as she saw Tracy, Selma opened her arms in an expansive gesture that took in the entire room.

"This is something else!" Selma's booming voice reverberated around the huge lobby. She paused long enough to gaze around, and then pressed her hand to her ample bosom, as if overwhelmed. Then she threw her arms around Tracy and gave her a bear hug, nearly choking the life out of her.

Drowning in Selma's overly powerful perfume, Tracy laughed and hugged her back.

"Thanks for coming," she said, fighting back tears. "Isn't the diner open tonight?"

Selma beamed. "Miss a grand occasion like this?" She turned to Joe, who looked more than a little uncomfortable in dress slacks, a starched white, long-sleeved shirt, and bolo tie. She jabbed him in the paunch with her elbow. "We're thrilled, aren't we, José?"

"Let me show you two around," Tracy offered, ready to usher them into the sitting room.

Selma shook her head. "You go ahead and greet your other guests. We'll help ourselves to refreshments and show ourselves around."

"What other guests?"

"The ones in the cars that pulled in behind us."

As Selma and Joe made their way into the sunroom, Tracy looked over and saw Geoff Wilson, owner of the Twilight Cove Gallery, and his partner Vincent Smythe walk through the door. Geoff had the exclusive rights to sell Carly's paintings in California.

The minute she saw Geoff, Tracy realized that this sudden influx of unexpected but very welcome guests had to be Carly's doing.

"Tracy!" Geoff grabbed her hands and leaned back to look her over. "You look *absolutely fabulous*. Doesn't she, Vincent?"

Vincent concurred. "Stunning. I *really* like what you've done with your hair."

Self-consciously, she fingered the French twist.

"Very retro," Vincent winked. "Very old Hollywood."

"Very Grace Kelly," Geoff added.

"Thanks . . . I think. I take it the gallery is closed tonight?" Overwhelmed with gratitude, Tracy wanted to cry. Downtown Twilight Cove was fast becoming a ghost town tonight. "Thank you two for coming."

"Mind if we look around?" Geoff asked, ignoring her question.

"Of course not. That's what tonight is all about. I have some guest rooms open down the hall to the right." She pointed the way. "There is plenty of wine and munchies in the sunroom."

They were a few steps away when Vincent suddenly turned around. "By the way, Tracy, if you ever, *ever* need help in a pinch, I've always wanted to play innkeeper."

Touched, she promised, "Thanks, Vincent. I'll remember."

Geoff rolled his eyes. "I'd pay you to hire him, just to get him out of my hair." The men laughed and continued on into the sunroom.

No sooner had they walked away when a trim young brunette with a deep tan and an exotic lilt to her eyes came through the front door. She paused to look around with obvious admiration for the setting. Spotting Tracy, she quickly walked up to introduce herself.

"I'm Kat Chandler." She offered her hand.

"I've heard all about you from Carly," Tracy said. "I'm glad to finally meet you in person."

"Same here." Kat Chandler was Jake's former partner in his private investigating firm in Southern California. House-sitting for the Montgomerys had led to Kat's subsequent marriage to a Twilight Cove local.

"My husband would have loved to have seen this place, but he's away on business for a couple of days." Kat's gaze lingered on the fireplace and the sitting area. "What a great room!"

"I'm glad you like it. It's my favorite." She explained that there were guest rooms open for viewing, and then Kat Chandler asked, "Are you booked up for the end of July?"

Don't I wish?

"Not yet."

"How many rooms do you have?"

"Nine, but one is occupied."

"I'll book the other eight and the ninth if it's available then. We'll need them for a week beginning Thursday the twenty-second of July."

"All my rooms for a week?"

Kat nodded. "My family is coming over from Hawaii, and you know how it goes. At first only three of them were coming, then it was down to two. Then seven of them, and now more of the kids have decided to fly over. There'll be around fourteen in all, so I'll reserve all the rooms to be certain."

"Are you sure?" Tracy couldn't believe she was reserving all nine rooms in one fell swoop until it hit her. "Did Carly and Jake put you up to this?"

Kat laughed. "No. Why?"

"They've come to my rescue a lot lately."

"Actually, the Montgomerys are innocent this time. The idea is all mine. We've been trying to figure out where to put everyone at our house, which would be impossible." She turned and pointed out the open front door. "See those lights on the point a couple miles down?"

Tracy nodded.

"That's the Chandler house. That's where we live."

They chatted a few more minutes while Tracy led Kat over to the reception desk and penciled in reservations for the eight rooms. When they finished, Kat strolled into the sunroom and Tracy realized that there had been a little over a dozen late arrivals, not all of them Carly's mercy calls. She made the rounds, speaking to travel agents and bed-and-breakfast booking service owners who gave her advice on Internet sites and brochures. Two of them took digital photos of the rooms.

When Carly finally reappeared a few minutes later, Tracy excused herself, leaving behind travel agents who were singing her praises.

"Thank you." At a loss for words, she threw her arms around Carly's neck.

"For what?" Carly's smile was infectious.

"For this." She indicated the guests with a sweep of her hand. "For coming to the rescue and calling out the troops." Tracy took a deep breath and wiped away a tear from the corner of her eye. "Most of all, for being such a great friend."

"That's what friends are for, isn't it?" Carly asked softly. "You've been there for me so many times over the years."

"Friends don't keep score," Tracy reminded her.

"Exactly." Carly reached over and carefully wiped a tear from beneath Tracy's lower lashes. "Enough, okay? You're going to ruin your mascara." She glanced around the room. "Have you seen the boys?"

"I thought I saw them go outside with Jake. Have you seen Chelsea? She's got some explaining to do."

Carly didn't try to pretend she had no idea what was going on.

"She is a wreck," Carly admitted, but she didn't make any excuses for Chelsea. "She forgot all about mailing the invitations until two nights ago, when she found them in the bottom of her purse. She tried to make up for it by calling everyone on the list to tell them the invites were on the way."

"Why didn't she just tell me?"

"She wanted to try to salvage the situation first. She really hated to let you down." Carly glanced around. "I see that quite a few of the travel industry guests made it after all."

"Fourteen out of seventy-five isn't a very good showing." As she gazed around the room again, she caught Selma in deep conversation with Geoff and Vincent, watched Joe and Palmer charm the ladies. Vincent was talking to Kat Chandler. New friends, old friends.

Tracy found herself fighting back tears again.

"Actually, it's worked out even better than I expected," she admitted, smiling through tears as she gazed around at all the people gathered in the sunroom. "If this hadn't happened, I might never have known just how many truly special friends I have in this town."

Wade was on his way back inside when he saw Chelsea step out onto the porch and pull her cell phone out of her purse. She looked as if she'd been crying.

Looking down at the phone as she hurried along the garden path, she nearly walked right into him.

"Are you okay?" He'd had to have been blind to miss the dark look she shot him.

"Do I *look* okay?"

He held up both hands. "Sorry I asked."

She looked like she was going to sidestep him and walk away, but suddenly changed her mind.

"What are you doing here, anyway?" she wanted to know.

"I was just checking on my bike and was headed back inside."

"I meant, what are you doing *here*, at the hotel? When are you going to check out?"

"Has Tracy said anything about wanting me to leave?"

"Tracy is way too nice to kick you out. Besides, she needs the money. Unlike her, I know what you're really after."

"You think so?" He tried to ignore the insult. "Tracy's a grown woman," Wade reminded her.

"My dad's not around to stick up for her, so I will. If you're waiting around for her to sleep with you, forget it. She was crazy about my dad. She's just lonely right now. You're nothing but a substitute for what she's really missing."

"You've got me all wrong, Chelsea."

"Oh, yeah? And what makes you different from most other guys on the planet?"

"I'm not most guys." She'd been upset when she walked outside, and he was pretty certain he wasn't the cause of her anger, but he was getting the brunt of it.

"If you're in a rotten mood, maybe you should go and pick a fight someplace else."

"Really? Where. There's no place to go in this town."

Just then, a red Corvette driven by a kid wearing glasses and a letter-man's jacket pulled up at the end of the driveway. Chelsea waved to him, then turned around.

"Do me a favor, will you?" she asked.

"Sure."

"Tell Tracy I went out with Eric for a while."

"When should I tell her you'll be back?"

"Whenever you want to."

"I meant what time?"

She called out over her shoulder as she headed for the Corvette, "I know what you meant. Tell her not to wait up."

CHAPTER THIRTY-THREE

Wade slipped into the foyer without drawing attention to himself and lingered in the shadows. His gaze unerringly found Tracy, and the moment he laid eyes on her, his heartbeat quickened.

He knew he was in serious trouble. A woman had never gotten to him so fast without even trying. She was in deep conversation with Carly Montgomery, her features alive with animation, her delicate fingers wrapped around an empty china teacup.

The light and shadows in the room danced over Tracy's porcelain skin, kissed her blond hair with highlights that sparkled like a halo of jewels.

Observing without being observed, he noticed every minute detail about her. He wondered: What was she like as a child? Then a teen? Had she always been so focused?

She had been thrown into a situation that could have destroyed a weaker woman, but she was bound and determined to make this venture work. He hoped for her sake that she was on the brink of success.

Not even half of the guests she'd expected had showed up, but there was no lack of love in the room. Those gathered around were laughing and chatting, and so was Tracy as she tried to make the best of a bad situation.

Tonight he was content to remain in the shadows, watching, wanting the best for her, wondering what might have happened if they had met

years ago, before she'd married. Before he'd made the biggest mistake of
his life in the name of success. If he'd met her then, both their lives could
have taken a different journey, one they would have traveled together. He
was sure that whenever, wherever he'd met her, he would have fallen in
love with her.

She wasn't like anyone else he'd ever met. She was the ideal he thought
he'd never find. Beautiful, intelligent, a woman who wasn't afraid to get
her hands dirty. A great mother. A caring friend.

He was a man on the run from himself and the public. A man haunted
not only by the memory of twelve murdered young women, but now, one
very persistent ghost.

Any dream he might nurture about a future with Tracy would forever
be just that—a dream.

That's what I want someday. That look. That feeling.

Tracy tried not to envy the way Carly and Jake smiled at each other
across the room when they thought no one was watching. Though the
Montgomerys had been married for over two years now, they still acted
like newlyweds.

So as not to get caught staring at them, she quickly glanced down at
her watch and realized that time had flown. It was nearly nine, almost
time for the gathering to come to an end. When she looked up again, she
saw Carly making her way across the room.

"I'll start cleaning up the kitchen," Carly offered.

"Absolutely not. I can handle it. You've been here all day. Go on
home."

"Are you sure there's not something I can do?"

Tracy thought for a moment. "Since you and Jake brought separate
cars, do you think he'd mind staying after everyone leaves to go over whatever he found out about the accounts? If he'd prefer to wait until tomorrow, I'll completely understand, but I know I won't be able to sleep
thinking about what he's going to say."

Carly's long, sun-bleached hair swayed around her shoulders when
she nodded. "I don't think he'd mind at all, as long as you're not too
tired."

"Not at all." *Tired?* Sleep was the furthest thing from her mind. When she hadn't been thinking about Wade, she had been worrying about what Jake was going to tell her.

As Carly walked away, Tracy headed for the buffet. Tossing used napkins in a nearby trash basket, she turned around and found Wade right behind her.

"You still look beautiful." He had the uncanny ability to make her feel as if she were the only one in the room with just a look.

"Thank you. And thanks for the gardenia. It's still fresh." She turned her head, inhaling the heady scent that had reminded her of him all night and made her feel as if he'd been right there beside her, though she hadn't really seen him all evening.

"I wish for your sake more people had shown up." His eyes spoke volumes. The last thing she wanted was him feeling sorry for her.

"There was a little snafu with the invitations, but thanks to Carly, things worked out. The point of tonight wasn't just to make contacts, but to celebrate. So instead of networking, I had a chance to share my accomplishment with old friends."

Whenever she thought of everyone who'd come over at a moment's notice, her heart felt lighter.

When he took her by the elbow and stepped toward the bank of windows behind them, that light heart started tripping over itself. Though her mind was still full of questions, her heart was powerless to resist him.

"I saw Chelsea out front."

She felt a touch of lightness ebb. "I was looking all over for her."

"She went out with Eric. She told me to tell you not to wait up."

His voice lowered to a more intimate level as he leaned closer. "I have a bottle of champagne on ice in my room. After everyone's gone and you've tucked Matt in, would you share it with me in celebration of all you've accomplished?"

No one had ever said anything remotely as romantic. The idea that Wade wanted to celebrate what she'd done nearly brought her to tears again.

"You really are an enigma, you know." She was tempted to reach up and rearrange his artfully tousled hair.

"How so?" He gave her a half smile, no more, as if some deep, lingering sadness prevented him from ever being completely happy. On him, that half smile was enough to intrigue, and entice. And to warm her to her toes.

She thought of the night he'd walked in out of the rain carrying nothing but his motorcycle saddlebag and helmet, how he'd said no more than half a dozen words to her before disappearing into his room.

That man was a far cry from the one she'd come to know as a talented writer, a professional who wasn't afraid to pitch in. And yet there was still so much to learn. He never talked about his childhood, never mentioned his family nor one single friend, not even in passing. She had no idea where he'd gone to school, how he chose his profession, or what he wanted out of life. She had no idea where he lived or where he was headed.

And she still hadn't gotten to the truth about his knowledge of Ezra Poole and how he knew about the location of the *Lantana*'s logs.

All she did know for certain was that for tonight it didn't matter. Tonight they'd agreed to not discuss it.

"You're still quite a man of mystery," she said, thinking aloud.

"Is that good or bad?"

"It's . . . interesting."

"Interesting enough to tempt you to have champagne with me?"

She looked around the room and located Matt. He waved to her, his smile perhaps not as bright as it used to be, but he was smiling again. She sighed, and when she turned to Wade, she knew she could give him only one answer.

"I'm afraid I'll pass on that champagne." She tried to hide her regret but failed miserably. "I wouldn't feel right, being alone with you in your room."

Hoping you would do God knows what with me.

She reminded herself that he had invited her only for champagne. She was the one assuming that things would go further.

"I could come upstairs," he suggested.

She shook her head. "That wouldn't work either."

"I didn't think so, but it was worth a try."

"I'm sorry," she finished lamely, wishing he weren't so close. She was tempted to reach for him. "I hope you understand."

"I knew it was a long shot, but you can't blame a guy for trying."

Did he sound as disappointed as she felt? She wondered what he would think if he knew just how close she'd come to saying yes.

CHAPTER THIRTY-FOUR

After everyone left, Tracy tucked Matt in and hurried back downstairs where Jake had slipped out of his casual sportcoat, rolled up his sleeves, and was seated at a bistro table in the sunroom, looking over papers in a manila folder. As she walked into the room, he closed the file.

Her mouth was suddenly dry, but she walked straight over to the table without stopping for anything to drink. Oddly enough, her palms were damp. She pressed them against her linen pants and then sat down across from Jake.

"It's bad, isn't it?" She would never forget that morning in David Sylvester's office when the accountant had told her about her financial status, or rather *lack* of one. She had that same hole-in-the-pit-of-her-stomach feeling now that she'd had then.

It didn't matter that she was surrounded by the fruits of her labor, that she'd pulled things together somehow and made a home for herself and Matt, or that she was on the brink of establishing a very viable business. She was waiting for another ax to fall.

Snap out of it, she told herself. *There's nothing you can't handle.*

The soft strains of the Eagles' "Hotel California" drifted in from the CD player in the sitting room. The scent of cinnamon coffee rose on the steam above Jake's cup.

She clasped her hands together in her lap, reminding herself that nothing he could tell her could hurt them now. Glenn was gone. If he had a drug habit, if he was heavy into gambling or God knows what else, that was behind her now. Knowledge is power. Hopefully she would learn something from whatever Jake had to say, but looking at his deeply concerned expression, she knew that whatever he had discovered was troubling. He seemed hesitant to begin.

"It's bad, isn't it?" She leaned forward, perched on the edge of the chair.

"I went over all of Glenn's books, looking for any misappropriation. I thought maybe someone who worked at the brokerage, a secretary or one of the other agents, might have found a way to siphon off money. It was a long shot, but that was my suspicion when I started digging."

He sounded perfectly calm, as if he were so used to dispensing terrible revelations on a regular basis that he had grown immune to it. But his eyes were still too expressive. The news wasn't good.

"That wasn't it, though, was it?"

He shook his head. "Glenn simply spent way more than he made. When money ran low, he took out second and third mortgages. Eventually he ran through an equity line of credit and wasn't able to borrow any more."

"Damn it. Why? Where did all the money go? Three years ago we had more than enough put away. It was money that was not commingled with the business."

She thought about the move from Twilight Cove to Canyon Club, the way Glenn spared no expense on decorating or buying himself a new Mercedes, all the investing he'd done in so many new development projects. Of course, she had worried, but he was constantly assuring her that everything was fine.

Jake's voice pulled her back.

"I'm not going to beat around the bush," he said. "There were things in the books that to the untrained eye wouldn't necessarily be seen as red flags. Things David Sylvester might not have questioned, but I can't believe he didn't."

"Glenn hired him because David is the best around."

"Were they close?"

She thought back. "I thought just acquaintances. They met through a business group, Rotary or something, in San Luis Obispo." She took a deep breath, twisted her wedding ring around and around. "We never went out socially with David and his wife." She tried to recall Glenn talking about David on a personal level.

"Tracy, Glenn had a mistress," Jake said quietly.

She froze, locked up from head to toe, and nearly stopped breathing.

A mistress.

"Are you certain?" She had no idea that she could feel such anger, or such betrayal.

"He had an affair with a woman for over three years before he died."

"Three years?" Suddenly, as if she'd been living life behind a fog bank, the mist began to clear.

Honey, I'm afraid I'm going to be late again. I hate like hell not to get home for dinner, but there's no way around it. Don't wait up.

Trace, I'm sorry, but I'm going to have to go back to Santa Barbara tonight. I've got a big meeting with the contractors on the Plaza town house project. I'll be back Tuesday."

Liar. All lies.

She'd suspected. Just before he died, she'd confronted him and still he'd lied.

"Are you having an affair, Glenn? If not, what's happening to us?"

"I don't know how you can even ask me that. I love you, Tracy. I love you and Matt and the things we've built together."

She had swallowed the lie, now she was choking on the pain.

He was *cheating on you.*

He had a mistress.

"How do you know? How do you know that for certain?" The blood in her veins was turning to ice, and slowly, her heart began to freeze, too. She could barely feel it pumping.

"Glenn was withdrawing large amounts of cash, large by most people's standards anyway. Ten and twenty thousand at a time. He purchased a very pricey fixer-upper in Montecito, nothing on a really grand scale, but you know how much property goes for down there."

Numb all over, she tried to fathom it. "A house? In Montecito?"

"I checked at the recorder's office, looked for grant deeds and holdings in his name. One was originally held in joint tenancy with the woman. The amount he paid in cash certainly accounts for the money shuffling he'd done. The house was transferred to her name a couple of months later.

"I also linked her to him through some checks he wrote to her personally. On the surface, some appeared to be legitimate business transactions."

"Who?" Who was the woman he'd ruined all their lives for?

"Tracy, there's something more."

"What?" *What more could there be?*

"They had a child together."

When the room started to spin, she unclenched her hands and propped her forehead on her palm. Jake was beside her in an instant, steadying her with a hand on her shoulder.

"Do you want to put your head down?"

She licked her lips. Her tongue felt coated with cotton.

"No," she whispered. "I'll be okay."

"Maybe we should go into the sitting room. Or do you want me to take you upstairs?"

"No." She shook her head and the dizziness slowly passed. Jake walked over to the sideboard and poured her some water. She took a sip, but it made her nauseous.

"How old is the . . . their child?"

"Almost two."

Somehow, though her heart was numb, her mind was still functioning. Her anger raw and real.

"You're absolutely sure?"

"I drove down to Montecito and took photos." He sounded as if he hated to admit it.

"Photos?"

"Surveillance photos."

Surveillance. She felt as if she'd suddenly been cast in a bad B movie. She must have looked stunned, for he gently reminded her, "Tracy, it's what I used to do for a living."

She'd forgotten. Now she tried to imagine Jake—big, smiling, kindhearted Jake Montgomery—skulking around behind shrubbery, sneaking photos of the woman who'd been sleeping with Glenn.

A woman who'd had a child with *her* husband.

"Who is she?" She almost welcomed her anger. It was at least an assurance that she wouldn't live out the rest of her life unable to feel at all. She tried to focus on Matt instead. He would need more than a brittle, angry shell of a mother in his life, but right now, she could see only red.

"Who is she, Jake? What's her name?" She wanted somewhere to direct her rage and, damn him, Glenn was gone.

Jake's shoulders rose and fell as he took a deep breath and let it go. *This isn't easy for him, either.*

"Willa Conner." Jake shifted toward the edge of his chair, as if ready to vault around the table and catch her if she fainted.

"What did you say?" She wasn't certain she'd heard him correctly. She couldn't *believe* she'd heard correctly.

"Willa Conner," he repeated.

Willa.

Her oldest friend. Willa, who had shared her high school years. Her college roommate. Willa, who had made the move to California with her. Willa, who'd sat in her living room a few days ago and wished her well.

"I thought she was ill." Incredulous, she remembered how worried she'd been about Willa.

"You know her?"

"She was here just a few days ago." A hollow laugh she couldn't stop bubbled out of her. There was no joy in it. "We've known each other for years. We were close once, a long time ago."

She had been the one who'd pushed Glenn into choosing Willa to decorate the Canyon Club model homes. She had been instrumental in getting them to work together. Willa was a talented designer, an artist, not to mention a beautiful woman, but Willa had never had much luck with men. She'd always claimed to be completely fulfilled by her career, but Tracy thought she'd seen a quiet longing in Willa, one she hadn't noticed until the first time Willa saw Matthew right after he was born.

"Do you have a picture of the . . . child?" She still couldn't believe it. She wanted to see for herself.

Jake slowly opened the file folder. Her gaze dipped to the photos lying there—upside down from where she was sitting—but there was no mistaking Willa's sleek dark hair and porcelain skin. Then Tracy saw a flash of red gold before Jake picked up the top photo and handed it over to her without a word.

She didn't need further proof than this. No paternity test in the world would shout the truth as loudly as the photo of Willa holding a toddler who had hair the exact same reddish gold as Glenn's and Matt's. The child's eyes were the same cerulean blue. Her little button nose matched Matt's at that age. Their baby photos could have been interchangeable.

And Willa? The image showed her carrying her little girl from what must have been her house to the Volvo. Impeccably dressed as always, Willa's arms were wrapped tightly around the child. She wasn't smiling. Violet smudges stained the shadowed hollows beneath her eyes.

She's grieving, not ill. Tracy couldn't tear her eyes away from the photograph of her friend. Willa was grieving for Glenn on a deep level of her own, grieving the way Tracy should have, had her memories not been shrouded with the strain their marriage had been under.

Willa was grieving for the lover she'd lost. Her baby's father. *For Glenn.*
She slid the photograph back across the table, finally met Jake's eyes. He must think her the biggest fool on earth.

But Jake was a professional. Amazingly, he comprehended her thoughts without her having said a word.

"There's no need to feel ashamed. Most people never suspect a thing in these cases, Tracy. Probably very few people who knew you and Glenn would ever suspect, either."

She thought of David Sylvester, his anally neat desk, his smug smile. His condescending charm.

"David Sylvester knew." She was sure of it now. Somehow, some way, David had known but hadn't told her. She was sure of it, but now that Chelsea was working at his office, hoping to land a scholarship, she hesitated to confront him.

Jake nodded in answer to her remark. "Maybe. Maybe not. He had to have seen the one-way cash flow. He may have even cautioned Glenn at some point."

She sniffed. "Believe me, Glenn never took well to being cautioned. Not once he set his mind on something." Her gaze traveled slowly around the room. "Look at this place. Surely someone must have told him he was crazy when he bought it, but did he listen?"

"Are you going to be all right?"

"Yes. Sure. Fine." She had no idea if she'd ever be *fine* again. One thing was certain, she'd never be such a blind idiot again. Never.

"Why don't you let me call Carly and have her spend the night?"

Instantly she looked up and shook her head. "No." The humiliation was too much when she thought of Carly knowing. "Did you tell her?"

"Not at all. I handled this whole thing as confidentially as I would have if you'd hired me."

"Would you . . ." she looked at her hands, "would you tell her for me?" She was on fire with embarrassment, but she didn't want to shut Carly out. She'd become too trusted a friend. Besides, she knew that Carly was not one to spread gossip.

Tracy reminded herself that she'd trusted Willa, too. Trusted her with Glenn. Pushed them into business together . . .

"Of course, I'll tell her." Jake sighed. "I just hate leaving you alone."

She thought of her precious boy asleep upstairs, and for a fleeting second she wondered where Chelsea was and if she was safe.

There was no way she could ever let either of them find out about Glenn and Willa. It was enough that her own love and trust had been dealt the final blow tonight—broken into an infinite number of blunt, jagged pieces. No, they didn't need to know.

"You'd better get home, Jake. It's late and Carly will be wondering where you are." She tried to smile, wondered if she'd be able to stand, if her legs would even hold long enough for her to walk him to the door.

"This is what I hate most about this job," he said.

"Being out late?" She couldn't think straight. Her mind was still reeling, still seeing the images in the photograph.

Jake pushed away from the table, gathered up the file, and offered it to her. She recoiled, as if it were a bomb about to go off.

"I don't want it. Burn it, for all I care." She tried standing. Miraculously, her knees held. "What was it you were saying? Something about what you hate?"

"Having to be the one to tell people that they've been cheated on. Telling them that the one person in the world they care about the most has betrayed them. It's why I quit taking on marital cases and started writing 'how-to' books."

"You know what *I* hate about this?" As they crossed the wide lobby, their footsteps sounded hollow against the bare wood floor.

"The whole thing, I imagine."

They paused just inside the front door. Jake looked so very concerned that, for his sake, she forced herself to smile.

"It's bad enough finding out that Glenn was unfaithful for years, but what really fries me is that he's already dead. Now I won't be able to kill him myself."

CHAPTER THIRTY-FIVE

At least she left Jake smiling as he walked out the door. She turned out the lights as she hurried upstairs, needing to see Matthew, needing to ground herself in the reality of her new life—in this place that didn't feel like a real home. In Matt.

Matthew was her world now. She didn't need to remind herself of that, she just needed to touch her baby, to make sure he was sleeping soundly, that he was warm and alive.

Because she was surely dead. She still couldn't feel a thing.

A pyramid of light streamed out of Matt's room as she walked down the hall. He'd fallen asleep propped up against his pillow. The lamp on his bedside table was turned low, the journal she'd given him lay open atop the comforter. His pen had rolled to the edge of the bed.

She picked up the journal, set the pen on the nightstand, and then gently sat down beside her sleeping son. Her initial anger receding, she was amazed at how calm she'd become. Her hands weren't even shaking anymore. Then again, she no longer felt anything, so why wouldn't she be cool as a cucumber?

Looking down at the open journal in her lap, she glanced at the last entry Matt had made and ran her fingertip over his unevenly spaced letters. Penmanship had never been his strong suit.

Saturday nite.

Dear Dad,
    Tonight Mom had a party. It was really grate. Chris was here and so was a lot of people that you know. That guy Wade is still living downstairs. He shooed his Harley to me and Chris and Jake. Jake liked it a lot and you wood, too.
    I think Wade is kinda nice now.
    I still miss you so much, tho.
                        You're dear son, Matthew A. Potter.

The letters blurred. Her vision smeared behind tears. Tears Glenn certainly didn't deserve. She scanned Matt's first entries and then closed the journal and set it on the table.

She pulled the comforter up around his shoulders and reached out to touch his hair. Her hand stopped poised above his strawberry blond hair. The image of Willa and Glenn's daughter flashed across her mind. A child with hair the exact shade as Matt's.

And Glenn's.

She smoothed Matt's hair back off his forehead with a feather-light touch. His lashes fluttered on his smooth, lightly freckled cheeks, and then his eyes slowly opened.

He smiled up at her. "Hi, Mom." His voice was thick with sleep. She knew he wasn't really awake.

"Hi, honey."

Still groggy, he rolled over to his side. "If you wanna talk to Dad, you can use my journal." His words drifted off to a whisper as he gently slipped back into his dreams.

She'd *love* to talk to Glenn right now.

But nothing she had to say was fit for her son's ears.

She turned off the light and made her way through the darkness to her own room. Light from the bathroom spilled across the king bed, a field of emptiness that dwarfed the compact room. There was no way she would sleep tonight. She found herself wondering if she'd ever get a good night's sleep again. Before she realized what she was doing, she'd pulled off her wedding ring and was walking toward the dresser. She opened the top drawer, dropped the ring inside, slammed the drawer.

The walls closed in on her. The room suddenly became claustrophobic.

She left the room, ran up the attic stairs, and burst out onto the widow's walk.

The wind had picked up. It was howling around the eaves again. She wrapped her arms around herself as a gust whipped long strands of hair out of her French twist. She didn't care. The air was damp with moisture off the water, the sea spray carried on the stiff breeze was chilly tonight. Another unseasonable storm was on the way. She didn't care.

"Damn you, Glenn!" Knowing her words would be muffled by the wind, she cursed aloud but found no real release, no satisfaction in cursing a man who couldn't hear her.

Unable to breathe, she grabbed the railing and clung to it, leaning over, drinking in gulps of air, but she couldn't catch her breath. She looked down, saw the light from Wade's window spilling out across the garden.

She wondered if he was awake, if he was writing. Maybe he slept with the lights on now that he'd made friends with Ezra Poole.

He had champagne on ice in his room.

"Would you share it with me in celebration of all you've accomplished?"

She'd turned him down because she always did the right thing. Always the good girl, she'd done the right thing all her life. She'd suspected Glenn, but hung on to hope, believing him long past when she should have, daring to hope that things would turn out fine. She'd put her belief in him though he hadn't deserved it. He hadn't deserved an ounce of her love, or her loyalty.

She took a deep breath, filled her lungs with cold, damp salt air, then she let it go in a rush.

She didn't want to be good or right anymore. She just wanted to *feel* something again.

Wade's mind was wandering in a million directions at once.

He'd tried reading through his notebooks, tweaking sentences here and there, tightening the writing. When he heard an unexpected knock on the door, he gathered up the notebooks and deposited them in the top drawer of the small bureau on his way across the room.

The instant he opened the door and took one look at Tracy's swollen eyes and tearstained face, he knew that something terrible had happened. Her smile was a caricature of the genuine article she always wore. Strands of golden hair had escaped the pins that held it in an intricate twist. Wisps straggled alongside her pale cheeks.

She hadn't changed. Nor had she taken off her corsage. She looked pale and shaken as she stepped past him into the room and looked around.

"Good. I see you still have that champagne." She nodded toward the plastic ice bucket on the low bureau. A bottle of Dom was standing in water with a few bits of ice floating around it.

"It's not ice-cold anymore."

She shrugged. "I don't mind. Am I still invited?" Her gaze barely grazed the bed before moving on.

"Certainly." He picked up the champagne, and droplets of water trickled off the bottle. He swiped the surface of the bureau with his bare hand and shrugged apologetically.

"Sorry."

She blinked, looked up at him. "For what?"

"Making a mess."

She shrugged, made no other comment.

"I'll be right back." He was half afraid to leave her alone.

He grabbed a hand towel from the bathroom and hurried back. The cork popped smoothly and he pulled it out, held the bottle up to the light, and watched the champagne bubble up inside.

Across the room, Tracy remained silent, her arms wrapped around herself in a protective, telling posture. He'd never seen her like this, and she was scaring the hell out of him.

He filled two champagne glasses he'd bought at the liquor store and walked across the room to where she was staring out the window into the darkness.

"Cheers," he said, handing her the glass and then touching the rim of his flute to hers.

"Cheers." The word came out on a barely audible whisper, and when her eyes met his, he saw such deep, raw sorrow in them that his heart contracted.

She finished the champagne in two long, smooth swallows and held the thin flute out to him again. He set down his own glass, walked back over to the bureau to refill hers.

"What made you change your mind?" He glanced over his shoulder, hoping she would open up to him.

She shrugged. "I felt like talking."

He indicated the only chair in the room before he sat down on the bed, leaned back against the headboard, and crossed his ankles. She sat.

"So talk." He noticed she'd already polished off half of the second glass of champagne.

She held the stem of the flute between her thumb and forefinger, lifted it to the light, and studied the bubbling liquid as if it were a science experiment. Finally she turned to him again. Tonight her eyes were pale, liquid turquoise, shimmering with unshed tears.

He set his glass down, got up, and crossed the space that separated them, then went down on one knee beside her chair. Strands of her hair had come loose and curled in soft wisps around her temples, like stray sunshine. He reached up, hooked his finger in one of the curls, and gently pulled it away from the corner of her eye. Her skin was as cool as the night air.

When he took her hand and then cupped her jaw and said, "What's wrong, Tracy? What happened?"—silent tears began to slide down her cheeks.

She bit her lips together, gave a slight shake of her head, and closed her eyes.

He took the glass from her hand, set it aside, took both of her hands in his, and led her over to the bed so that he could sit beside her. With his arm around her shoulder, he drew her against him and let her cry.

She didn't make a sound, something even more disturbing than having her break down sobbing. She sat there with silent tears streaming down her face.

Not knowing what else to do, he drew her against his chest and held her. The moment she lay her cheek against his heart, she started sobbing in earnest. When her heart-wrenching sobs slowly subsided and she rested her head on his shoulder, he brushed her tears off her cheeks and kissed her brow.

He wanted to throttle Chelsea for the mix-up with the invitations. Obviously, all the work, the pressure, the poor turnout, had finally gotten to Tracy.

Her head moved against his shoulder. He felt her breath catch on a mingled sigh, and then her hand slowly covered his. She slipped her fingers between his and held on tight.

"What would you do if you found out your whole life was a lie, Wade?"

His whole life *was* a lie right now. *Does she know?* If she'd somehow found out, she wouldn't be sitting here crying about it. She'd be kicking his sorry ass out onto the street.

"In what way?" he asked.

"In every way," she whispered.

He slipped his fingers beneath her chin, gently forced her to look at him. Her lashes were spiked and matted, her complexion mottled red. Still, she was beautiful to him. He was so very tempted to kiss her, to try and make her forget whatever had upset her so, but he couldn't take advantage of her weakness.

"Tracy, what happened?"

She took another ragged breath. "I met with Jake after the party."

"Carly's husband."

She nodded. "He's a private investigator."

He'd been afraid of discovery, and all this time Tracy's closest friend's husband was a *P.I.*?

"He told me . . . he told me . . ."

She pressed her fist against her lips and stopped. Her shoulders heaved beneath his arm. Slowly, she calmed again, pulled herself together.

"Tracy, I'm so sorry." *Jake told her. Jake had discovered the truth and now she knows I've lied to her.*

"There's no need for you to be sorry," she said, shocking him. "It's not your fault. I *knew*, damn it, but I didn't press him. I lived with it. I swallowed his lies."

"Who? Press who about what?"

"Glenn was having an affair for more than three years and I didn't do a damn thing about it." A short burst of sound escaped her, something between a laugh and a sob. "Is it still called an affair when it lasts that long?" She looked to him for an answer. "Do you know?"

"I have no idea." The schmuck who'd left her penniless had been screwing someone else?

"They even had a child together." She pulled away, blinked, and wiped her hand across her eyes, a valiant effort that only destroyed her mascara. He reached over, tried to thumb off the dark streak beneath her eye.

"And what did I do about it? Miss Merry Sunshine? Miss The-World-Is-Such-A-Wonderful-Place? I let him convince me that things would be all right. That he was working himself to death to provide for us, to give us the world. Not that I'd ever asked for it, mind you, but because he said he wanted the best for all of us."

She was working herself up to a full boil, which he suspected he could handle a whole lot better than the misery she'd been mired in a moment ago.

"And all that time, he was sleeping with her." She covered her cheeks with her palms, but her blue eyes shone over the tops of her fingertips as she stared back. "She had his daughter, and I had no idea."

She was trembling now, her hands shaking violently when she pulled them away from her face. She was no longer wearing her wedding ring.

He picked up her glass, filled it to the top along with his, and carried it back to her.

"Here's to starting over." He lifted his own glass to toast her, knowing without a shadow of a doubt that starting over wasn't all that it was cracked up to be. Sometimes it was downright impossible. "You're a fighter, Tracy. You'll be all right. If I had to bet money on anyone putting this behind them and moving on, it would be you."

"You want to know the best part?" Ignoring his last comment, she knocked back half the glass of champagne. "I'm the one who threw them together."

"You know her?"

"Oh, yes, I know her. She's an old friend." With a quick shake of her head, she gave another bitter laugh. "Her firm was allied with Glenn Potter's development projects. We were friends back in Indiana."

He took the glass from her, set it aside, took her in his arms. As he held her tight, he gently swayed back and forth. Her arms tightened around his waist and she drew closer, burrowing deeper into the security of his embrace.

Gingerly, he pulled the pins from her hair and then ran his fingers through it, watched it fall around her shoulders. The blond skeins were soft as silk, light as moonbeams.

Her breath came on a soft, warm sigh against his neck. For a moment his own caught and held when he felt her warm fingertips tease the skin above his shirt collar.

She turned her face up to his. Her eyes were closed, her lips kissably close.

No man in his right mind could resist her, though he was pretty well convinced that he wasn't in his right mind most of the time now anyway.

Hungry for the sweet, alluring taste of her again, he kissed her without hesitation. There was no resistance on her part as she kissed him back, parted his lips with her tongue, tasted, delved, hungered for more.

She pressed her hips against him, as if she couldn't get close enough. He splayed his hand against the soft curve of her spine at the small of her back and moved against her, made her aware of what she was doing to him, how quickly she'd brought him to a full erection.

She moaned against his mouth and slipped her hands beneath the hem of his shirt, pulled it up, teased his ribs and abs with her nails—urging him without words to walk backward, toward the bed.

He complied, the fever in him stoked by the feel of her body against his. Unpinning her corsage, he set it on the dresser. Then he slipped his hands between them, started unbuttoning her blouse. When he backed into the edge of the bed, he went down, drew her down with him, rolled her beneath him.

Their hands were all over each other, fighting with fabric, tearing away buttons. When her zipper went down, the sound was loud as a freight train breaking the stillness of the night.

The only other sounds in the room were Tracy's moans and sighs. They mingled with that of his labored breathing.

He unclasped her bra, slipped it open to reveal her perfect breasts. She arched, offering them up to him. He suckled on her nipples, one, then another. Lifted her higher. Her fingers tangled in his hair, urging him to take more, to take whatever he wanted.

She was writhing beneath him, grinding against his fully engorged erection.

She clasped his face between her palms.

"Make love to me," she rasped into his ear, her voice throaty, full.

He wanted her more than he wanted to see the sunrise in the morning. Wanted her more than he'd ever wanted anything in his hopelessly damned life. In a blinding flash of realization, he knew that he'd do anything for this woman, give her anything, give up anything, just to make her happy.

And in that moment he also knew that making love to her tonight would be the worst thing he could ever do to her, or for her.

She was tracing a path from his neck to his belly with her lips when he shoved his fingers through her hair, gently forcing her to look at him. Her breath was coming rapid and shallow, her eyes were bright, her cheeks damp with tears.

He took a deep breath, slowly shook his head. Her smooth brow slowly creased. Questions filled her eyes.

"Not like this, Tracy."

She froze and her sky blue eyes widened. When she moistened her lips with her tongue, the innocent move was almost his undoing.

He slipped his arms beneath hers, gently tugged her up higher, until she rested her cheek against his chest.

It felt so real, so natural to have her there. This wasn't a dream or a hallucination. This was real.

All the more reason why he had to tread very carefully. To make her understand.

"Not tonight. Not out of anger, Tracy."

"But—" She shook her head, tried to deny it.

He wouldn't hear of it.

"You don't want this any more than when you turned me down earlier. You're here because you're hurt. You're here because you've been betrayed, not because of what we might find together, or what we can give each other. You want to get even with your husband."

She grew very still, unmoving. Then she lifted her head and stared up at him. The turmoil was raw and real in her eyes, and then he saw the one thing he feared seeing before he turned her down.

Her cheeks flamed before she quickly paled. She lowered her eyes in shame.

"Don't, Tracy. *Don't*." He tried to lift her chin, to get her to meet his eyes again.

She tried to pull away, to slide off of him, but he held her tight.

"There's no shame in your coming to me tonight. The shame would be mine if I took advantage of your weakness. I can't do that to you and I won't. I care about you too much."

"Please," she whispered. "Let me go. Let me up."

He sat up with her, gathered her blouse in his hands, helped her cover her naked breasts. She grabbed her bra, clung to it.

Her hair fell like a gossamer curtain across her face, hiding her expression from him, hiding her embarrassment. He brushed it back, tucked it behind her ear.

"I'm sorry," she whispered, getting to her feet, slipping on her sandals. "I'm so sorry, Wade."

"Don't be." Barely under control, he tugged on his Levi's, buttoned his fly. "God knows you have every reason to need this tonight." He wished she'd look at him again, but she was already walking toward the door.

In two long strides he'd outpaced her, grabbing the door handle first to keep her from running out. He refused to move until she raised her eyes.

"If we were to make love tonight, you'd never forgive yourself for acting on impulse. You'd never forgive me for letting you. I don't want to hurt you, Tracy. Not ever. I know that when you're thinking straight again, you'll realize I'm right."

Tears sparkled in her eyes, but she didn't look away.

"Come on, I'll walk you upstairs." He opened the door. Lamplight spilled out into the dark hallway ahead of them.

"I'll go up alone."

"Are you sure?"

She nodded. "I'm sure."

"I'll see you in the morning, okay?" He kissed her softly, tenderly on the mouth. "Meet me in the sunroom."

She stepped out into the hall and he thought she was going to walk away without another word. Suddenly she stopped and turned around, clutching her bra as she held her linen blouse closed with her hands. The smile she gave him was bittersweet and wistful. Her eyes were sad, but luminous.

"Thank you, Wade," she whispered. "Thank you for being so honorable."

CHAPTER THIRTY-SIX

All around her, shadows filled the deep pockets of darkness in the far recesses of the lobby and adjacent sitting room. She clutched her bra, trying to move soundlessly across the bare wooden floors. Her breathing was rapid and shallow, the sound filling the emptiness.

She felt Wade watching her. She'd seen him lean against the doorjamb after she walked out, his arms crossed, his mouth drawn in a tight line. When she reached the bottom of the stairs, she finally heard the door to his room close.

Dear God in heaven, what was I thinking?

She nearly tripped on the wide hem of her pants, let go of her blouse to brace herself, and dropped her bra. Ashamed of sneaking through her own house, she shook herself and pulled her blouse together.

By the time she reached the apartment, she was shaking like a leaf, her head already pounding from too much champagne. Her conscience screamed as she stepped into the dark living room and felt her way past the overstuffed chair and ottoman before inching her way down the hall to her room.

A night of revelations. She'd learned more about her life and about herself tonight than she would have ever thought possible.

Why paint a pretty picture? Glenn was a bastard. He'd cheated on her, ruined their lives, put Matthew's and Chelsea's futures in jeopardy. And for what? So that he could carry on a long-term relationship with Willa?

And Wade Johnson? Yesterday she'd suspected him of lying to her in order to get into the attic. Tonight he'd proved that he had more scruples than Glenn ever had. Thank God Wade was the man he was, that he had the honor to do what only a handful of men would have done in the same situation. He'd sent her packing.

Not only had she discovered the depths of his honor tonight, but she had finally faced the truth. She had gone to him seeking solace, longing for his touch, needing him to soothe her battered ego by making love to her, and, somewhere between acting on her pain and hearing Wade turn her down, it hit her with blinding clarity that she wanted him because of who he was and what she felt for him. Not merely to get back at Glenn. Not to salve her own ego, but because she'd fallen in love with him.

She wanted him with a need kindled that first night when she'd taken a chance and let him into her hotel and into her life. She wanted to make love to him, to have him make love to her. To give as much pleasure as she would surely get in return.

Her anger and betrayal paled beside her explosive desire for the man downstairs.

Even knowing that Wade intended to walk back out of her life as surely and as suddenly as he'd walked into it, she still wanted him.

When she heard the soft sound of a footstep in the hall, Tracy's first and only thought was *Wade*.

A heartbeat later, there came a quick knock on her half-open door. She whirled around, the slip of her white lace bra clutched in one hand, holding the front of her linen blouse closed with the other. It was Chelsea, not Wade, who pushed the door the rest of the way open.

Tracy was suddenly paralyzed, right there in the middle of the room.

"My sorority sisters are always sneaking back into the house like this." Chelsea's disbelief was loud and clear. It was a night for surprises.

Tracy tried to straighten her tangled hair and gave up. "I'm not sneaking."

"You look like a deer caught in the headlights."

As Tracy turned around, she stuffed her bra into the dresser. Though her hands were shaking, she somehow buttoned the middle two buttons on her blouse.

"I looked for you when I came in. I went up to the widow's walk, but then I figured you were with him." Then Chelsea whispered something Tracy barely heard.

"What did you say?"

"I said, what about *Dad*? He loved you so much! How could you do this?" The words were loud and bitter, filled with hurt.

Tracy crossed the room on long, angry strides, walked right past Chelsea, and quietly closed the door. "Keep your voice down or you'll wake Matt." She fought for calm, struggled to sound in control.

Chelsea didn't move. "You wouldn't want Matt to know you've been downstairs fucking Wade, would you?"

Tracy's hand shot out before she knew that she had even moved. The sound of her palm connecting with Chelsea's cheek cracked unbelievably loudly in the silence of the night, imprinting itself forever on her mind and her heart.

Before a second passed, Tracy grabbed Chelsea, and though the girl struggled, she refused to let her go until she had succeeded in wrapping her arms around her.

"Oh, my God, Chelsea. I'm so sorry. I'm so, *so* sorry." She'd never struck anyone in her life. Never laid a hand on Matthew or Chelsea before. She'd never laid a hand on anyone in anger.

"I loved your father." She was quaking so hard she could barely stand, ashamed and appalled at what she'd done. "Once I loved him with all my heart."

Slowly, carefully, Chelsea slipped out of her arms but she didn't run out of the room as Tracy expected.

"This isn't about Dad, is it? It's about tonight. You're pissed because I didn't mail the invitations on time, aren't you?"

Tracy shook her head, feeling completely disjointed. "The party is already light-years away now."

"I'm sorry about the invitations. I put them in my big leather bag, the one I haul back and forth to work. They ended up on the bottom and I forgot all about them. Once I found them, I tried to call everyone."

Tracy held up her hand. "Please. It's all right. That doesn't really matter anyway, does it? What matters is what I just did." She closed her eyes, pressed her fingertips against her forehead, and rubbed it. "I don't deserve your forgiveness, honey, but I want you to know that I'll never, ever forgive myself for slapping you." She dropped her hand, met Chelsea's eyes, on the verge of tears again. "I'd do anything to take it back, but I can't."

Chelsea shrugged. "My mom wouldn't have thought twice about it."

"I'm not Monica."

"Definitely. That's why I've been so worried about you and this Wade guy. My mom's a pro when it comes to men, but you're so different. You and my dad had something special, and for a long time I was jealous. Tonight, on top of the mess I made of your party tonight, when I came in and saw you standing there with your eyes all puffy and your hair and clothes all messed up, I snapped."

"There are worse things than a low turnout at an open house." Tracy felt as limp as a wet washrag.

"But it was your big night to show off the place, and now . . ."

It was my big night all right.

"Go to bed, Chelsea. It's late, and we're both tired."

Chelsea didn't move. Instead she stared back at Tracy, her gaze sweeping her from head to toe.

"Did he attack you?"

"What?" Tracy drew back, startled.

"Wade Johnson. Did he attack you downstairs?"

"Of course not." She walked over to the low dresser on the other side of the room and stared out the closest window. The sky was ink black. There wasn't a star to be seen. She closed her eyes and took a deep breath, wishing away all the things Jake had told her, wishing she could take back slapping Chelsea. Wishing she could start the whole night over again.

Then she thanked God that the girl was so resilient and, apparently, so forgiving.

Then she quietly admitted, "I'm lucky Wade Johnson is the man he is. *He's* the one who kept things from going too far tonight."

Chelsea hesitated. "What's really wrong, Tracy? If you aren't upset about the party, what is it?"

"Nothing you need to worry about. Nothing either of us needs to worry about tonight. I'm just tired. Everything will look better in the morning."

"Are you sure?"

Tracy nodded. "I'm sure."

She somehow held on until Chelsea said good night and left. Then she ran into her bathroom and threw up.

"Mom?"

Lost in a dense fog, Tracy struggled toward the sound of Matthew's voice.

She was asleep and yet completely aware that she was dreaming—a strange, convoluted saga in which Glenn and Willa had shown up at the Heartbreak, luggage in hand, asking for the best room in the place.

Wade, walking around in low-slung Levi's and nothing else, was the bellboy. He tried to serve them a plate of cinnamon rolls burned to the size and consistency of charcoal briquettes while Palmer Biggs danced around the sunroom with a naked Selma Gibbs. Palmer was so short that his nose was wedged between Selma's ample breasts. And now Matthew was there dressed as Spider-man, calling her name.

"Mom?" Matthew again, shaking her shoulder.

She opened her eyes, finding herself facedown in her pillow. The inside of her mouth tasted like the Gobi Desert. She sat up too fast and her head started clanging like the bells of Notre Dame. She'd fallen asleep completely dressed.

Shoving her hair out of her eyes, she stared over at Matt, who was beside the bed in pajama bottoms and a fleece sweatshirt, his arms folded across his chest, his brow creased in a deep frown.

He looked exactly like Glenn.

Glenn. Suddenly the awful truth came rushing back.

Glenn and Willa.

They had a child together.

"What is it, hon?"

"The roof is leaking."

"What? Where?" She clamped the sides of her throbbing head with both hands.

"In the kitchen. It's dripping all over the kitchen. I put bowls and pans under the drips, but water is pinging out onto the linoleum."

"Did a pipe break?"

"It's *raining*, Mom."

Raining. Again. And hard, too, if the sound of it was any indication.

She glanced over at the clock on the bedside table and realized she'd slept right through the alarm.

Jumping up was a bad, bad idea. Her head started to spin, so she braced a hand against the wall and closed her eyes.

"Mom? Are you okay? How come you slept in your clothes? Your eyes are all puffy."

She swallowed. "I'm fine. I ate something salty. I got to bed late. Have you had breakfast?" She wondered what Wade was thinking when she didn't take coffee and rolls downstairs.

"I had Cap'n Crunch."

"Where's Chelsea?"

"Gone to meet Eric someplace."

"Go down to the laundry room and bring back the yellow plastic bucket to put under the worst drip, okay?"

He nodded, suddenly important for having been given a real chore. "I will."

She looked up, remembering that her room was beneath the attic. She'd have to go check it for leaks up there, too.

"If you run into Mr. Johnson, tell him that I'll bring the coffee down shortly."

"Okay, Chief." He saluted before he charged out of the room.

She refused to look in the mirror as she walked past on her way out of the room. The kitchen felt cold and damp. Rain streaked down the windows facing the ocean as the storm blew onshore.

She measured out coffee before going back to her room to clean up.

It took fifteen minutes to shower, pull her hair into a ponytail, and use enough eyedrops and makeup to hide some of the damage.

She poured herself a cup of coffee and, before she could change her mind, dialed Willa's number. Clutching the phone to her ear, she closed her eyes and thought she was ready, but she wasn't prepared for the shock of hearing Willa's voice.

"This is Tracy," she managed somehow after Willa said hello.

"Tracy!" There was a slight pause. "How was the party? I'll bet it was fabulous."

Hot coffee sloshed over the rim of the mug. She barely got it into the sink before she let it go. *Willa*. The woman had no idea she knew everything.

Her hand tightened on the phone.

"Tracy? Are you still there? Can you hear me?"

A blessed, icy calm came over her. "Yes. I'm here." She took a deep breath. "The party was fine. Great." *Just peachy.*

"I'm sorry I had to miss it."

I'll just bet you are.

Willa sounded drained. No wonder. Her lover, the man who'd given her a child, the man who'd bought her an expensive home in one of the most exclusive areas on the coast, was dead.

"How are you doing, Willa?"

There was a pause. "Fine, why?"

"I was worried about you after you left the other day. You looked so . . . sad."

Another pause. "I'm all right."

"That's good." Tracy paced over to the middle of the room and watched rainwater plunk into her pottery mixing bowl.

She felt completely disconnected, thoroughly unemotional. As if she were another woman entirely.

"You know, your visit got me thinking. It's been *way* too long since we've had lunch together. How long has it been? A couple of years?" Using the toe of her tennis shoe, she adjusted the position of the bowl beneath the drip.

Willa's voice was so soft, Tracy could barely hear it. "I have no idea when I'll be up in your area again."

"No problem. I have to drive down there to pick up a special order this week anyway," Tracy lied. "I'd love to take you to lunch."

"I'm not sure—"

You're not getting off that easy.

"Oh, come on. It's been years. I'm not taking no for an answer. What day this week is best?" She heard Willa shuffling pages, imagined her at her desk, checking her calendar.

"Tomorrow at one. That's probably too soon."

Not even if I have to walk all the way.

"I'll be there. Should I pick you up at your office?"

"I'll meet you at the Brown Pelican."

"That would be great. I haven't been there in ages."

"If the weather stays bad . . ."

Tracy glanced toward the window. Rain smeared the glass, distorting the view.

"I'm sure it will clear, but I'll call if I can't make it. I'll see you tomorrow at one, Willa."

They said good-bye. It wasn't until Tracy hung up and set the phone down that she realized what she'd done. She leaned against the kitchen counter, staring at the coffee mug in the sink and the coffee staining the porcelain around it.

"Mom?" Matt came running into the kitchen with bucket in hand, barely missed the mixing bowl, and pretended to be gasping for breath. "I saw Wade and told him to come get his own coffee."

"Oh, no!"

"Well, I already told him to." He set the bucket on the floor and started to pick up the mixing bowl.

"Let me do that." She started across the room and almost died when she realized that Wade had followed Matt in.

"I'll get it." Wade picked up the full mixing bowl and Matt swiftly replaced it with the bucket between drips.

Tracy's heart stumbled when Matt held up his hand and exchanged a high five with Wade the way he used to do with Glenn.

Dear Dad. I still miss you so much.

"Can I watch Nickelodeon, Mom?"

Trying to keep it together, she nodded. "Okay, but keep the volume down."

He started to run out of the room and then halted in the doorway, his expression serious. "I turned on the vacancy sign."

When she thought she hadn't any left, she felt a rush of tears. "Thanks, honey." She collected herself and then told Wade, "If he keeps this up, I'm going to have to put him on the payroll."

Wade walked over to her as soon as Matt was out of sight. She looked everywhere but into his eyes. He touched her shoulder, ran his hand down her arm to her wrist. His fingers were warm and gentle where they rested against her pulse point.

"How are you doing?"

Drawn by the kindness and genuine concern in his voice, she smiled. It was feeble, but it was a passable smile. "Not as bad as I thought I would be. I'll live."

"Good." He smelled like soap and shampoo and filled the small galley kitchen with his raw masculinity. Hard, but giving.

"Coffee?" She had a hard time forming a complete thought whenever he touched her.

"Sure."

She kissed him as he poured himself a cup of coffee.

"I'm sorry," she apologized. "I overslept."

"I was worried you wouldn't sleep at all."

She shrugged and admitted, "I was up most of the night."

He leaned back against the counter, crossed his ankles, and blew on a sip of black coffee.

She collected her own cup from the sink and started over.

"So, you're meeting Willa tomorrow?"

She glanced up quickly, as if caught doing something forbidden. "You heard?"

"I didn't mean to. I followed Matt in. I'm sorry."

He didn't look sorry. He looked curious and, more than that, he looked concerned. "She doesn't know that you know everything yet."

It wasn't a question, merely a statement. He'd crossed the room to stand in front of her. She felt drained and hollow, tempted to lean into him, to tap into his physical strength.

"No, she doesn't know."

"Why put yourself through it, Tracy?" When he reached for her, she let him pull her within the circle of his arms.

She closed her eyes, pressing her cheek against his shirtfront. A button on his new denim work shirt dimpled her cheek.

"Because I still don't know everything, and I need to. I don't know when it started. I don't know how she could do this to me and Matthew and Chelsea." The memory of slapping Chelsea hurt as much as the actual act. She took a deep, shuddering breath. "I need the truth."

"I can't see you wanting to make her suffer, not even if she deserves it."

"I'm *not* doing this to make her suffer. I'm doing this for *me*. I need to see her face when she tries to explain. *If* she even tries."

He moved slightly and she heard the clink of his coffee mug against the counter. Then he pulled her closer with both hands, nuzzling his lips against her hair.

Drawing strength from his comforting embrace, she remembered the look on Chelsea's face last night, her anger, her shock.

I'm human, too, not some perfect sitcom mom who has all the answers. I'm flesh and blood. I need love, too.

Even if it's not forever.

As Tracy slipped her arms around Wade, she couldn't help but think of how differently things could have gone last night if not for this man's honor.

She raised her face to him and whispered, "Just a kiss?"

"Of course." He brushed her lips, slowly, tenderly.

And suddenly she was lost in sensation—until the *Rugrats* theme song drifted in from the living room.

"Thank you," she said. Though her world was still rocking, she found herself able to smile, to step back. "That was nice."

More than nice, it had sizzled. Right now though, the last thing she needed was a stimulant.

He reached for his coffee. "Don't go to Santa Barbara tomorrow."

She shook her head. "I have to."

"What about Matt?"

"I'll call Carly. She won't mind having him over."

"Are you going to tell her where you are going? Does she know about Glenn?"

"Jake was supposed to tell her for me. And no, I'm not going to tell her I'm meeting Willa." She hoped she made her point when she added, "And you aren't either."

"What about guests? What if someone wants to check in?"

She remembered Vince, Geoff's partner, offering to help out last night.

"I have someone who can fill in for me."

"I see you have this all thought out, but I can fill in for you," he offered.

"You've already done more than enough, Wade. Besides, it's a good idea for me to train someone to take over if I ever need help. Vincent will be great." *And you won't be here forever.*

She glanced out the window again. The rain was a hazy gray sheet still battering the coast. The swells were dark and angry, topped by whitecaps that rose and sank beneath the roiling water.

Capt. Ezra Poole flashed through her mind.

Her whole life was riding out a typhoon and only she had the power to keep it from capsizing.

"Why don't you take some time to go through the *Lantana*'s logs in the attic?" she suggested.

"I'm not opening *that* can of worms again." He sounded determined to not discuss the logs or his writing again. Their argument seemed light-years away now.

"For whatever reason, you've come here to tell Ezra's story . . ." she began.

He cut her off. "Tracy, look, I didn't come here to tell Ezra's story. I still have no idea how it came to me."

"Please, Wade. I don't *care* how it happened right now. Please, use the logs. Learn all you can about Ezra Poole."

"You still don't believe me."

She searched his eyes, knowing that *he* believed what he was telling her.

"Everyone deserves a little personality quirk."

"The other day you weren't as forgiving."

"I've been on a roller-coaster ride since then. Finish your story. It's wonderful. People need stories about lasting love, today more than ever."

He was silent, thoughtful. She could tell that he didn't approve of what she had planned for tomorrow—but he didn't try to argue.

No matter what he might have said, come hell or high water, she was going to talk to Willa face-to-face.

CHAPTER THIRTY-SEVEN

Monday the sky was brilliant blue without a wisp of a cloud in sight. The storm had washed away the smog, and every tree and shrub, every blade of grass sparkled with vibrant shades of green—lime, emerald, chartreuse.

A few minutes before one, Tracy pulled into the parking lot and walked down the curving sidewalk lined with fan palms toward the Brown Pelican, a restaurant tucked into a cove on the beach in Santa Barbara.

It was a casual, popular spot right on the sand of a broad, level beach. The decor was typical funky waterfront with rough, weathered wood siding and old pier pilings cut in staggered heights bordering the flower bed. A wall of windows faced the ocean. Today the Pacific was so calm, it was hard to believe the storm ever happened.

Glancing at her reflection in the window, forcing herself to walk slowly, Tracy hoped that her nerves didn't show. She'd chosen her outfit carefully, changing three times before finally deciding on her favorite Tommy Bahama beige silk slacks, a matching sleeveless shell, and, in case the mercurial weather changed again, a thin silk sweater tied around her shoulders.

Tracy saw Willa immediately after stepping through the front door. She paused at the hostess station.

"I see my party," Tracy told the twenty-something hostess. The shapely, tanning-bed-bronzed blonde grabbed a menu and led the way to Willa's table.

As yet Willa hadn't seen her. She was sitting at a table for two beside the front window, staring out at the water with her chin propped on her hand, her eyes deeply shadowed. She looked completely miserable.

And why wouldn't she? Her lover is dead.

Did betraying her best friend ever enter her mind?

Willa looked completely startled when she realized Tracy was already there, standing beside the table. The hostess quietly slipped away as Tracy pulled out her chair and sat down.

"You're here." Willa's smile faltered, then slowly reappeared.

"Is everything all right?"

Willa slowly nodded. "I've been wanting to see you again, actually."

Tracy fingered the napkin wrapped around the silverware, took a deep breath, and forced herself to stay calm.

"It's been a long time since we've done this." Her voice sounded far off and tinny, as if escaping an old Victrola.

There was a distance in Willa's eyes as she nodded. The even, blunt ends of her smooth dark hair brushed her jawline.

Tracy unwrapped her silverware and spread her napkin on her lap. There was a lull while the waitress took her order. She chose a simple garden salad, knowing she would have to force-feed herself. Actually tasting anything would be impossible.

Tempted, she denied herself a martini, deciding to stick with club soda and lime. She didn't want to end up on *Eyewitness News.*

Betrayed wife kills husband's mistress in local eatery.

"Remember years ago, when I first met Glenn and would vent about all the little things that bugged me about him? All the dumb little things that didn't really matter? You were such a good listener. So sweet to put up with it."

Willa didn't flinch, but there was a faraway look in her eyes again. Tracy swiftly changed the subject. "How's the decorating going?"

"Fine. I'm finishing up a few projects."

Their salads were delivered to the table along with a small basket of bread. Tracy chose a piece and tore off the crust, one crumb at a time.

Willa didn't even lift her fork, but kept her hands in her lap. "How are you doing now that you aren't focused on the open house?"

"Funny you should ask." Tracy popped a bite of hard crust into her mouth. It could have been cardboard for all she cared. Willa seemed to be dissolving right before her eyes.

She took a deep breath, swallowed the bread crust.

"Life is always interesting, don't you think? I mean, six months ago I was married. Everyone thought I had a devoted husband and was living a fairy tale life. But now . . ." She paused, leaned back, and realized that she wasn't nervous at all now.

There was so much strength in knowledge. So much power in having the upper hand.

"But now Glenn's gone and I'm running a hotel on my own and . . ." She paused again, leveling her gaze on Willa, ". . . and not only is my husband dead, but I found out that he had been sleeping with an old friend . . . for years."

Slowly what little color that was left in Willa's cheeks drained away. The violet circles beneath her eyes deepened as her hand went to her throat.

She opened her mouth, but nothing came out. Not a sound. Tears welled in her eyes. She did nothing to stop them as they slipped over her bottom lashes.

The woman looked positively pitiful.

Tracy felt nothing. Not even triumph when she played her trump card. The betrayal was still too raw, still too real.

When Willa finally spoke, Tracy could barely hear her over the chatter around them.

"How long have you known?"

"Long enough."

"You didn't say anything when I came by . . ."

Tracy thought about that day. How sad Willa had looked. How she'd assumed that her friend was simply sharing her pain. Empathizing with her.

"I didn't know then."

"Who told you?"

"A private investigator."

Willa's mouth dropped. She leaned forward. "You hired a private investigator?"

"To go over Glenn's books. To see if I could find out how he got into such debt. The trail led back to you. To his cash withdrawals. To the house he bought for you—"

"Tracy—"

"— to the daughter you had with him."

"I know what you must think of me."

Tracy shook her head. "No. You have no idea. Actually," a tight, angry laugh escaped her, "it's funny, but there's really no way to express what I feel, or what I've been thinking since I found out."

Willa shoved her plate aside, shook her head, and leaned forward. "Believe me, I never planned to fall in love with Glenn. It just happened."

Tracy quickly cut her off.

"How did you let it happen, Willa? How does a woman let her feelings go beyond attraction for another woman's husband? To an old friend's husband? What kind of woman lets that happen? How could you, of all people, let that happen?"

"I couldn't help myself."

Glenn's handsome, boyish smile came to mind. His shining sandy hair, deep blue eyes. His ready laugh. He'd always been attractive to women. Handsome and successful. It was a tough combination for some women to ignore.

Willa turned toward the window as the waitress approached them. The girl glanced down at their untouched plates.

"Is everything all right?" she asked.

Tracy dismissed her with a nod and a quick, "Fine, thanks."

It was another moment or two before Willa could even look at Tracy again.

"He loved you, Tracy." There was no trace of spite or envy in Willa's tone. She sounded sincere, caring as always. "He said he'd never divorce you. He made that clear right from the start, and I would never have asked him to."

"So, you were content to sleep with him and take his money?"

"It wasn't like that."

"No? Then how was it, Willa?"

"It was . . . like nothing I've ever felt for anyone. I didn't care that he could only give me stolen hours. I knew going into it that he'd never, ever leave you. He wouldn't do that to you, or to Matthew."

Most especially to Matthew.

Tracy knew how much Glenn always regretted the effect his divorce from Monica had had on Chelsea. She could see him wanting to avoid doing the same to Matthew.

"I can believe he stayed for Matthew, but if he *truly* loved me, he would never have slept with you."

"Don't you think it's possible to love more than one person?"

Two nights ago she had been ready to sleep with Wade, and she'd known him a month. If she were completely honest with herself, she knew she had been attracted to him almost from her first glance. But if she'd still been married? Or if Wade was married?

She didn't have to think twice about what choice she would have made then.

"Glenn took a vow to be faithful, Willa."

"You must have suspected something," Willa said softly.

"Certainly, things were . . . different." There was no way she was going to let Willa know exactly how things had been between her and Glenn those last few years. She changed the subject, asking one of the questions she'd been wrestling with for two days now.

"What about your child? What were you going to tell her when she was old enough to understand? 'Your daddy has another family? A real family?' "

"I was going to cross that bridge when, and if, I came to it."

"So, you *were* hoping Glenn and I would divorce."

"No."

When Willa reached for her water glass, Tracy noticed that her hand was trembling wildly. For a second she thought the woman was going to drop it.

Willa took a quick sip of water, no more, and looked pained.

"My daughter's name is Mary Jane."

"After the shoes?"

"After my grandmother."

Tracy tried to not care what Willa and Glenn had named their daughter. She tried to forget how much the child looked like Matt.

"I know about all the money, Willa."

"No," Willa shook her head, "you don't."

"I know that Glenn gave you a sizable stipend every month for the last year, and that he bought you a house in Montecito."

"It was all for Mary Jane."

"And you."

"But you don't—"

"What? I don't *what*? I know everything, thanks to Jake Montgomery."

"Tracy, let me finish a sentence."

Tracy didn't want to *let* her do anything. How Willa could sit there and justify anything was beyond her. Her anger at Glenn, at both of them, was back—hard, cutting, and bitter, and she hated feeling this way. All this anger didn't fit. It hurt like nothing she'd ever felt before—like walking a mile in a pair of shoes that were two sizes too small.

She looked down at her salad, at the crumbs of bread crust scattered everywhere, and resisted the urge to sweep them onto the floor.

"Fine, so finish." She dared Willa to make any more excuses.

"I'm dying, Tracy. I have leukemia and it's reached the terminal stage."

CHAPTER THIRTY-EIGHT

Tracy's gaze quickly touched on Willa's sunken cheeks, the dark circles beneath her eyes, the way her veins showed like blue lines on a road map across the backs of her hands.

"Dying?" Not mourning Glenn so deeply that she had lost an inordinate amount of weight. *Dying?*

"Are you sure?" The woman was only in her mid-thirties.

"They've tried everything. The last experimental drug nearly killed me."

"Did Glenn know?"

"Of course. That's where most of the money went. The disease showed up when I was pregnant with Mary Jane. I couldn't have treatments then, of course. After she was born, it came on with a vengeance."

"Does she have it, too?" Dear God. Tracy could never wish that for a child, any child.

Willa's face mirrored her deeply embedded relief.

"No, thank God. She's fine." She took a deep breath. "My insurance would pay for only so much. Glenn is . . . *was* paying for my treatments. The cost was exorbitant."

She looked down at her hands as if more ashamed at having to take the money than for the affair.

They fell into an uncomfortable silence.

Tracy's anger had fizzled like a bad Fourth of July bottle rocket. The hurt was still there, deep and searing as a terrible burn, but the fury of her anger was gone.

As she looked across the table at Willa, at this new, pale, emaciated version of Willa, those long-ago years full of laughter and friendship they'd shared in Indiana battled the weight of her hurt and anger.

Her positive outlook on life had always been her mainstay. It had pulled her through the worst of times and kept her going. It had given her the strength, the will, to start over with nothing but the Heartbreak Hotel and a vision.

Now the attitude that she'd fought so hard to nurture all her life was fighting her need to strike back for what Glenn and Willa had done.

"The house . . ." Willa's words drifted away. She looked as if she were about to collapse as she reached for her water again.

"Maybe you should try to eat something."

Willa shook her head no and set the water glass down without taking a drink. "The house was a fixer. It was in terrible shape when Glenn bought it, but he saw the potential in buying in Montecito. He had one of his contractors remodel it and we moved in. The house was never for me, Tracy. It's for Mary Jane. The equity in it is her trust fund. Glenn promised to take care of her." Her lower lip trembled as her eyes filled with tears again. "Now he's gone."

Tracy tried not to care, but that was simply too tiring. She felt like a ship becalmed. All the wind was out of her sails and she was exhausted.

Willa rested her elbows on the table and rubbed her temples.

"I had my mind made up to tell you today. I know you probably don't believe me now, but it's true. When I dropped by the Heartbreak in May, I didn't come to visit. I was there expressly to tell you, but I couldn't do it. Now there isn't much time left, and I wanted you to know."

"So now I know." Tracy thought of how she'd walked into the restaurant ready to take no prisoners. Ready to see Willa squirm.

"I need your help, Tracy, though I don't have the right to ask for it."

"No. You don't. I can't forgive you, Willa. Not this." Her mind suddenly flashed on Chelsea. *I'm so, so sorry, honey.*

She forced herself to focus on Willa.

She's my oldest friend. In my life long before Glenn. Before California.

"I'm not asking for your forgiveness," Willa said. "I know that would be asking too much. What I want is for you to take Mary Jane after I'm gone."

"*What?*"

"Raise my daughter, Tracy. I have no family. No one else. Besides, there's no one on earth I'd trust her with but you."

The image of the smiling redheaded little girl flashed through Tracy's mind. The little girl who looked so much like Glenn. So much like Matthew.

As if Willa had read her mind, she quickly reminded her, "She's Matt's half sister, Tracy."

She's Glenn's child.

Would Glenn have come to me? Would he have laid it all on the table, the affair, the money, the house in Montecito? Would he have asked me to raise his and Willa's daughter after Willa was gone?

"Was that Glenn's plan?"

"For the first time in his life, Glenn had no plan. He refused to believe the treatments wouldn't work. He kept going from day to day, pushing his projects, pushing himself. I tried to tell him that it was past time he told you. I only have a few more months, maybe even a year, but only if I'm lucky. Who knew Glenn would go first?"

Reeling, Tracy sat in stunned silence, staring.

Willa shuddered. "I know that if things were different, if I asked you to raise a child of mine who wasn't Glenn's, that you wouldn't bat an eye. You wouldn't hesitate to say yes."

"But this is too much."

"I know."

"I feel like I'm the lead in a soap opera. The next thing you know, Glenn will walk through the door telling me it wasn't really him we buried, but his evil twin, one that no one even knew existed." Despite the gravity of the situation—or perhaps because of it—Tracy laughed.

Even Willa smiled, though weakly. "*That's* what I want for Mary Jane, Tracy. I want her to be able to laugh in the face of adversity, to make lemonade when life gives her lemons. It's something I've never been able to do. I want you to pass that on to my daughter."

"Willa, I *can't.*"

"Don't refuse me outright. Go home and think about it. I know that if anyone can make sense of this situation, if anyone truly understands what would be best for Mary Jane, it's you."

"Just because I'm able to laugh when I feel like crying, don't make me out to be Mother Teresa. I'm human, Willa, and right now I'm mad as hell."

"You're the one who has always done the right thing. You're the one who truly believes in herself. That's why I want you to raise Mary Jane."

Somehow Tracy managed to pay the check. She left Willa sitting at the table and walked out of the Brown Pelican. She was across the parking lot, standing beside her car, before she realized she'd even moved.

Just as she pressed the lock button on her key ring, she heard the sound of a Harley starting up across the lot and thought of Wade. As she opened her car door, the sound grew louder. Looking up, she realized it was Wade as he came riding across the parking lot, headed in her direction.

He pulled up in the empty parking space beside her and killed the engine. He was off the bike, taking her in his arms in two long strides.

"Tracy."

"Is something wrong at home? Is Matthew all right?" Her words were muffled against the front of his leather jacket.

"Matthew's fine. Everything's fine. I was worried about you."

She drew back, still in his arms. He was frowning as he thumbed away her tears.

"You don't sound happy about it."

"Yeah, well, I don't much like to worry. I wanted to make sure you weren't too upset to drive home."

"Some tough guy you are."

"Hey, it was a beautiful day for a ride anyway." He shrugged, trying to make light of the fact that he'd ridden all the way down here just to be sure she was capable of driving herself back.

She looked around, not wanting Willa to walk out of the Brown Pelican and see her wrapped in Wade's arms. She didn't want to see Willa at all. She took a deep breath and stepped away from him.

"I'm okay. Really." *Confused. Empty.* She tried to smile and failed miserably.

"How did it go?"

"Certainly not the way I expected."

"Want to talk about it?"

"I don't know how to explain what just happened in there." She hadn't yet come to grips with what Willa had asked of her. She certainly wasn't ready to try to tell anyone about it. Not even him. "How are things at home?"

"Vincent actually checked in three guests. A couple on their honeymoon, and a single man."

"Maybe I should leave more often. Maybe it's me," she mumbled.

"I'm worried the single guy might be competition."

She found herself smiling. With Wade beside her, the whole sordid stew her life was in seemed a little less bleak. She couldn't bear to think of him leaving tomorrow, let alone ask if he were still planning to go.

He rubbed her arm. "You ready to head back? I'll follow you."

"I'm ready. I'm *so* ready."

Despite the turmoil inside her, Tracy realized that she was desperately looking forward to getting home. There was so much to think about, so much she didn't want to face yet—though she would have to sooner than later.

Willa and Glenn. Willa's illness and her impossible request.

And Wade. His life, his work, was in L.A.

They hadn't spoken of his leaving since Saturday night. She hadn't been foolish enough to believe that he would stay, that at the very least he'd ask if he could keep in touch, if he could see her again.

She chose to deal with things later. She'd had enough for now.

She slid into her BMW, started the engine, and headed out of the lot. As she headed up the coast, she realized that for the first time ever, she was thinking of the Heartbreak as home.

CHAPTER THIRTY-NINE

The sun had already set and the sky was getting dark as Matt sat on the top porch step waiting for Wade. He watched the tall man come walking up the bluff path and waited until he reached the garden walk behind the hotel before running out to meet him.

"Hey, Wade. Mom says you're leaving tomorrow." The Harley was way cool and Wade wasn't so bad. He might even miss him a little.

"I'm heading out in the morning." When they were at the back steps, Wade sat down on the porch and stared out at the ocean.

Matt sat down beside him. "You coming back sometime?"

"Maybe."

"You gotta go back to work or something?"

"Something like that."

Matt noticed that Wade sure wasn't talking much tonight. Neither was Mom. He hoped that she wasn't going to be too sad after Wade left. He hadn't thought about it much before, but maybe she needed a grown-up around to talk to. He didn't know how to talk Wade into staying a little while longer, so he just sat there thinking about how much he'd miss sneaking out to sit on the Harley. He remembered the day Wade went shopping with them, and then he had a great idea.

"Wait here, okay, Wade?"

"Sure."

Matt jumped up and ran back into the house and up to his room to grab the disposable camera off his dresser. When he ran back out to the porch, Wade was still there.

"Here," he said, holding out the camera.

"Want me to take a picture?" Wade turned the camera over in his hand.

"I used all the film. You can have it."

"Don't you want to get them developed?" Wade was looking up at him, trying to figure it all out.

Giving Wade the camera made him feel really good. So good he couldn't stop smiling.

"You can take it with you and keep the pictures. That way you'll always remember your vacation here."

Wade tried to hand the camera back. "That's really nice of you, but it's yours."

"It's a going-away present. I want you to take it with you." Matt sat down beside him again. It was getting darker out. It was hard to see the ocean now, but he could still hear it.

Wade didn't say anything. He just sat there holding the camera in his hands, staring at it. Finally he looked over and said, "How about this— I'll get doubles made of the photos and send them to you."

"Wouldja?"

"Sure."

"Way *cool.*" Matt wondered if he'd feel this bad every time guests checked out. He thought about the new guy who had checked in earlier and decided: *probably not.* He had a feeling that Wade was different. That if he stayed a little longer, they might get to be real good friends. Then he had another great idea.

"Since you're leaving, you think you could give me a ride on the Harley?"

This time, Wade laughed. "Is that why you gave me the camera? Is this a bribe?"

"No. I gave you the camera so you won't forget us. So how about the ride?"

"Your mom would kill me if I gave you a ride. I think you know that already."

"Yeah. I know. I just thought I'd ask." He rested his elbows on his knees and his chin on his fists. The porch lights came on, making it even harder to see what was out beyond the garden.

"Matt?"

"What?"

"Thanks again for the camera."

"That's okay."

"Even without photos, I won't forget you."

Alone in his room a few minutes later, Wade carefully stacked the *Lantana* logs on the dresser. That evening he'd sorted and scanned through fifteen years of shipping details from the late 1800s, right up to the year Ezra Poole's ship had been lost at sea.

Ezra was through dictating. The renovations were finished. It was time to go.

His saddlebags were packed and lying on the chair across the room. Leaving wasn't something he wanted to do. For the first time in his life he'd met a woman who he could actually imagine sharing his life with, someone he would look forward to waking up with every morning. But Tracy deserved far more happiness than he could offer her.

She'd never know how much her trust, her smile and determination, her warmth and caring meant to him. She'd never know that his taking refuge here for a few weeks had saved his life. He would never forget her or the Heartbreak.

He reached for a log written the year before the ship went down and headed for the bed, intent on making a last few notes, when there came a soft knock on the door. It was late, too late for Matt to be up, and, knowing it could be only Tracy, he wondered if his longing to see her had somehow conjured her up.

"Hi." She was carrying an open bottle of Pinot Grigio and two wineglasses. "May I come in?"

"Of course."

She glanced over at the stack of ship's logs. "If you're working—"

"No. I was making a few final notes." He closed the door behind her.

She walked immediately to the desk and poured two glasses of wine. He couldn't take his eyes off her as she crossed the room and offered him one.

The confrontation with Willa had affected her deeply. She not only seemed a world away, but there was a hesitancy about her, an uncertainty, as if she were treading very rocky ground, watching every step.

"Here's to life." She lifted her glass in a toast.

"To life." He raised his own goblet, touched it to hers. His mouth touched the rim of the cool glass. He would rather be savoring the sweetness of her lips.

"How's the writing coming?"

"The dreams stopped the day the story ended with Ezra taking that swan dive over the bluff." After another drink, he shrugged and added, "It's still a goddamn romance."

"Literary fiction has its place, but give me a happy ending any day. I wish I still had time to read." As she laughed softly, the sound settled heavily around his heart.

"Ezra killed himself," he reminded her. "You call that a happy ending?" He thought about his own ending—which may not have been much different than Ezra's if he hadn't checked in.

"So, that proves that technically, you *didn't* write a romance. The hero never, ever dies in a true romance novel." She walked over to the French doors. He saw her become perfectly still when she noticed his saddlebags lying on the chair.

"You're really leaving," she said softly.

"Yes." He ached with the wish that he had made love to her last night.

She set her empty wineglass on top of the dresser. When she turned to him, a wistful smile lifted the corners of her lips. "What if I asked you to stay?"

He set his glass down, crossed the room, and stopped short of holding her.

"If you asked me, I'd have to tell you that that was impossible."

"But you won't tell me why."

"No."

Her eyes searched his face. "Have you done something illegal?"

"It's nothing like that, believe me."

"What if someone asked the impossible of you, what would you do?" She was watching him closely.

A few weeks ago, he thought writing again was out of the question, that living was impossible. Staying here any longer would make it impossible to ever leave. And eventually, that would make life impossible for all of them.

"I can't stay, Tracy." It hurt to say the words.

"I'm not asking you to."

She stepped closer to the window and stared out into the dark night.

"Willa asked me to do something today that would require me to be a far better person than I am. I don't have it in me."

"She asked you to forgive her?"

"She's dying."

Shocked, he had no idea what to say.

"Willa's dying, and she asked me to raise her and Glenn's daughter."

"No one would blame you if you refused." He went to her, took her hands in his. There were no tears in her eyes tonight. Only confusion. Only questions. "What about her family?"

"She doesn't have anyone."

"Before she was Glenn's lover, she was your friend. Someone like you, someone with a heart as big as yours would find her request hard to ignore."

"Her daughter is Matt and Chelsea's half sister."

"Exactly."

"I'm no saint, Wade. People would think I'm crazy."

"From what I gather, they thought you were crazy for taking on this place."

"I had no choice."

"There's always a choice. I learned that the hard way. But tough choices don't scare you. You've proven that here. If anyone can do what Willa's asked, you can. I know the welfare of that child means more to you than what people would think."

"What would I tell Chelsea and Matt?"

"Chelsea is old enough to handle the truth." He thought of the disposable camera tucked in his backpack. "Someday, when Matt's old enough, you'll explain it to him. He'll know you made the only choice you could make."

"How can you be so sure?"

"He's your son."

"It won't be easy."

Unable to resist, he went to her, took her in his arms, and struggled to find the right words.

"Life isn't ever easy. But I've learned something being here with you, watching you pull your life back together. It's not what happens to us that matters as much as how we take the experience and make something out of it."

"Thank you," she said softly, holding tight to his hands. "You've given me a lot to think about."

"You'll do the right thing."

"I hope so." She seemed in no hurry to leave his arms, and though it was sweet torture, holding her close, he couldn't let her go.

"Matt fell asleep early," she dropped her gaze to their hands, "and Chelsea agreed to work late tonight."

He went perfectly still, unwilling to break the spell, sensing a distinct change in her.

She pulled away slightly, just far enough to look up into his eyes. "I want you to make love to me. I guarantee that I'm not hysterical tonight. I haven't had too much to drink, either."

"Tracy—"

She sighed and pressed her fingertips against his lips before he could respond. "Hear me out. Please."

Refusing her once was the single hardest thing he'd ever done. He had no idea how he was going to do it again.

"This has nothing to do with what Glenn did, nothing to do with salvaging my ego. I want this night to remember you by when the days are long and the nights are longer. I want *you* tonight, Wade. I'm not asking for anything else. You're leaving. I know that. My own life is in chaos. If you don't feel safe enough to tell me whatever it is that's going on with you, I'll accept that . . ."

"Tracy, I *would* tell you if I thought it would change things, make things better, not worse—"

"Don't make me beg you," she whispered.

"You make it impossible for a man to say no."

"I don't think there are many men who would have said no the first time."

"Just the fools."

She shook her head as she wrapped her arms around his neck. "Just the heroes."

"I'm no hero, Tracy, believe me. I am no hero."

"You could have fooled me."

"You don't know me."

"I know that you've got a kind heart. That you're willing to help someone in a bind. That you're caring, intelligent, and talented. I've looked forward to talking with you, to being with you, kissing you. Isn't that enough?"

When she drew his head down, stood up on her tiptoes, and pressed her lips to his, so pliant and willing, he lost the will to resist. Her lips parted beneath his, her hands moved to gently frame his face. They were both breathless when the kiss ended.

He opened his eyes, found her staring into them with a need that matched his own.

"I can't do this without telling you everything."

She put her fingertips against his lips. "*Don't*. Not if it will change things between us."

"Tracy—"

"Will it? Will it make me see you differently?"

"Probably. I don't see how it wouldn't."

Unshed tears glistened in her eyes. "I really can't take any more right now," she whispered. "Please, just leave it alone. Leave things the way they are and make love to me."

"Come here." He led her over to the bed, waited until she sat down before he left her, collected their wineglasses, and refilled them. After handing her the wine, he sat down on the edge of the bed. It sagged beneath his weight. Her heart was pounding in her ears, drowning out the sound of the sea. She took a hearty sip of wine, keeping her gaze riveted on his face.

She could see that he was still haunted by what he had wanted to tell her, but she didn't want to hear it. Not any part of it. Not tonight.

She wanted *him*—the Wade she'd come to know. She wanted to remember him just the way she'd known him, but he looked so grave, she had to lighten the mood.

"Are you afraid Ezra is watching?" She pretended to be looking for someone and even peered into the corners.

At that, Wade finally smiled. She slipped her arm around his waist, amazed at how perfectly she fit against him.

"Now that I've written his story, Ezra's through with me." He finished his wine and leaned around her to deposit the glass on the nightstand. "I don't want to waste what precious time we have left talking about a ghost. Besides, you're the only one haunting my dreams lately."

She missed his warmth when he left her to close the curtains.

Nervous beyond belief, she slipped her hand into the pocket of her khaki slacks and withdrew a handful of small foil packets. There had to be a half dozen of them.

She wanted to die of embarrassment. She'd never purchased a condom in her life.

"I bought these on the way to Santa Barbara the other day." The foil packets shone on the palm of her hand. "I didn't know if you had any."

"Are you all right? You look like you're going to faint."

"I've never done this before."

"Then how'd you have Matt?"

She found herself laughing. "You know what I mean."

He took her in his arms, kissed the crown of her head. "I'm honored." He palmed the condoms and tossed them on the bed.

"Do you know," she began softly, letting a slow smile tease the corners of her lips, "they sell some that glow in the dark?"

"Is that what you bought?"

"Heavens, no!" She suddenly paused. "Should I have?"

"No. Those are fine." He eyed the pile. "Think you got enough?"

"Will we need more?"

"If we do, we'll work something out."

"Have you slept with many widows?" Slowly, hoping provocatively, she drew her blouse over her head, dropped it, then reached for the hem of his shirt.

"You're my first."

The moment her fingers connected with the warm, smooth flesh of his abdomen, she felt emboldened. "I want to see you naked," she whispered. "I want to feel your skin against mine."

He helped her tug his shirt over his head, threw it toward the desk. It missed, slid off, crumpled on the floor.

She grabbed the waistband of his Levi's. He sucked in his breath when she touched his skin, slipped her hand down inside his jeans and cupped him, gently massaging him, startled by the hardness of his erection.

He was staring into her eyes when she wrapped her hand around his erection. There was no room for shyness between them tonight. Amazingly, every move she made felt perfectly right.

She had almost convinced herself that he would leave and she would never know him intimately. Never feel him inside her. Never touch him this way.

She sighed, licked her lips, closed her eyes, and slid her palm up and down along his hot, turgid skin. He gasped, then forced her head up and brought his mouth down over hers. Kissing her deeply, he began to walk her backward toward the bed. His hands were wrapped in her hair, his tongue delving into her mouth, sliding against hers.

She let go of him, drew her hand out of the front of his jeans. She fumbled with the buttons on his fly until it opened and he was free.

He shucked off his pants, kicked them aside.

She paused, unable to avoid staring in silent admiration of his body. She crooked a brow, smiled in appreciation.

"No underwear?" she whispered.

"Waste of time." He grabbed her around the waist, pulled her down onto the bed with him, and rolled over her. "Time you got naked, too." He made short work of her bra and khaki slacks. She blushed when he ran his fingertip around the elastic of her bikini briefs and smiled down at her.

"What's so funny?"

"I would have guessed, that's all."

"You weren't expecting a thong, were you?"

He shook his head. Smiled. "Definitely not. But you could easily wear one and look great."

"I'm somebody's mother," she reminded him.

"So is Madonna."

His gaze slowly moved over her, from head to toe. When she tried to cover herself with her hands, he grabbed both her wrists and held her arms over her head. He pulled off her panties.

"Touch me," she whispered. "Touch me, Wade."

He let go of her wrists, slid his hand down to the apex of her thighs. She was embarrassed, knowing that she was already hot, already wet and ready for him. She wanted him to take it slow, wanted to give him as much pleasure as she wanted to enjoy.

She wanted it to last so that the memory would be unforgettable.

She wanted him to take that memory with him, too.

When he ran his hands over her, gently touched the slick, moist folds of skin that blossomed for him, she couldn't hold back a moan of ecstasy. Unexpectedly, she climaxed. The pleasure pain ripped through her and she cried out, writhing against his hand, pulsing around his fingers.

As her throbbing climax slowly faded and she came down to earth again, she savored the feel of the firm, muscular body draped over her. It seemed that he was touching her everywhere at once and then suddenly, he was gone.

She gave a soft cry of protest, opened her eyes, and realized he'd left her only long enough to slip on a condom. Long enough for her to settle back again, to close her eyes.

This should be the beginning, not the beginning of the end.

She wanted to be able to remember this night for the rest of her life. To remember the feel of his weight, the gentle touch of his hand, the scent of the salt air mingled with that of their bodies. She wanted this to be a night that Wade would never forget—no matter how far away he went. She wanted him to think of this night, to remember her, for the rest of his life.

"Promise me something." He slipped his arms around her again, held her close, stroked her tenderly.

"Anything." She owed him that much. She'd begged for this. Initiated it. She would never, ever regret this night.

"No good-byes," he whispered.

She knew why. She couldn't bear it either. "No good-byes." Suddenly her heart was breaking. The image of Ezra and Violette standing on the widow's walk flashed through her mind. Their parting had been forever.

"Promise?" He kissed her temple.

"I promise."

When he slid inside her, she gasped, clung to him, urged him to fill her completely, in one swift thrust. She cried out, held him tight, dug her fingers into his buttocks.

Overwhelmed with the intensity, the unleashed passion, tears leaked from the corners of her eyes. She treasured each and every sensation, every movement, every thrust as he rode her higher and higher, faster, until she was panting, clinging to him, begging for release.

He demanded more, inspired more. She arched against him, cried his name. She couldn't hold back any longer.

When she climaxed again, he came with her. It was a bone-shattering release.

Already a memory emblazoned on her mind.

Wade opened his eyes and found her lying on her side, smiling down at him. Her fingers trailed across his chest, teased his nipples.

She'd never know that he would be dreaming of this night for a long, long time to come. Him, the guy who couldn't remember the name of the first girl he'd ever slept with. Until now, until Tracy, none of them ever mattered. He never thought he'd experience this kind of desire, this kind of sharing. It was the stuff of trite novels, of sappy songs.

He'd never believed in this kind of emotion, this kind of need. Then again, he'd never believed in ghost stories, either.

The saddest thing in the world was that he believed now—and it was too late.

Not only would he be haunted by her memory, but by the thought that someone else would eventually check in to the Heartbreak who would surely fall in love with her, seduce her. Worse yet, maybe even break her heart.

She was a warm, vibrant woman.

She had so much to give. She deserved to love and be loved. She deserved more than what her husband had done to her.

She definitely deserved better than him.

He found her gazing down at him from beneath her lashes, eyes lazy, glazed with passion and desire. Those rich blue eyes open as he slipped his fingers inside her again. He stroked her until her eyes drifted closed. She arched against him, softly cried out, and savored another release.

When she was back inside herself again, she pushed him back against the pillow, trailed her lips down his chest to his navel, captured his erection in her mouth. It was almost more than he could bear. She drove him wild, coaxing him with lips and gentle nips of her teeth.

Then before he realized she had even moved, she was on her knees, then moving over him, taking him into her, sliding down the length of him.

She rode him until she wrung a cry from his throat, until his eyes were strangely moist and their hearts beat as one.

The room was dark when Tracy opened her eyes and found herself alone in Wade's room. Exhausted, satiated, she'd drifted off to sleep in his arms. They'd used half the condoms.

A glance at the clock and she knew she'd slept no more than twenty minutes. She reached over, touched the indentation in his pillow. The fabric was still warm.

"Wade?" The only sound beside the ocean's roar was that of her own breathing. She slid out of bed, ran to the bathroom, and pushed the door open. It was dark inside. He was already gone.

A sound escaped her, a cry that came from the depths of her soul. She covered her mouth with both hands, stood there naked in the middle of the room, her shoulders heaving, dry sobs welling up from her toes.

Suddenly a rumble of sound cut through the night.

Wade's Harley.

She'd never hear a motorcycle again without thinking of him.

He had to have walked out a moment before she woke up. Had he been somewhere in the hall? Heard her stir before he let himself out? Had he been tempted to turn around? To take her in his arms and stay?

"No good-byes."

"No good-byes. I promise."

She ran to the French doors, threw them open, and ran out onto the porch. From there she could see the driveway. Helpless, she watched him turn the bike in the direction of the road.

If he looked back, he might see her standing there naked, bare to the elements, her heart stripped bare, too. Did he know he was taking it with him? Would he care?

He gunned the engine, pulled out of the drive, and headed south. He didn't look back.

The chill of the sea spray kissed her skin as she focused on the Harley's taillight. Tears blurred the red glow that grew smaller and smaller until it was reduced to the size of an ember, bobbing in the darkness as the bike hugged the curves in the coast road.

She slipped back inside, locked the doors, gathered up her clothes. She thought of taking a shower, then decided she wanted to wear Wade's scent awhile longer. She threw on her clothes and went upstairs.

Chelsea's bedroom door was closed, which meant she had come in sometime earlier. Had the girl looked for her downstairs? Had she walked down the hall? Heard them making love?

She hoped not. Things had been all right between them since the confrontation after the open house. Chelsea may have forgiven her, but every time she looked at the girl, she still felt ashamed.

Tonight she felt no shame about what she'd done with Wade, though. No shame at all.

She looked in on Matt. One of his plastic Transformers lay on the floor beside the bed. She picked it up, set it on his bedside table, kissed him on the forehead, and went into her own room.

Wrapping her favorite faded terry robe over her clothes, she went up to the widow's walk. Her skin still tingled from his touch. The cool night air was damp, but it didn't faze her.

She didn't know she was crying until she reached up to brush her hair back off her cheek and found her skin wet with tears.

For a while, couldn't she simply pretend that he was still downstairs, still in his room? Wouldn't it be easier to pretend, at least for now, that she would see him again in the morning? That she'd find him sitting in the sunroom, sipping hot coffee, going over his notes, leafing through the morning news?

It was easier to think about looking up to see him coming down the hall in his loose, easy stride, his jeans riding low on his hips, that slow, sensual half smile on his lips.

Easier to pretend, just for a little while, that she would see him again.

She was still alone, but no longer lonely. She had added a new chapter to her own story. A new memory. She'd survived Glenn's death and ultimate betrayal.

She would survive Wade leaving. She had to, no matter how much it hurt.

As she wiped her face on her sleeve, she pictured a secret spot deep inside her heart, a corner where she could safely tuck away a scrap of hope that their paths would someday cross again.

CHAPTER FORTY

The next morning the sun was struggling to shine through a cloud bank as valiantly as Tracy struggled with her aching heart while serving coffee to the guests who had arrived while she was at lunch with Willa.

Henri Brochard was a Frenchman in his mid-seventies who wore a bad toupee that stuck out around the sides of his head. His skin was the color of grade school paste, his hands and fingers long and tapered. He waved them around his head whenever he spoke, which was often.

Henri was taking his coffee and date nut bread with cream cheese in the sunroom at a table where he could sigh over the view. He wore a long silk dressing gown over striped pajamas. A burgundy fez rode his toupee.

A bittersweet ache filled her as she remembered Wade teasing her about the single male guest who might steal her heart.

A couple from South Dakota had taken their breakfast into the sitting room, where they sat opposite each other on the two sofas. Both of them were deep into novels, the wife so absorbed that she merely nodded and didn't even look up when Tracy asked if they'd like their coffees topped off.

She noticed the woman was reading a paperback, *An Even Dozen*, by Edward Cain. What seemed like light-years ago, someone at Global Mortgage had given Glenn a hardcover copy of the book when it first came out.

She wondered if it was upstairs in a box someplace and then thought: *Who am I kidding? As if I have time to read.*

She left the guests to themselves and went back upstairs, where she found Matt in his room, drawing. Needing a few minutes to catch up on paperwork and balance her checkbook, she was on her way to her room when she heard the water running in Chelsea and Matt's bathroom.

Chelsea usually left for work at seven and it was well past eight. She gathered up her bookkeeping, intending to work at the small breakfast bar. On her way, she knocked on the bathroom door.

"Chelsea? Are you going in to work today?"

She hoped there wouldn't be another confrontation about Wade this morning. *Not today. Please.*

"I've got a headache. I called in sick."

"Want some breakfast?"

"No, thanks."

Great. Exhausted from lack of sleep and feeling as if she were constantly picking up the pieces of her life, Tracy went back to the kitchen and dived into the bills, a daunting job to say the least. By the time she looked up, a good thirty minutes had passed. She stretched and went back to knock on Chelsea's door, wanting to see for herself that Chelsea was all right. Needing to talk to her if she was upset about last night.

She had to knock twice. "May I come in?"

There was a long pause before Chelsea finally answered, "Sure, come on in."

The girl was curled up in an overstuffed chair by the window and didn't turn around when Tracy stepped into the room.

"Is there anything I can get you? A Motrin, or anything?"

"I'll be okay." The answer was a little too quick. It also lacked conviction.

"If this is about last night, I was with Wade when you came in." Tracy closed the door and walked over to the bed.

"I figured." Chelsea chewed on her bottom lip.

"He's gone. He checked out." She hated saying the words aloud. Hated making it real.

"He did? Really?" Chelsea sounded surprised but not relieved.

There was a gnawing hollow in Tracy's stomach as she confirmed it. "Really."

"Is he coming back?"

Is he coming back? She pictured the hopeful corner of her heart and shrugged. "I have no idea. Not anytime soon, anyway."

"Are you okay with that?"

Surprised that Chelsea cared enough to ask, Tracy crossed the room and sat on the corner of the bed closest to Chelsea's chair.

"No. I'm not okay with it. I'm going to miss him. I . . . I came to care for him deeply." She was surprised at how easily the truth came out this morning.

"Why didn't he stay?"

"He just couldn't. The timing wasn't right for either of us."

Finally Chelsea turned her gaze away from the window. Her usually bright eyes were dull, filled with sadness and confusion. "I hope he didn't leave because I was rude to him."

"When?"

"The night of the party. I was pretty upset about the invitations and all." She took a deep breath. "I told him he was just a substitute for Dad."

"Honey, that's not true. You know that."

"I was so bummed that night, so mad at myself. But when I saw Wade, I took it out on him. I was going to apologize, but I didn't get the chance."

Just then the sun broke through the haze and came streaming in the window. Tracy couldn't keep her gaze from drifting to Chelsea's cheek, to the spot where she'd slapped her. Every time it happened, her stomach tied itself into a knot. The slap hadn't even been hard enough to leave a mark, but the memory would forever be a stain on her own heart.

"You're white as a sheet, honey." Gently, she laid her hand on the girl's shoulder and Chelsea reacted with a shudder. Tracy's heartbeat accelerated. Something was going on that had nothing to do with her or Wade.

"You know you can tell me anything, don't you?"

She watched tears well up in the girl's eyes and spill down her cheeks. Instinctively, she slipped her arm around Chelsea's shoulders and drew her close, the way she did with Matt when he was upset. Chelsea's breath hitched and, after another second, she buried her face in her hands.

"I hate David Sylvester."

He wasn't at the top of Tracy's list of favorite people, either. He never had been. Since Jake had told her about Glenn's affair, she'd been fairly certain that David had known, and kept the truth from her.

Rubbing the girl's back, Tracy coaxed her over to the bed to sit beside her. She let her cry without questioning her, waited until Chelsea wiped her eyes and sat with her hands clenched between her knees.

She could think of only one thing that David might have done to upset Chelsea so much, and then she remembered that Chelsea had been working late last night. Anger erupted out of a reserve deep in every mother's heart, anger reserved for those times when they need to fight for their children in any way they can.

"Did he do something inappropriate? Did David come on to you?"

Chelsea shook her head no, but continued to stare at her hands.

"Tell me, Chelsea."

"He asked me to work late, and then when everyone else was gone, he . . . he offered me a glass of wine." Then she shrugged. "That's no big deal. We . . . I've had wine at parties." She finally looked up, met Tracy's eyes. "You know that, right?"

Tracy nodded. She knew very well what went on at sorority and fraternity parties. The first time Chelsea came home from college, Glenn had even offered her wine with dinner. But for David Sylvester to do so, especially at the office, was inexcusable. He knew better than to put himself in a compromising position with an eighteen-year-old girl.

If he didn't, he was certainly going to hear about it as soon as she was out of this room.

"Did you have a glass of wine with him?"

"I told him no. I wanted to leave because I didn't like the way he was looking at me, you know?"

Again, Tracy nodded. Chelsea was a vibrant young woman, full of energy, ripe with sensuality, still possessing the innocence of youth—a tempting combination.

"He told me I was beautiful," Chelsea said. "I told him I had to get home. But he said 'What's the rush?' "

"I said that Eric was waiting for me downstairs, in the lobby."

Thank God for Eric Nichols. A freshman at Cal Poly, San Luis Obispo, Eric was on the tennis team. From what she could recall, he was well-mannered and soft-spoken. He had curly brown hair and always wore dark-rimmed glasses. She had no doubt that he was probably head over heels in love with Chelsea, though they didn't seem to be officially dating.

"What did David say? Did he tell you to go on home?" Tracy rubbed Chelsea's shoulders and back, thankful that the girl was confiding in her.

"He said he was attracted to me. I told him I wasn't into married men. That's when he said he wasn't *that* married." She finally faced Tracy again. Her breath hitched, but she didn't break down this time. Her own anger was finally taking hold. "It made me sick to my stomach. He told me things weren't going all that well at home, that his wife Kathy was overly devoted to their daughters, and that she didn't have time for him. I guess I couldn't hide how disgusted I was.

"He said he didn't like the way I was looking at him. How was I *supposed* to look at him? He's married for God's sake! He's got his wife's and kids' photos all over his freaking desk! He said making passes was what guys did. *All* guys. Then he started talking about Dad, Tracy. He told me that Dad had women on the side, too. I called him a liar, and he laughed at me. He said that Dad had a lot to hide. A *whole* lot to hide."

Tracy's suspicions confirmed, her own anger was simmering close to a boil. How dare he throw Glenn's infidelities in Chelsea's face, thinking it would help him plead his own case? How dare he tell her?

"Did he keep you from leaving? Did he touch you?"

She shook her head. "No." A smile flitted across her face, but then dissolved a heartbeat later. "Not after I threw a glass of wine in his face and ran out without looking back. I left the sweater you loaned me in my cubicle." Her eyes filled with tears that started rolling down her cheeks. "It . . . was . . . your . . . your favorite pink one," she sobbed.

Tracy knew she wasn't crying over the lost sweater as much as her lost innocence. She held the girl close, desperately angry at David Sylvester, so furious that she could barely sit still. Her anger was tempered only by the pain she felt for Chelsea.

It wasn't but two minutes later that Chelsea mopped her pajama sleeve over her face and turned red-rimmed eyes on Tracy.

"Did Dad play around?"

Tracy knew that the minute she didn't immediately deny it, that the instant she hesitated and weighed the consequences of telling Chelsea the truth, the girl would see through her.

"Tracy, tell me it's not true."

"Honey . . ."

"Dad fooled around? Did you *know?*"

"No." Easy, so easy to tell that truth. She hadn't known, not really. "Not for certain. Not until a couple of nights ago."

She had no recourse but to tell Chelsea what Jake had discovered when he went over the account books. How, apparently, Glenn had had a mistress, but she stopped short of telling Chelsea about Willa and Mary Jane.

"Oh, my God, Tracy. I can't believe it."

Suddenly the tables were turned and she found herself the recipient of Chelsea's sympathy. It was nearly her own undoing when Chelsea took both her hands and clung to them.

Slowly, she admitted, "I didn't want to believe it, or I'd have pursued it sooner. And I would have done everything in my power to keep you from finding out. I'd have told you myself before I let you find out this way." It was easy to see that Chelsea was still in shock. So much so that she was no longer crying.

"I never thought Dad would do something like this to you. I thought he loved you so much."

So did I.

"There's no doubt that he loved you, honey. No doubt. This doesn't change the way things were between the two of you."

"You don't think so? He was living a lie."

"Just remember, you were his princess." She wondered what Chelsea would say if she knew that Glenn had another daughter.

Chelsea sighed and pushed her hair back over her shoulder. "I told Eric to get my sweater for me when he went in today. Obviously, I won't be going back there again."

"Don't worry about the sweater. I'll get it myself."

Chelsea's hand tightened on Tracy's. "You *can't.*"

"Oh, yes, I most certainly can, and I will. There's no way I'm letting that man get away with this."

Chelsea jumped up. "Please, don't. I'm *all right.* Nothing happened. If you go in and make a big deal of this, people will talk. David's wife might find out. His little *girls* might find out. He has two precious little girls."

Tracy remembered the photo of those darling children in their matching tartan dresses. It was on display, front and center, on David's desk. She couldn't wait to see the look on his face when she went marching into his office.

"We can't let him get away with this."

"But I don't want those girls' lives shattered the way mine was when Dad moved out and left me behind with Monica," Chelsea cried.

It was the first time she'd ever opened up about how her parents' divorce had affected her. The first time she'd ever admitted how deeply she'd been hurt, though her pain and confusion had been evident from the minute Tracy had met the sometimes sullen, more often sad-eyed little eight-year-old.

"I understand your feeling that way." Tracy hoped that she appeared calm, when what she was really feeling couldn't be further from the truth. "But I can't look the other way and give David a chance to do this sort of thing again." She stood up and walked to the middle of the room. "Now, you go shower and have some breakfast. I'll need you to stay with Matt until I get back."

"Are you really going to David's office? Right now?"

"You bet I am." She started for the door, ready for an argument, determined not to be swayed.

"Tracy, wait." Thankfully, Chelsea sounded resigned, not angry.

Tracy paused with her hand on the doorknob. "What, honey?"

The girl summoned a trembling smile and whispered, "Thank you."

Two hours later, the employees bustling around the offices of Sylvester, Lease & Lynch all appeared to be intent on what they were doing, all definitely in a no-nonsense mood when Tracy walked in.

An attractive twenty-something receptionist with long straight hair and a conservative shirtwaist blouse that failed to hide an ample bustline looked up from her desk. She made the mistake of giving Tracy a practiced smile behind the phone headset she was wearing.

"May I help you?"

"Tracy Potter to see David Sylvester. I don't have an appointment, but I'm sure he'll see me."

The brunette blinked a couple of times. "Why don't you have a seat?"

She indicated a bank of chrome-and-leather sling chairs lined up between huge potted palms.

"I'm fine right here." Tracy silently dared her to argue.

The receptionist picked up the phone.

"Yes. A Mrs. Potter. Okay." She hung up and smiled apologetically. "He's all tied up for the rest of the morning. He said he's sorry, but that if you make an appointment—Hey!" She jumped up so quickly that she pulled the headset out of the phone. Tracy was already through the doors to the right of the desk. "You can't go in there!"

Once she was in the hallway beyond the waiting-area doors, Tracy ignored the receptionist and kept going past a maze of cubicles and doors until she reached David's office. She hadn't been here more than a couple of times since that terrible morning last March, but she knew the way. She didn't bother knocking, not as long as she'd gotten this far. She barged all the way in.

Shoving the door open, she marched across David's paisley-print carpet and didn't stop until she was standing across the desk from him. He'd jumped to his feet the moment she'd stepped through the door and quickly concealed his shock. Carefully, with a great show of purpose, he slipped his Montblanc pen in the ebony holder on his desk, shot his cuffs, and noted the time on the gold watch on his arm.

Then he did the worst possible thing he could do, given the circumstances. He smiled.

"You bastard," she said softly. "How dare you stand there smiling when you know very well why I'm here."

"And why is that?"

"You not only tried to seduce Chelsea last night, but you told her that her father was a player."

"Prove it."

"It's her word against yours, is that it?"

"No one else was around. Obviously she's been unstable since Glenn died. She was under the false impression that she had a chance at the scholarship we award to a deserving intern every year, and she thought that seducing *me* would be the way to assure she got it. Unfortunately, I had to fire her last night." He raised his arms, shrugged. "I'm sorry that she's angry enough to accuse me of something so sordid."

"I see you've got it all figured out." Tracy stepped away from his desk, her gaze traveling over the well-appointed office. "In fact, you've got such a well-rehearsed answer that it sounds like you might have thought this all out *before* you sexually harassed Chelsea." It was a moment or two before she saw what she was looking for.

"Do I need to call security to show you out?"

Though she knew it would be his word against Chelsea's, she didn't count herself out yet, and he shouldn't have, either.

"Actually, no. But I'm sure your assistant has been in here this morning. And you've already seen clients, haven't you?"

"So?"

"You no doubt have a cleaning service that comes in every evening to straighten things up, right?"

"What are you getting at Tracy?"

"I'm sure all of them, if forced to testify, would tell the truth if they were asked if they noticed that red wine stain on your carpet."

She watched the blood creep up from the tight button-down collar around his neck. He shot a glance down at the carpet right in front of her feet where there was, indeed, a red wine stain the size of a dinner plate. It was obvious that someone had tried to clean it up. It was faded, but noticeable right there in the open.

"Chelsea told me she threw red wine at you."

"I spilled that myself. I was so shocked by her behavior."

"Did you wear your dirty shirt home? How did you explain what happened to Kathleen?"

"I spilled it myself."

"Chelsea threw wine in your face. It would be on your collar. All over the knot of your tie. Maybe even your shoulders. Not exactly where you'd spill it on yourself. How would you explain that?"

His confidence was paling as his face grew redder. "Who do you think you are?"

"A mother. A mother who is mad as hell. Nobody messes with one of my children without paying for it, David. Nobody."

"She's not even yours."

"Oh, yes she is. She's been part of my life for ten years, and no matter what Glenn has done, no matter whatever happens from here on out, she's still mine. Now, will you admit what you did, call Chelsea, and apologize, or do I call Kathleen and tell her everything?" She knew that in the long run, she'd be doing Kathleen a favor by calling her.

"You keep the hell away from my family."

"You keep the hell away from your interns from now on. And stop covering for your clients. I found out about Glenn before you said anything to Chelsea. I had help from a private detective, and I won't hesitate to have him dig up everything he can on you, David. Every sordid detail he can uncover. I'm sure that this isn't the first time you've harassed one of your employees."

"What is it you want?"

"I want you to tell me that this will be the last time you try to take advantage of a woman. And I want that scholarship money for the fall semester."

"Blackmail? You'd resort to blackmail?"

"I think the politically correct word is reparation." She took a deep breath. "And David? I'd resort to almost anything where my kids are concerned."

CHAPTER FORTY-ONE

A complete calm washed over Tracy the minute she walked out of Sylvester, Lease & Lynch with her pink sweater in her hand and a hefty check for Chelsea's fall tuition in her purse.

Now, alone in the kitchen in her apartment, she was concentrating on scooping a measuring cup full of flour and dumping it into a white crockery mixing bowl. She heard footsteps behind her and turned to look over her shoulder.

Chelsea walked up beside her and stared at the recipe card for scones. She picked up a stick of butter, and then, shoulder to shoulder with Tracy, measured out three-quarters of a cup by slicing through the silver wrapper.

"I hated you when you married my dad," she said softly.

Tracy knew how hard it was for the girl to admit to what she thought was a secret she'd been harboring for years.

"I know." Tracy leaned toward the sink and filled a smaller cup with water.

"You did? You knew?"

"Kids are pretty obvious."

Chelsea's complexion reddened. "I wanted Dad to come back home, not marry someone else. I blamed you for his not coming back to us."

"You were only eight." Tracy's hands stilled. "I didn't break your parents up, you know that, don't you? I didn't even meet your dad until after he was divorced."

"Monica used to tell me that you two had something going on before he left us."

"That simply wasn't true. I hadn't even been living in California long enough."

"I figured that out when I was in high school." Chelsea picked up the recipe card and turned it over and over.

"Tracy, I'm so sorry."

"It was a long time ago. We've both grown a lot since then."

Chelsea wiped away a tear. A small laugh escaped her. "I haven't cried this much since the day you called and told me Dad died. I just hope you know how sorry I am. I treated you pretty badly for a long time, and all you've ever been is good to me. You didn't deserve it."

She wiped the back of her hand across her eyes. "You were so great this morning, listening the way you did. Taking my side. Monica would have told me not to make such a big deal out of what happened. She'd tell me to go back and apologize to David, that if I wanted that scholarship, I should have been nicer. She probably would have told me that I should have let him . . ." She closed her eyes, unable to go on.

"Look at me," Tracy said softly. Chelsea opened her eyes. "You did what was right. Your dad would be proud of you. And I'm proud of you."

"I'm sorry for all the times you made my favorite dinners and I wouldn't touch them."

"Chelsea—"

"And I'm sorry for the time we went to the Grand Canyon and I didn't talk to you all week."

Tracy laughed. "You insisted on wearing a towel on your head in the car so you didn't have to look at me. I'd forgotten all about that trip."

"After you let me move in with you this summer, I told you that I wouldn't be caught dead cleaning rooms in this—dump. I feel like crawling under a rock and never coming out. I'd be more than willing to have that job now, if you still need me."

Tracy took her by the shoulders. "Enough. Stop this now or . . . or I'll have to send you to your room for a time-out."

At that, Chelsea finally smiled.

"Clean slate. Okay?" Tracy offered. "From here on out we start over. Deal?"

Chelsea nodded, though she did so slowly. "I still can't believe what David said about Dad, but I believe you, so I know it's true."

"The best thing you can do is let it go." Tracy wished she could follow her own advice. "Just remember that he loved you."

Tracy embraced her and Chelsea hugged her back.

Tracy picked up a wooden spoon, her heart fuller than it had been in months. Then she heard Chelsea ask, "How did you end up being such a good person?"

Good person?

Tracy set the spoon down and closed her eyes. Willa's face, her voice, filled her mind.

"I want you to raise my little girl."

Her gut reaction had been to laugh in Willa's face, but she'd been too stunned. Wouldn't a truly *good* person, a selfless person, be able to forgive and honor Willa's request?

According to her Baptist grandmother, a truly *good* woman would never have slept with a stranger, a man she would never see again, especially with her son asleep under the same roof.

"I'm not that good, believe me."

"Yes, you are. You're exactly the type of person I want to be, if it's not too late."

"You're already a good person, Chelsea."

"You think so?"

"I know so. You made the right choice last night."

Chelsea left the kitchen with a smile on her face.

She left Tracy frowning down into the scone batter. Chelsea only meant to compliment her, she knew that, but unknowingly, the girl had forced her to consider the biggest challenge she would ever face.

A few minutes later she was just about to put the scones in the oven when the phone rang. She answered and heard nothing but silence on the other end of the line, a silence so still it was deafening. When she heard her heart beating through it, she knew without a doubt who it was.

"Wade?" Her fingers tightened around the phone.

"How are you doing?"

"I miss you." She released a long sigh. Hearing his voice again jolted the truth out of her.

"I wasn't going to call," he said.

She wrapped her arm around her midriff. "I watched you ride away."

"I thought you were asleep."

"Where are you now?"

"Down the coast. How is everything?"

"Let's just say life is never boring around here." She cut out the last scone, set it on the baking sheet, and brushed her hands off over the sink. He didn't need to know what had happened this morning, though she was proud of standing up to David. Wade wasn't part of their lives anymore.

"Have you had any more guests check in?"

"No. The weather stinks." Then she thought of Henri and smiled. "The Frenchman is still here, though."

"Still in his robe?"

"It's growing on me."

They laughed, too short, but very sweet sounds, before they fell into silence. She closed her eyes. Imagined Wade right beside her.

"There's a package coming in the mail for Matt. FedEx," he told her.

"Really?" She wondered what he'd found that Matt would enjoy. "That's so thoughtful. He'll be so excited to get a package."

There was such a long pause that she thought the connection had been broken, but then he said, "Tracy, last night with you—"

"I know," she whispered. "I know."

They drifted into silence punctuated by the distance between them. There were no words for what had happened for her last night. She could only hope it was half as good for him. *Just come back. Why don't you just come back?*

She wanted to scream at the injustice of fate.

How could she have possibly fallen in love so soon?

Even an amateur psychologist could see that she was rebounding. She'd needed reassurance, needed to rebuild her self-esteem, and she'd fallen into the arms of the first man who'd looked her way. Literally, almost the first man who had walked through the door. That was the most rational explanation.

But when was love ever rational?

Deep down inside, she wanted to believe that what she felt for Wade was more than an easy fix, more than a knee-jerk reaction to her loss, her pain, and ultimate humiliation.

It certainly felt as real and as true as the love she'd once had for Glenn.

But the voice of reason warned her to remember how that had ended.

She tried to remember, too, that Wade had reasons of his own for moving on. Reasons that she'd refused to let him talk about last night. Things that he was convinced would change the way she saw him, the way she felt about him.

"I've got to go, Tracy," he said softly.

"I know." She bit her lips together to stop their trembling, refusing to cry any more. She'd proved just how strong she was this morning in David's office. Her heart was strong, too. Strong and resilient, and hopeful.

The silence deepened. She was afraid he'd already hung up, but then she heard him sigh.

"Be safe, Wade," she whispered.

"You, too," he said. And then the line went dead.

The scones forgotten, she hung up and stared down at the phone.

"Mom! Mom!"

As Matt came charging into the apartment, she hung a smile on her face.

"What's up?"

"You better get downstairs quick. That crazy old French guy is walking around in the lobby in a striped Speedo!"

CHAPTER FORTY-TWO

The Best Western Inn by the Sea on the Pacific Coast Highway in Dana Point held none of the charm of the Heartbreak, but Wade wasn't looking for charm when he checked in.

In a room decorated in eighties mint green and peach pastels, a standard-issue motel television was bolted to the dresser. For three days the local news channels had focused on "the storm of the century." Obviously the producers had already forgotten that they had dubbed last month's storm the century's worst.

He'd been on the road for a month now and didn't have to watch the news to know the weather sucked. All he had to do was look out the window. Not only had an El Niño weather pattern hit the coast from San Diego to Seattle; in a move that further crippled the tourist industry, the Department of Homeland Security had raised the terrorist alert level from yellow to orange.

Travel plans had been canceled all over the country.

Neither the weather nor the alerts had ever mattered to him back when he'd been mired in his own egocentric world, working to keep his Edward Cain books in front of the public eye.

Edward Cain, national bestseller, wouldn't have cared if a widow living in a monstrosity outside of a burg like Twilight Cove was affected by the latest catastrophic storm, fire, *or* pestilence. Before he became the notorious author of *An Even Dozen,* Edward Cain had never cared about anything but his career.

But Wade MacAllister, a.k.a. Wade Johnson, did care.

He cared a hell of a lot, and now that his sensitivities had kicked in, there was no turning them off.

Staring out the window at the downpour that was sending a river of water pouring down the gutter and into the storm drains along the highway, he dialed the number of the Heartbreak Hotel for only the second time since he'd left there.

He recognized Chelsea's voice the moment she answered.

"Chelsea, this is Wade."

"Oh!" Her surprise was more than evident. He expected a curt reply and a hang up, but instead she quickly said, "Tracy's not here. She ran into town to pick up some milk and the mail. She'll be so disappointed."

He pictured Chelsea in the lobby, leaning against the dark oak registration desk, and strained to hear the Elvis music in the background.

"How are things going?" he asked.

"Not good," she admitted. "It's really slow everywhere. Even Pismo is nearly deserted. The shops in Twilight are empty. We've only got a couple of rooms rented this week, but that's better than last."

"I'm sorry to hear it." He realized it wasn't just an empty phrase. His heart ached for Tracy. He thought about having Bob send her money. He'd even thought about Schack arranging to buy the place for him through a broker so that she could move out and not have to worry about money at all.

But if she ever found out what he'd done, she might never forgive him, and he still wasn't ready to live with that yet.

"Wade, I never got a chance to tell you how sorry I was about the way I acted the night of Tracy's open house."

The girl's apology took him completely by surprise. He wondered what caused such a change of heart.

"Apology accepted, but I can't fault you for looking out for Tracy."

"Thanks."

"You keep it up, okay? Take care of her." He stopped short of adding . . . "for me."

"Why not come back and take care of her yourself?"

He couldn't tell her that, by keeping his distance, he was doing them all a favor.

"I wish I could, but that's not possible." He walked over to the dresser where the photos Matt had given him were lying in plain view. He picked up one of Tracy standing on the front steps, smiling into the camera.

"Listen, I've got to go. Thanks for the apology, Chelsea."

"She misses you, Wade. She hasn't said anything, but I can tell."

He closed his eyes, still saw Tracy's smile.

"Thanks again," he said, helpless. Feeling low, he hung up after Chelsea told him good-bye.

Debating how to help Tracy, he realized that apart from donning a clown suit and waving a cardboard arrow at passing cars in front of her hotel, the only thing he knew how to do, besides spend money, was write.

If he really wanted to help, then he had to do the one thing he did best.

Before he could talk himself out of it, he phoned information for the number of the *L.A. Times* features editor and then had the number put through. Thankfully, he didn't get a voice mail. He had no intention of leaving a callback number.

"Jim Kemerer."

Wade recognized the voice immediately, though he hadn't spoken to the man since Jim had been an editorial assistant at Ballard Publishing.

"Hey, Jim. This is Edward Cain. How's it going?"

"Holy shit!" There was dead silence on the other end of the line before Kemerer recovered. "Where are you? Man, everyone thinks you dropped off the face of the planet."

"Good. That's how I want to keep it."

"Do I get an exclusive? Is that why you called?"

Wade knew that Jim was already seeing dollar signs and a Pulitzer nomination for an interview with the elusive Edward Cain.

"Maybe down the line. Right now, I need a favor. Big time."

"Shoot."

"I'd like you to run a travel article about an inn up the coast."

"A travel article."

"Right."

"What's the hook? Aside from the fact that I assume you're staying there."

"I'm not there. Actually, I'm on the other side of the continent," he lied. "I'm doing this as a favor to a friend—and there is a hook."

"Okay. Shoot."

"The place is haunted."

"Haunted. As in, by a ghost?"

"Right."

"That's it?"

"Come on, Jim. You know people are attracted to that kind of thing. Ghostly mansions, haunted museums and hotels, all of that—stuff." He would have said "all that crap" before. Not now.

"Have you actually seen the ghost? Got any photos of it?"

There was no way he was admitting he'd been anywhere near the place, or even in California. "No, but I have it on really good authority."

"Hell, I'll run anything you want to send me."

"Yeah. Well, there's a catch. I don't want an Edward Cain byline. Use Staff Writer if you want. Anything but the Cain name. Got it?"

"Why did I have the feeling you were going to say that?"

"Will you keep the name Edward Cain off it?"

"Is that how it has to be?"

"It's important to me, Jim."

"I hear ya. When do I get the copy?"

"I'll FedEx it to you with a couple of photos. You'll have it by five to-morrow. You think it'll make the Sunday travel section?"

There was a long pause. "I'll have to kill the lead feature, but for you, sure. I'll put it on the AP wire, too. Where can I reach you in case any questions come up?"

"Nice try. You can't. There won't be any problems. Count on it."

"What do you get out of it?"

"Like I said, I'm doing a friend a favor."

"Okay, fine."

"And the Cain name stays off."

"Sure."

"Thanks, Jim. And if Edward Cain ever surfaces, you'll get the first in-terview."

Wade hung up, grabbed his jacket, and headed out to buy computer time at a Kinko's a couple of miles inland.

On Saturday afternoon, Tracy sat curled up on the couch with Matt tucked in beside her. There were no guests downstairs, and since it was pouring buckets outside, she had popped some corn as they settled in to watch a *Trading Spaces* marathon.

"Mom?"

"What, hon?"

"Do you think Wade's been riding his Harley around in all this rain? Or you think he got a car?"

She stared at the television, watched as a too-cute carpenter sawed an old table in half to make a recycled bookshelf, and imagined Wade riding through the rain. She had no way to contact him, no way of knowing if he was even in California at all. He could be very near, or he could be a thousand miles away. All she knew for certain was that a day didn't go by that she didn't think of him and remember every second of the night they'd spent in each other's arms.

"I doubt it." She hoped he was warm and dry. But more than that, she hoped he wasn't holed up in another hotel somewhere, charming the pants off of someone else.

"He hated for all that chrome to get dirty," Matt mumbled around a mouthful of popcorn.

"He told you that?"

"I could tell. He was always polishing it." He reached for another handful of popcorn, leaving a trail of kernels between the bowl and his mouth.

"I kinda miss him. Do you, Mom?"

"What?"

"Do you kinda miss Wade?"

She refused to lie to a nine-year-old.

"Yes. I kinda do."

"Maybe he'll come back."

"Maybe." She'd begun to doubt it, though.

Earlier in the week, she'd come in toting plastic bags full of groceries. Sopping wet, she almost made it through the front door when Chelsea appeared and helped with the bags. She'd said that Wade had called to see how they were doing, and Chelsea had told him all about the bad weather and lack of guests.

Hearing that she'd missed his call, Tracy had fought the urge to sit down in the middle of the lobby and bawl her head off. Instead, she'd calmly trailed Chelsea up the stairs, emptied the grocery bags, and told herself that, even if she hadn't spoken to Wade herself, at least he'd called. At least he was still thinking of her.

Suddenly the phone rang unexpectedly. She hoped it was him and that he could sense how much she'd been thinking of him. She grabbed the portable phone off the sofa beside her.

"Heartbreak Hotel."

"Do you get the early weekend edition of *The Tribune?*"

Tracy immediately recognized Carly's voice and smiled.

"Nope. I get it on Sunday. What's up?"

"I hope you have a good supply of cinnamon buns and scones in the freezer."

"Of course I don't. I serve them fresh. Why?"

"Because your phone is going to be ringing off the hook, that's why. There's a travel article that's going to be in the Sunday edition. It's credited to the *L.A. Times* travel section."

"If it's about how tourism is sucking big-time right now, *puleeese,* you don't need to read it to me."

Carly laughed. "Actually, it's about a very colorful, very romantic inn on the central coast. A place named Heartbreak Hotel."

Tracy sat up so quickly that Matt tipped over and spilled half a bowl of popcorn.

"Someone stole our *name?*"

"No. Someone wrote an article about *your* Heartbreak Hotel."

"Henri. It had to be Henri. I knew there was more to that old codger than the fez, Speedos, and silk robe."

"Not Henri. Edward Cain."

"Edward Cain?" She frowned. "The name rings a bell, but I can't put a face to it."

"Edward Cain is that novelist. *The* novelist. The one who wrote *An Even Dozen?* Remember?"

"Kind of. Oh, yes! The woman from South Dakota was reading it while she was here last month. Is it good?"

"The big deal about it is that a real killer committed twelve murders that he copied *exactly* as Cain wrote them. It was pretty grisly. Eventually the killer was caught, but Edward Cain was sued by some of the victims' families. He even received *death threats,* and then dropped out of sight as soon as the trials were over. I just saw an article about him in *People* a few weeks ago. I've still got that issue around here someplace . . ." Carly muffled the phone, but Tracy could hear her yelling to Jake to hunt through the back issues of *People.*

"How would Edward Cain know anything about the Heartbreak?"

"Tracy, the article was also about *you.* There were paragraphs singing your praises. He said there was a ghost haunting the place. Specifically, a ghost named Captain Ezra Poole. The article had some details about Ezra's past, and Twilight Cove. It even mentioned Palmer Biggs and the historical society. How come you never told me you had a ghost?"

"Because I *don't* have a ghost, Carly."

"He described you, your delicious coffee, and fabulous home-baked goods. He made the place sound so romantic and inspiring, and he even went so far as to say it was a better stop on the coast than Hearst Castle."

Tracy thought back through the handful of guests who'd checked in over the last few weeks. She was barely making enough money to keep the lights on, let alone break even. She'd just about decided that if things didn't pick up soon, she'd have to think about signing the place over to the historical preservation society just to keep from having to pay the utilities and taxes.

"There was even a picture of the place. A photo of you standing on the front steps. And there was a crooked shot of the neon sign out front."

"That sounds like one of Matt's photos from the set Wade sent to Matt the day after he left . . ."

"Tracy, don't you get it yet? *Edward Cain.* Edward Cain is obviously a pen name for the only writer who ever stayed there long enough to know the place so well."

There is only one guest who knows anything about Ezra Poole. One guest who ever admitted to being a writer. Only one person who had access to those photographs.

"Ohmygod. Wade?"

"Right! Wade." There was a pause and then Carly added, "Tracy, the guy has to be worth millions."

Her Wade—with his worn-out cowboy boots and low-slung jeans, his slow smile and dark, sad eyes that looked into her soul. Her Wade, the man who'd walked in a stranger and become so much more. *Wade writes as Edward Cain?*

She thought she knew all she needed to know about him. She'd slept with him and she hadn't really known him at all.

"Tracy? Are you still there?"

"I'm here." *Somewhere. I'm in here somewhere.*

"Want me to bring the article over?"

Outside, it was still raining cats and dogs. She thought about Carly making the winding drive down Lover's Lane and then through Twilight Cove. The carpenter on the TV was painting the recycled bookcase a puke shade of green that reminded her of strained Gerber peas.

"That's okay. Matt and I will run down to the Paper Sack and get a copy."

"Unless I miss my guess, you'll be so busy from now on that you won't be going much of anyplace. I still can't *believe* it. Wade is Edward Cain. I never even saw him in anything other than Levi's and a T-shirt except for the night of the open house."

The night I begged him to make love to me.

He tried to tell me. He wanted to tell me the truth.

She thought back to that night, tried to recall every word.

"I can't do this without telling you everything."

"Don't. Not if it will change things between us. Will it make me see you differently?"

"Probably. I don't see how it wouldn't."

"Tracy?" Carly's voice shook her out of her reverie. "Are you there?"

"Yes. I'm here."

"I can't *believe* Jake didn't recognize Wade as Cain. I told him he must be losing his touch. He was so into that whole case. He is going through a stack of old *People* magazines right now. If we find it, I'll save it for you. Why don't you go Google Edward Cain?"

Tracy promised she would before she said good-bye. Matt was still eating popcorn off of the sofa. The cute carpenter on TV was trying to squeeze the bookcase through the door, but he'd measured wrong and it didn't fit. A paint-spattered couple in *Trading Spaces* shirts didn't look hopeful.

Wade is Edward Cain.

She remembered that Chelsea had told him exactly how badly things were going at the beginning of the week.

The travel article was his valiant attempt to try and save the Heartbreak for her.

CHAPTER FORTY-THREE

For three solid days it had rained almost nonstop, and even so, the hotel had been surrounded by news vans and reporters on Edward Cain watch. The phone had been ringing off the hook with reporters and publicists, and despite the barrage, she couldn't turn it off because, amid the flurry, people were calling with inquiries about legitimate reservations.

It was afternoon and still raining outside as Tracy put the finishing touches on a bouquet in the sunroom. When she heard footsteps in the lobby close by, she whipped around, wielding her pruning shears, prepared for just about anything.

It wasn't a reporter, but Chelsea, who came walking in wearing a baseball cap and sunglasses.

"Calls still coming in?" Chelsea glanced at the phone. "Who knew the Heartbreak Hotel would end up being *the* place to stay on the coast? And the only one filled to capacity."

Tracy had opted to not step outside after she'd opened the front door to answer it and nearly been toppled by reporters, microphones, and cameramen. Sunday night had been so unbelievable that they'd smuggled Matt out to Carly's car in a pile of linens, and she'd driven him up to their place for an overnight.

"I hope things calm down soon," Tracy said. "We're already all booked up clear through next summer." She set the shears down. "Are you going out?"

"To the store. Did you notice that most of the news crews have left?

There's only one truck left out there." Chelsea had all of her long hair wound up beneath the baseball cap. "Where did they go?"

Tracy charged over to the window and drew the curtain back an inch. "Do we really care, as long as they're gone?"

"It seems weird, though. First they all descend, and now they've taken off again like a swarm of locusts."

Not only had the press descended, but two days ago an exorcist called, guaranteeing he could get rid of Ezra Poole for five thousand dollars. Tracy told him she wanted to keep Ezra. A publicist for New Zealand's world famous medium Jennie Crawford called, proposing a seminar and psychic training sessions at the hotel for those who wanted to hone their ability to speak to the spirit.

A couple from Roswell, New Mexico, phoned to say they didn't believe that Ezra Poole was a ghost. No, they had proof that Ezra was a code name for an alien being known as Arze. After she hung up, she realized Arze was Ezra spelled backward.

Yesterday the FedEx carrier delivered a résumé from a self-certified ghost-buster.

Matthew was already charging his classmates for tours. He'd tried to bribe Chelsea into hiding in the closet draped in an old sheet to scare his customers. She would have been more upset about his new enterprise, but he hadn't been this happy in months. Chelsea was getting adept at sneaking out of the hotel in disguises, sometimes using the guests as shields.

"Sylvester, Lease and Lynch called while you were in the shower," Tracy told her.

Chelsea paled. "Did they say what they wanted?"

"It was Lease himself. David Sylvester quit. He relocated to Denver. They wanted to know if you could come back and work for them next summer. He also apologized for any 'inconvenience' we may have suffered."

"What does that mean?"

"That's exactly what I asked him. He said that they received an anonymous letter suggesting that they look into David's 'indiscretions,' and it seems there were quite a few. He was asked to take a payout and leave."

"Did you write the anonymous letter?"

"I wanted to, but I didn't. I know how strongly you felt about David's family finding out."

Chelsea was thoughtful a moment. "I have a feeling it might have been Eric. I think he's the only other one who knew."

"Don't be angry with him, Chelsea. He obviously cares a lot about you." Tracy then added, "Mr. Lease said that they would be happy to have you back next summer, if you are interested. He insisted that you keep the 'scholarship' check David wrote, whether or not you decide to go back."

"There's no time to go back this year." Chelsea finally smiled again. "Maybe when you sell this place, Jake will take you on as a P.I. You certainly took care of David Sylvester like a pro."

"Has Wade called back?" She hadn't given up hope.

"Not yet."

She sighed, still battling her confusion. As much as she wanted to talk to him, she was jumpy and nervous about it. He wasn't just Wade Johnson, writer on hiatus anymore, he was a bestselling novelist, extremely wealthy, and a hot topic. Certainly not the man she thought she knew. In her heart of hearts she knew he hadn't written the story to hurt her, but she found herself wishing he had given her some warning before the story broke and she was blindsided.

She'd researched Edward Cain on the Internet, found his Web site. The information there hadn't been updated for over two years and, of course, there was no mention of the murders. His bio was scanty at best, and in his photos he was barely recognizable as the man she'd come to know. She'd read plenty of archived news articles that detailed not only the grisly murders but the subsequent hearings that Wade had endured.

She longed to talk to him, but she didn't know where to start.

When the front doorbell suddenly rang, she and Chelsea both jumped at once.

"It looks like a woman." Tracy headed for the door. Check-in wasn't for hours yet. She glanced through the window in the door and noted that the caller was a young woman in her early thirties, dripping wet, carrying a sopping canvas overnight bag. Dressed in a wraparound skirt and T-shirt that looked as if she'd slept in them, the caller looked harmless enough.

Even so, Tracy opened the door cautiously. "Do you have a reservation?"

"Not really." Before Tracy knew what hit her, the woman shouldered her way right past her into the lobby and shook out her tangled, curly hair like a wet puppy.

"I'm sorry. I'm afraid we're completely booked." Tracy hated to send her off in the rain. She thought of all the nights the place had been empty over the last month. Now she didn't have even a cot to spare.

The young woman sat the overnight bag down. She didn't look at all disappointed or worried. Nor did she look like she was going anyplace. Chelsea stepped out from behind the reception desk and joined them.

"You must be Tracy Potter." The young woman turned to Tracy first and extended her hand.

"Do I know you?" Tracy tried to place her.

"Lauren Westin, from *World* magazine." She pulled a business card out of a side pocket in her purse and handed it to Tracy.

Tracy tried to hand it back. "We aren't talking to reporters."

Lauren turned. "You must be Chelsea."

"We aren't giving interviews. If I have to call the police, I will," Tracy warned her.

"Hear me out first, okay? Surely you've heard of *World*."

"All the news that's not fit to print." Tracy reached for the woman's overnight bag. It was so light that it had to be empty. "Since you won't be staying, I'll just carry this out to the porch for you."

Lauren Westin snagged the handle and a brief tug-of-war ensued. "Hey, we're the biggest little newspaper in the world. We're at every checkout counter in every English-speaking country on the planet."

"I've seen your rag," Chelsea told her. "What was the headline a couple of weeks ago? 'Cro-Magnon man comes out of cave dwelling to abduct Bush daughters'?"

"One of our all-time bestsellers." Lauren actually looked so proud that Tracy laughed.

Her laughter quickly halted when Miss Westin, seeing an opening, turned on her. "Is it true you had an affair with Edward Cain?"

"Who said that?" She jerked the suitcase out of the woman's hand and headed for the door.

Lauren Westin was hot on her heels. "So it is true?"

"I didn't say that."

"You didn't deny it, either."

Chelsea stepped between the reporter and Tracy. "Look, leave us alone."

"*World* will pay for a story. Just give us what you can on Edward Cain. Give us anything you can. How long ago was he here? Where did he go? How has he managed to stay out of sight for so long? Has he had extensive plastic surgery?"

"You need to leave." Tracy opened the door and set the suitcase outside, fully prepared to pick up Lauren Westin and toss her out after it if she had to. "Bye now."

"Did you sleep with him? How often? How did you two meet? How long was he here?"

"I've never met Edward Cain." Not exactly a lie.

"We wouldn't reveal your name. We'd quote you as 'a source close to Edward Cain.' My publisher is prepared to pay as high as twenty-five."

"You have to be kidding." *Sell out Wade for twenty-five dollars?*

"Okay, fifty thousand, but that's all I'm authorized to offer without calling my boss."

"Fifty *thousand* dollars?" All she had to do was tell this hungry reporter with the sloppy fake-leather purse and run-down shoes what she knew about Edward Cain and she'd make *fifty thousand dollars*?

Tracy glanced over and noticed that Chelsea was stunned and staring at the reporter. Fifty thousand dollars would go a long way toward paying for the rest of her education. Tracy held her breath.

"How about you?" Lauren focused on Chelsea, on her obvious interest. "That's a lot of money. At least think about it." Lauren pulled out a pen and wrote "$50,000" on her card, and then she handed it to Chelsea, who stared at it in disbelief.

"Think about what fifty thousand can buy, and call me when you change your mind. Just remember, no one wants old news, so don't wait too long."

Lauren Westin sailed through the door, grabbing her overnight bag as she crossed the porch. Tracy shut the door behind her.

Chelsea was still staring at the card, running her fingers around the edges. "Can you believe it? Fifty thousand dollars?"

Tracy's heart caught in her throat. Chelsea was no doubt thinking about how she could make a small fortune if she chose to tell *World* magazine, or any other media outlet, that the night before Edward Cain checked out, he and her stepmother had slept together. If anyone got wind of what Chelsea knew, or thought she knew, there would be a bidding war for the rights to the story.

Then Chelsea slowly smiled. "You know what I was just thinking about?"

Tracy didn't know if she wanted to hear. "No. What?"

"Out of nowhere, I suddenly flashed on those hokey birthday dinners you always make me. One for every single year since you married Dad. And those old tacky paper cone hats we always wore, and that pitiful kitty candle you've saved since I was eight—and all I could think was, *as if. As if* I'd sell you out for a *measly* fifty thousand dollars.'"

Chelsea laughed and tore the business card in half, then quarters, then eighths before handing it to Tracy. As the pieces sifted into her palm, Tracy couldn't say a word. She was too busy fighting tears.

The legendary Hotel Del Coronado on Coronado Island in San Diego opened in 1888 and boasted resident ghosts in rooms 3312 and 3505. Since both rooms were already booked, Wade decided that having a drink in the hotel's Babcock & Story Bar would be as close as he wanted to come to another ghostly encounter.

Despite heavily overcast skies, surf lessons were under way on the beach in front of the hotel as he sat at a table on the outdoor terrace. He punched Bob Schack's number for the first time since the article came out on Sunday and took a sip of a tall, icy mint *mojito*.

"Bob-o." He had a feeling his agent would be in as sour a mood as he was himself.

Bob didn't even bother with hello. "You could have warned me you were doing that article, buddy, so I could cover my ass. You know what it's been like in this office since your name surfaced again?"

"Yeah? Well, that article wasn't *supposed* to have my name on it." He'd bought the *Los Angeles Times* the day the story ran and was thankful he was a three-hour drive from L.A. or he'd have come out of hiding long enough to track Jim Kemerer down and give him more than a piece of his mind.

As it was, he'd had to wait until Kemerer was "at his desk" and settle for a far from cordial phone conversation that left him frustrated and angry, but it was far too late to do anything about it.

"You didn't bother to get anything in writing, obviously," Schack chided.

"Exactly what Kemerer told me. I didn't think I'd have to. He says he never gave me his word, but then he tried to blame the byline on his copy editor. Jim *conveniently* left the office for the weekend *after* telling his assistant that the story was by Edward Cain. He claims he gave the assistant specific instructions to leave the name off, but that the story was nothing unusual without it and the assistant editor acted on his own."

"Well, buddy, the good news is, book sales have spiked again. I don't have to tell you the bad news. The media is all over that hotel."

"Yeah, I know. That's the last thing I wanted." Thinking about the aftermath that hit Twilight still set Wade's teeth on edge.

"I take it the blond in the photo was behind your writing that piece. Am I right? I would have never guessed a woman could flush you out of hiding."

Tracy. He'd done it for her, to help her. He'd wanted to spotlight the hotel, not turn her world upside down. He'd watched the television reports taped outside the hotel on all the local news spots. The Heartbreak had already been featured on *Entertainment Tonight* and *Extra.* The copycat murders were to be revisited on *20/20* and *48 Hours Mystery* at the end of the week.

Palmer Biggs and the mayor of Twilight Cove had already given interviews.

Tracy was refusing to talk to the media. Reporters had dubbed her "Mrs. Muir," after *The Ghost and Mrs. Muir* movie. It seemed that the lovely, mysterious widow who'd lured Edward Cain out of hiding was refusing to make a statement.

He'd tried calling over and over but never got past the hotel answering machine. He couldn't leave his number, so he'd hung up, hoping that, eventually, Tracy would have to answer.

"Wade? Are you there?" Bob's voice jarred him back to reality. He watched a big set of waves roll in, tossing amateur surfers right and left in its wake.

"Yeah. I'm here."

"Are you in or near Twilight Cove right now?"

"No."

"Thank God. I've been going nuts, praying you'd call in again. The day after that story hit, I had a frantic call from Geraldine Farley."

The woman's face came to mind immediately. Sixties, overweight, the pale skin of a Midwesterner in midwinter. Her daughter had been victim number seven. Mrs. Farley was one of the survivors' relatives who hadn't sued him.

"She's decided to sue after all?" It would mean going back to court, facing life as Edward Cain.

"That would have been better than what she had to say. A couple of days after the story broke, her son, Franklin, went missing."

"What do you mean, missing? As in kidnapped?"

"No. As in he left home." Bob suddenly paused, as if hesitant to go on.

Suddenly Wade remembered Farley. Early thirties, mentally unstable, his sister's death had hit him hard. He'd made death threats already.

"Let me guess—"

"His mother is afraid he's headed out to the coast looking for you."

"He really dangerous?"

"Does the phrase 'He's off his meds' mean anything to you?"

Wade broke out in a cold sweat.

"Why don't you come to L.A.?" Bob suggested. "Let me put you up someplace."

"I'm not worried about myself, damn it." He could care less what happened to him, but his mind raced ahead of the implications. It was imperative that he live long enough to get back to the Heartbreak.

"When did this guy leave Minnesota?" Wade's mind raced as he calculated driving time.

"Three days ago."

"He could already be out here."

"Look, Wade—"

"I'll call you back."

"Wade, wait—"

He hung up before he wasted any more time. Knocking back the rest of his drink, he stood up and tossed a ten-dollar bill on the bar and walked out.

As soon as he got back to where he'd parked his bike in the parking lot, he pulled out his cell phone again and dialed the Heartbreak Hotel.

In the mess that was her kitchen, in the middle of the cracked linoleum floor, Tracy was carefully lifting cinnamon buns off a hot baking sheet with a spatula when the phone rang. She paused, listening to an intercom connected to the answering machine on the reception desk downstairs.

"Tracy? Are you in there? *Pick up the phone!*"

Her breath caught and her heart started hammering. It was Wade, a.k.a. Edward.

She raced across the room, realized she was still balancing the bun on the spatula, stopped halfway to the phone, and headed back to the cooling rack on the counter.

"Don't hang up!" Though she knew he couldn't hear her, she hollered at the phone anyway as she dumped the bun. She tossed the spatula in the sink on her way back across the room.

"Tracy, this is Wade. It's important. For God's sake, pick up. I'm afraid you might be in—"

The intercom went silent.

"Damn!" She grabbed the phone and picked it up. "Wade? Wade?" All she heard was dead silence on the other end of the line. She flicked the receiver up and down but couldn't clear the line. Nor could she get a dial tone. The weather had played havoc with the phone lines. For the last couple of weeks, service had been on again, off again all over the area.

She hung up, ran out the apartment door, and headed downstairs, yelling, "Chelsea? Grab the phone, would you?"

She mumbled to herself as she ran downstairs. *"I'm afraid you might be*—what?" What was he going to say?

Might be mad? Up to my ass in reporters? Trapped in the house, afraid to go out onto my own porch? Afraid someone will shove a microphone in my face and ask for the "real" story?

"Have you met Edward Cain? When did he stay here?"

"Did you have an affair?"

"What does he look like now? Is he planning another book?"

Wade—no doubt he was calling to apologize for turning her life upside down, for creating a media frenzy outside her door—for giving her what she'd wished for—a successful inn with a calendar full of reservations.

She could forgive him the circus outside. The spotlight would eventually move on. All the vans but one were already gone. All she had to do was wait out the storm.

"Chelsea?" She ran to the reception desk and finally remembered that Chelsea had slipped out for groceries. The answering machine light was blinking so she played back the messages, skipping ahead until she got to Wade's. There was nothing more than what she'd already heard. *"I'm afraid you might be—"*

She clicked the receiver button up and down. There was no dial tone on the downstairs phone, either.

She had no way to reach him, even if she used her cell. He'd never given her his number.

Listening, hoping the lines would be working soon, she stared out the front windows, watched the rain fall, and waited. A few minutes later she checked the line again.

The phones were definitely dead.

CHAPTER FORTY-FOUR

Operator. May I help you?"

Wade forced himself to speak slowly and distinctly. "I'm trying to get a call through to a number in the Twilight Cove, California, area." He'd pulled over at the rest stop at Leucadia, gave the operator the number, and waited while his intestines wound themselves into a coil.

"The lines are down in the area due to heavy rains. They'll be operational again as soon as possible."

"Can you try the Twilight Cove police?" *Surely they have a contingency for a phone outage.*

"Sorry, sir. The line for the Twilight Cove sheriff's station isn't working, either. If this is an emergency, I can connect you to the San Luis Obispo police."

"That would be great."

Within seconds he had the 911 dispatcher in San Luis Obispo on the line.

"I need you to send a squad car to the Heartbreak Hotel. It's on Route 1, just north of Twilight Cove. Their phone lines are down and—"

"What's the emergency?"

"Tracy Potter, the owner of the hotel, may be in danger."

"*May* be in danger? And your name, sir?"

"Wade MacAllister."

"Mr. MacAllister, what makes you think Ms. Potter is in danger?"

He wanted to yell, *"Shut the hell up and send over a squad car!"*—but he knew that would get him nowhere. He forced himself to sound calm instead.

"Someone is out to get me and I'm afraid he might go through her to do it."

"And who might *he* be?"

"Franklin Farley. He's from Minnesota and he's made threats on my life."

"Do you know for certain he's in Twilight Cove at the hotel at this moment?"

"We think he may be headed there."

"You and Ms. Potter?"

Wade sighed and clenched his teeth so hard he was afraid he'd crack a crown.

"Look, my agent called and said that Farley's mother warned us that he's been off his meds. He's out for revenge against me. I'm Edward Cain."

"You said you were Wade MacAllister."

"Do you read the papers at all?" Sarcasm won out.

"Look, sir, we're short-staffed here as it is. I can't send out a squad car just because you think someone who's from Minnesota *might* be headed to the hotel."

"Farley threatened my life. He may believe I'm at the Heartbreak Hotel. He may try to lure me out of hiding by using Mrs. Potter."

"Are you in Twilight Cove?"

"No. I'm just north of San Diego, but—"

"And you're hiding because?"

"Because of the media and—"

"Hey, wait a minute. Are you *that* writer?"

Finally. He'd never been so glad to have his name recognized.

"Yes."

"We still can't send anyone out there on a hunch."

"I can't get through to the Twilight Cove sheriff's office."

"There is a bridge closure four miles down the highway, which is where most of their squad cars are needed."

"The bridge is out?" His heartbeat slowed. If no one had access to town, then Tracy would be safe until he could get to her. "No one can get into Twilight?"

"Yes, sir, they can. The canyon route is open but it's slow and go. We've got a couple of small landslides up there."

"You won't send anyone to the hotel?"

"We can't do anything until there's an actual emergency in progress."

Wade hung up and cursed. The weather was cloudy with occasional drizzle this far south, but he'd be heading into worse weather on the bike. No picnic. It would be a miserable ride in the rain, but all his time on the road had conditioned him to riding in any weather. Once he got there, he'd have the advantage of being able to skirt backed-up traffic.

He quickly punched in Schack's number. This was no time for pleasantries. "Have you heard from Mrs. Farley again?" he asked the instant he heard Bob's voice.

"She still hasn't seen or heard from Franklin."

"Okay, listen. I want you to call the top security company in the San Luis Obispo area. Hire a guard to watch the Heartbreak Hotel and get him there right away. If Tracy Potter walks out of the hotel, I want her trailed. If anything looks the least suspicious, have them follow up. I don't want the occupants of the hotel alarmed or alerted."

"They'll need a photo."

He described Tracy and then added, "Have them check the Net. Try Twilight Cove real estate sites. She used to have a license, and Realtors always have headshots. There's a long shot of her in front of the hotel that ran with the article. It might be online on the *L.A. Times* site. If not, have them check the archives."

"Right. Okay. I'll get on it."

"I've got to go."

"Wait!"

He gave Schack one more minute. "What?"

"Be careful, Wade. I don't represent dead authors."

Matt was having the time of his life. He couldn't believe it when Tucker Hannah and Willie Schmidt showed up at four that afternoon. The twins were the most popular guys in the sixth grade and would never have given a fourth-grader the time of day—unless that fourth-grader had access to a real live ghost.

"So, this is the room, huh?"

Tucker stared at the door to Wade's former room and Matt nodded. He'd turned the hall lights off earlier, just to make it spookier. His mom kept asking why the lights kept going off, but he'd just shrugged and hoped she wouldn't call an electrician.

She'd told him to stop with the tours, but she was so busy that he was still able to sneak kids in.

He pointed to the door and lowered his voice.

"This is where Edward Cain met the ghost of Captain Ezra Poole." He'd memorized the article about the hotel, at least the parts about the old sea captain and how he had been marooned on an island like Tom Hanks in *Castaway,* how Ezra almost starved before he got rescued. Then he'd pause dramatically and lower his voice before he told how Ezra jumped off the cliff behind the house and splatted on the rocks below.

He now knew why Wade was always in his room scribbling. He was thinking about becoming a writer himself. He'd almost filled the whole journal with letters to his dad, and some of them were whoppers. It was a gift that he didn't know he had, but he figured he ought to be able to make up some really good stuff and get paid for it.

He put the key into the keyhole and slowly cracked the door ajar.

"Can we go in?" Willie whispered.

Matt pretended to think about it. "I dunno."

Willie nudged Tucker with his elbow. Tucker bribed, "We'll give you seventy-five cents extra."

Matt sighed and pretended to think about it. "Okay. I guess. But don't touch anything."

Chelsea and his mom would kill him if the bedspread got wrinkled or messed up before the guests checked in later.

"And *be careful,*" he warned the guys. "Ezra won't come out if he doesn't like you."

"What's not to like?" Tucker elbowed Willie hard and laughed. A shoving war ensued.

"Hey, keep it down or you'll scare him off."

The older boys quieted down and walked into the room, their eyes wide and full of awe as they turned full circle to take it all in. When the curtains at the oceanside window billowed up, lifted by the breeze, they both jumped, bumping into each other.

Willie shoved Tucker. "Fartface."

Tucker shoved back. "Shithead."

"I'll have to end the tour if you don't shut up," Matt warned, suddenly feeling a rush of power. He waited in the hallway so that he could keep an eye out for Chelsea and Mom. If Mom caught him again, she'd for sure make him give the guys their money back.

When a deliveryman walked into the lobby, Matt glanced back into the room to make sure Tucker and Willie weren't touching anything before he hurried down the hall.

The deliveryman was holding a huge vase of roses with a card sticking out of it. He lowered the vase. "These are for Tracy Potter. Is she here?"

"My mom's upstairs." He was afraid that if he called her, she'd come downstairs and he'd get busted for operating the tour again.

"Just leave 'em on the registration desk," he suggested.

"Sorry. She has to sign for them."

Matt sighed and impatiently pointed to the stairway on the opposite side of the lobby. "She's up there. Go on up."

As soon as the flower deliveryman started toward the stairs, Matt hurried back to Wade's old room. It was time to slam the door on the guys and pretend it was Ezra's doing. It was the best part of the tour as far as he was concerned. Even better than the quick peek and maybe even a walk around the haunted attic.

Christopher had called last night to say that he heard from one of the kids in their class that the Haunted Heartbreak Hotel tour was almost as good as Disneyland.

Matt couldn't help but smile. By the end of summer, he was going to be a *gazillionaire.*

Tracy was headed for the stairs when she turned the corner and nearly ran into a deliveryman already halfway up with a bouquet of huge ivory tea roses in his arms. They almost hid him from view.

The man peered around the roses. "Are you Tracy Potter?"

"How did you get in?"

"The kid told me to come up."

Remembering Lauren Westin posing with an empty overnight bag, she asked, "Are you a reporter?"

"No." He had a vacant look, as if he had no interest whatsoever in his surroundings or her. His job was to deliver the roses and leave. Charm wasn't a requirement. "The Daisy Drop sent me."

"Come on up." She stepped aside to let him pass when he reached the landing, and then ushered him into the apartment, where stuff was piled everywhere, a sure sign that her life had gone haywire.

I'm going to need more help.

"Put them on the coffee table." She found her purse and started digging for a tip as he set the flowers down and then pulled a receipt out of his pocket.

She glanced at the bouquet, anxious to read the card stuck on a plastic pitchfork. The roses were lovely—breathtaking in fact. The Daisy Drop was the oldest and best florist in Twilight, and they always did an outstanding job.

The deliveryboy was no boy. He had to be close to thirty. His hair was thinning, nearly the same length all over. His eyes were deep-set. He was looking around the room.

"Sorry the place is such a mess." She immediately stopped when she realized she was apologizing to a deliveryman. "Here you go."

She handed him three dollars. He stared at it for a second before he pocketed it, looking more uncomfortable by the second.

"Well, then." Surely he wasn't stalling for a bigger tip. "Thanks for bringing them upstairs." She started for the open door, hoping he'd get the hint and walk out before she had to tell him to go ahead and leave.

"So, where's Edward Cain?" He glanced around the room.

"You *are* a reporter." She shook her head, closed her eyes, and prayed for patience. "I'm getting really sick and tired of you people."

"I'm not a reporter. Just curious."

"Edward Cain is *not* here. Now please, leave."

"Is he coming back?"

"I really have no idea." The guy was beginning to creep her out, but she couldn't exactly put her finger on why. Maybe it was because his lackluster gray blue eyes never really settled on anything. There was nothing suspicious about him, really. He seemed mild-mannered, almost shy. His features were so average that he would easily blend into a crowd and barely be remembered.

She glanced into the kitchen, thought of going for the phone. Last time she had checked, the line was still dead, but he couldn't know when service would go back on. She opted to walk out into the hall and if he didn't follow her out, she was going to bolt down the stairs, find Matt, and head outside to where the news van was parked across the road.

"Well, then—" She was three feet from the door when he came bolting past her, slammed it shut, and leaned against it.

As her pulse shot up and her ears started buzzing, she fought to focus.

Where are you Matt? She prayed he wouldn't come upstairs. Chelsea was out shopping and due back soon. She didn't want her walking in, either. There was no other way out except through the door to the widow's walk, a fine alternative in case of fire, but not with someone trailing after her. Still, if she could get there before he could stop her, if she could run to the stairway that led upstairs, get there before he—

Her thoughts were hopping around like a jumping bean. She decided to keep him busy, keep him away from the kids at all costs. He was between her and the stairs to the lobby. She could try to get to the kitchen, to the knives, if she had to.

But with a knife in her hand, she might be putting herself in greater jeopardy.

I have to do something.

"Whatever you're thinking, don't." With more speed than she would have given him credit for, he pulled a switchblade out of his pocket. It sprang to life, a glittering silver stiletto that flashed deadly, even in the gray light streaming through the front window.

Not today, she thought. *I don't want to die today. I won't die today.*

Matt, stay downstairs. Please, please. Chelsea, take care of him. You're a smart girl.

She prayed that Chelsea would somehow divine that something wasn't right. *But how?*

Finally she managed to find her voice again. "What do you want?"

"Edward Cain."

Death threats. Wade had received death threats. She'd wondered just how bad things could be that he'd had to change his looks and keep moving. Now she knew.

This is how bad it can be.

"He's gone. I didn't even know he was here."

The intruder shook his head as if shaking off a pesky fly. He frowned. "But he knew you."

He leaned against the door, a casual posture that belied the way his gaze was darting around the room and back. He pulled a piece of crumpled newspaper out of his pocket. She stared at it. The Heartbreak feature story, creased and faded.

Quoting the article word for word without even looking at it, he recited, "Tracy Potter, innkeeper. A consummate hostess who serves baked goods that melt in your mouth. She met a challenge head-on by creating a welcoming, homey atmosphere that tempts guests to linger by the fire on a chilly day, or take in the view from the sunroom. Who can go wrong lingering awhile in a place where a rose garden grows wild beneath the California sun, and gulls play over the water?"

He shoved the article back into his pocket. "How *cozy* were you two?"

When she didn't immediately respond, he laughed. The sound chilled her blood.

"Please, my son might come in. Tell me you won't hurt my son," she pleaded.

"I don't hurt kids." He didn't sound all that convincing, though. "I don't really want to hurt you either, but Cain has to pay."

"For what?" Keep him talking, she decided, thinking of all the detective series she used to watch while she was waiting up at night for Glenn to come home. *Keep him calm. Keep him away from Matt.*

"Cain deserves to die. My sister was one of the even dozen. She was pretty, just like you. She was younger, though. She never asked for trouble, but because of Edward Cain's book, she's dead. And so are all the others. He got off easy, but I'm going to make him pay. God told me I have to make him pay. Now, I want you to call him. Get him back here."

CHAPTER FORTY-FIVE

I don't know how to get ahold of Edward Cain." Despite the cloudy weather, Tracy could feel sweat trickling down her temple.

"Do I look stupid?" her assailant asked.

"Not at all." *You look dangerous. Demented, but not stupid.* "The phone lines are out. They've been out since this morning."

"Don't patronize me. I can read your thoughts through your eyes, Ms. Potter."

"Try the phone."

He made her get it for him, bring it to him. She obeyed, and when he punched it on, there was no dial tone. Raising his arm as if to throw it across the room in frustration, he immediately thought better of it and shoved it into his waistband.

"I have no idea where Wa . . . Edward Cain is—"

"Where's your room?" He moved quick as a snake, grabbing her arm.

"Why?" She dug her heels into the carpet. Though he didn't appear to be in all that great of shape, she was no match for his strength.

He stepped away from the door and dragged her across the room. She bumped into the coffee table and winced.

"My son is downstairs. If he comes looking for me, the first place he'll go is my room. You don't want him to find us, do you?"

Oh, Mattie. Think. Think. Breathe.

"There's an attic. No one ever goes up there. Take me to the attic." She prayed she hadn't just signed her own death sentence.

He stopped in the hall just outside the door to her room. "Show me."

The front window in the attic looked down on the news van still parked out front. All she needed was to attract the attention of someone, anyone, a reporter or member of the crew. Maybe someone would see her if she waved, if she could just attract their attention. Maybe someone could help her. Save her.

If she could just get someone's attention . . .

His fingers dug deep into the tender underside of her arm as she pointed toward the door at the end of the hall, and he dragged her through it and then up the steps. At the landing he paused.

"Which door?"

She pointed to the attic door.

"What's the other one?"

"It goes outside. Onto the roof."

He opened the attic door and, once inside, hooked the door lock. The space was tidy now, thanks to Wade. The boxes and crates were all labeled and stacked. There was nothing in sight that she could use to defend herself. At least nothing that jumped out at her. Wade was the last one to touch most of the boxes. Somehow, the thought comforted her.

She thought about darting over to the front window, but he was right there, breathing down her neck. Though it was raining out, the air held a hint of tropical moisture. It was stuffy in the room.

"How long do you intend to keep me up here?"

"Until the phone works and you can call him."

"I already told you—"

"We'll sit here until he comes back!" he yelled.

Tracy groaned. "But he's *not* coming back. What part of that don't you understand?"

His voice dropped almost to a whisper and, as if he were explaining to a three-year-old, he fell into a singsong rhythm. "Sooner or later someone's going to notice you're missing. It will make the news. Then Edward Cain will come back to help you, to look for you."

She thought for a second she was going to throw up. Not Wade, but eventually the kids would be looking for her. Then what? Knowing how often she went out there, they would naturally look on the widow's walk, and then they would think to check the attic, too.

Her gaze flew to the small iron hook that he'd latched on the inside of the door.

"My children will notice I'm missing and they'll come up here. How do you plan to keep all three of us quiet?"

The question gave him pause, heightened his nervousness. "I don't know. I don't know. I don't know." His gaze shot back and forth. "Shut up."

"Have you thought this through? What's your name?"

"Franklin."

"Franklin, you know, you still have time to walk out of here before you get yourself into real trouble. I won't hold it against you if you change your mind right now and let me out. You can walk out. Did you drive? Is your car out front?" Surely someone had seen him come in with the flowers. Wouldn't they notice that he hadn't come out?

"Please *shut up.*"

"Cain will never come to my rescue."

"If I kill you, he'll come then. He'll come after me because he'll know it should have been him, not you. He cares about you. I can tell by what he wrote about you."

Her hands had been trembling, but now they were shaking uncontrollably. She clenched them together, tried to make herself look weak, thankful that he hadn't tied her up. It was obvious Franklin had no idea what he was doing, but with the stiletto in his hand, he was holding all the cards.

"I really don't want you to die, like my sister and the others. But if I have to kill you to get Cain's attention, I will. Now, please sit down."

She stared around the room. Glanced over at the front window. Too far. She wouldn't have a lot of chances, but she could try to get to it. If she had to, she'd kick it out, scream bloody murder. But that might enrage him and he would still have time to kill her, run downstairs, and find Matt.

"Where should I sit?"

"On that one." He pointed to a box in the middle of the floor. It was filled with Ezra's logs. She'd boxed them up herself the day after Wade left and brought them back up here.

He sat within arm's length of her, stretched his legs out in front of him, and was tucked into the dark space where the angled ceiling met the floor.

"How? How did your sister die?" She tried to not choke on the question. Her one goal was to keep him talking.

"You haven't read the book?"

"No." She knew now that she never would be able to bring herself to open it. And she knew why Wade had looked so desperately lost and lonely that first night.

"My sister was number seven. Simple murder wasn't good enough for Mr. Cain. The killer he created, the spawn of his imagination, not only raped his victims, but at the end, he slit their throats. And Cain even took it a step farther with each victim."

She saw the knife in his hands. He was staring at the gleaming tip.

"Cain's killer dismembered them before he killed them. One piece at a time. Toes. Fingers. Feet. Hands. He tied off the wounds, made certain they didn't bleed out. Kept them alive, in pain, in terrible agony, Ms. Potter. He did different horrible things to each of them. Tortured them in twelve different ways before he slit their throats. Killing them was actually the most merciful thing he could do. And it was all Cain's design."

"It was fiction," she whispered.

"It became fact. My sister didn't deserve to die that way. None of them did," he said sadly.

"Edward Cain is certainly not the only author writing that kind of novel. What about the people who buy and read them? Aren't they just as guilty? Is it Edward's fault that someone decided to replicate the murders?"

Franklin drew his legs up close to his body and looped his long arms around his knees. The knife was ever in his hand.

He was glaring at her, his eyes focused for the moment. Determined. His expression made her shiver.

"I suggest you shut up, Ms. Potter. This isn't something you can fix by mixing up a batch of 'mouthwatering cinnamon rolls.' You should start thinking about what I might have to do to you."

If he was waiting for her to break down, to grovel, then he was going to have to wait until hell froze over. She was determined to stay strong, to not show fear.

"Edward cares only about himself. He won't care what happens to me."

Nothing was further from the truth. Her death would be one more burden for Wade to bear. In writing the travel piece about the Heartbreak, he'd risked his own anonymity for her. How many people like Farley were out there seeking revenge?

She broke into a cold sweat when she heard a creak on the stairs' outside the door.

Franklin shot up lightning fast and without a sound. In a second he crossed the room and covered her mouth with his hand. She felt the hot prick of the cold blade at her throat.

"Don't move. Don't make a sound." His breath was stale, his skin so cool it felt reptilian as he whispered in her ear. "If you even twitch, I'll kill you. I swear on your kid's life."

Her eyes widened above his hand and she watched as the door handle slowly turned back and forth, back and forth. Then her heart almost stopped when she heard Matt's voice on the other side of the door.

"Weird," Matt said.

"What's weird?"

She didn't recognize the second voice, but it sounded like another boy.

"The door is supposed to be open, but it's stuck. Or maybe it's locked from inside." Matt sounded puzzled. The knob rattled as he tried to open it. Tracy willed him to give up and leave.

After what was only heartbeats that seemed like hours, she heard his voice again. "I guess Ezra doesn't want us in there."

"Yeah, right. Somebody else locked it."

"There's no keyhole, see?"

There came the sound of a scuffle to see and then a third voice complained, "What a gyp."

"Come back and bring friends—maybe Ezra will let us in next time."

The stairs creaked and footsteps echoed hollowly as the boys went back downstairs. Tracy's relief was as great as her fear when she knew that Matt and the others were leaving.

Suddenly her mouth was free. Franklin had let her go. He walked across the room but hovered beneath the eaves where he could see her, where he was close enough to reach her if he had to.

She told herself to hang on, to think straight. She was still alive. She'd come too far in the last few months to give up now.

Stay alert. Stay strong. Wait for a chance to escape.

Surely he'll get tired, if he doesn't crack first.

He can't watch me every second.

As long as she was alive, there was a chance.

Thank God for the Harley.

Wade skirted the traffic jammed along the canyon road as if it weren't there.

The minute he cleared the bend in the old road and saw the Heartbreak standing on the bluff against the misty, smoke gray sky, an odd mix of relief and anxiety hit him at once.

Carefully negotiating potholes and puddles, he tried to temper his anticipation with caution. There was no need to panic, or to panic Tracy, either. Farley might very well be back in Minnesota. He could have just been making idle threats.

The hotel, with its eclectic mix of architectural styles, its widow's walk and dormers and wide porch, gave him a sense of homecoming—the likes of which he'd never known in all the years of shuffling around New York from apartment to apartment.

That sense of homecoming was surely inspired, not by the sight of the hotel, but by his feelings for Tracy. He'd been a fool to not tell her who he was and how he came to be there, even though she'd told him that she didn't want to know.

As the bike quickly ate up the last half mile to the Heartbreak, his desperate need to hold Tracy again, his need to see her safe, to feel her in his arms and tell her how much she meant to him, was almost overwhelming.

As he drew nearer, he finally and completely understood Ezra, his love for Violette, and how it had kept him alive—and why he couldn't live without her.

A news van was the most recognizable vehicle on the road, with its tall antenna and bright station logos painted on the sides. So was the nondescript navy blue sedan parked at the curb. A three-hundred-pound security guard was taking up half the front seat.

Noting a couple of other cars out front, he blew past the *Eyewitness News* van and pulled into the driveway, continuing on up to the house as if he had every right to be there. He left his helmet on, with its tinted face shield, dismounted, and hustled up the walk to the side door. He was inside so quickly that no one from the van had time to move, let alone stop and ask questions.

He didn't pull off his helmet until he was safely inside the lobby, where he found a couple standing beside their suitcases at the registration desk.

"Do you work here?" the woman wanted to know.

"No, but maybe I can help. What do you need?" He glanced around, wondered where Tracy might be.

"We're here to check in. The Kormanicks?"

Wade opened the big drawer in the desk and pulled out a room key.

"Here you go," he said, tossing it to them. "Mrs. Potter will take a copy of your credit card when she gets in. The rooms are right down the hall. Make yourselves comfortable."

He pointed them in the right direction, then checked the sunroom and the laundry. Both were empty. He headed for the apartment stairs, taking them two at a time.

Relief washed over him when he heard Matt's voice coming from inside the apartment.

Matt was fine. Tracy was fine. Everything would be fine. It had to be.

Matt was headed down the stairs with two older boys trailing behind him. He stopped the minute he recognized Wade, and his two friends ran into him. Launched into the air, Matt came flying at Wade, who caught him before he ended up knocking them both all the way back to the lobby.

"Wade! Wow. You came back. Did you see the *Eyewitness News* van outside? There were five of them out there yesterday, until the mudslide. They were waiting for—"

Wade cut him off immediately. "Will you come upstairs with me, Sport?"

"Sure." Matt drew himself up, suddenly important. "Bye, guys," he told the other boys. "Be sure to tell everybody about the tour."

Wade started up the stairs behind Matt. "Tour?"

"Yeah. The Heartbreak Hotel Ghost of Capt. Ezra Poole Tour." Matt stopped, forcing Wade to stop in his tracks, too. "You're a writer, Wade. You think I should name it something else?"

"You could add the words 'world famous.' The World Famous Heartbreak Hotel Ghost of Capt. Ezra Poole Tour."

"I think that's too many words."

"It worked for Sargent Pepper's One and Only Lonely Hearts Club Band."

"Who?"

"Never mind."

"Maybe I'll try it." But he sounded doubtful.

Wade took a deep breath as he stepped over the threshold of the apartment. Everything seemed quiet inside. The windows were slightly open to the view and the ocean, just wide enough to let the salt air in and keep the rain out. There was still a hint of cinnamon in the air mingled with that of roses. He thought of Tracy. Ached to see her again.

He and Matt called out to her at the same time.

"Tracy?"

"Mom?"

Emptiness echoed back. Wade walked into the kitchen, where everything looked to be in place, but the longer he stood there, the longer he had the strangest feeling that something was wrong. The feeling grew stronger when Matt came running back into the kitchen.

"She's not in the bedroom or the bathroom. Maybe she went to the store." He sounded more than a little hesitant. "She would'a told me she was going, though."

"Is Chelsea here?"

Matt shrugged. "Mom wouldn't have left me by myself."

They moved into the living room together, Matt sticking to him like glue. It wasn't a bad feeling at all. "You wanna watch TV, Wade?"

He wondered how he'd missed seeing the gargantuan bouquet of roses in the middle of the coffee table, but then he realized he'd been looking for only one thing—Tracy.

The bouquet was so huge it was better suited for the lobby.

Wade walked up to it and gently pulled the card out of the plastic flower pick in the middle of the bouquet. He opened the small envelope and stared at the card.

Tracy,
Thinking of you.
Love, Edward.

The Daisy Drop was the local florist where he'd bought Tracy's gardenia corsage.

He stared at the card from "Edward" and his blood ran cold.

He hadn't sent her flowers, and if he had, he certainly wouldn't have sent them signed from Edward.

He dropped the card on the coffee table and turned to Matt.

"Where did these come from? Do you know? When were they delivered?"

The boy shrugged. "Some guy brought 'em a while ago."

"When did he leave?"

Matt turned on the TV and started channel-surfing. Wade walked over and stood in front of the screen.

"Did you see the flower deliveryman leave?" He tried to keep the strained urgency out of his tone, but Matt immediately picked up on it and looked concerned.

"I was busy giving the tour. I never saw him leave. I told him to bring the flowers up here, and then he did."

Wade paced over to the front window, stared out at the news van. The security guard was sipping something in an oversized take-out cup.

Wade shoved his hands into his pockets.

"Hey," Matt said, hopping to his feet, "maybe she's in the attic. Or on the widow's walk."

Wade's pulse picked up as he pictured the close, pitched roof. The room where he'd found the *Lantana*'s logs and questioned his own sanity. Matt was talking, calling his attention back. "What did you just say?"

"I said, the attic was locked when I tried to show the guys. Right before you saw us. There's no key, but there's an old hook on the inside of the door. The kind you slip through a little ring. I told them Ezra locked it, but it had to be Mom, right? Ezra's not real, is he, Wade? Mom said you made him up so we'd get more business, but I'm not supposed to tell anyone that part of the story. Did you make him up?"

There is an old hook on the inside of the door.

"Sure. Did you knock on the door?"

Matt nodded. "Maybe Mom went in there to take a nap. It's been kinda weird around here. We got all kinds of people trying to talk to her and—"

"Listen, Matt. I'm going to need your help."

Matt turned off the television and jumped to his feet. "Cool. What are we gonna do? Wash the Harley?"

Wade pulled out his cell phone and dialed 911. He was connected to the San Luis Obispo dispatcher again. He told her to hold on a second. He went down on one knee and put his hand on Matt's shoulder.

"Listen up, okay? This is really important. Go out front and ask the big guy parked out there in the dark blue car if he has a two-way radio. Ask him to have his company call the police. Tell him to stay out there with you and watch the house, okay. Can you do that?"

"Sure." He didn't look sure. He looked scared. "Where's my mom?"

"Probably at the store, like you thought. Or maybe she did go to the attic to get away from all the newspeople."

Matt shook his head. "Not my mom. Why do you need the police?"

Wade told the dispatcher to hold on again and then told Matt, "Time to get going. You ready?"

"But . . ." Matt dragged his feet.

Wade started to walk him to the door, but before Matt could step out into the hall, Chelsea breezed in with two plastic shopping bags dangling from her hands.

Wade automatically took them from her and set them on the kitchen counter. Chelsea looked none too pleased to see him. She followed him into the kitchen.

"What are you doing here? Where's Tracy?"

Wade nodded to Matt. "Go ahead. Take off. Now." He looked to Chelsea for support.

"Go ahead, Mattie. I need to talk to Wade alone."

"Why?"

"Just go."

As soon as the boy was out the door, Wade got back on the cell. The line was dead. He walked over to where he'd dropped his saddlebags, opened one, and pulled out the Colt.

"What are you doing?" Chelsea started backing toward the door.

Wade tossed her his cell phone. "Call 911."

The gun had been loaded since Bob warned him about Farley. Wade took the safety off. "If you can't get anyone, try San Luis Obispo. Tell them there is an armed robber in the house."

"Is there?" Her eyes went huge and her face drained of color.

"I don't know."

"But . . ."

"Tell them whatever they need to hear, just get them out here. Go outside and wait with Matt. Stay with the security guard out front."

"*What* security guard?"

"The guy in the blue car."

"I saw him sitting out there. I thought he was a reporter." Her gaze flashed between the gun in his hands and his face. Her blue eyes were wide with fear and confusion. Her freckles stood out like specks of cinnamon across the bridge of her nose.

"I don't understand." She shook her head. "What's going on, Wade? Why are you doing this?"

"Tracy's in trouble."

"She's been in trouble since she let you in the front door."

Frustrated, he took a step toward her and when he saw her recoil in fear, he remembered the gun and quickly backed away. "I'd never do anything to hurt any of you," he swore.

"Then why are you standing here with a gun in your hand? Where is she?"

"There's someone out to get me and I think he may have walked in here earlier posing as a flower deliveryman. Matt never saw him leave, and Tracy's not around. Matt said the attic is locked from inside."

"*Ohmygod,*" she whispered. "I thought the copycat murderer was dead."

"Someone else threatened revenge."

She punched 911 into the cell phone.

"What should I tell them?"

"The only thing that'll get them here. Tell them there's an armed intruder inside the house, then get out and go stay with Matt."

Already on her way out, she paused at the door. "Want me to send the security guard up?"

He shook his head. "He's a rent-a-cop. I'd rather wait for the police."

"But, if Tracy's up there, if someone does have her—" Someone was on the other end of the line. "Hello, this is an emergency."

Wade signaled that he was headed upstairs.

Chelsea ran back in and grabbed the sleeve of his jacket. "Maybe you should wait for the police, too."

The gun was awkward and heavy in his hand. He was a writer, not a hero. Not by a long shot, but he had created a monster in *An Even Dozen,* and in turn that monster had infected the mind of another crazed and tormented soul.

Unfortunately, he knew exactly what his own monster had been capable of—but he had no idea what was going through Franklin Farley's head. Nor did he have the luxury of time to find out.

As Chelsea demanded immediate help over the phone, he tried to silently run down the hall to the stairway, hoping he had jumped to conclusions. Maybe the attic door was jammed. Maybe his imagination was working overtime. But he couldn't take a chance.

He crept up the stairs with his heart hammering out of his chest, stopping at every creak and groan. When he reached the top, he pressed his ear to the door, heard nothing.

Slowly, barely breathing, he reached for the old brass doorknob, turning it gingerly so that it didn't make a sound. He tried opening it, but Matt was right, it was barred from the inside.

CHAPTER FORTY-SIX

When Tracy heard the Harley, she covered her face in her hands, afraid her reaction would give Wade away. She listened, knowing he had pulled into the driveway and stopped.

Wade's here. Wade's back. Dear God, Tracy prayed, *don't let him come up here.*

Seconds became minutes. Her mouth was dry and her butt was numb from sitting on the box. A second ago she thought she saw the doorknob move ever so slightly, but her vision wavered and she decided she was hallucinating.

Farley was becoming more disoriented and confused with every passing minute. At one point he'd taken to softly humming a meandering, unrecognizable tune. Absorbed, he almost seemed to have forgotten she was there.

"Could you open the window, please?" She tried to sound as casual as she would talking to anyone. If Farley wanted to see her scared, he had a long wait coming. She'd be damned if she'd let him know how petrified she was, not for herself, but for Wade.

When he didn't answer, she turned to look over her shoulder and found her captor seated against the far wall, staring at her with a glazed look in his eyes.

"Franklin, *please* open the window a little wider. It's stuffy in here."

"Wrong. It's raining outside. But you'd like that, wouldn't you? You'd like me to show myself to those newspeople out there, wouldn't you?"

"They don't even know you."

"No, but they will."

"Don't you realize that while you're sitting here, Edward could be getting farther away? It might be hours before anyone starts looking for me."

He shook his head. "I don't think so. Soon your boy is bound to notice you're not around. Boys notice things like that . . . like when their moms are gone. Or when their sisters are killed. They notice."

His voice sounded distant, as if he were slipping back to another time and place.

A place he inhabited only in his mind.

Wade closed his eyes and released a pent-up sigh when he heard Tracy ask Farley to open the window.

He bowed his head. The gun in his hand wavered like a mirage, but this was no mirage. No dream. No fantasy he'd concocted. This was as close to hell as he ever wanted to get.

For now, Tracy sounded as if she were holding her own. All he had to do was sit tight and wait for the police. They were the experts. He'd researched enough police procedure to know that they knew the best tactics for getting Tracy out alive.

Hang on, Tracy. Hang in there.

He crouched outside the door on one knee, listening—recalling how Ezra had prayed to a God he never believed in for rescue, prayed that he and his Violette would be together again.

Interminable silence on the other side of the door was finally broken by the screech of tires against the pavement out front. Footsteps echoed behind the attic door.

And then, Farley's voice. He sounded frantic. "It's the police!"

Wade's hand involuntarily tightened around the gun. He pressed his palm against the door. It was old and locked—if Matt was correct—by a flimsy hook and eye.

You're only a writer. You're no damned hero.

Suddenly it didn't matter who or what he was—if he didn't hear Tracy say something by his next heartbeat, he was going in. He whipped the gun behind him, shoved it into the waistband of his pants, and covered it with his jacket.

"The police are out there!" Farley scooted across the floor, crawling away from the window like a disjointed crab, heading right for her with the switchblade open.

Tracy gauged the distance to the door, thought about trying to make a run for it. She knew she'd never make it.

There had been no sirens, no slamming of car doors, just a screech of tires that had immediately sent Farley darting over to the window. She could see that he was frantic. There was no guessing what he might do now.

"It's not too late to let me go. I'll convince them this was all a big mistake," she offered.

"Shut up! Let me think." He reached her in seconds, sweat beading his thin upper lip.

"You aren't going to get out of this any other way. The police aren't going to let you go unless I assure them that you're innocent."

His gaze darted from one side of the attic to the other, to the window, back to her face.

"*Now* Cain will come."

She dropped her gaze, terrified that he would see the truth in her eyes, that he would surely realize that the man he knew as Edward Cain had come back.

Wade was out there somewhere. He was here because he must have known about Farley. He had to have been the one to call the police. She remembered his voice over the answering machine earlier. *"Tracy, I'm afraid—"*

Now what he'd tried to say was all too clear. He'd called to warn her about Farley.

He'll have taken care of Matt, and Chelsea, too. She knew it in her heart. Wade would make sure her kids were out of harm's way.

Suddenly without warning, Franklin grabbed her by the arm and jerked her to her feet. She'd been sitting in one cramped position for so long that without thinking, she cried out in pain.

"Shut up! Or I'll kill you! I swear I will!" He shook her, whipped her around, and wrapped his arm around her in a viselike grip. He pulled her up against him, pressing the deadly knifepoint against her throat. His hand was shaking so violently that the switchblade jabbed into her throat.

A loud crash ripped through the room. The old door frame splintered as the door flew back on its hinges and banged into the wall.

Wade rushed into the attic and froze. "Let her go, Farley. It's me you want."

"Wade!" The minute she opened her mouth, the knifepoint pressed deeper into her throat. Something warm and terrifying trickled down her neck.

"Why not let her go, Farley?" Sounding as casual as if he were asking the man to pass the salt, Wade took another step into the room. He was unarmed, but he looked and sounded completely calm, perfectly in control.

"How does it feel?" Farley's voice had gone up an octave. "Now you can watch her die. You won't have to imagine what it's like to have someone you care about carved up into pieces. You can witness it firsthand. You'll have a chance to see what a *real* murder looks like."

Tracy was afraid to breathe. Every time she inhaled, the point of the blade was that much closer to sliding into her throat. She hung on Farley's arm, watching, listening. Wishing she could tell Wade to get out, to save himself. Wishing she could say all the things that she had been foolish to not tell him before, foolish to think it was too soon.

It's never too soon to tell someone you love them. Never.

Better too soon than too late.

She had to tell him now, before it was too late. "Wade . . . I . . ."

"Shut up! Shut up!" Farley's arm had tightened so tight that she was afraid he'd break her ribs.

Wade hadn't moved an inch, but his tone was no longer casual. He was furious, no longer hiding it. "You want to carve someone up, Farley? Make it me. Prove what a man you are. Come on. Kill me." Wade spread his hands wide, stepped closer.

"No!" Tracy cried.

Farley shook her. "Shut up!" he hollered.

"The police are downstairs." Wade was deadly calm again, speaking slowly, as if explaining the situation to a five-year-old. "If you want me, you're going to have to take me before they get up here." Wade spread his arms wide, palms up, in surrender. "Come on. You want me? It's her or me, Farley. You make a move to kill her, and I'll be on you before you can stop me."

Farley was humming now, a low, strained, wandering tune that sent chills down Tracy's spine. And now he was quaking like a leaf, scratching the switchblade across her throat.

While Farley wavered with indecision, her gaze was drawn to shadows shifting in the stairwell behind Wade. Then, without warning, the stairs creaked loudly. Farley shoved her aside and sent her reeling. Struggling to keep her balance, she hit her head on the low underside of the ceiling.

As she fell to the floor, she saw Farley rush Wade with the switchblade aimed at his chest. She screamed and, as if seeing everything in slow motion, watched Wade whip one arm behind him, and a gun instantly appeared in his hand.

Farley lunged at Wade at the exact moment an armed sheriff's deputy burst into the room. Wade fired at Farley. The officer fired at Wade. The two rounds echoed simultaneously.

"Wade!" Tracy screamed as she watched him pitch forward.

Farley clutched his side and staggered back before colliding with the low ceiling and crumpling to the floor in a heap. As the fingers of his outstretched hand opened, the switchblade fell onto the floor.

"Wade! Oh, God. Wade!" Tracy pushed herself up onto her hands and knees and started crawling toward Wade as a flood of sheriff's deputies poured into the room. Seeing stars, she staggered, got to her feet, and started toward Wade just as a deputy nudged a gun out of Wade's hand with his toe.

"What have you done?" Blood was pouring from a wound in Wade's back, low on his shoulder. Falling to her knees beside Wade's prone body, she shouted at the deputy, *"What have you done?"*

A young, blond deputy, his thick chest fortified by a Kevlar vest, reached for her arm to help her up, but she shrugged him off.

"We got a call about an armed assailant." He stared down at Wade and the gun lying beside him.

She pointed over at Farley's crumpled form. "That's the assailant. He was holding me hostage, threatening me at knifepoint." Kneeling beside Wade she cried, "This man was trying to save me."

She struggled to turn Wade over as another officer went down on one knee and pressed his fingers against Wade's neck, feeling for a pulse.

"Get the paramedics up here!" he shouted. "He's still alive."

An officer across the room was kneeling beside Farley, handcuffing him. "This guy's just grazed," he said.

Tracy covered the wound in Wade's shoulder with her hands, leaned over to try and stop the flow of blood.

"Get some help up here!" she screamed at the county sheriffs as Wade's warm blood pumped through her fingers. "I need some towels! Where are the paramedics?"

"They're on the way, lady."

Around her there was nothing but noise, deputies yelling for the paramedics, two-way radios squawking, the heavy footfalls of men running up and down the stairs and moving around the crowded space.

She ignored them all as Wade's face drained of color.

"Wade?" She leaned her lips close to his cheek as she pressed down on the wound. She could feel his heart beating, almost beneath her hands. *So close,* she thought. His heart was too close to where her hands were covering the bullet wound.

"Please, hold on, Wade. Please stay with me. You're going to be all right." His skin had gone ashen. Behind her, the sound of another two-way radio crackled as paramedics finally hustled in. The attic was crowded with men in uniforms. "Wade? Listen to me. I love you. I love you. Do you hear me?"

She watched his face, desperate for a sign, the flicker of his eyelids, the merest trace of movement on his lips. Something. Anything to let her know that he had heard, that he understood that she loved him. That it wasn't too soon.

She prayed that it wasn't too late.

Someone knelt beside her—a woman, one of the emergency medical response team. They exchanged a look that conveyed feelings without words. *Finally,* Tracy thought. *Finally someone who understands.*

"Let me," the young Hispanic woman said softly.

Finally Tracy let go and moved aside, relinquishing Wade to the young woman's capable hands even though she wanted to wrap her arms around him, to cup his face and will him to open his eyes, but he needed more than just her will now.

She looked down at her hands, helpless, and saw that they were cov-ered in blood.

"We need to move him, ma'am. We need to get him out of here." A paramedic who didn't look any older than Chelsea was kneeling on the other side of Wade.

"I want to go with him," she appealed to the woman. "May I please go with him?"

A deputy stepped between her and the stretcher they were carefully shifting Wade onto. "We'll need a statement from you first, ma'am."

"But—"

"I'm sorry, but you'll have to stay here."

CHAPTER FORTY-SEVEN

Though Carly and Jake were waiting downstairs, she didn't see Chelsea or Matt anywhere. It wasn't until the Montgomerys came rushing toward her that the grim reality of what had happened hit her all at once, and she started sobbing.

"Where's Matt? Where's Chelsea?" She grabbed Carly, forcing her friend to look her in the eyes. In her heart of hearts, she felt Matt and Chelsea were safe, but she needed to hear it from her friend.

"Chelsea called and told us to come over. We had her drive Matt up to our place. They're with Christopher. Geoff and Vince are both on their way over there, too, so the kids won't be alone."

She knew that Geoff and Vince would pamper the kids, comfort them with food, exhaust themselves cheerleading.

It wasn't until Jake took her arm and walked her toward the small bathroom off the sunroom and said, "Let's get you washed up," that she remembered there was blood all over her hands.

"I'll run up and get you a clean top," Carly volunteered, but the sheriffs wouldn't let her up the stairs.

When Tracy heard a siren blare outside, she tried to veer toward the lobby.

"Where are they taking him?"

"They're headed for the hospital in San Luis Obispo."

"But—"

"Let's get you washed up, and then after you talk to the sheriff, we'll drive you straight over there."

Jake handed her over to Carly when they reached the small half bath off the solarium. Carly started the hot water and then pumped hand soap onto her friend's bloody hands. Tracy closed her eyes rather than watch the deeply red-stained water swirl around the bowl and down the drain.

Once she was cleaned up, Jake led her back into the solarium, where the deputies were waiting.

"Some of the guests were supposed to have checked in by now." She glanced around. Real life—bookings, check-ins, room rates, vacancies—seemed light-years away.

"We sent the early arrivals to Selma's, where she's giving them complimentary dinners. I called Kat Chandler, and she's going to come over and sit at the desk until you get back. She'll check the guests in and send them to Selma's. The police said that as long as no one goes upstairs, they'll be allowed to get into their rooms in a couple of hours."

Tracy thought her emotions were under control, but upon hearing of Selma's kindness as well as that of a woman she'd so recently met, her tears started flowing again.

"I don't know how to thank you." She tried to wipe away her tears, but more kept coming.

"Don't even think about it." Carly hugged her, then grabbed a napkin off the buffet in the sunroom and tried to dry Tracy's tears. "Friends don't keep score, remember?"

"Is Mom dead?" Matt was shaking by the time he finally found the courage to ask Chelsea the question that had been haunting him since they'd left the Heartbreak.

He'd seen the sheriff's deputies pull up and run into the house. He'd heard gunshots. Right after that, he'd leaned over and hurled his lunch right there in the gutter beside the security guard's car.

No one told them what was happening when the paramedics rushed inside, not until Carly and Jake drove up a second later. Jake got real mad and showed everyone his P.I. identification and went inside, but Carly told Chelsea to drive him and Chris back to their house. Geoff Wilson and his friend Vincent came driving right behind them. They rushed them all into the house and then started cooking.

Geoff turned on the music video channel and took the remote into the kitchen with him, but not until after Vincent had threatened to drive them around in the car for hours if they dared to turn on the news.

It reminded Matt of the day his dad died. The Montgomerys had picked him up at school and taken him to their house. He'd stayed for dinner, and the whole time, everyone was acting really weird. Finally, by the time it was dark and cold outside, his mom had shown up and she was crying.

That's when she told him his dad was dead.

Now he was back at the Montgomerys' and everything was creepy and almost the same, except that this time Chelsea was with him. But she wasn't talking.

"Chelsea? *Is Mom dead?*" He realized he'd barely whispered before. This time he almost yelled at her.

Chelsea turned away from the TV screen and looked at him. Really looked at him.

"She's just fine. Jake and Carly drove her to San Luis Obispo to see Wade. He's in the hospital there."

"Did he get shot?"

"Yes."

"Is Wade gonna die?"

"I don't know." She shook her head and patted the sofa beside her. "Come here, Mattie."

He walked over to his half sister and let her hug him.

"Chelsea?"

"What?"

"Do you think Wade will die?"

"I hope not."

"Me, too."

She hugged him even tighter than before, and then she cupped his face between her hands and looked him right in the eyes.

"No matter what, you know you'll always have me, don't you?"

He used to think he'd always have his dad, too. Now all he had were some photos and a dumb old journal full of letters instead.

"Something might happen to you. Everybody dies."

"Mattie, Tracy's fine, and I'm fine. We're not going to die anytime soon. I promise."

He wanted to believe her, he really did, but ever since Dad died, he'd been feeling the way he had the year he was in kindergarten and somebody told him there wasn't really any Santa Claus.

He knew that nobody, not Chelsea, not anybody, could promise that they wouldn't die. Nobody.

And just like the truth about Santa Claus, it was something he wished he didn't know.

Two hours later, Jake ushered Tracy through a cluster of media people and into the Sierra Vista Regional Medical Center. Suddenly the weather and bridge closure were old news. The latest up-to-the-minute reports were all about Edward Cain, Franklin Farley, and the drama that had unfolded at the Heartbreak Hotel.

It took ten minutes, Jake pulling out every piece of identification he had on him and having an intense discussion with the deputy stationed at the front door, to get Tracy up to the waiting room near where Wade was still in surgery.

The minute she walked into the waiting area, she was approached by a harried but handsome man, tall, balding, confident, but obviously very shaken.

"Ms. Potter? I'm Bob Schack." He extended his hand. "Wade's literary agent. I recognized you from the news clips." He led her over to a chair.

"How is he?" she asked. Her nerves taut as wire, she perched on the edge of the vinyl chair when both Schack and Jake started encouraging her to sit.

"He's in surgery. The doctor said the bullet went clear through him, which is the good news. They don't know what damage he's sustained though."

"Did he ever regain consciousness?"

The agent shook his head. "Not that I know of."

"What about Farley?"

"The good news is, Wade is a lousy shot and Farley was barely nicked. He's under arrest in the psych ward."

Hating this helpless, useless feeling, she thought of Wade in surgery, visualized the doctor's capable hands on him, healing him, helping him. Short of praying, there was nothing she could do to help Wade. Nothing.

He risked his life to save me.

She clasped her hands together, refusing to break down, refusing to give up hope.

"He wrote that article to help me fill the hotel," she whispered, thinking aloud. Thinking of how he'd unwittingly put himself in danger by having his pen name surface again.

"The Cain pseudonym wasn't supposed to be on it." Schack sighed and rubbed a hand over his bald head.

The air-conditioning was set on arctic. Chilled, Tracy rubbed her arms, got up, and started walking around the small room, giving in to the need to move.

"Isn't there *anything* we can do?"

Bob Schack shook his head, failing miserably at smiling. "All we can do is wait."

By the time the surgeon in green scrubs appeared in the waiting area, Tracy felt like a used pillowcase—crumpled and empty.

He immediately walked over to where she was seated between Jake and Bob Schack. "Are you all here for Wade MacAllister?"

MacAllister? She watched Schack stand.

"We are. How's he doing, Doctor?"

"He's actually awake and out of recovery. You can see him one at a time, but only for a few minutes. His prognosis is great. Much better than I expected when he got here."

As he went on to explain the extent of Wade's injury and the surgery, Tracy tuned him out. She'd heard what she needed to hear. Wade would be fine.

She was as relieved as she was confused.

MacAllister? Wade MacAllister?

"Why don't you go in first," Schack offered.

Before she left to follow a hospital guild volunteer waiting to take her to Wade's room, she looked up at the literary agent. "MacAllister?"

He nodded. "That's right. Wade MacAllister."

"He told me his name was Wade Johnson."

"He used aliases to protect his identity."

She left him to follow a pink-smocked volunteer down the hall. The woman chatted all the way, no doubt hoping to put her at ease, but it wasn't working. She paused on the threshold of the private ICU room, not knowing what to expect.

It certainly wasn't seeing Wade awake and alert. He was lying in a web of tubes and wires, surrounded by monitors. The moment he saw her, he smiled.

Later, she wouldn't remember crossing the room, only that she was suddenly at his side. Carefully, she reached for his hand, and though he didn't say a word at first, he clung to her fingers.

"Oh, Wade," she whispered, fighting not to burst into tears in front of him as she stared into his eyes. "Your eyes are blue." She couldn't believe it. They were as blue as her own.

He blinked. "They must have taken out my contacts."

"What else, Wade? What else don't I know?" She remembered that he was not Wade Johnson, but Wade MacAllister, a.k.a. Edward Cain, grossly successful thriller writer.

She'd had him cleaning paintbrushes and putting together bed frames.

"My hair is really light brown," he confessed.

She sighed. It wouldn't matter if his hair were fluorescent purple. She rubbed her thumb over the back of his hand, content to just watch him breathe.

"Are you in pain?"

"I feel like I have a sizable hole in my shoulder," he confessed. "Can you forgive me for lying to you?"

"You tried to tell me the truth, remember? I wouldn't let you." She smiled, and then added, "How can I be mad at someone I don't even know yet?" Then she shook her head. "Actually, I am feeling a lot of things right now. Grateful, relieved, concerned, confused. But not angry."

When he tried to move and winced, she immediately reached for him but didn't know what to do. "What is it? Do you need the nurse?"

"No. I need you."

She closed her eyes at the stark, horrendous memory of blood pouring out of his shoulder, the close air in the attic, the acrid smell of blood in the air. Over and over, she reminded herself that the doctor had assured her that he would be fine.

She opened her eyes, holding tight to his hand. A chair was wedged into a small space between the bed and the wall. She lowered herself into it.

"I'm so sorry, Tracy. I never wanted anything but good for you." He paused, tried to shift positions, and his pillow slipped sideways. She automatically leaped up to help him, gingerly reached around him, raised him just enough to adjust his pillow. As she drew back, she was so close that his warm breath was caressing her cheek.

"The article worked. The Heartbreak is booked up for the next year," she told him.

His eyelids drifted shut and, thinking him asleep, she tried to slip her hand out of his. His eyes flew open.

"You should get some sleep," she urged.

"Don't leave yet. I want to talk."

"I'll sit right here," she promised.

"The night I checked into the Heartbreak, I had no intention of checking out."

She couldn't tell if he knew what he was saying, for she had no idea.

"What do you mean?" She wondered if he was talking about his writing, about how he knew about Ezra Poole and the ship's logs stored in the attic, if he was finally going to tell her why he'd showed up that night.

"I was going to commit suicide."

She thought she'd heard wrong. "Suicide?"

When he nodded slowly, she added, "In *my* hotel?" Vivid images flashed through her mind. She saw herself walking down the hallway, opening the door, finding his body. Calling 911. The police. The reporters. The room that would always be a reminder.

"How? Why?"

"How? I bought a gun for protection. Why? I was sick of running from myself and from the world. Sick of not having a life. Sick of the guilt I couldn't shake."

"You told me your name was Johnson, not MacAllister. Why?"

"One more level of protection. You didn't ask to see my driver's license. I didn't know if I'd ever talk to you again."

She rubbed his hand, had to know, "Why . . . why didn't you do it that night? Why didn't you kill yourself?"

"The nightmare. The dream. I don't know what it was, but that night

I had the first real sleep that I'd had in months. And I didn't dream about the Even Dozen murders. I dreamed of Ezra, almost as if I was there, re-living it with him. Maybe he wanted to keep me from doing what he'd done, from taking my own life the way he had. I don't know. But for whatever reason, those dreams forced me to write again and kept me alive."

He paused, took a deep breath, and winced.

"Wade, you need to rest. Please." She started to stand again.

"No. Not now. There will be time for sleep later." His gaze locked on hers. There was nothing but heat in his ice blue eyes when he looked into hers. "It might have been the dreams, the writing, that kept me at the hotel at first, but it soon became you, Tracy. Your own attitude toward your situation, your determination, your vulnerability. I stayed because—whether you'd ever admit it or not—you needed help and I needed some-one to help, someone to care about. I decided early on to stay until more guests started checking in and you and your kids weren't alone anymore."

"So you left me with Henri?" Though she was smiling, his simple ad-mission had moved her more deeply than anything else he might have said.

"I left to save you from the very thing that ended up happening."

"I know. How well I know that now." She rose out of the chair, unwill-ing, unable to keep from kissing him. Aware of the IV line, of his ban-dage, she leaned over him, touched her lips to his. She kissed him lightly.

His eyes drifted closed again. This time he struggled to open them.

"I'm going to let you sleep," she said softly. "I need to see Matt, to let him know we're all right."

He mumbled, "As much as I hate for you to leave, I know he needs you, too. Will you send Schack in before I'm out for the count?"

He was right. She hated the thought of leaving him, but she couldn't wait to see Matt, too. To assure him that she was fine, that Wade was going to be all right. She kissed him again, quickly, carefully.

"Do you have family you want me to call?"

"No. No one."

The simple admission broke her heart.

"I'll send in your agent," she promised.

"How will you get back?"

"Jake is here." She turned away again, reaching for the door.

"Tracy?"

She turned, barely hearing him when he said, "Come back soon?"

She would forever remember him bursting into the attic to save her.

"I'll be here in the morning when you wake up," she promised. When she found the courage to whisper, "I love you," she saw that he was already sound asleep.

CHAPTER FORTY-EIGHT

The next morning, Wade opened his eyes and, just as she'd promised, Tracy was there, making his heart beat faster, making the whole world brighter.

"Hi," she said softly, instantly on her feet, taking his hand, touching his cheek. "I thought you'd never wake up."

It hurt to swallow, but he managed.

"Hi." His voice sounded hoarse and his shoulder hurt like hell, but her smile was the only drug he needed to make the pain go away.

"How are you feeling?"

"I've been better. More important, how do I look?"

She laughed. "You want the truth?"

"That bad, huh?"

"That bad."

To dispel her worry, he reached up and touched his hair, which was flattened against his head.

"I really need some gel. And contacts. Would that help?"

Her smile faded. "No more hiding, Wade. Not from me, anyway."

Her words, softly spoken but with her meaning perfectly clear, left him no room for argument.

"No more hiding. Bob and I spoke last night. I want him to fly me down to L.A. as soon as I'm released." He saw the disappointment on her face, the worry, but he wasn't going to lie to her anymore. He watched her gaze sweep the room and then rest on the monitor, which was beeping with a steady even rhythm.

She hesitated before asking, "Do you know how soon that will be?"

"Tomorrow, probably." He could see everything she wasn't saying in her eyes. "As soon as I'm able, I'll start giving interviews. Hopefully, if I give the press and the public what they want, sooner or later they'll get bored with me and leave me alone. It'll be easier to accomplish that in L.A."

"Are you sure that's what you want?"

He nodded. Catnapping off and on, lying alone in the dark last night, listening to the sound of his heartbeat echoing in the monitor, he'd had nothing but time to think about what he wanted. For now, for the future.

"I'm sure. I've had time to do some thinking, too. If I go home with Schack, it'll draw the media away from here."

A shadow crossed her face, but it was fleeting. "You think I can be intimidated by a few more sound crews and news vans? I'm getting used to it."

He wished he could joke about it, too, but the memory of hearing Farley telling her to shut up yesterday, hearing him threaten to kill her, was still fresh in his mind.

"You've seen the dark side now, Tracy. You've seen what can happen."

Her smile slowly faded, but her hand tightened around his. "We made it through together, remember?"

"I don't want any of you in danger."

"I noticed there is still a security guard outside the hotel. This morning I spoke to him, and he said he was hired by the Schack Literary Agency."

"Something Bob Schack knew I'd want. There will be a guard there as long as it takes," he assured her. "I love you, Tracy. You know that, don't you?" He watched her carefully, willing her to understand. He couldn't take a chance with her life again. Couldn't put her and her family in harm's way. "I love you and I know you love me, too, or you wouldn't be here right now. If you *didn't* love me, you'd have never forgiven me for not telling you everything in the first place."

"I know," she whispered. "Just as I know I'll never forget that you almost died for me yesterday."

"Help me believe that I can work this out, that there will be a time when the worst of this will all be behind me and I can come back to you."

There was a wistful sadness in her eyes. "Do you really think that there's a right time, a perfect time for anything? We can't plan our lives that easily. Things happen, Wade. Things we don't expect to happen that suddenly do—things like birth and death and—"

"Falling in love?" he asked.

"And falling in love," she whispered. "I don't want you to leave."

"I don't *want* to leave you again, but if I can do anything to make all this go away—and sooner rather than later—then that's what I have to do. And I need to believe that you understand, that you'll wait until I work this out. I need to believe in your love more than I've ever believed in anything in my life."

Trust him, her heart whispered.

Trust in your love for this man.

Tracy forced herself to smile down into unfamiliar blue eyes and fought a wave of anxiety. Letting him go again would be one of the single hardest things she'd ever do. She knew that Bob Schack would see that he was being well cared for, protected—but he would be in the spotlight and, after what had just happened, she feared for him.

"Tracy?" He pulled her close, slipped his fingers into her hair, kissed her lips. "Hopefully it won't be long. I'll call you every day."

When she drew back, she saw his determination. Just like before, he was doing what he thought was best for all of them. He was leaving.

Tears stung her eyes, blurred her vision, but she refused to cry in front of him. She silenced the nagging voice inside her that reminded her that she'd trusted once before, that she'd loved before. But this time things were different. This time she was walking into love with a heart that was a little battered, but wiser for it.

"Come here," he whispered, tugging her hand. She got up, leaned against the chrome bed rail, and was about to kiss him when the door opened and an Asian American nurse came breezing in carrying his chart. Her short, straight hair was bright fluorescent purple. She wore a smile from ear to ear.

"Nurse Robin!" Wade's face lit up just looking at her. Tracy couldn't stop staring at her hair.

He lifted a brow suggestively. "She's promised to give me a dye job."

"Not until you get me an autographed copy of your book," the nurse shot back.

Tracy saw that it was a struggle, but Wade finally laughed again. "Only if you can get me outta here in record time."

"Are you kidding? We need the room already." Then the nurse turned to Tracy. "Your daughter's waiting for you in the hall," she said matter-of-factly.

Tracy's heart rate spiked.

"What's wrong?" Wade looked as concerned as Tracy felt.

"I have no idea. She's supposed to be home with Matt."

He wouldn't let go of her hand until she promised to come back and tell him what was going on. In the hall she found Chelsea with her arms folded and her forehead creased with deep concern.

"Where's Matt?" Tracy could barely get the words out.

"He's at the Heartbreak. I called Vincent and he came right over. Everything's fine at the hotel."

"But *something's* wrong."

"You had an emergency phone call. I tried to call your cell phone—"

"They aren't allowed on up here," Tracy explained.

"I thought I should tell you myself, anyway." Chelsea took a deep breath. "A woman called about your friend, Willa. A hospice worker. She said Willa is asking for you."

Willa's home was surrounded by sycamore trees in an exclusive neighborhood dubbed the American Riviera, where parcels were at least an acre and homes cost in the millions.

Bone-tired and dreading what she was about to do, Tracy rang the doorbell and took a deep breath. Within seconds a woman with big, soulful eyes and long brown hair greeted her at the door.

"I'm Theresa Bonaducci, Willa's neighbor," the woman said. Tracy introduced herself and Theresa said, "I'll take you back to Willa's room."

Theresa led her through the beautifully appointed house fit for an *Ar-*

chitectural Digest spread. Custom furnishings of exotic woods, slate and hardwood floors, and high wood-beam ceilings all worked together to make what was once a simple, one-story, California ranch–style house a lovely home.

Willa's room was decorated in calm, cool colors—peaceful shades of the sea and sky. Soft classical music filled the air. Another woman, who introduced herself as the hospice worker, welcomed Tracy and stepped out so that they could be alone.

Shocked when she realized that the person lying in bed was actually Willa and that she was watching her from across the room, Tracy said the first thing that came to mind.

"It's nice here."

"A nice place to die."

"Oh, Willa."

The longest walk Tracy had ever had to make was across the pale celery–colored carpet to Willa's bedside. Once more she found herself sitting beside a hospital bed, but in this room there was no relief, no hope for another, brighter tomorrow. She stared at the hollow shell of what was left of Willa. The woman's hair had thinned to next to nothing. Her skin was the color of ash.

Guilt nearly swallowed Tracy whole. She'd avoided making any decision about Mary Jane, but—even consumed by her own drama, in Wade, in running the hotel—she'd never forgotten Willa's request.

She had almost waited too long to answer.

As if Willa could read her mind, she said, "I don't have long, they say." Her smile was a grotesque parody of itself, her speech halting whenever she paused to take a ragged breath. "I feel like . . . I'm already a hundred years old. I'm not even sure what day it is."

She paused again as if each word, each sentence, was an effort.

"Theresa saw the story about the . . . intruder on the news yesterday." Willa seemed too weak to go on, but asked for details.

Tracy told her in as few words as possible about Wade's identity, how Farley had held her hostage, and how there were still reporters outside the Heartbreak.

"So, you see," she ended on a sigh and added, "so you see, there's no way I would feel right exposing your daughter to that kind of—"

Willa interrupted, saying something Tracy couldn't quite hear.

"I'm sorry." She leaned closer. "What did you say?"

"Is . . . Matt . . . there? At the hotel?"

Tracy nodded. "Matt and Chelsea both."

"I want Mary Jane to be with them."

Tracy's heart sank. "Willa—"

"It's up to you," Willa added.

Tracy closed her eyes against the pain of seeing her former friend like this, tried not to think about Willa's daughter growing up without her mother, tried not to think of how and why all their lives had changed irrevocably because of the affair.

Her gaze strayed to a framed photograph on the table beside Willa's bed. Surrounded by pill bottles, a plastic water carafe, a plastic cup with a flex-straw, a box of tissues, the vibrant face of a lovely little redheaded girl was smiling back at her. Thankfully there were no photos of Glenn, or of the three of them together.

"That's her," Willa rasped. "That's Mary Jane."

Despite everything, Tracy's heart, a mother's heart, truly ached for the woman.

"Where is she now?" *Who is caring for her? Is she with strangers, or somewhere here in the house?*

"It's her nap time. Theresa's been Mary Jane's sitter since she was born."

"Have you made arrangements for her care? Since you didn't hear from me . . ." She had to look away and found herself wondering if perhaps Theresa was close enough to want to adopt Mary Jane.

"My lawyer . . . found a young couple who wants to adopt her."

The notion should have freed Tracy, but with stunning clarity she realized that the idea of a nameless, faceless couple waiting to adopt the child in the photo bothered her more than she could have imagined.

"I had the lawyer . . . draw up two sets of adoption papers. I told the couple to not get their hearts set on the adoption." Willa struggled to swallow.

When Willa started coughing, Tracy automatically reached for the carafe, filled the plastic tumbler, and shifted the flex-straw so that Willa could take a sip.

By the time Tracy set the tumbler back on the table, she was shaking like a leaf. She'd been more composed in the attic with Farley than she was now—seeing Willa like this—knowing that the woman she'd befriended so long ago was facing life's unavoidable, ultimate test. In that split second, as she watched Willa wince and struggle to swallow, Tracy knew that, right or wrong, there was only one choice she could live with.

Careful to not disturb Willa, she lowered herself to the edge of the bed, closed her eyes, and forced herself to forget everything else and remember the day they'd first met. Tall and gangly at thirteen, Willa had definitely been an ugly duckling, but she'd been blessed with hair the color of iridescent black satin and flawless alabaster skin. Both would help her create an image that was unforgettable.

"Tracy?"

She glanced down. Willa's eyes were closed, her breathing ragged.

"I'm here," she said.

"I'm afraid." A tear leaked out of the corner of Willa's eye and slid down her temple.

Tracy had to swallow a lump in her throat before she could speak. "I am, too."

There was only one way she could help Willa find peace, only one thing she could do.

"I'll raise Mary Jane for you," she promised.

"Are you sure?" Willa's eyes fluttered open.

Am I sure? She was sure of only two things right now—her love for Wade, and the fact that she wouldn't be able to live with herself if she didn't agree to adopt Matt and Chelsea's half sister.

"She'll become part of our home and our lives, as dear to me as Matthew. As special to me as Chelsea."

"What will you tell her about me?" Willa whispered.

"What do you want me to tell her?"

"That once, we were best friends."

Tracy nodded, fighting tears. "I'll tell her. I promise."

"Thank you," Willa whispered. "I thank you with all my heart. Someday, when she understands what you've done for us, Mary Jane will thank you, too."

When the hospice worker came back and told Tracy that it was time for Willa's pain medication, she left the room, shaken, but determined to live up to her promise to raise Mary Jane as her own.

It hit her that explaining Mary Jane to Matt wouldn't be as hard as telling Chelsea. Chelsea was old enough to take one look at Mary Jane and, if not immediately put two and two together, ask questions. Facing another truth about her father would be a second tremendous blow.

In the living room, Theresa smiled warmly, but it was obvious she'd been crying.

"I still can't believe it." She shook her head and sighed. "I prayed for a miracle." She pulled a handkerchief out of her pocket and mopped her eyes. "It's almost time for Mary Jane to wake up from her nap. Would you like to see her?"

Mentally exhausted, Tracy nodded.

"Can I get you a cup of tea?" Theresa offered. "You look like you could use one."

What she could use was a good, strong drink.

"Herbal, if you have some." She had a long drive home ahead of her. The last thing she needed was liquor or caffeine. She was too tired for alcohol, and the stimulant would only add to her anxiety.

"Are you . . . will you be adopting Mary Jane? I know how much Willa was hoping you would."

Tracy wondered exactly how much Theresa knew and decided that she was too tired to care at this point. What Theresa obviously knew was that Willa had chosen her to raise the child, so that's what she talked about.

"I'm hoping you can help me make this a smooth transition for her," she said.

Together they decided that it would be best if Tracy brought Matt and Chelsea down to meet Mary Jane here. Tracy hoped that she could make more than a few visits over the next days or weeks, just so the child could grow comfortable with her.

By the time she'd had two cups of hibiscus tea and a long chat with Theresa, they had worked out an arrangement.

Am I really doing this? Am I bringing this child into my life? Into all our lives?

She knew that what she was doing was bound to affect her and Wade's future, but there was no way to predict how until she could talk to him.

Theresa walked her back down the hall, past the closed door to Willa's room. This time Tracy was ushered into a nursery right out of the pages of a fairy tale. She found herself immersed in a world of sensory memory, of baby powder and lotion, plush toys, the melody of a wind-up mobile. Diapers, pairs of tiny socks, of soft flannel and sunshine-fresh cotton.

Across the room, Mary Jane was awake in her crib, her eyes still puffy from sleep. When Tracy and Theresa walked in, the child pulled herself up and stood at the crib rail in a buttercup yellow sundress. Her plump bare legs and feet were pumping up and down.

"Ma?" She tried to look past Theresa as the sitter walked over to the crib.

Theresa's eyes filled with tears, and Tracy had a hard time holding on when Theresa rubbed Mary Jane's back and said softly, "No, honey, Mommy's sleeping right now."

She lifted Mary Jane out of the crib and held her high on her hip as she turned to Tracy.

"Say hi to Tracy, honey. This is Mommy's friend."

Mommy's friend.

Mary Jane silently took her in with huge, innocent blue eyes. Slowly, a trusting smile bloomed across features reminiscent of both Matt and Chelsea, and yet distinctly her own. Then she opened her arms wide, giggled, and strained toward Tracy, begging, without words, to be held.

Automatically Tracy reached for the little girl without thought or hesitation. Theresa handed her over, and when Tracy enfolded Mary Jane in her arms, all traces of doubt dissolved. She knew, deep down in her soul, that no matter what happened after today, she'd made the right choice.

Later, after Willa had fallen asleep, Tracy left the house and drove north with the radio blasting. Tears streaming, she forced herself to sing every oldie at the top of her lungs. By the time she reached San Luis Obispo, she had stopped crying and entered the state of euphoria that always hit her when she went beyond tired. She felt as if she'd crossed over some invisible threshold and was running on warp speed. Her mind was fooling her body into thinking she would never need sleep again.

After calling Chelsea to check in and hearing that she and Vincent had everything under control, she decided that for once she'd *buy* baked goods for the guests so that she could spend time visiting Wade before she headed down the canyon to the Heartbreak.

Once she reached the hospital, she had to talk her way around the nurse with the purple hair before finally walking into Wade's room with a new, determined spring in her step.

CHAPTER FORTY-NINE

Wade was channel-surfing when she walked in. Clicking the remote off, he set it aside and watched her cross the room.

"You're glowing," he said, amazed. "Should I worry? I didn't expect to see you until tomorrow."

"I couldn't go back to the hotel without stopping by."

"I'm glad. How did it go?"

"The best and the worst. Willa's dying." There was no satisfaction in her voice, only sorrow.

"And Mary Jane?"

"She's coming to live with us." She seemed to be waiting for a reaction, as if her adding another child to her home would faze him, as if she was worried that he might think twice about having a relationship with a woman with not one but two kids at home and a part-time daughter in college.

"I knew you'd take her." He smiled to let her know it was all right.

"I didn't. In fact, I tried to turn her down."

"And yet you didn't. Are you all right with it now?"

"Actually, I feel great. I'm not looking forward to telling Chelsea, but I can't put it off. There's no way to know how long Willa has." Her smile dimmed. "The hospice worker said it could be two weeks, or it could be days. I may be picking up Mary Jane before I know it."

"I wish you could get away, maybe come stay with me in L.A. for a while. Bob could hide us someplace for a week or so, until I'm really up and around. Whenever you needed to, you could come back and move Mary Jane into the Heartbreak." He could see that she was tempted, but she slowly shook her head and then sat down on the edge of the bed.

"It sounds like heaven," she said softly, "but I've got a hotel to run and a life I can't just walk away from anymore." She paused, traced the back of his hand with her fingertips, and then looked into his eyes. "I've been thinking about your going back to L.A. I thought about it all the way back up here. I've decided you're coming home with me when they release you. I want you to stay at the Heartbreak. I've already called Matt and Chelsea and they both agree. Matt volunteered to sleep in Chelsea's room on a futon until she goes back to school. You can have his room."

"You're coming home with me."

The idea that she still loved him after everything that had happened, that she wanted him back in her home after what he'd done to her life already, still astounded him.

"I can't ask you to do that, Tracy."

"You didn't ask. Come home with me. Let me take care of you. Let *us* take care of you."

"I can't let you do this," he insisted.

"Why? Because you'd rather have Bob hire some fake-breasted tall blond nurse in L.A. to take care of you?"

At that, he couldn't keep from laughing. "Yeah, that's it. You got me." He sobered when he realized how intent she looked.

"I'm doing this for purely selfish reasons, Wade. I don't want to let you go."

What she was offering was a life the likes of which he'd only briefly glimpsed during his stay at the Heartbreak. He tried to imagine himself settled in Matt's room, surrounded by LEGOs, Transformers, Hot Wheels, and plastic action figures. Tried to picture himself living in the heart of a family of more than two—something he'd never experienced in his life.

He knew what it was to be a loner, but not what it meant to be part of a real family that had just added one more. For as long as he could remember, he had lived his life in self-imposed isolation, immersed in his work.

A writer writes. A writer needs solitude. It was his mantra.

But he wasn't a writer anymore. The problem was, he didn't know what he was.

She was staring back at him, waiting for a decision, looking at him as if he truly were a hero, as if he had all the answers. He didn't know if he could live up to her expectations, no matter how small. Nor did he for one minute believe that his troubles were behind him.

"As you just said, you've got a hotel to run and a family to care for."

"You don't think I can take care of you, too?"

"I *know* you can take care of me." He lifted the back of her hand to his lips, pleased when she blushed at his kiss.

"Then let me."

"Tracy—"

"You left before, Wade. You walked out of my life because you didn't want to bring the media down on us, and look what happened."

"I'm sorry, you know that."

"I don't want you to be sorry. I want you to stop running. I want you to stay here. No matter what happens, we can survive it. There's no need for you to run anymore. Whatever happens, we can survive it together. The least we can do is try."

"Are you sure?" He didn't want to leave any more than she wanted him to.

"Willa asked me that same thing earlier and, you know what? I realized that one of the only things I was sure of was my love for you. I think we both deserve some happiness right about now, don't you? Give this a chance. See what happens."

"See if I pass the test, you mean?" He pictured himself riding down the coast road on the Harley someday soon, finally giving Matt that ride he'd been begging for.

"See if Matt, Chelsea, Mary Jane, and I pass. What do you think?"

"I think I'd better call Schack and have him cancel the jet."

The next day Tracy and Chelsea were having breakfast together at the narrow bar that separated the kitchen from the living room. Each morning they went over the reservation schedule for the day, talked about which guests were checking out and which rooms had to be prepped for new arrivals.

"So, is Wade going to be staying here or going back to L.A.?" Chelsea picked up a bear-shaped plastic container and started squeezing honey onto a piece of toast smothered in peanut butter.

"It was a hard sell, but I finally changed his mind." Tracy picked up the honey when Chelsea finished and dribbled some into her hot coffee. "We'll have the media to deal with again, but hopefully not for too long."

Chelsea smiled. "It won't be forever. Besides, we're getting pretty good at handling them, don't you think?"

"I think we are." Tracy would never have guessed that the trials they'd faced over the previous few weeks would have brought them closer, but they had. She just hoped that what she was about to say wouldn't jeopardize the new bond between them. She was finally having the kind of relationship she had always wanted to have with Chelsea—the kind she'd always hoped for.

"What a shock about your friend, Willa." Chelsea reached for more orange juice and poured herself another glass. "Did you know she was sick?"

Fate had just handed Tracy the perfect opening, and she knew she'd better take it.

"Not until recently." *There were a lot of things I didn't know until recently.* "Yesterday, when I went to see Willa, I made a decision that concerns all of us, but it was mine to make. I hope you'll understand."

Chelsea lowered the toast without taking a bite. "This sounds serious."

"It is." Tracy dived in headfirst. "It's about your father and Willa." She lowered her hands to her lap, clasped her fingers together.

"They worked together sometimes," Chelsea remembered aloud. "Didn't Willa decorate the Canyon Club models? I haven't seen her in years."

"She was—" Tracy's throat closed. She took a deep breath and blurted, "She was his mistress."

"Willa?" Chelsea's brow scrunched. "And my *dad*? Wasn't she an old friend of yours?"

Slowly, Tracy nodded. "Yes, she was."

Chelsea's eyes grew huge. "Is that . . . is she the one *David* was talking about when he said Dad was a player?"

Tracy had to clear her throat. "Yes." She took a quick sip of her own juice and let Chelsea mull over what she'd just said before she hit her with the second round.

"You didn't know?" Chelsea asked.

Tracy shook her head. "Not until the night of the open house."

"It really wasn't about the invitations. *That's* why you were so upset."

Another nod. "Yes."

"Did she beg for your forgiveness from her deathbed? My God, Tracy. I can't believe you went!"

"That's not why I went. I drove down there because Willa and your dad had a child together—a little girl. Willa asked me to adopt her."

"A little girl?" Chelsea paled. Her breakfast sat ignored, the toast going cold as melted peanut butter dripped over the crust and pooled on her plate. *"Dad?"*

"Yes. And Willa."

Chelsea opened her mouth to say something, closed it again, and slowly shook her head. "I can't believe it," she whispered. "Are you sure?"

"Yes. Her name is Mary Jane, she's almost two, and she looks a lot like both you and Matt."

"Do you have a picture of her?"

"I should have asked for one, but I didn't." She wondered if Jake still had the file of photographs, but decided it would be too painful to ask him, to see those photos again. If she'd only asked Willa for one, then she remembered. "I was hoping that you would go with me this week, down to Montecito, to meet her."

"Are you . . . I can't believe it. Are you actually thinking about adopting her?" She covered her lips with her fingertips. Her eyes searched Tracy's.

"Yes. Yes I am."

"How can you even stand to look at her and not think of what Dad did to you?"

"I wondered that myself, believe me, but Mary Jane is the innocent one in all of this. She's just a baby, Chelsea. And indirectly, she's part of you, and part of Matt. She's not to blame."

"She's my half sister."

"That's right."

"Just like Mattie."

"Just like Matt." Tracy slid her empty plate back and traced the edge of her place mat with her fingernail. "Willa found a couple who is willing to adopt her . . ."

It wasn't too late to tell Willa that she'd changed her mind—but this wasn't about Willa or Glenn or even what Chelsea wanted anymore. This was about Mary Jane, about a two-year-old who had a half brother and sister who stood to gain as much as they would give by having her in their lives.

In the stillness that fell on the room, as the second hand ticked quietly on the fat-faced clock above the sink, Tracy waited for Chelsea to digest everything she'd just said.

"This couple," Chelsea leaned back on the bar stool, still frowning fiercely. "Who are they? Does Willa know them? Is she related to them?"

"No. Her lawyer found them. She doesn't have any relatives." It was the one thing they'd had in common growing up. Tracy was raised by her grandparents, Willa by a maiden aunt. If anyone knew what it was to want for family, it was Willa.

"Well," Chelsea stared down at her toast a few more seconds before her gaze drifted back over to Tracy, "we have to take her, don't we? I mean, she is my half sister."

"I'm so glad you agree—because I already promised Willa that we'd take her." The second half of the hundred-pound weight that Tracy had driven home under yesterday suddenly lifted, and she felt like crying with relief.

"What about Mattie? What will you tell him?"

"For now, just that Mary Jane is my friend Willa's daughter, and that Willa died and wanted us to adopt her."

Chelsea nodded in agreement. "He'll be excited, I think."

"I hope so."

Chelsea grew thoughtful again. "When do we get to have her?"

"It could be a week, maybe a little more, or it could be today. There's no way of knowing." Tracy couldn't help but think of Willa.

"There are only a few weeks left before I have to be back at school. Maybe I should move to Monica's until then since Wade is moving in, and now Mary Jane, too."

"I've been thinking about contacting one of the parties due in today to see if I can't work something out with them."

"Like what?"

"Like getting them booked into Rose Cottage in Twilight instead, and offering them a free booking next summer." She noticed Chelsea's hesitation. "Unless you *want* to move to Monica's."

"No, I don't want to go, but—what if the guests refuse to take you up on your offer?"

"Dealing with a couple of irate, disappointed guests is nothing after what I've been through this week. We'll manage. Just remember that I want you here as long and as often as you want to be here, Chelsea. This is your home, too."

"Thanks, Tracy."

"I love you, honey. I know you're going to love Mary Jane the minute you see her."

Just then Matt came strolling in, tripping over the hems of his sagging pajama bottoms, the oversized T-shirt he'd slept in hanging past his knees.

"Who's Mary Jane?" He rubbed his eyes, walked over, and started eating Chelsea's peanut butter and honey toast. It dribbled down the front of his shirt, but he didn't seem to care.

Tracy and Chelsea exchanged a glance.

"Hop up here." Chelsea indicated the empty bar stool beside her with a pat. "Tracy's got a really *big* surprise for you."

When they moved him back into his room downstairs at the Heartbreak, Wade felt more at home than he ever had in his upscale apartment in Manhattan.

Sitting up in bed on his fourth night back, he was content to watch the curtains billow in on the breeze and listen to the sound of the rolling surf. His shoulder was stiff and painful beneath his bandage, but he was diligently working on the exercises the therapist had assigned him. The therapist was due to stop by in the morning to check on his progress.

There had been a media mob in front of the hospital the afternoon he was released, but he and Bob had put their heads together to come up with a plan that had his agent as excited as a kid in a candy store. Schack held a formal press conference, promising that after a month of recovery and intensive physical therapy, Wade MacAllister, a.k.a. Edward Cain, would be available for interviews. Until then, Mr. MacAllister was going to be resting up in seclusion at a private home in Malibu—which Bob just happened to own.

Then, with much fanfare, "Wade"—or rather, an out-of-work actor from Pismo Beach posing as Wade—was swiftly wheeled out of the hospital covered by a lap robe and wearing a baseball cap, huge dark glasses, and a turtleneck pulled up to his lips.

He was filmed boarding a private jet at the airport and, again, disembarking at Van Nuys. Schack's Malibu house, the "undisclosed location," was covered night and day. Paparazzi had ample opportunities to get shots of "Wade" whenever he would occasionally dart past a window or quickly step out onto the sundeck for a second before ducking back inside the house.

In the meantime, the real Wade had slipped out the back door of the hospital in scrubs provided by Nurse Robin, who, it seemed, was completely shameless as long as she could get her hands on autographed copies of his books. It didn't matter which books, just so long as his signature was in them.

Bob immediately started booking interviews, and the last time he called to check in, Oprah and Barbara Walters were butting heads over who would have the first on-air time with Wade.

Meanwhile, the real Wade was in his room at the Heartbreak, a room he no longer shared with a ghost. Someone was constantly at his side making sure he wasn't bored, hungry, or lonely. In the past few days he'd played more hands of Uno with Matt than he cared to recall, and, much to Matt's chagrin, he was becoming an expert at Game Boy.

He was also adept at going over the USC class catalog and fall schedule with Chelsea. She confessed that she was tempted to major in journalism, that was until he told her that writers like Lauren Westin made hardly any money—their publishers kept it in reserve as payment for their sources.

Whenever Tracy could spare a few minutes, she'd been right there beside him, fluffing his pillows, asking if he was doing his shoulder exercises, plying him with food. She brought him every meal, ate with him, tempted him just by being in the same room. His first day back, he'd playfully asked if she'd sneak down and spend the night with him. She laughed and thought he was kidding.

She didn't seem to realize that even though he'd been shot in the shoulder, his penis still had a mind of its own.

According to his watch, it was 8:30 already, and she still hadn't come down to say good night. Last night they had sat out on the porch, listened to the waves, and talked for hours.

By 9:00 he was antsy and missing her, so he got up, tested his strength, and left his room for the first time in three days.

There was an intrinsic, peaceful stillness about the hotel. Even with every room filled, there was still a settled kind of quiet that was missing in most places these days. There were no distractions, no cars constantly humming along the road out front, no streetlights. Here, the night sky wasn't faded to gray by city lights. The stars looked close enough to touch.

The hotel seemed to glow with its own warmth, pulse with the beat of its own heart.

Passing through the lobby, he half expected to see Tracy at the reception desk and was disappointed when she wasn't there. Two couples were in the sitting area sipping wine and chatting amiably as he walked by. No one paid any attention to him other than to nod.

Everyone knew that Wade MacAllister was in Malibu recuperating.

Memories assailed him as he climbed the stairs. The aroma of cinnamon and spices lingered. Aged wood and the accumulation of years added to the homey atmosphere. As he started up to the apartment, he noted that the stairs still creaked. The wallpaper in the stairwell was faded almost beyond description, but it seemed right somehow, that aside from adding a new coat of paint and a bucketful of hope to the place, Tracy had hardly changed a thing.

At the top of the landing he had to stop and catch his breath, and hoped he hadn't popped anything under his bandages. He figured he could have walked right into the apartment, but it was a familiarity he hadn't yet acquired, so he knocked and waited.

It wasn't Tracy, but Chelsea, who answered.

"Wade! Are you all right?"

"Is Tracy around?"

She gently took his arm and led him in as if he were a centenarian out on the loose alone.

"She's up on the widow's walk. Sit down and I'll run up and get her." She tried to steer him over to the sofa.

He motioned toward the hall. "I want to surprise her."

"Do you need help?"

"Not with what I've got planned."

She blushed to the roots of her hair. "Oh, Wade."

"I'm just kidding. Besides, I can barely stand." Not exactly a lie. The climb up one flight already had him feeling weak as a kitten.

She wouldn't let go of his arm until he told her he was only kidding again.

Down the hall, the light was on in Matt's room, the door open a foot or two. Inside, Matt was propped up against his pillow, writing in his journal. He must have sensed that someone was watching, for he looked up, and when he recognized Wade, he tossed the journal aside.

"Come on in!" He pulled himself up straighter in bed.

Wade quickly held his finger up to his lips and walked into the room.

Matt whispered, "What are you doing up here? Are you better already?"

"I'm getting there. I came up to surprise your mom."

Suddenly Matt was grinning from ear to ear. "She's up on the roof."

"I know."

The boy shrugged. "So are you gonna go up and try some kissie, smoochie stuff on her?"

"You think I should?"

"Women kinda like it. That's what Christopher told me." He lowered his voice and glanced toward the door. "Chelsea does. She's always out in the driveway smooching with Eric when she thinks nobody is watching."

"Maybe I'll give it a try." He noticed the journal. "That's not Spider-Man anymore, I see."

Matt looked proud. "Naw. I filled that one up already. I'm gonna be a famous writer. Like you."

When Matt beamed up at him, Wade's confidence stumbled. He'd certainly never had published anything worthy of a child's praise.

"Go on up and surprise Mom, then come back and tell me what happened, okay?"

"It's pretty late. I think you'll have to wait until tomorrow to find out."

Thoroughly disappointed, Matt sighed, but he didn't argue.

"Will you please turn out the light for me?"

"Sure." Wade stepped close to the bed and Matt handed him the journal. Setting it carefully on the nightstand, Wade turned out the light.

"Mom leaves the door open a crack."

"Okay. Night, Sport." Wade stepped out into the hall and made certain he left the door open a crack behind him.

CHAPTER FIFTY

Clear, warm nights were Tracy's favorite times on the widow's walk, yet there had been very few of those this summer. She'd splurged on two matching teak deck chairs, figuring she owed it to herself now that the hotel was constantly booked. Besides, she would have another windfall as soon as she sold her wedding ring.

Dressed in comfortable lightweight sweats, she stretched out on the deck chair and stared up into the night sky, content to watch the stars and listen to the song of the sea for a few minutes before she went down to tell Wade good night.

She liked to imagine that Ezra's Violette might have come up here at night, too, watching the same stars and constellations, listening to the waves' soothing, monotonous tune as they rolled in over the rocks, the sound soothing her as she waited for Ezra to return.

A moment ago she'd been thinking of Wade. She couldn't help but smile as she remembered the junk-food wrappers in his wastebasket. Twinkies and Cheetos. And tequila bottles. Not exactly brain food. After all that alcohol, sugar, and those preservatives, it was no wonder he thought he'd heard Ezra's ghost.

She took a deep breath and closed her eyes—just for a minute.

The next thing she knew, someone was calling her name. She imagined it was Wade, that he was right there, beside her—so close that she could hear the sound of his voice over the waves. Slowly she opened her eyes and realized she must have drifted off to sleep.

"Tracy?"

She quickly sat up and there he was, kneeling beside her deck chair, staring into her eyes, as if he were trying to look into her very soul. It was a shock seeing him there, where she hadn't expected him to be.

"How did you get up here? Are you all right?" She reached out, cupped his jaw with her palm. His skin was clean-shaven and, looking at him now, she tried to picture him as he had appeared in his Edward Cain headshots. So sober. So cool and distant. It seemed impossible.

"I'm fine. I was downstairs all alone, missing you."

Glancing down at her watch, she realized that, somewhere, she'd lost a good twenty minutes. "I either fell asleep just now or," she looked up at the star-spattered sky, ". . . I was abducted by aliens. There's close to twenty minutes unaccounted for," she teased.

"I hear they can't possibly do all that testing and get you back to earth in less than forty-five. You must have just dozed off."

When she stopped laughing, she wanted to know, "So, you really missed me?"

She watched his hair move with the wind off the water, tempted to run her fingers through it. She didn't know this version of him with his light brown hair growing out beneath the darker hue, and sky blue eyes that seemed to see right into her heart—but he did look very, very good. Better than good, he looked delicious.

"Like crazy. I was forced to crawl out of my sickbed and come looking for you."

"I'm glad you did, but I hope you didn't wear yourself out." Whatever else she was going to say was swallowed by his kiss. She let the taste of his lips, the touch of his hands, sweep her away from everything, infuse her with the warmth and energy she needed tonight.

"That's the least of my problems tonight. You seem tired, though." He smoothed her hair back behind her ear.

"I'm not really tired, just running in too many directions at once. If you'll be all right alone, I thought I'd see if Vince can come in while I drive the kids down to Santa Barbara tomorrow to meet Mary Jane. The sitter called and said that Willa's much worse."

"I'll be fine. Don't worry about me. I wish I could go with you."

"It's a long ride and, besides, you're supposed to be hiding out. Earlier I found myself thinking about everything I have to do and wishing we all had more time. Time for Mary Jane to get acquainted with us before we bring her home. More time before Chelsea goes back to USC, because I'm really going to miss her this year." She got to her feet, took his hand, and walked with him to the railing. She wrapped her arm around his waist and lay her head against his good shoulder. "I wish there was time for just the two of us."

"We'll have plenty of time, Tracy."

"You think so?" She knew better than to count on it now. No matter how positive she tried to be, no matter how much she looked forward to the future, life had taught her some hard lessons over the past few months—lessons she wasn't going to forget anytime soon.

"I sure hope so," he whispered.

She closed her eyes and leaned into his embrace. "Whenever I come up here, I can't help but think about Ezra and Violette as I look out to sea or watch the gulls fly over the bluff. Do you think they're together now?"

"Ezra and Violette?" He smiled into her eyes. "I know they are."

"Did he tell you so?" The darkness hid her smile.

"He didn't have to. I could tell when I walked into my room again. There's a new lightness there. Ezra's definitely gone. Where else would he be, if not with Violette?"

His arm was hanging over her shoulder. She touched the back of his hand with her index finger, stroked it lightly, tenderly. Over the past few days they'd talked of many things, of Chelsea's coming school year, of Farley, the Even Dozen, the trials. She'd let him talk, sensing that he hadn't ever opened up to anyone else.

They'd talked of everything but their future. Though she hungered for him night and day, right now it was enough to have him near. They hadn't actually spoken of love again since that day in the hospital.

So she was completely caught off guard when he said, "I've never been in love before, you know. Not like this. Not with anyone. I never knew much happiness, Tracy. Not as a child, not as an adult. Sometimes I think I would have made a great poet. I was born melancholy. I was always looking toward the future, dreaming of becoming a star, of making my mark in the writing world. I was forever chasing the gold ring. I was never happy in the moment. I planned to be happy when I finally had it all. The trouble was, I wasn't happy once I had it all, either—because of the way I'd made all that money.

"I always thought that love and happiness were illusions until I walked in your front door and saw them in the way you treated Matthew and Chelsea, in your friendships, in your hopes and dreams for this place. I've seen how you derived happiness from the simplest of pleasures, setting out your china cups and plates, baking something fresh every day, making sure people felt at home here.

"I felt them both the night I pinned that corsage on your shoulder, and the night we made love—when you gave, asking nothing in return.

"Being with you has taught me that it's not the big events or achievements, not the 'wow' moments that make us happy, it's the little things, the humdrum ordinary things that happen between heartbeats that should bring us joy, love and happiness, and loving memories. Those are the moments we have to celebrate, and I want to celebrate all those everyday moments with you, Tracy." He slipped his arms around her and drew her closer. "I want to share all the joy and all the memories to come with you and your kids for as long as fate lets me."

He claimed to have never loved, and yet he'd just expressed his love in the most eloquent of terms. She turned in his arms, reached up, and carefully looped her arms around his neck.

"What about the not-so-joyful moments? Will you be willing to share those with us, too?"

"Love is what's seen you through the good times and the bad. If you'll marry me, I'll never give you reason to have to doubt my love for you."

"Marry you?" Despite everything he'd just said, she hadn't seen the proposal coming.

"Will you?"

"I love you, Wade. Most of the time, almost desperately. I thought of you today right in the middle of serving breakfast and wondered if anyone would notice if I just walked out of the sunroom, slipped down the hall and into your bed."

"I wish you would have."

"I believe you were in the middle of a hot hand of Uno at the time."

He groaned, kissed her, but didn't give up. "About that proposal . . ."

"This isn't something you should rush into—"

"Say you'll marry me, Tracy. It doesn't have to be this week, or this month. Not even this *year,* if you don't want to, but I need to hear you say you'll marry me."

"Marry a crazy writer who hears ghosts?"

"A crazy writer who's head-over-heels in love with you. A writer who happens to have enough money to hire a staff to keep this place running so that you can spend all your time with me if you want."

"I don't care about your money." Truth be told, she still had to remind herself about Edward Cain, his books, his success, his notoriety. To her, he was still just Wade. Her Wade.

"That's one more reason why I love you, and I don't want to let you get away." He laughed.

"I'm not going anywhere."

"I saw Matt on my way up. He gave me some man-to-man tips. Said women like kissie, smoochie stuff."

"Is this a conspiracy?" She couldn't help but laugh. "That's surprising. Lately whenever the subject of girls comes up, he can sum everything about them up with one word—yuck!"

She wrapped her arms tight around his waist, lifted her face to the stars. "I think this is where you definitely need to try some kissie, smoochie stuff," she whispered.

"You think a couple of good kisses will convince you that I'm not an invalid, and that you should come downstairs and tuck me in?"

"Try me." Her heart was soaring. She was ready to savor the moment, to celebrate the joy that was theirs right here, and right now. "Somehow, I have the feeling you can be very persuasive."

EPILOGUE

Four months later . . .

The Heartbreak was dressed for Christmas. Carols were playing in the lobby. A huge tree sparkled with lights and replica ornaments from the turn of the century, when the building was constructed.

For Tracy, welcoming guests would never be routine, not with such a wide variety of people visiting from all over the world. She was just finishing checking in a couple from Hawaii.

"Thank you, Mr. and Mrs. Sparks, and welcome to the Heartbreak Hotel. Let me know if you need anything else. Once you're settled in, you might want to wander out on the back porch, where wine and cheese will be served at sunset. It's a good time to get to meet some of the other guests, if you care to. Whatever you do, feel free to make yourselves at home."

They thanked her profusely and headed for the hall, stopping to ooh and ahh while they gazed at the Christmas tree. Then, as the Sparks wrestled their bags down the hall, Tracy crossed their names off the reservation ledger.

The day Tracy walked into the hotel for the first time, she would never, ever have guessed that she would find happiness here—but the Heartbreak had truly become a place where not only she had healed, but so had Matt and Chelsea—and Wade.

For all of them, time had soothed hurts, faded scars, and gilded memories. Willa's death had affected her more than she would have ever thought possible, given what had happened. In losing Willa, she'd lost the last connection to her own past in Indiana. Willa's death was one more reminder of how very short life is, and of how every precious moment is a gift.

Tracy heard footsteps on the stairs and watched Chelsea come strolling into the lobby with Mary Jane riding on her hip. The little girl started playing peekaboo with Tracy the minute she saw her, burying her face behind her hands and peeking out through her fingers.

"I've got the wine and glasses set up outside on the porch. All you need now are the cheese and crackers," Chelsea said.

Chelsea was home on holiday break, helping out with the rooms, taking care of Mary Jane, running things behind the desk, greeting guests, and generally filling in. She came home at every opportunity and always slipped right into helping out. She enjoyed the challenges so much that she'd decided to major in hotel management.

"Thank you. Are you going out?"

"Eric called and asked me if I wanted to go to the boat parade of lights at Gull Harbor. Do you need me tonight?"

"Go," Tracy encouraged. "The last guests just checked in."

"Great, I'll call and tell Eric I can go, then."

The front door opened and Jamie, the FedEx deliveryman, walked in.

"Hey, Jamie. How are the kids?" Tracy took the box he handed her and set it on the counter, then she signed for it and listened while he gave them an update on his new twin boys.

The minute he walked out, she picked up the box and looked at the packing slip. It was from the Robert Schack Literary Agency in L.A., but addressed to her, not Wade.

"What is it?" Chelsea was at her elbow, trying to see. "Another package from Wade. I think these Twelve Days of Christmas surprises he keeps sending you are just great. What did you get yesterday?"

Tracy blushed with embarrassment. "Tickets to Paris."

"You're kidding! Open this one." Chelsea nudged her. "Quick."

Tracy pulled the tab and the box opened. Inside was a book, hardbound, with an aqua dustcover and a picture of the California coastline below the embossed title, *The Life and Times of Captain Ezra Poole.*

She ran her fingers over the glossy finish, tracing the raised letters: "By Wade MacAllister and Capt. E. Poole."

"He did it. He published Ezra's story," Chelsea sounded awed. "But not as Edward Cain."

Wade had, indeed, given the press what they wanted for a good two months. He had entertained interviews from a hotel room at the Beverly Hilton and had gone on the talk show and news magazine circuit.

And so far, his plan was working. Getting more air time than Michael Jackson, the press soon got their fill of him. Another Jennifer Lopez wedding scandal soon overshadowed the demand for Edward Cain appearances.

And somehow, through it all, he'd managed to put the finishing touches on Ezra's book and sent it to the publisher without telling her that he'd even finished.

"Is there a note?" Chelsea picked up the box and shook it, but nothing fell out. "Wow. Did you know this was coming out?"

"I had no idea."

Matt came downstairs and immediately walked over to join them. "What's up?"

Tracy looked at Matt standing next to Chelsea and wondered if he had grown a foot since summer. "Wade published the story of Ezra Poole."

"Cool!" The sparkle in his eye told her he was thinking of a new moneymaking scheme.

"Don't even think about giving tours again, young man."

"We could sell copies of the book," Chelsea suggested. "Wade could autograph them and we could show them here at the front desk." She automatically drew Mary Jane's hand away from her long hair and then untangled the strands wrapped around the toddler's fingers.

"See if Wade already autographed it," she urged.

Tracy set the book on the counter and, lifting the cover, realized there was something inside. She let the book fall open on its own, and there, pressed and dried, was the gardenia blossom from the corsage he'd given her the night of the open house.

"That's just about *the* sweetest thing I've ever seen," Chelsea said softly. "That's the kind of thing Eric would do."

"Who put a dead flower in the book?" Matt scrunched up his nose and winced. "Weird. What does it say?" He tried to see over Chelsea's shoulder. Mary Jane grabbed his hair and wouldn't let go. He started emitting painful yowls.

Chelsea winked at Tracy when they heard the Harley pull into the driveway.

"Looks like hubby's home." Chelsea grabbed Matt by the collar and turned him in the direction of the stairs. "Come on upstairs and I'll fix you a snack."

"Why? Why can't I stay here, Mom?"

"Because she and Wade need some adult time," Chelsea told him as she gave him a nudge.

"They sure need a lot of adult time. How about I go with you for a dollar?"

"Quarter," Chelsea countered.

"Fifty cents."

"Deal."

As they bickered their way up the stairs, Tracy carefully placed the gardenia back in the middle of the book and turned to the title page. There was no autograph written there.

Wade walked in the side door, set his helmet down on the bar stool behind the reception desk, and wrapped his arms around her from behind. She leaned into him, closed her eyes, and knew she was the luckiest woman alive.

"I missed you," she whispered.

"I missed you, too. And to think I only went to the post office," he laughed.

"Still—"

"You got the book!" One-handed, he reached around her and picked it up. "Did you see the dedication?"

She shook her head. "I looked to see if you autographed it."

He flipped the book open and put it into her hands. When she looked down at the page, her heart skipped a beat as she read his words, printed for all the world to see.

Words more precious to her than any trip to Paris, than anything money could buy.

To my wife, Tracy,
Ezra and I both thank you.
Never forget . . . true love stands the test of time,
I love you.
Wade.

ABOUT THE AUTHOR

JILL MARIE LANDIS lives with her husband in California and Hawaii. Her list of award-winning books includes *Come Spring, Blue Moon, Sunflower, Just Once, Summer Moon, Magnolia Creek, Heat Wave,* and *Lover's Lane.* She loves hearing from readers at www.jillmarielandis.com.

ABOUT THE TYPE

This book was set in Garamond, a typeface originally designed by the Parisian typecutter Claude Garamond (1480–1561). This version of Garamond was modeled on a 1592 specimen sheet from the Egenolff-Berner foundry, which was produced from types assumed to have been brought to Frankfurt by the punchcutter Jacques Sabon.

Claude Garamond's distinguished romans and italics first appeared in *Opera Ciceronis* in 1543–44. The Garamond types are clear, open, and elegant.